CROSS-HAIRS

ALSO BY CATHERINE HERNANDEZ

Scarborough

CROSS-HAIRS

— A Novel —

CATHERINE HERNANDEZ

ATRIA BOOKS

New York   London   Toronto   Sydney   New Delhi

An Imprint of Simon & Schuster, Inc.
1230 Avenue of the Americas
New York, NY 10020

First Atria Books hardcover edition December 2020

ATRIA B O O K S and colophon are trademarks of Simon & Schuster, Inc.

For information about special discounts for bulk purchases, please contact Simon & Schuster Special Sales at 1-866-506-1949 or business@simonandschuster.com.

The Simon & Schuster Speakers Bureau can bring authors to your live event. For more information or to book an event, contact the Simon & Schuster Speakers Bureau at 1-866-248-3049 or visit our website at www.simonspeakers.com.

Interior design by Jill Putorti

Manufactured in the United States of America

1 3 5 7 9 10 8 6 4 2

Library of Congress Cataloging-in-Publication Data is available.

ISBN 978-1-9821-4602-3
ISBN 978-1-9821-4604-7 (ebook)

Pulse Nightclub, Orlando.

Here is what I dreamed:

They were there.

Forty-nine of them.

Crowding the light of a bathroom.

Playfully fighting for space along a smudged mirror.

Fingerprints of those who came before us.

To place upon lips a shine.

To dull a shine upon the nose.

Ready to dance.

Let me tell you: They were beautiful.

Dressed to impress.

All name-brand.

All bought on sale.

Skin Black and Brown.

It was twilight and we could hear the music,

loud and thumping,

Somewhere beyond.

The ones who came before

Our ancestors

were ready for us

in that nightclub high above the clouds.

"Let's go!" one of the forty-nine said.

There were cheers.

The forty-nine worked as a team building a spiral staircase

Made of magical dominoes

Suspended in midair.

Despite heels

Despite tight pants

They built it together

I looked up and saw we were approaching a hole in the sky

They used the domino staircase to enter the hole

Then they all looked down at me through the circle

Gesturing me to come up and join them.

"Not now," I said sadly. "I'm not ready yet."

They waved goodbye.

I will never forget the image of them waving from that hole in
the sky.

These people I never knew who could easily have been any one
of us.

They waved.

To the people of privilege,
You will survive your discomfort while reading this book.
But many like me, who sit dangerously at various intersections
of identity,
will not survive long enough for you to complete the last page.
What will you do?

AUTHOR'S NOTE

There are slurs used by the fascist regime in this book, which are meant to illustrate the oppressive power of words.

For clarity, characters who use the singular "they/them" pronouns are referred to with an asterisk when they are first introduced.

CROSS-HAIRS

1

Evan. My beautiful Evan. Here in the darkness of this hiding place, I write you these words. Without paper, without pen, I trace these words in my head, along the perimeter of your outline. Watch this sentence travel along the meat of your cheekbone. See my teeth dig into your flesh playfully. Watch these words ball into your hand along with a fistful of bedsheet, which you pull over us to create a tent. I imagine you now, lying across from me, improvising a silly song about the smallness of my ears. Ironically, you sing it half in tune, half out of tune.

"Maybe you're the one with the small ears," I suggest, and you scrunch your face in embarrassment. You're talented at many things, but music isn't one of them. Sometimes the image of you is clear, right down to the curl of your eyelashes. Sometimes, especially when I'm hungry, I recall the shape of your smile and nothing more. Watch these phrases ink across an imaginary page, a Whisper Letter, folded twice, placed in an envelope and mailed to wherever you may be. I will never forget your name, Evan. And I pray you will never forget mine.

If by some miracle my whispered words reach you, I want you to know that I'm safe on Homewood Street where Liv has hidden me in her basement.

No room in Toronto is ever used in the way it was originally intended. That's what happens in a city always trying to reinvent itself.

Like it has an itch it can't scratch. Like it has a commitment problem. This place was meant to be a cold cellar. A place where, before the invention of refrigeration, the woman of the house would have likely stored things like butter or eggs. That's why even in the heat of the summer, the heat of this hellish summer, I feel like I'm swimming in the cold breath of ghosts. I'm wearing all the clothes I ran away in. Five layers, which you told me to wear. There is no finding me. At least I hope so.

To ensure that I am hidden, I have set up my bed beside Liv's furnace. My bed consists of two layers of cardboard boxes cut to fit in the corner of space behind the furnace, and a pile of Liv's old winter coats, which I use as blankets and a pillow. The idea is, if I need to leave again and in a hurry, what remains behind won't resemble a hideout for me: a Queer Femme Jamaican Filipino man. Anne Frank, minus the diary.

It is here where I await news, where I hope for your arrival, where I wait for Liv to feed me or to tell me it's time to run again. I am unsure of exactly how long I have been here, as counting days is its own form of torture. Instead, I understand the passing of time by watching the moon's cycle from the basement window. Maybe you are doing the same. Lunar crescents have grown fat and then thin across the night sky almost six times. And at the swelling of every moon, Liv has replenished my supplies. It is through this same basement window that I have watched a raccoon give birth, pushing those kits out, one at a time, in the space between the spiderweb-stained glass and the corrugated metal framing. I have been here long enough to watch them grow too large for the cubbyhole. Long enough to watch the mama bite the collars of each of her whimpering kits and carry them to the surface of the world, high above me.

In the dead of winter, under a waxing fingernail moon, I jogged in place to keep my limbs from feeling wooden and numb. In the spring, when the flooding began once again, I would stand in ankle-deep filthy water. Under a new moon, with flashes of lightning as my only guide in the darkness, I filled buckets with floodwater and passed them to Liv through the hatch to pour down the kitchen drain. Since summer has returned, and the moon is pregnant-round, I am thankful the musty smell of mold has dissipated a bit.

I can see the sky peeking through the opening of the basement window like a half-circle picture-perfect blue. I'm not sure what is better: to look outside the window and long for sunlight or to lie on my dark makeshift bed, close my eyes, and dream of bicycling with you through the city, fast and free.

When I first arrived, I kept to my cardboard bed and wept, seeing the basement as my prison, my tomb while the Renovation unfolded at ground level. Then, as time passed, as the moon scratched a wound across the sky, I began to inch my way around the concrete to witness the untold history of the home with my curious hands and squinting eyes. At the opposite end of the basement, where a broken stove sits, just beyond the reach of its power cord's coil, is a washroom rough-in. Three unfinished pipes poke through the solid concrete like necks without heads. I picture a couple in the early 2000s renovating the basement to create a separate apartment, then halting their construction as the stock market crashes. In the adjacent corner stands a dusty wooden bar and dysfunctional sink. I imagine a husband in the 1970s, wearing his paisley shirt, sneaking through the bar's shelves in search of his favorite brand of whiskey. A mysterious series of headboards from several different time periods from several different occupants lean against the cold walls.

Every corner of this basement tells a tale and so too does every inch of my body. The landscape of every curve is a map of my traumatic experiences. Evan. Take your first two fingers and make a compass. Walk your compass between the mounds of my kneecaps to find bodies of water, deep with your touch, remembered. The distance between my belly button and my throat is measured in increments of miles run in my escape and the sequence of events that led me here, to this nightmare lived. The canyon of my palm is where I feel everything and everyone I have lost in the last several months. And constantly echoing through these vast mountain ranges of bones and sifted garbage heaps is the sound of first screams and final goodbyes. The cartography of memory. The navigation through valleys of scars.

Tonight, the light comes. I hear the kitchen table slide roughly across the floor, and then the hatch is lifted.

"Kay!" Liv says to me.

The light is painful beautiful. The light is ugly perfect. I squint my eyes and open them as wide as I can all at the same time. I want that light inside of me. It feels so good. As usual, when Liv opens the hatch, I stack the milk crates to raise myself high enough to reach Liv's hand. Our hands touch, and she hoists me out onto the ground floor. We land on our bums on the linoleum tiles with a soft thud and she begins crying. I usually hate seeing white folks cry because it means I have to assure them that I, as a Black person, do not think less of them. But Liv is different. I know she wouldn't cry unless she had reason to do so.

"What's wrong?" I ask gently. My voice is hoarse, speaking for the first time in ages.

She doesn't answer me. She pulls her shirt up to wipe her wet face. I look around to see if there are tissues, but I don't see any in the kitchen, so I let her continue with this sad wet-shirt business. Her breathing calms enough for her to let her shoulders relax finally. By then her shirt is wetter than her face. Whatever it was has passed, it seems. I am too scared to ask.

"Are you hungry? Can I make you something?" she asks while standing herself up. A few sniffles escape her mouth like a hiccup.

"Yes, please." My stomach growls. "Do you want help?" I say, knowing I have few calories to spare.

"No, no. Just chill."

I sit at the kitchen table and chew my cheek. Once I taste the threat of blood in my mouth, I will myself to ease off, for food is on its way. The sound of a podcast transmits from Liv's phone. A recording of the ambient sound of an industrial kitchen with the occasional calling out of orders slowly crossfades with a raspy voice. "My name is Khalil. I'm twenty-eight years old. I have been in charge of the kitchen here at the Don Valley workhouse for three months now . . . "

With one hand, Liv wipes her chaffed nose with a tissue, while the other begins opening and closing cupboard doors and the fridge; she shakes her head at the lack of choice. She settles on grilling strips of bacon and making it a stir-fry with leftover rice and frozen veggies. I swallow hard, watching the bacon fold in on itself with the heat and sizzle. I feel like passing out from anticipation, so I focus on amplifying the podcast by placing the phone in a clean coffee cup on the table. The voice of a journalist can be heard over Liv's cooking.

"It is a crisp Wednesday morning. Khalil blows warm air on his hands, as his silhouette spirits across a fiery dawn toward the mess hall," the journalist narrates. The sound of cutlery clinking. Plates being piled. Barely coherent words of thanks from a lineup of people. "After mass environmental displacement, homelessness and hunger once plagued the lives of these workers. But not today. Despite the lofty task of feeding hundreds of people at this factory, Khalil still finds the time to check in with those enjoying the meals his team has made and to shake the hands of everyone sitting at each table. This includes the children of the workers, who, despite the rumors of separated families, are schooled and housed on the compound alongside their parents. With his apron still stained from today's prep Khalil makes his way to a little girl holding her teddy bear."

The microphone shifts and catches the audio of a small girl's sweet voice. "Can Bear-Bear get a muffin too?" she pleads.

"You betcha!" Khalil replies.

The sound of the mess hall crossfades with the clunk of cans being stacked on a shelf.

"There isn't a moment to spare today. Once the breakfast plates are cleared, Khalil is busy with planning lunch and tracking inventory. I finally ask him the question that's been on minds around the world in the wake of reports smearing the Canadian government with charges like 'genocide' and 'fascism.'"

Ambient noise of Khalil counting cans. Finally, "So what do you say when people call the workhouses 'concentration camps'?"

He scoffs. "Absolutely not. They're not concentration camps. I'm in charge of cooking three meals a day for these workers, seven days a week. We're all housed. No one's getting hurt. No one is starving. Even with the food shortages and floods, the compound helps people get access to free meals and clean water. You wouldn't call *that* a 'concentration camp.' That's called 'teamwork.'"

I wrap my hands around the cup to feel the vibrations of the podcast reverberate through my palm. I feel the power of connection through the device, of the ability to connect with others and be seen online. I resist the urge to scroll through Liv's social media. No one, including you, is reachable anyway.

Khalil continues, "If it weren't for the workhouses many of us would be homeless, useless. As the Renovation creed says, *Through our work, our nation prospers. Through our unity, we end conflict. Through our leader, we find peace. Through order, we find tranquility.*"

"And what does that mean to you, Khalil?" asks the interviewer.

Khalil's voice is determined. "It means all this was for the best. We need to pull together and stop fighting each other. Know your place and do the work that's needed. The Renovation taught us that. Mother Nature taught us that. When she stepped in and showed us who's boss, we had no choice. We all had to pitch in. Others like me have to put our talents to good use, instead of fighting each other and arguing over who has what."

At the sound of this, Liv lets out a heavy sigh and reaches for the phone. "I'm so sorry," she says. One tap of her thumb and the podcast is paused. "I download and listen to it for appearances, in case my phone is seized." Two plates are collected from the cupboard and the stir-fry is served. "As if Khalil isn't white and Christian. As if Khalil is his name. As if he even exists. We can't even see him. It's a fucking podcast. And yet, people still believe it."

We sit quietly as I devour the meal, making sure to leave the fatty ends of the bacon for last. Every onion, every pea, every piece of shredded carrot has that delicious bacon grease on it, so I eat until all that is left are smears across the plate. An oil painting. I drink heartily.

"It feels so damn good to resurface every now and then to drink running water and eat perishable food." I chuckle to myself even though Liv's mind is far away. "Jesus be a juicy burger. Jesus be a glass of cold milk. Jesus be a plate of freshly fried potatoes."

Now that I have finished eating, I will fill containers for my rations. Anything that can stay in my hideout for extended periods of time and not rot. When I first started hiding here, Liv's instructions were clear: If I had to run, I was to stack the containers without any crumbs onto the canned-goods shelf, to lean my makeshift bed against the wall, and toss the coats into a pile so that it wouldn't look like anyone was staying there. It would just look like a messy basement. Before I go back to my dank hidey-hole, I begin restocking all the things I once loved and now abhor after eating them again and again. Wasabi chickpeas. Purple tortilla chips. Dried snap peas.

"You don't have to do that now. We can wait. You need to stretch your legs a bit."

Don't I ever. The ceiling downstairs is low enough to graze the top of my unkempt hair.

"Our usual?" she asks me.

I nod. I am so happy she asked. Liv takes my hand, and we go upstairs. She is quiet again. I stay quiet with her.

Liv draws me a bath. I sit silent on the toilet as she attempts to get the remaining bubble bath soap out of its bottle by filling it with water, swishing it around, and dumping it out. My skin is so hungry for that heat that I get goose bumps.

After one last swirl of her hand in the bath, she dries her hands. She searches the cabinet and places a pink razor and a toothbrush on the counter.

"Remember to just hide the razor and toothbrush in the garbage after you're done." She leaves the bathroom to give me privacy. I want to tell her that I don't want privacy. That being aboveground means light. It means speaking. It means seeing people's faces. It means hearing things clearly rather than muffled through the floorboards. But she is gone before I am brave enough to ask. I see her feet walk away through the slit under the door.

I undress. It feels incredible to peel off these sorry clothes. I scratch my skin heartily and watch tiny parts of me fall like snow onto the bathroom tiles. It feels so good to be naked. As usual, I open the bathroom door a bit to leave my clothes outside for Liv to launder. She always refuses to let me do it.

I test the water with my toes, and it is delightfully hot. My hair stands on end, and I remember to grab the razor and place it on the ledge of the tub. I sink into the hug of this bath. This bath that reminds me of who I am.

Who I am. Who am I? Oh yes. I am Kay. And I marched.

During the Pride festival, the LGBTQ2S community would emerge from their closets or lack thereof to march and be proud of their identities. I marched with them to the horizon of asphalt, heat mirages snaking into the air. I applied makeup in alleyways—a compact mirror sitting on a void of missing brick—to ready my face and parade down the path of cheering crowds. We marched in the name of screaming nights; us queens circling lampposts like stripper poles, circling stripper poles like lampposts. We marched in the name of sparkles and leather, mesh and feathers. We marched for those who could not march. We marched south on Yonge Street, the main artery of the city, turned the corner at Carlton, then dispersed among the dense crowd along Church Street toward the center of the gay village. To the tune of bull dykes drumming, we danced through streets, baring all; our sweaty shoulders shiny against the sun like apples waiting for a hungry bite. And we ate. We ate at the bounty of us, this buffet of body, at the bathhouse or club. We ate. We ate well. Some of us grew families. Some of us grew gardens. Some of us were lucky enough to grow older. Some of us did not survive.

Evan, do you remember watching me perform at Buddies in Bad Times Theatre? On the dance floor, I would give you a kiss before heading downstairs to the dressing room, to peel off my sweaty pantyhose. Once inside that postered and bright room, I would shake off my damp wig and count out my tips. Drag was a humble living but enough to get us a post-show burger and groceries for the next day.

I still remember that day, one of the last days. There were three of us queens removing our faces, making a pile of dirty wipes on the counter. It was one of the many gigs I shared with my roommates, Fanny and Nolan. Fanny, still in costume, went to the adjacent washroom to piss. Her Chihuahua, Sedgewick, was celebrating our return to the dressing room with his sharp yelps. Nolan remained at the counter, meticulously wiping perspiration from his armpits with an old shirt.

"Who's up for brunch tomorrow?" I said, flashing my tips.

"Oh, look, Fanny," said Nolan while rolling his eyes and scrolling his phone.

From the washroom Fanny flushed the toilet and then reentered the room. "What?"

"Kay is buying us brunch."

"I'm not buying anything for you thankless bitches!" I threw my pantyhose at Nolan's face. I had the worst aim, so it drifted to the floor instead. Nolan flashed me a belittling smile. I tucked the cash into my jacket pocket and averted my eyes to save my dignity. "I'm just lucky that there happened to be a bachelorette party in the audience for my 'Going to the Chapel' number tonight. That ugly-ass bride was like a cash cow with a dollar-store veil on her head. And did you see the bills she had on her? All twenties, no fives, no tens." I removed my false eyelashes in two dramatic movements for emphasis.

"You can have them, Kay. To hell with all those drunken bridesmaids with their feather boas and dick drinking straws. I couldn't stand the sound of them butchering 'Single Ladies' during my Beyoncé set. They all ruined it with their . . ." Fanny flipped her hand back and forth to demonstrate the bridal party's sad imitation of Beyoncé's choreography, and I burst out laughing.

With his show dress still undone and bunched at his waist, Nolan rose from the counter, trying to catch the Wi-Fi signal from the theater upstairs. It was always weak down below in the dressing room. With his phone in hand, he tried various positions near the door, cursing in between each one. When a healthy signal was achieved, he gleefully gestured us over. "Who wants to see my latest *Party Crashers* episode? My editor just sent me the link."

One of Nolan's regular gigs was to host a popular web series where he crashed political events in full drag and interviewed attendees. Bare-chested and sweaty, we rushed to his side as the video buffered. It faded in to the tune of Vivaldi's "Spring." Establishing shots of a convention center filled the screen. Catering staff prepared trays of hors d'oeuvres. Cascading floral arrangements were placed on tables. Fancy people in fancy suits shook hands. The video cut to a shot of the Ontario premier Walt Ogilvy shaking hands with said fancy people while cameras flashed. To the right of the screen Nolan entered in Connie Chung drag, complete with larger-than-life blown-out wig, tailored pantsuit. One manicured hand held a glittery microphone while the other arm bent upward like a teapot to hook an oversize handbag. The music changed to a hard, rhythmic guitar as Nolan's gait was emphasized by dramatic slow-motion video.

"Damn!" I said. "Was the wind blowing when you were shooting this? Did you plan it that way?"

"What can I say?" Nolan shrugged. "I try to change the world one slow-motion shot at a time."

The video continued with a shot of Ogilvy walking with his colleagues down a hallway. Cameras flashed. Nolan approached Ogilvy with his microphone arm outstretched.

The premier's ruddy and round face snickered at the sight of Nolan. I could see in Ogilvy's eyes that he thought this was a prank, or the entertainment portion of the event.

"What do we have here?" More laughs. His compadres joined in, laughing at the man in a dress. Security guards stepped forward to protect him, but Ogilvy waved them off with a hearty guffaw.

Nolan's face remained pursed with Connie Chung–like discernment and journalistic downward inflections. "Good evening, Premier. Are you confirming that you can actually see me?" Nolan pointed the microphone in the politician's face and waited for an answer.

Ogilvy looked around the room, balking at Nolan's strange question. "Of course I can see you and all this that you're wearing. Whatever it is. Whatever you are. How can anyone not see you?"

"Then if you can see me, Premier, is there a reason why your party denies the presence of Trans and gender-nonconforming folks in the current sex-ed curriculum?" At the end of this sentence, Ogilvy's face shifted and he began walking away.

"I think you are a very confused individual," he said over his shoulder dismissively. Two security guards intercepted Nolan as the premier made his way down the hall. The media scrum suddenly divided between covering Ogilvy's arrival into the event space and recording the drag queen in hysterics.

"I'm not confused, Premier! I'm clearly channeling Connie Chung meets Vera Wang meets Armani!" Nolan cried. "And even if I was confused, at least you acknowledged that I indeed exist. Just like"—

in front of the puzzled media scrum, Nolan reached into his hand-bag and pulled out a pile of papers covered in images; one showed a doctored photo of the premier's face on a porn star's body, jacking off—"masturbation exists!" He shuffled to another print, this time, a photo of Ogilvy at a press conference denying allegations of sexual assault. "Consent exists!"

The video ended with Nolan exiting the convention center, his arms playfully around the security guards as they escorted him out. Fanny and I gazed at Nolan, our mouths agape.

"I am . . . I am . . ." Fanny could barely find the words. "I am so damn jealous of you. I wish all of us Homos could give that closeted asshole a piece of our minds. Drag him."

"Wow, Nolan." I shook my head in wonder. By the looks of the view counter, the video was already well on its way to going viral. "You are brave."

"Why, thank you, Kay." Nolan curtsied and put his phone in his show bag. "Okay, bitches. When we get home can we finally catch up on *Zombie Country*?"

The skin where his eyebrows once were rose in a plea. I found it hard to read his emotions without his full drag makeup. He was one of those queens who had no lips or eyebrows unless they were drawn on. I had to rely on dramatic pauses or comedic timing to understand his expressions.

Sedgewick yapped at the sight of Fanny struggling to remove her pantyhose and foam bum. Nolan groaned at the sound.

"Yes, Sedgewick, Mama has to pack her ass into a plastic bag." Fanny sighed with relief when her control panties were finally inched off her fat belly, giving her generous rolls breathing room. "I'm game for watching *Zombie Country*, but you need to promise to sit right next to me. That show is scary as fuck. I don't know why we watch that. It's like torture."

"We watch it to prepare ourselves," said Nolan, slipping on his boy underwear and adjusting his penis under the fabric.

"For what?" Fanny began combing out her bobbed wig. "You think we'll have a zombie apocalypse?"

"No. This is metaphorical. The zombies are like a real and present evil within all of us, taking over."

"That's bullshit."

"How is that bullshit?"

"You think the creators of *Zombie Country* are thinking metaphors and symbols? I think they're thinking about what kind of show makes money. That's all."

"Sure, Fanny. There's that too." Nolan combed his hair into a tight ponytail. "But my parents came from Cambodia after surviving the Killing Fields. The way my dad describes the events that led to the Khmer Rouge taking over and forcing everyone into labor camps . . . it sounds just like a zombie apocalypse to me!"

"Bitch, how did this conversation turn so sour all of a sudden?" Fanny chuckled.

We all laughed nervously.

"No, for reals. I think there is evil in all of us. All it takes are the right circumstances and we're in the same situation as Nazi Germany." Nolan tossed his dirty makeup wipes into the trash and applied lip balm.

"Okay, Nolan." Fanny slipped into an off-the-shoulder sweatshirt she purchased at a secondhand shop the week before. "So you tell me: How is this show, this internationally popular television show, preparing you for impending disaster?"

Nolan rubbed the stubble coming in on his eyebrows. I could see him partly thinking about his response and partly taking a mental note to pluck before his next gig. "It reminds me to look for hiding places. It reminds me to consider who I can count on in case of emergency."

"What emergency is that?" I asked, my heart skipping a beat. I realized I was behind in undressing. I still had my head wrapped in tape and pins. I had forgotten you were upstairs waiting for all of us to undress. I quickened my pace.

"In case . . . the small things we experience every day become so big we have to run. I mean . . . look at what I just did to our premier. We can't even exist in textbooks. Where else are they going to erase us?"

We were silent for a moment. Nolan lovingly touched Fanny's forearm. It was badly bruised after her last run-in with a cop. The cop had catcalled Fanny just after she finished a gig at Sirens Nightclub. She did not respond and chose to jaywalk to avoid contact with him. He then issued her a ticket for jaywalking. When Fanny protested, the cop strong-armed her, calling her a she-male. Fanny pursed her lips and looked away.

Nolan broke the silence. "Could you imagine drag queens fighting an apocalypse?" Nolan pretended to sword-fight with me. "We'd be like 'Fuck, the enemy is coming! Hurry, get your heels! We need to stiletto these bitches to death!'"

"Or you know how in the movies, just before a revolution starts, the leader does that inspirational speech? We'd do that, but one of us would be lip-syncing the speech from a playback track of a speech. That's how drag it would be," Fanny said, joining in with a smile.

I watched quietly as Nolan and Fanny took turns lip-syncing in dramatic drag queen fashion (including quivering lips for vibrato) while the other recited William Wallace's *Braveheart* speech in a Scottish brogue: "'They may take our lives, but they'll never take our freedom!'" Even Sedgewick joined the two humans above him with his high-pitched barking. I smiled but had nothing to add to the joke. Instead, I wondered what could possibly happen in my lifetime that would have me running. What would mean enough to me to fight for it?

I remember us all meeting you upstairs and heading home that night together, me on your right arm, Fanny on your left. Nolan up ahead smoking a cigarette.

"See? Look at Evan. This one's a keeper, Kay," Fanny said to me, while hitting your chest playfully with her purse. "He knows to walk slowly after an entire show wearing stilettos."

I scoffed. "Oh, enough! You've already changed into those ugly-ass nurse shoes."

"I will have you know, these are called high-tops and kids nowadays are all about them."

We laughed. Maybe a bit too loudly. You tightened the grip on our arms and whispered, "Keep walking. Keep quiet."

Nolan looked back, confused. "What is it? What's wrong?"

"Turn around. Keep walking," you said.

Under the light of the bug-stained streetlamps, we did not question you. Being followed at night (or in the morning or afternoon, really) was a familiar sensation. It was becoming more familiar as the days wore on. Making our way toward Church Street, our casual stroll became a speed walk as did the pace of the person (or people?) behind us. I could not hear their footsteps but could hear their breathing. I did not dare look back. Just as Fanny began to cough with exertion, an open plastic cola bottle was thrown in our path. It spun in flat circles along the concrete and the smell of piss rose into the air. We stopped before our toes could touch the filthy puddle.

"TRANNY N_ _ _ _RS!" a voice yelled before disappearing into the night.

We sidestepped the mess and continued walking toward our apartment, where we went inside and shared a spliff. I remember your hands shaking while rolling the buds into an imperfect cylinder. I remember you pulling the drag longer than usual and pretending everything was all right. We all pretended that night.

But that was then. Before Nolan left us. Before we all had to disappear ourselves. Before we begged Fanny to run.

I wonder sometimes where Fanny is and if she is safe. We aren't white boys who can take off the gay like a coat, hang it up in a closet, then lock ourselves in that closet. People like Fanny and me don't have a choice. You can't take off the skin. You can't take off the femme. So that's why I ended up here in Liv's house, sitting in her tub, writing this Whisper Letter to you.

*   *   *

Filth runs off me. I scrub the overgrown hair on my head angrily. I shave my legs, my sad legs, then pull the plug in the tub. I rinse off my body, this body that is mine, under the shower as the last of my filth and hair goes down the drain.

When I walk into Liv's room, she already has her closet open for me.

"Kay, sometimes—well, no—*every* time we do this, I think to myself, you must hate my wardrobe."

I do. Her formal wear is boring. All capped sleeves and knee-length skirts fit for corporate arm candy. Her casual apparel is hideous. It's like what those ladies used to dress up in at Lilith Fair in the 1990s. All paisley skirts and slouchy sleeves. But it will do for now. For this one moment.

"I don't hate your wardrobe." I roll my eyes and make my way to the closet. She knows I'm lying. I slip Liv's fake kimono off the hanger and onto my true skin. The bottom edges of the fabric brush against my newly shaven legs, and it feels like a kiss. Wrapping the belt around my waist I admire my reflection in Liv's standing mirror. I'm thinner, but you will be happy to know, the shelf of my bum can still be seen through the fabric. Liv smiles at my towering slender reflection, and I smile back.

"Shoes?"

"Ummm . . . yes!" I know her feet are too small, but I manage to squeeze myself into a pair of white peekaboo-toe heels. I look again in the mirror and flex my calves. I walk and pivot back and forth from the mirror to make Liv giggle.

When her laughter dies down, she says, "Do you want to have some time alone in here?"

"Hell no. If you have a moment, I'd love to talk to somebody. I just want to say things and hear things. Anything."

I sprawl myself across the width of her soft bed. I raise my legs up with the high heels still on. Damn I look good. Damn I feel good. Damn this entire life.

Liv's side table contains both her sex toys and her nail polish collection, so it smells like a strange combination of rubber, bubble gum, and acetone. I choose the reddest-of-red color. I choose it because it's a similar shade to the first red lipstick I stole from Shoppers Drug Mart on my thirteenth birthday. It is red like newly bloomed poppies and red like blood from a fresh wound.

"I'm glad you chose this color. It was my wife's favorite . . . It *is* my wife's favorite." Liv has a problem with tenses too, which are dependent on how hopeful we are of reuniting with those we have lost.

I slip the heels off and prop my feet atop Liv's lap as she weaves a rolled-up tissue between my toes. She gathers her bleach-blond hair into a messy bun, exposing the dark brown at her roots, then begins polishing. I love listening to stories about Erin, so I keep quiet, hoping she will tell me more.

"When Erin got pregnant, she still wanted me to paint her toenails, even though she could barely see her own feet by the end of her third trimester. I loved doing it, though. She'd fall asleep every time."

Each nail looks like a race car when she is done, shiny and perfect. We both admire her work for a moment. Liv looks at the blood red of my nails and she begins to shake. When she kneels next to the bed, I can tell her head is heavy with thinking, so I reach my hand out to hers and hold it tight. That's when she speaks truth. "It's time to run again."

My heart sinks. My skin is suddenly cold against this silk robe. This fake silk kimono. There is a sour smell to the sweat of my armpits against this fabric. Every pore on my body touches the kimono in pins and needles. It's time to run.

Arranging for Liv to not only cross paths with Charles Greene but also to engage with him meaningfully took a substantial amount of planning and patience. The Resistance strategically placed Liv as a

server at Legal Tender, a bar located in the heart of Toronto's financial district, where Charles was a regular.

After two months of Liv being on the job, the two finally met. It
was Cinco de Mayo. Despite the incessant rainstorms, the bar was
packed with executives who embellished their tailored suits with
tourist sombreros on their heads and handlebar mustaches on their
faces. There wasn't a Mexican in sight.

Charles sat at a booth with two men who clinked their Coronas.
One had a reddened face and bloodshot eyes. The other had smart
spectacles and a loosened tie. Charles, on the other hand, appeared
soft and disarming in his blue golf shirt and khaki slacks, casual Friday to their power suits.

Over the sound of faux mariachi music and dudes screaming
"¡*Ándale!*" at random, Liv approached his booth to take food orders.

"Are you hombres ready to order some tapas?" With a listless face,
Liv turned the page of her notebook and clicked the nib of her pen
into position. Charles removed his sombrero and finger-combed his
boyish haircut.

"Uh-oh! Someone's trying to fill us up on some food because we're
gettin' too rowdy," Bloodshot Eyes said, half speaking, half spitting.

"Speak for yourself," Loose Tie said through even looser lips.
"Charles and I are being perfect gentlemen."

Liv looped her bleach-blond hair behind her ear and recited the
specials. "Well, the chef has two amazing platters tonight and—"

"What about you? Do we get you on a platter?" Bloodshot Eyes said.

Loose Tie put his hand around Liv's waist. "Don't scare her away!
Look. She's scared. She's scared."

"Two of the platters. Just bring one of each," Charles intervened.
He looked at Liv apologetically as she retreated to the kitchen.

When their table was just about finished for the night, another
drunken suit approached Liv.

"I need to settle my bill, beautiful," he said sloppily, pretending he
didn't know Liv, pretending they had not trained together for months

for this very moment. Liv began processing his receipt. In Charles's plain view, Drunken Suit began stroking Liv's triceps with the surface of his knuckles. Liv swatted him away like a fly, and like a fly his hand returned.

"Can I help you, sir?" Charles said to Drunken Suit, aggressively putting his arm around him, like they were pals.

"I'm paying my bill."

"How about this: you can go back to your table and put down two crisp fifties and call it a night."

"I don't think so. I just had four beers."

Charles stepped toward the man until they were practically nose to nose. "Put down the money at the table and leave the lady alone." The man wavered and did as he said.

Liv made a face. "Yikes. Thanks. I'm sorry you had to do that."

"Are you kidding me? I'm sorry you've had to deal with fools like that all night, including my friends over there." His pale blue eyes flashed toward his booth. Bloodshot Eyes and Loose Tie were struggling to get their jackets on.

Liv waved off his concern. "It's part of working here. The bankers are the worst. Lawyers a close second."

Charles rubbed his boxed beard with a sly grin. "And the businessmen like me?"

"They're okay, I guess." Liv pretended to fight back a grin and made eye contact, long enough for him to remember her face.

The next morning, at his office on King Street, Charles looked up and saw Liv distributing the paperwork among his colleagues. Their eyes met and she made a face, the same face she made in the bar, before quietly exiting the meeting.

Later that day, Charles leaned on the doorframe of the staff lunchroom while Liv waited for her food to microwave. "Hi, intern."

Liv held up her hands defensively. "I swear I didn't know who you were when I met you last night."

"Moonlighting?"

"That's my part-time job so I can afford the life of an intern."

"I hope you know who I am *now*."

"Of course I do. You're Charles Greene, CEO of CAN Create." Liv looked to the side, blushing. "And you're a great fighter of drunken men who manhandle waitresses. Thanks again, by the way."

Charles smiled a slow smile, interest alive in his face.

They both threw protocol aside and shared dinner at Flax, Toronto's latest organic farm-to-table restaurant. By the end of their dinner, the two were sharing dessert.

"Okay . . . I have to ask. What's it like? Being a CEO of this multinational corporation? God, I hope I don't sound like a hick saying that."

"You sound like you think I'm a superman or something."

"Well, you kind of are, aren't you? I mean, your company occupies the top seven floors of a skyscraper that has the best views in the city. You have thousands of employees. These people have houses because of you. They can feed their families and send their kids to school."

A waiter approached politely. A Black man, hands behind his back, smiling gently. "How are we enjoying the dessert?"

Charles paused with his spoon in the air and snarled, "How about you let me eat without you asking me questions that interrupt our conversation?"

The waiter's smile faded slightly before he attempted to reinvigorate it at its edges. He failed. He bowed and receded to the kitchen. Charles threw Liv a look, and she snickered.

Wiping the edges of his beard with his napkin he continued. "I dunno, Liv. It's a little more complicated than that. There are thousands of employees here in Canada and thousands more elsewhere. Take this dessert we're enjoying right now. This ridiculous toasted-pumpkin-seed, beetroot-reduction, cane-sugar-crisp whatever dessert. I want you to consider the hands that processed the pumpkin seeds, harvested the beetroots, and extracted the sugarcane juice. In order for us to even afford organic food we have to ensure those very

hands are not paid well. And in order for those people to be willing
to be underpaid . . ."

"They have to be desperate." Liv scooped another spoonful into
her mouth, careful not to smudge her lipstick.

"Exactly. Just last month, in one of our facilities in China, those
desperate people we employed were ravaged by a third typhoon in
two years. The Chinese are hardworking. They know how to take
orders. They do things quick, and they do things cheap. It saddens
me to think of how many of them were lost. Truth is, a bunch may
die, and they have millions more willing to take their place." Charles
tossed his napkin onto the table.

"I'm sorry. That's a lot to handle."

"Meanwhile, here in Canada, we aren't desperate enough. There
are people here, especially after the floods on the east coast and the
droughts on the west coast, who should be begging to keep their
hands busy with repairing what we have left. But instead they're asking for handouts. You have these Others wandering around aimlessly,
when they should be proving themselves and being useful."

Liv chimed in, playing along. "There's this one waitress over at
Legal Tender who drives me up the wall with her hipster discourse
about fair trade. We're all folding napkins and wiping wineglasses;
meanwhile she's preaching to us about how important it is for us
to buy vintage clothing to 'divest' from sweatshop operations." Her
fingers made rabbit ears in the air at the word "divest," and Charles
pressed his palm to his forehead, closed his eyes. "But no one thinks
of how, even if this little Bengali girl is making five cents a day making
my sweater, it's a hell of a lot better than her selling her body in some
brothel. 'Divesting' without giving actual options to these Others is
talk I don't have patience for."

Charles waved his hand in agreement. "Here's the thing. Your coworker feels bad about these little Brown children making shoes, because unlike China or Bangladesh or the Philippines, people here in
Canada, no matter how poor, are not willing to do this kind of work.

It frustrates me to no end seeing these Others who would rather ride a gravy train than put their skills to good use. And when people like this"—he pointed his fork toward the waiter—"accept handouts, they become dangers to our society. But I want to change that. That's why we'll be ending our overseas manufacturing within a year and have everything Canadian-made."

"You can afford that?"

"There are ways."

They left Flax and strolled east along King Street's theater district, with its marquee bulbs blinking rhythmically over the faces of restaurant hostesses hoping to lure passersby to their overpriced menus. Everything was overpriced due to the shortages. The more expensive the food, the bigger the hostess's smile. At each intersection, partygoers sat on lines of sandbags to enjoy their cigarettes, the swollen lake lapping at the other side. Some were inebriated enough to stand knee-deep in water that had yet to recede back into the lake, splashing each other, with high heels hooked in one hand and a smoldering spliff in the other. Some sat on the roofs of halted streetcars, unable to move in the deluge, and playfully shot plastic pistols at passersby.

In a dry clearing stood a hot dog cart with the promise of street meat sizzling on its grill. Liv turned to Charles.

"Be honest with me. Are you still hungry after that organic meal?"

"Starving. But I'm sure these hot dogs are organic free-range something or other."

Charles sat on the edge of a concrete tree planter to eat, and she perched on his lap and leaned in close to grab a bite.

"Great. Now I've got ketchup down my bra."

They laughed. They held hands. They kissed.

They kept strolling, until the crowds from the clubs and bass-heavy music dissipated among the quiet of the skyscrapers in the business district, stopping to kiss heatedly in the shadows of buildings. At the sight of his Adelaide Street East condo building Charles said, "Come upstairs."

Just as Liv was about to play the nice girl and shrug her shoulders coyly, Charles pinched her chin between his thumb and forefinger. It was rough enough to throw her off-balance. He held her steady and gazed directly into her eyes. His breath was heavy and labored. Liv hardly breathed at all.

"That wasn't a question." He let go to retrieve his keys from his pocket.

She straightened her blouse and went through the door.

From elevator to hallway to Charles's penthouse, the pair vacillated between licking to choking to sucking to pushing to fucking. By the end of the ordeal, after he finally orgasmed, Liv sat at the edge of Charles's bed, an ice pack placed on her swollen cheek. The twinkling lights of the sprawling city and south across the lake could be seen from his expansive window. In the foreground of St. James Park below, clusters of tents glowed with the goings-on of the newly homeless, thankful for a dry place to rest their heads. Yet another tent city.

"Here." He surprised her with a lollipop.

Liv was able to resist the urge to flinch. He unwrapped the lollipop and handed it to her. She didn't move.

"Take it," he said firmly.

She placed the candy in her mouth. Strawberry.

Softly he said, "Good girl." He kissed her temple, then headed into the shower.

Sucking the lollipop, Liv tried to look around the bedroom, considering what information she could gather from its numerous drawers and cabinets. But she could only think of Erin and their baby.

Time passed. Just as quickly as the relationship had bloomed, she resigned from her internship at CAN Create and her waitressing job at Legal Tender. Over the course of a year, Liv traded in photocopiers and pencil sharpening for executive luncheons, company soirees, and more-casual catered barbecues at lavish estates. She shook hands with numerous bigwigs the Resistance had been watching closely over the last several years. Footwear tycoons. Firearms distributors. CEOs of social media networks. Government officials. For Liv, feigning ignorance was easy when she pretended to be more fixated on backsplashes and light fixtures in people's homes than the hushed conversations happening between businessmen and politicians in corners.

"Who was the father of the bride, again?" Liv asked in bed while Charles massaged her sore feet after an epic wedding. "His speech tonight was hilarious."

"Quincy Rutger of Q Tobacco. He's one of our affiliates."

Liv pretended to luxuriate in Charles's touch and adjusted her body so he could massage the other foot. "Whoa. Isn't Q Tobacco under investigation because of that murder on that plantation? Is that the one?"

Without warning, Charles pulled Liv's leg until she slid down and was pinned underneath him.

"You ask a lot of questions."

Liv smiled. "Just trying to make conversation. I really don't care."

"You don't? Because you should." An aggressive kiss was placed on Liv's mouth before he grabbed a fistful of her hair. "Do you know how difficult it is to manage thousands of workers, only to find out one of those Jamaicans has been siphoning goods? Do you know how difficult it is to make an example of that person so that others don't do the same?" His weight was unbearable.

"You're right. That is difficult."

"It won't be difficult for long. Things are going to change for the better, Liv."

At a fundraising gala for the Elita Norwich Foundation for Breast Cancer Research, Elita's daughter, Maureen, approached the podium. She positioned her reading glasses and unfolded the pages of her speech.

"I am thrilled to bring up to the stage a man who inspires us all: CEO of CAN Create, Charles Greene. CAN Create's pilot project, the Renovation, is making bold and necessary changes to this city.

Facilitated by the help of the skilled—and may I say, *handsome*—new special forces, the Boots . . ." Maureen paused for comedic effect. Giggles tickled the audience as their heads nodded in the direction of a lineup of Boots standing at attention at the stage-right wing. Collectively the Boots remained still. They did not smile back. "His dream of unity and peace in the face of disaster will put marginalized and vulnerable populations to work while housing and feeding them and their families. And this evening, we are celebrating Charles's generous donation of $2.5 million toward the construction of the Elita Norwich Wing of St. Cecilia's Hospital, dedicated to the care of breast cancer patients. I truly believe this tremendous individual can add the words 'philanthropist' and 'visionary' to his title."

Liv applauded along with the adoring crowd, her new solitaire-cut engagement ring twinkling with each clap. Hundreds of chairs shuffled wide from banquet tables to allow for a standing ovation.

Wearing the newly designed Boots black leather regalia, Charles, with mock modesty, took to the stage, where Maureen waited with an oversize check. While he posed in various handshakes and embraces, shouting was heard at the back of the hall. Everyone turned to look, curious about the commotion.

"Charles Greene!" screamed a Black man who was making his way past the line of sandbags at the entrance of the reception hall, toward the stage. Trails of floodwater followed in his wake. He tilted his chin up toward each corner of the room, ensuring his voice carried to the bewildered crowd. "You have blood on your hands, profiting from forced labor and—"

Two security guards hurriedly made their way to the man. He shifted left and right in an attempt to escape.

"CAN Create and its affiliates profit from forced labor!" he managed to say before the guards dragged him past the sweets table, past the line of sandbags, then finally off the premises, kicking and screaming. Venue staff discreetly mopped up the water left behind from the unexpected kerfuffle.

Maintaining a smile, Charles waved, and the audience applauded again.

"Can you believe someone would do that? He's so generous," a woman at the same table whispered into Liv's ear while clapping her white evening gloves in rhythm. Others chimed in.

"And then you wonder why Charles is doing all this in the first place."

"Ungrateful."

"He'll be thanking Charles once he gets a job."

"Doesn't he look handsome in his Boots uniform?"

"Love a man in uniform."

Liv nodded in pretend agreement. "What can you do? Can't please everyone."

During the taxi ride home, Liv caressed Charles's cheek. "That was awful. I'm sorry." Charles grabbed Liv by the wrist.

"The only person who'll be sorry is him." He let go of her wrist and looked back at the taxi driver's concerned face in the rearview mirror. "What are you looking at, Paki? Drive."

One week later, that Black man, Leo Ebil Amodo, prison reform activist, father of two, was found dead, supposedly from suicide.

Liv removed her panties, stuffed them into her purse, hopped onto the examination table, and placed her feet into the stirrups. A knock at the door.

"Ready?"

"Ready."

Dr. McKay entered with a file folder under his arm and closed the door. "Let's take a look," he said, crisp and professional, his sunburned baldness reflecting the office lighting. He wheeled his chair to Liv's face and squeezed his hands into the squeak and snap of latex gloves. After switching on a directional floor lamp just beyond Liv's legs, he shifted to a tender tone. "How you doing, Liv?"

"I'm okay."

"We're all thinking about you."

There were no words. Dr. McKay put a gloved hand on Liv's forearm, and the two shared a knowing look and a forced exhale.

"Shall we get started?"

At Liv's nod, Dr. McKay opened the file.

"As you can see here, our boy Charles has been busy." Liv adjusted herself sideways for a better view, her feet still in the stirrups. Photos of Charles traveling through the city. Charles shaking hands with tough guys. Tough guys who had served prison sentences for what were called hate crimes long before hate crimes became the norm. Tough guys who were done cooking meth and would rather burn the Others alive. Tough guys humiliated by Black women who had put them into the friend zone. Tough guys who were traumatized after being carjacked by Asian gangs. Tough guys who hated Indigenous boys for getting their teen daughters pregnant.

"Yup. Got it."

Dr. McKay shuffled through the photos until a series of drone shots of industrial warehouses made it to the top of the pile.

"And here are the workhouses. So far, we've counted seven of them in the Greater Toronto Area. According to our sources, some of them are outfitted for garments. Some are outfitted for food production. Some for electronics. Each one is different, depending on their stakeholders. And we're talking multiple international corporations having some skin in the game."

Dr. McKay pushed back on his wheeled chair to sort through the photos until he arrived at the one he was looking for. "Aha. Here we go." He dug his heels into the floor to close the gap between him and Liv. "See here?" He adjusted the neck of the lamp to shine on a drone photo. His gloved hand pointed to what looked like a gaping scar opposite a warehouse. From above, what appeared to be several dots of people encircled the scar.

"What is that?" Liv strained her eyes at the pixelated image.

"We asked the same thing. Our drones recorded them digging this ditch over the course of a few days. Other warehouses had them too, of varying sizes, but all located within walking distance of the compounds. Then we got these images from one of our Boots from the inside of the Junction workhouse."

Dr. McKay filed the drone shot to the back of the pile and looked at the next photo for a brief moment before revealing it to Liv. The lower-left corner of the photo was obscured by fabric, perhaps the pocket of the undercover Boot and the curve of a fingertip.

In the photo, three Brown men sat at the edge of a ditch with their hands interlaced behind their heads, their eyes fixed forward. They were naked, and their clothes were piled beside them. About ten feet from them, in the lower-right quadrant of the photo, was their future: a tangle of lifeless legs and arms. How many? It was unclear. What was clear was the outline of a Boot in the upper-left quadrant of the photo, aiming a rifle at the head of the first of the three men.

Liv took the photo from Dr. McKay's hands and looked closely at the men's eyes, searching for the solace that their souls had already left their bodies, like a sheep that goes still and blank in the face before the kill. But the closer she looked the more the pixels obscured their legacy cut too short. She stopped herself from bending the edges of the photo with her hands, now shaking and wet with perspiration.

Dr. McKay placed another photo in front of the one Liv was holding. The image was of a large room in a warehouse with a concrete floor. Around the perimeter of the room was a chain-link fence. People were lying on mats, blanketed by foil sheets. "This one has better image quality, and here's why." He pointed at one Boot in the photo, gesturing toward the people, as if waking them up.

"So we've got one Boot who guards them. We've got their surveillance camera right here." Dr. McKay pointed to a device affixed to the fencing in the right-hand corner of the photo. "But this workhouse, my friend, is a converted All-mart store. And our guy managed to give us a live feed from the All-mart's surveillance system."

Dr. McKay positioned the photograph in front of him like a show-

and-tell, pointing at the blanketed figures. "So we know these are not just people. These are children. And we can confirm they have been separated from their parents. Between the execution images and these jailed children, we're not talking workhouses, Liv."

"They're concentration camps."

"Exactly."

Liv took a deep breath and leaned back, looking at the ceiling tiles, searching for order in their lines and cracks. She shifted her bum, and the paper crunched over the examination table.

"The bad news is, we don't have a lot of time. Others are being rounded up quickly, and we certainly aren't able to hide everyone, even though we're all going to try. There are only so many allies willing to shelter people, inside and outside the city. Good news is, because the Renovation is unfolding so quickly, each compound has its security flaws, which means—"

"We may be able to get some people out?" said Liv.

"More than that. There's a plan, especially given the number of Boots we're recruiting to the Resistance from the inside." Dr. McKay removed his rubber gloves and threw them into the trash bin under his desk.

"Which means we're moving ahead with an uprising," Liv said to the ceiling tiles. "When? The way things are going, we need to move quickly."

"I know, Liv. It's a lot. Know that Erin sends her love and the baby is doing okay."

Liv sat up quickly. "She sent you pictures?"

"Sorry, bud. But she wanted me to tell you the baby isn't a baby anymore. He's officially a toddler."

Dr. McKay wheeled his chair to his workstation and pushed the photos through a paper shredder. Liv dressed herself to the sound of the machine's blades transforming those horrific images into slivers of indiscernible smudges. For many of these Others, these would be the last photo taken of them.

Liv touched Dr. McKay's shoulder one last time before exiting the clinic, pretending she had seen nothing.

The return of flooding in the preceding summer had led to water contamination at shorelines across the country, which led to endless lineups of people begging for food, water, and shelter. The relentless currents made river rocks of everyone. Wading hip-deep through the rainbow streaks of gasoline, people found shelter on rooftops and bridges, no longer mighty. Arms poked out of office buildings, waving at passing helicopters, pleading for rescue.

"I have been standing here since seven this morning," said an Indigenous woman on a news segment. A large warehouse stood at the top of a rolling hill, the surrounding trees wavering in the wind and rain. A front-facing carrier held her sleeping baby while another young child burrowed his face into her side. The woman firmly held the stem of the microphone alongside the uneasy reporter. "Our Tyendinaga Mohawk Territory is just east of Belleville, Ontario, and I was told this depot in Peterborough, 77 miles northwest of us, was the closest place I could get water and food for my two children."

The news reporter nodded, feigning concern, while trying to pry the mother's hands off her beloved microphone. "The rule is, according to that warehouse sign over there, a maximum of one five-gallon water container and one box of dried goods per family. But I've been watching these white families backing up their big SUVs to the warehouse, practically mowing all of us down and carrying out boxes and boxes of goods to their trunks! Who is allowing this to happen? What gives those people the right to take more than any of us?!"

On the Confederation Bridge, hordes of people fled the northeast province of Prince Edward Island for the higher elevation of neighboring New Brunswick. Motor vehicles braved the bridge's seven-and-a-half-mile span over tumultuous waves. The piers were stunted by rising sea levels. But members of the island's Muslim community were forced to go by foot.

"Everyone on our street was forced to leave their cars behind. They couldn't move through the water," said a teenage Muslim girl to a news camera, as she shouldered the weight of her grandmother. High winds and the numbness of her lips obscured the audio, then finally: "The people who could drive to New Brunswick took extra people. But they turned us away. So we just have to walk."

"What made the motorists turn you away?" the reporter asked, struggling to keep the windsock on the microphone. He turned the device back to the girl, the sleeve of his trench coat catching the gusts like a khaki-colored kite.

At the sound of this question, the girl and her grandmother were already moving on. Still, the microphone managed to catch the girl's voice: "Look at everyone on foot, sir. What do we all have in common?" The camera zoomed out on a line of Brown folks bracing themselves against the tempest of water and air, salwar kameezes and hijabs damp against their bodies.

In southern Ontario, the concrete jungle of Toronto was transformed into a shallow bayou. Park benches sat in water like rafts in muck. Beneath the surface of floating detritus, curbstones and fire hydrants grew fluffy with green algae. Metal posts wavered in the tide with submerged bicycles still chained to their stems.

Some citizens continued to commute to work, as if denying within themselves the truth of the environmental crisis, as if putting on their pantsuits and packing their lunches would somehow make the city run again. Business as usual. But when the flooded subways had to halt operations, and when people began posting live videos on social media of being stranded in the streets atop recycling bins, holding on for dear life to a lamppost, the calamity finally became palpable.

One live video was of a Black man with his toddler daughter. He held up his phone to show his child sitting in her white plastic baby bathtub like a makeshift boat in the rising water, waving at the camera. He turned the camera toward his face and explained: "This is the way my girl and I are making our way through the city. Right now, we're trying to find any dry land where we can sleep tonight because our basement apartment is swamped." He kept the camera on himself as he waded through the hip-deep water, holding the edge of the floating bathtub, his daughter cross-legged and wearing a small rain jacket. "We ask that if you have a home that's elevated, that has any dry land, please, please, please, let people in. Help people. Feed them. Let them stay there for as long as possible. Share supplies. We all have to help each other. I don't even know who can see this video. But please share this."

The video went viral. People did share the video, not to answer his plea for help but as a warning of things to come.

Lower-income areas of the city sat in the stench of overflowing sewage, leaving their occupants to flee north toward elevated areas like Forest Hill, Sunnybrook, and the Bridle Path. These affluent communities, spared from the floods, closed access to outsiders begging for shelter. Members of the media requesting interviews with households that refused to assist the displaced were briskly turned away. People from around the world watched footage of the once-quiet streets of the rich being swarmed with land refugees, their Brown and Black faces trying to push through newly erected barriers, their tight fists wrapped around the fencing and begging for justice.

Candlelight vigils were held.

"This is day seven," said a Latina woman on her live video. "Me and my kids live in a high-rise on the twelfth floor. No electricity. No elevator. Water flooded the ground floor and below. We hoped these people in their big houses would have opened their doors to us by now, but we'll have to settle for dry ground to sleep on. We're just gonna take this day by day."

The Others sang throughout the night, hoping to turn the tide. Instead, the police were called, and the Others were forced to disperse.

A reporter shot a walk-and-talk segment with her videographer steadily shuffling backward to follow her movements along a muddy city street. "According to the Toronto Police Service, early this morning two men have been charged with aggravated assault against a police officer," she said before gesturing to a series of broken windows. "And instances of looting at grocery stores continue to be rampant. The special task force, the Boots, has joined first responders by handing out much-needed supplies and rebuilding our devastated city." She timed the end of her phrase with her arrival at a Boot who was handing out blankets to a lineup of citizens. "The police chief urges those displaced to honor the laws and allow city services to respond."

By the fall, the floods subsided, the Others returned to mildewed, rotting homes and high-rises with dysfunctional elevators. The privileged were finally left alone. The city tried to operate as a soggy version of itself, but the exhaustion from the crisis soon turned to rage.

Over the course of three days, climate activists donned cheap yellow rain boots and began marching in a large circle at Toronto's city hall, spanning all of Nathan Phillips Square. News outlets captured drone footage of hundreds of Others stomping around the expansive urban plaza in the demonstration's signature yellow boots.

"Toronto the Good, I see you for who you are!" a climate activist said over a megaphone. "If there was any sign of racism, if there was any sign of religious, gender, and class bias in this city, the flood showed it *all*!"

The crowd responded with "Shame! Shame! Shame!"

The yellow boots were seen in Ottawa, the nation's capital. This time, clustered in front of the Parliament building. "Shame! Shame! Shame!" From Vancouver on the west coast to Halifax on the east, the Others in their yellow boots shut down transit stations, blocked roadways, and staged sit-ins. "Shame! Shame! Shame!"

To offset media coverage of climate activists calling for governmental accountability, Prime Minister Marshall Pollack launched a two-pronged campaign. One side of his jowly mouth urged Canadians to band together in the face of environmental disaster while the other spoke about issues of national security in the presence of groups he classified as extremists, bogus refugee claimants, illegal immigrants, and sexual deviants.

"It is the nature of these instigators that they target us when we are the most vulnerable, when this nation is treading water, while claiming to stand for equality. This is not the time for people to 'Other' themselves by declaring the importance of their so-called identity. This is a national emergency! We cannot waste our valuable time and energy on protecting Others. Covering women as if they are in ancient times is a choice that True Canadians have a right to dispute. Jumping the line into our beautiful nation instead of going through the proper protocol is a choice that True Canadians have a right to dispute. Presenting yourself in a way that is deceitful to those around you is a choice that True Canadians have a right to dispute. These Others think they can distract us by demanding for their rights. We are not fooled by their rhetoric. We know better than to believe that the needs of Others override the needs of True Canadians," Pollack said at a press conference celebrating the erection of a new landmark in Ottawa. "Today is a celebration of all that this country holds dear: teamwork, positive thinking, and a vision for the future. Through our work, our nation prospers. Through our unity, we end conflict. Through my leadership, we find peace. Through order we find tranquility." He gestured dramatically behind him and two stagehands pulled ropes to reveal a statue. The cast-iron sculpture was of a dinghy, with waves licking its underbelly. Inside the boat were hopeful passengers: a father, a son, a mother holding a baby. All of them were frozen with their arms reaching up and smiling at an angel in midair. The cameras clicked. The audience applauded.

In Toronto, once the colder months hit, the white "True Canadians," from laid-off pencil pushers to small-business owners whose shops had been vandalized by the hungry, considered their options. Instead of lining up for limited supplies they joined the Boots, who offered free room and board.

"Through our work, our nation prospers. Through our unity, we end conflict," they recited before demanding IDs from citizens on the street; their eyes scanning all points of suspicion: clothing, skin color, mobility, gender expression. *"Through our leader, we find peace. Through order we find tranquility,"* they recited before dividing up supplies found in the homes of Others. It was easy to believe the creed when they were fed and warm.

White folks whose attachment to their upper-class comfort outweighed their desire to speak out against injustice watched the Renovation unfold and did nothing. They were the ones who chose to draw their curtains and turn up the volume on their television while Others were patted down outside their windows.

White folks whose sensitivity to injustice outweighed their attachment to their own comfort covertly joined the Resistance. They were the ones who considered how to leverage their access to supplies and information.

Those who straddled the line between being Others and being wealthy tried their best to steer away from conflict but soon realized that they were not immune to the demoralizing effects of a Boots checkpoint. Whether you drove a Lexus or a bicycle, Others were stopped and questioned. Whether you carried a Hermès purse or a plastic bag, Others' belongings were searched and often confiscated. With what little dignity they had left, they quietly coordinated passage out of the country.

By December, the Renovation was in full swing and the international community, dealing with environmental crises of their own, from hailstorms to droughts, watched and did nothing. In the months that followed, Liv spent her days leading Others into hiding and her evenings toasting Charles's success.

Tonight, things were different. He wanted to meet at her house on Homewood Street. Liv was touching up her makeup in the washroom, her stomach clenched as she thought of me in her basement. Under the harsh vanity light she delicately placed concealer on the bruise near her cheekbone using staccato strokes with her ring finger.

"Gary told me it's probably best to put my house up for sale in the fall," she called out to Charles in the bedroom. "That gives me enough time to focus on the wedding, then stage the house and do some minor renovations. It may mean we'll have two homes for a bit. But he says it's worth the return on investment."

There was a long pause.

Finally he said, "Hey, where were you this afternoon? It took you forever to text me back."

Liv gulped before answering calmly. "Wedding planning. Oh, and another appointment with my gynecologist. You know . . . woman problems."

"Ugh. Say no more."

She didn't want him to question her whereabouts any longer. It had been a busy day of relocating Others, disseminating information.

"Hey, you wanna see something?" Charles persisted.

"See what?" Liv wiped away the smears of mascara from under her eyes. She tried to remain casual, but the knot in her stomach continued to coil at the sound of his voice.

"When you're done in there, we can go for a walk."

"Sure!" Liv said, relieved to leave her house where I was hiding. "Are you treating me to dessert?"

He did not answer. They headed outside into the darkness of the night. Carlton Street was unusually quiet. Liv wished she had put on a pair of pants and boots instead of a skirt and sandals. It was the first night in a while without rain, and it was colder than one would expect in Toronto in May, so she folded her arms around her shivering torso, following Charles to God knows where. They walked north on Church Street, where the Others all used to party and march. Now many of the buildings were abandoned and mildewed at the base. The rainbow-colored crosswalk had since been replaced with an ad for chewing gum; a blond model breathing out mint leaves and snow-flakes. "Icy fresh, minty cool!" the ad read.

They passed the spiderweb of a broken window. Liv peeked inside at what was once Glad Day Bookshop, which she remembered from the few times she had visited the LGBTQ2S store. The place had been ransacked. Books lay burned and torn along the floor. The bar and some tables remained. A pigeon walked aimlessly back and forth over a toppled bookshelf, which was covered in bird poop and fuzzy gray down.

"Liv. Come on." Charles beckoned her to hurry. Liv stepped away, first seeing her own refracted reflection, then refocusing on the spray-painted words "DIE FAGGOTS!" on the broken glass.

They continued past what used to be the 519 community center to the park at its rear. The strings of rainbow lights had been removed, leaving the joists that once held them to resemble four barren crosses. The AIDS Memorial plaques were also dislodged, leaving a border of plain concrete slabs like unmarked graves. In the middle of this darkened void of erased history, a towering beech tree stood, daring to grow in an island of patio stones. They stopped.

Charles pivoted around and stood with his hands clasped behind his back, as if in a choreographed arrival, like the beginning of a dance.

Liv was confused. She looked around. "What? Why did you bring me here?" She twisted her arms tighter to stave off the cold wind.

From the adjacent trees, four white men emerged, also with their hands clasped behind their backs. They looked rough in comparison to Charles's upscale demeanor. In the dim light of distant streetlamps, Liv could barely see their faces but could make out fragments of their persons. One had a studded earlobe. Another had a blond ponytail pulled into a neat braid. A tattooed scalp. A wrist with a leather cuff.

Liv smiled calmly, taking slow deep breaths, the way she was trained to do. "Hello."

The men offered a silent nod.

"Look up." Charles pointed toward the tree canopy. She saw a foot dangling above her. Her eyes followed the foot up, barely registering what she was seeing. Spit began to gather in her mouth. A human being was hanging in the tree. A human being was hanged. A human being was lynched. Her knees felt weak. Her hands were in fists. With all her power she upturned her lips into a smile and laughed like it was a pleasant surprise.

"Wow!" she said, laughing like a jackal. Laughing like her life depended on it. "When did that happen?"

"I got the call about it just before I saw you tonight."

"You've all been busy today," Liv said to the men.

"They've been busy for a while, Liv."

"How did this happen?" She smiled in simulated wonder at this amazing feat.

Charles looked at the man with the blond ponytail. "Care to tell Liv how this happened?"

The man stepped forward, voice raspy and dutiful. "The boys and I saw this one walking down the alley. He had propped up a bunch of skids so he could reach into a garbage bin. Probably looking for some free food like a rat. We tried to get him to safety, bring him to the workhouse for a meal, but he wouldn't have it. He ran, and we had to catch him. Teach him a lesson." The man nonchalantly tapped the bare skin of the person's heel. The tap made the body swing from side to side slightly.

Charles's eyes caught the light of the streetlamp, and Liv could see him assessing her. She laughed. She laughed. She laughed. She wiped snot off her nose. She laughed. She kept the tears in the corners of her eyes. She did not let them fall. She laughed. The men collectively took a step closer toward her, watching her.

She saw two navy-blue leather flats scattered on the grass that once belonged to this human being. This human who once had a name. Liv's belly button felt like it was on fire. But she smiled.

The man continued, "I could tell from a mile away it wasn't a girl. I could tell he was pretending. Like he was trying to fool us. You see them all over Church Street. They're still around, even after the Renovation. We're gonna leave this one out for a while. Make sure anyone who sees it knows whose neighborhood it is."

Liv breathed shallowly enough to stop the bile from rising in her throat. Charles took her by the waist and suddenly they were slow dancing under this hanging person, this person who once had dreams. They were dancing to what song? She hadn't a clue. She could hear only her heart beating frantically.

She looked up at this human being, this human being who once had a favorite movie, a favorite food. This person's hair had been cut. Their* brown hands were once graceful. On their wrist was a thin gold bangle.

Charles whispered something into Liv's ear, and she couldn't understand what he was saying. She couldn't understand this moment. She wanted to scream. Instead, she whispered back. "I can't . . . What did you say? I can't hear you."

"Tonight is a celebration, Liv."

She smiled back as if her life depended on the quality of her smile. "What for?"

"The Boots' budget has been quadrupled."

"But you've already done the Renovation. What else is there to do?"

Charles grabbed her by the arm and she startled. The men around her stepped forward.

"That was just a pilot project. Our investors wanted to test things out in Toronto first, see how the general public would respond to the changes. Now that we've proven the success of the workhouses and the benefits to all of us, it's officially going to become a national initiative. I'm leading the deployment. The Boots are going to clean house across the country. Thousands of jobs for the Others. Millions of dollars back in the nation's purse. It's exactly what this country needs, Liv." Charles looked around at the other men, knowingly. A pause. "But first, we need to clean house here."

"You already did that."

"No, Liv. A Summit of Nations is scheduled in Toronto. The entire world—dozens of delegates and international media—will be watching to see the glory of the Renovation's national expansion. We need to lock it down. And if we're to do that, we need to know everyone we're associated with is ready and willing. Do you understand?"

"Are they ready and willing?" Liv pointed at the other men. They did not react.

"We've done our homework on each member of our team. And when things don't add up, there are ways we can correct things. A process of elimination." Charles looked at her expectantly.

Swallowing the bile at the back of her throat, Liv approached the person hanging. She took off her own sandals, slipped on the blue leather flats that once belonged to this person, and twirled in the circle of men to show off her acquisition. "My size. How lucky." She smiled at Charles.

He approached and gave her a soft, gentle kiss. A confirmation.

After receiving a nod from Charles, the men silently retreated into the darkness.

With her nose still touching Charles's cheek, being careful not to seem too inquisitive, Liv asked, "When's this gonna happen?"

"The summit is happening July first. Canada Day."

"That's quick."

"We have to be quick, before the rest of them go into hiding."

"I guess you just have to round them up again?"

"One by one."

"I'd like to see one of these workhouses."

Charles laughed. "The Renovation needs you, Liv. You can be such an inspiration to the many women who want to join the Boots because of what we stand for."

Liv smiled. She grabbed the lapels of his jacket and kissed him. In her mind, she imagined tightening her grip until she strangled him with his own jacket. But she knew she had to spread the word and tell the Others. She kissed him instead.

*   *   *

Liv pauses and awaits my reaction.

I rub my chin and feel the stubble already emerging from my pores. "When do I have to leave?" I ask her.

"Tonight." Liv has her cheek sitting on her knee, now wet with tears.

I don't understand. I feel like screaming.

Liv takes a breath before explaining. "After hearing the plans for the Renovation, our first plan of action was to get everyone we could into hiding. That's what got you here. That's why you're safe."

"And now?" I ask, my jaw tight.

"Now . . . we can't waste any time. We have to do more than keep you safe. Over the last few weeks we've arranged to get as many people as possible relocated to somewhere else."

"But why? How will Evan find me?!"

"If Evan is alive and in hiding, he will most likely be relocated as well. And if everything goes as planned, neither of you will have to hide at all."

I hold my breath at the thought of this, the possibility of trading in memories of you for your touch.

"Kay. I'm going to miss you. I'm going to worry about you every day until I see you again."

"You think you'll see me again?"

"If everything goes as planned"—she closes her eyes saying this phrase again, like a mantra—"I will see you again."

She takes the acetone from her nightstand and moistens a cotton ball with it. The cotton ball erases my femininity, cleaning the edges of red from the cuticles of my toenails. I remove the kimono as if in a ceremony, like a shell, like a shadow, and place it in her arms. I stand there, naked, unsure of myself in my in-between place.

"You will need to leave once your clothes have been cleaned." She goes to her night table and retrieves an indelible marker. She begins writing on my forearm. "This is an address."

I swallow hard. "Okay." She is looking at me, speaking like every word has to land, like every word is a newborn deer that has to learn to walk.

"I need you to get there before dawn breaks three days from now. A black Grand Caravan will park just north of the stop sign. When the door slides open I need you to get into that van." She sees in my face my attempt at committing it all to memory.

"Do you understand? I need you to get into that van."

"Yes."

"You get in that van and someone will bring you somewhere safe. Please, promise me you will do that."

"What's going to happen?"

"If you choose to, you're going to learn to fight. You're going to fight back."

Before I beg for more details, we hear the buzz from Liv's clothes dryer go off, and then silence. She leaves the bedroom and returns with a pile of my clothes, clean and warm. I get dressed back into this shadow of a person. I dress myself into the corners. I dress myself into the darkness.

When Liv opens the back door of her home the wind is loud and I can see the sun drawing a crimson line along the horizon of Toronto. She hands me a sealed manila envelope and instructs me to tuck it into the back of my pants.

"I need you to give this to the person driving the van."

She does not hug me goodbye.

I regret looking back. I see Liv, opening the curtains of her house, preparing breakfast in her kitchen as if nothing happened. I know this is an act. I know this is to protect me. But my heart hurts with her pretending.

2

My mother was not like your mother, Evan. My ma never greeted me hello. Ma would breeze into our apartment in St. James Town, arms full of groceries, mouth full of complaints after a full day caring for the Wright family children in the Forest Hill area northwest of us. She would kick her mule sandals off her chapped feet and begin her rant about the horrible state of transit between the wealthy upper northwest of Toronto and the poverty-stricken southeast high-rise we lived in. Being a Filipina working for the wealthy was not a walk in the park. In fact, working for the Wright family was more like strolling barefoot over hot coals, with their three entitled children wearing their private school uniforms and spitting their peach pits into Ma's face after snack time.

The plastic grocery bags' handles were stretched and worn over Ma's fists, and she placed them by the front door with a thud. A six-pack of rough, thin toilet paper. A sticky bottle of mushroom soy sauce. Cans of Spam with keys missing. A tin of potted liver pâté wheeled down the parquet and I caught it with the edge of my sandal.

"Not with your feet, *anak!*" she said. "Keith. Wash that, please. I don't want your feet on our food." I hated the sound of my name.

While Ma began sautéing the onions and garlic for corned beef, I continued working on my *Lord of the Flies* book report. Or rather, I continued to pretend that I was working on my *Lord of the Flies* book report. I opened up the pages of the paperback to where my bookmark—a wallet-size print of Randell Sampson's school picture— was placed. I'm embarrassed to tell you, my first love had a face that was both goofy and astute thanks to his prominent jaw and wide smile. One could tell by his large hands and his slender wrists that he still had some growing to do. Soon he would be even broader across the shoulders, with more girth in his thighs. I calmed my erection by biting my lip. For the millionth time, I turned the picture over to see his writing. Blocky, aggressive, staccato handwriting in the bluest of blue ink. "See you after school." Nadine, his girlfriend and my class- mate, had dropped it while clumsily trying to slip it into her Avery binder during chemistry class. I had managed to steal it off the floor tiles, pretending to tie my shoelaces.

"What is this?"

I shut the book quickly. My mother's hands ran through my hair, the knotted twists, like it was a tangle she could never undo. A prob- lem she could never solve. And I was a big problem. Compared to her five-foot, ninety-pound frame, I was practically a monster. Her wispy eyebrows furrowed in worry at the sight of me.

"Nadine knotted my hair for me. It's the style right now, Ma."

"Who's Nadine?"

"Remember? From school?"

Hair knots were the closest I could get to looking like the guys from De La Soul. I told Nadine I didn't want to look like this half- breed something or other. I detested the wideness of my nose as much as I detested the soft angle of my eyes. Between my dark skin and my plump lips I looked like a mutt with a capital *M*. More than anything I wanted my hair to decide which side it was on. I wanted to be Black. My mother, on the other hand, didn't want me at all.

"You look dirty."

"That's my hair."

"Did you try the thing I got you?"

"What thing?"

"The . . . *ano* . . . the thing. The hair thing."

"The conditioner you got from Mrs. Robles?" I laughed. Mrs. Robles had a granddaughter who, like me, was living evidence of her son's bed jumping.

"What?"

My voice cracked from puberty and indignation. "It's conditioner. It's not some magic potion that will change my hair straight like yours, Ma. This is just my hair."

Every night from then on, she tried. I sat on a stool in front of the bathroom mirror, a shivering sixteen-year-old skinny Black boy with my right hand holding a towel draped around my shoulders as she applied layer after layer of this supposed magical conditioner that was to transform me into the son she always wanted. Lock after lock, she slathered on the jaundiced yellow cream, then attempted to run her rattail comb through the tangles of curls. Thick curls forced to pass through such thin slots of unkind plastic. She would stop only after seeing blood on my scalp. The sound of her Christian radio channel, full of static and praise, would fill the void between us, this Brown woman at odds with her mistake of a child. This child at odds with his body. Shame kept my arms still. Duty to my mother kept my voice from screaming. I never fought back.

After washing my hair of cream and blood, I cried myself to sleep, praying myself into another body, another life. Sure enough, I would wake up the next day, still as Black as I was the night before, my mother tsk-tsking at the sight of me. Perhaps she didn't apply enough. Perhaps she didn't wait long enough before rinsing. Perhaps she should have never.

These ten fingers, these ten toes, this head of hair were the product of Ma's one-night stand with a man she met at Aristocrats Bar. Back then, Ma was working as a live-in caregiver for the Edelson family at Bathurst and Eglinton, another upscale enclave. Twin infant girls with red hair. Both were lactose intolerant and had explosive poops. Live-in caregiver was another name for night-and-day-whenever-I-need-her nanny. This meant being on call throughout the night to change, feed, and soothe the twins into sleep, and getting up at the crack of dawn to care for the twins at various playgroups. Live-in caregiver was another name for all-the-time mom to cover for the twins' absent wealthy mom who loved her sleep.

On her only day off Ma wrestled her winter coat on in the Edelsons' mudroom while the twins, now toddlers, embraced her legs, begging her not to go. If she hadn't been working toward her Canadian immigration papers, Ma would have kicked those two brats to the wall like misbehaving humping dogs. But alas, she had no choice but to gently remind them that the maid, a Guatemalteca woman by the name of Luz, would arrive just in time to cook them dinner.

Ma headed out the door, not looking back at the twins, whose noses were pressed against the glass window crying out Ma's name.

"*Ah-tay* Gabby! *Ah-tay* Gabby!" The twins butchered the Filipino term for "big sister."

Ma swore under her breath, looked behind her briefly to give a weak wave goodbye to those thankless kids, then trampled through the snow toward freedom. She loved how fast she could walk without those horrid girls wandering about, sucking on broken glass they found in the sand or crying over rocks in their shoes.

At that time in the late seventies a new phenomenon had broken out called karaoke. Straight from Japan, it was the biggest craze among the Filipino community that gathered every Friday night at Aristocrats Bar and Lounge. Ma wanted to have her song choices prepared before entering. She had managed to steal a couple of the request chits for future visits and filled them out with her favorite ditties. Before taking off her winter coat, she made a beeline for the karaoke host, Lex, and handed him her chits.

"You got it, Gabby." Lex wiped his bald white head with his sleeve and placed Ma's requests at the top of the pile.

"Put your hands together for Gabby, who is going to sing 'Summertime.'" Everyone in the bar cheered. They knew Ma could sing, and at least for the next three minutes and forty seconds, at least, they could enjoy a nice voice instead of a drunken, off-tune one. But to one person, my father, this was news. He had never been to this bar before and just happened to tag along with his Filipino friend Benny, from the automobile demolition center. My father watched as this diminutive Filipina removed her winter coat while the intro music began. She didn't even need the screen; she knew the lyrics. She tried to suppress her accent, but the overpronunciation of consonants and overuse of diphthongs revealed that she was new to Canada. And that was okay. So was my father. Keith Watson Smith, Jamaican born, had teeth so white that Ma remembered his smile widening in the dark of that bar many years ago.

The song that Ma sang that night on the karaoke stage was the same song she sang into Keith's ear after they made me on his springy mattress. The length of his body tented over the smallness of Ma's body. She attempted to kiss him on the lips as he did his business, but he was so tall he could only manage to kiss her forehead. Ma remembers watching Keith, capped by the globe of his Afro, smoke a cigarette afterward, staring down at the bleakness of Eglinton West on a winter morning. His second-story apartment sat above an Orthodox Jewish wig boutique.

"You should stay. It looks like there's a blizzard coming."

"All snow looks like blizzards to us," Ma said, laughing about their tropical origins. "I have to go back to the twins."

Ma never saw Keith again. Benny, his friend from work, informed her that he had been arrested. His work permit was false despite his contributions at work being true. Benny had no other information about Keith other than a mailing address clumsily scribbled onto a chit of paper. When Ma wrote to the address to inform my father of my impending birth, she received no word back. She grew in belly and worry. She gave birth at Women's College Hospital on November 2, 1977, in the presence of strangers.

Another Filipino family shared her hospital room. The woman

had given birth by C-section to a baby girl. The father, dressed in a tan leisure suit and matching wide tie, rushed from his job as an engineer at McDonnell Douglas Corporation to hold his new child while the mother slept painfully in recline, nursing her stitches. Once the mother stirred and the medication wore off, Ma watched as the father took the baby girl, still swaddled and swollen in the face, toward the pleading mouth of the mother who kissed the baby and whispered sweetly into her ear.

I, on the other hand, with my dark brown body and slick curls, lay in my bassinet screaming and flailing for attention because I was hungry and wet. My mother refused to look at me, as she did not have answers nor the heart to carry on.

From hungry and wet, I grew to be lonely and confused. When I was in fourth grade at St. Joseph's Catholic Junior School, our teacher, Mrs. Rossi, set us up into pairs. Nadine rolled her eyes at the sight of me, cursing her luck for being stuck with the most awkward boy in class.

"Well?" Nadine's come-hither gesture was vigorous enough to shake the cherry-shaped bobble hair ties that anchored her perfectly braided pigtails. "Come on, Keith. We gotta get started."

Mrs. Rossi gave each pair of us a lamp, which we pointed to a large piece of paper taped on the wall. Our job was to take turns sitting in front of the lamp while the other traced our silhouette. I let Nadine sit first. I traced her profile, marveling at how her chin stood erect and confident. Her nose was pointy. Her eyelashes were curly and long. There wasn't a single stray hair in her silhouette. Just as I got to her lips, Nadine told me to hurry the heck up.

"Your turn," she said, and pointed to the plastic stool. I had hoped the bell would ring before we would change places. Nadine removed her tracing and replaced it with a fresh sheet. I sat and looked at the paper with my shadow cast upon it. My hair was unkempt. My blue turtleneck was fuzzy and ill-fitting.

"You gotta look to the side, Keith. I can't draw you if you're looking right at the paper!" She sighed and cocked her hip to the side, as she usually did when she was exasperated. I took a deep breath and nervously obliged. Nadine got to work.

"Isn't your mom the nanny?"

"Huh?"

"Look to the side, Keith. Don't move." Nadine adjusted my chin to match the outline she had already made. "You know. The Chinese lady. Isn't that your mom?"

"She's Filipina."

"Yeah. The Filipina."

"Yeah. So?"

"Then why do you have hair like this?"

"I dunno."

"You must look like your dad, then."

I realized I had never seen a picture of my father. The Keith Watson Smith of my mind was nothing more than the bright smile and dark skin my mother had described, but without a face. Mrs. Rossi made us stand in a circle and show each other our tracings.

"Hold it up, Keith."

I raised my paper half an inch higher. My classmates laughed at the outline of my head.

"Hey! Shut up!" Nadine screamed.

"No thank you, Nadine. Watch your language. She is right, though. It's wrong to laugh at other people."

My classmates stifled their snickers until one of them exclaimed, "It looks like he has a wig on!" Then the class erupted into full guffaws.

"Stop it! That's not nice!" Nadine screamed again.

"Enough!" Mrs. Rossi paced the room, preparing us for another one of her inspirational speeches. She placed her hands on the waist of her polyester slacks and looked each one of us in the eye. "Everyone is perfect just the way we are. We have to tolerate each other's differences. Do you know what diversity is? This class is diverse. And you know what? That's the way it should be. Whether you have curly hair like Nadine"—Mrs. Rossi caressed one of Nadine's braids, and Nadine's eyes widened incredulously, her hands closed into fists—"or matted hair like Keith's"—Mrs. Rossi's fingers stroked the surface of my head as if I were a llama at a petting zoo—"we are all God's beautiful creatures." With each word in this last sentence, she patted my head for emphasis.

I thought the torture was over, but Mrs. Rossi then made us sit at our desks and embellish the outline with our facial features. I stared at the edges of me unable to manifest an understanding of my own face without a clear image of the man who contributed in making my features. Did my father's nose slope at this angle? Was my father's neck slight like mine, with barely a sign of an Adam's apple? When I sucked my bottom lip out of nervousness, was this his habit as well?

As I grew into a teen, the act of piecing together the shadow of my father overwhelmed me so that all I could do was lie on my bed each night, stare into the darkness, and hold the photo of Randell Sampson, a buoy in a sea of my confusion. "See you after school," I imagined he would write on the back of the photo, this photo meant for me to keep.

"It's for you to keep," said my mother to me the day she presented me a tricycle. My tiny fingers ran along the edge of the stickers of illustrated pistons, which made the plastic frame appear to be a high-end motorcycle rather than a beat-up, plastic hand-me-down toy. I sat on the low-lying seat and twisted the throttle back and forth like I saw in an episode of *Miami Vice*. Sand trickled onto our parquet floor. When I pushed down on the pedals, the wheel was so worn it spun in place. I giggled with glee. Maybe I was too fast.

"That came from Pastor Michael. But he says you can call him Tito Michael."

"Who's that?" I pressed the stickers illustrating multicolored buttons along the console.

"He's from Winchester Eternal Life Church. That's our church now."

Winchester was not a Gothic building like the Catholic church we'd left. It looked more like a friendly community center with a friendly wheelchair ramp and a friendly larger-than-life poster of friendly, running children. "Spreading the word at lightning speed" the poster read just under the children's clasped hands.

Pastor Michael, the provider of plastic tricycles, was also the deliverer of arduously long sermons. He gripped his congregation with his pious dissertation on surrendering to Jesus the way he gripped the wood veneer pulpit: tightly with white knuckles and pink face from effort. He conducted the orchestra of each singsong sentence, waving the sleeves of his oversize taupe suit jacket, which bookended the width of his red paisley tie. He frequently shared his stories of emigrating from Dublin in an attempt to connect with the immigrant and refugee population of the parishioners, even though he came from an upper-working-class, English-speaking family who came to Toronto by choice and not under duress. On our first visit, a hymn's lyrics were projected onto a large screen and the four-piece band began its number with a steady rock rhythm. Our fellow worshippers raised their arms into the air in praise and swayed side to side in time with the drum kit. Ma looked around and copied, albeit with some self-consciousness. An usher, an elderly Black man in suspenders and khaki pants, approached Ma quietly, interrupting her manufactured awe.

"Did you want to bring your son to the daycare?"

Ma couldn't believe her ears. She smiled and grabbed my wrist. I was brought downstairs, feet dragging.

"And what's your name?" a young South Asian woman asked with a charismatic smile. I had never seen a grown-up crouch down to my eye level, and the change in size and scale perturbed me, so I looked away. From the side of my eye I could see that her voluminous head of curls was tamed into a thick braid. Her slender hand gently capped her knee for balance as she patiently waited for an answer.

"His name is Keith." Ma pushed me gently so I would join the rest of the children in the daycare area. I whipped around and buried my nose into Ma's crotch. I felt a tap on my shoulders. Another first. No one had ever asked permission to have my attention before. I turned toward the woman but kept my eyes closed in protest.

"Did you know we have a water table? I can teach you how to blow bubbles the size of your head!" I opened my eyes in shock.

"*My head?*"

The woman nodded. Her teeth were bright tiles of white against her dark skin. I took her hand and joined the masses. I looked back to serve my mother an obedient smile, but she had already gone. About thirty of us, ranging from babies to toddlers, ran about while our parents worshipped upstairs and rejoiced in the free daycare. From our playroom, we could hear a combination of muffled singing and testimony. At the sound of the congregation erupting in thunderous applause, the toddlers would clap too, then return to throwing sand on the floor.

I never left the water table. I marveled at the rainbow cast across the surface of each giant bubble before it popped into oblivion. Where did the soul of that bubble go? I wondered.

"Pop! Another bubble gone to heaven," said Youth Pastor Vandna, the South Asian woman who had greeted me.

I looked at her, wondering if she was reading my mind, wondering if she was magic.

"Have you ever thought about heaven?"

I shrugged.

"That's what they're doing upstairs. Making sure we all learn ways to let God into our heart." She grabbed a fistful of soapy water and looked at me the way magicians ready their audiences for a special trick. She blew into the hole of her fist and out the other end a giant bubble emerged. I was enthralled. Another round of applause from the congregation upstairs. I clapped too. All service long, Pastor Vandna and I played with the water. Hours passed, and I was wet from my sleeve cuffs to my collar.

"Service is almost over, Keith. We'd better get you dried up." She took me to the daycare washroom, where cubbyholes were filled with toilet-training seats, diapers, and spare clothes. "Go ahead and get your clothes off."

Ma had put me into those darned overalls again. I fumbled with the buckles. "I need help."

"Here. Stay still." Pastor Vandna undid the buckles with two swift pulls, then slowly lowered the overalls to my ankles. I wavered slightly with my ankles bound by wet denim. "Whoa!" She managed to hold me up by my armpits, and I jerked away from her tickling. She placed me back in my equilibrium, and suddenly things became very quiet.

"Uh-oh. What's that?" She pointed to my small erection.

I had no idea what it was, so I stretched the elastic of my underwear to take a look.

"You have to push it down to tell it to go away," she said as she pushed the tiny bulge. It did not make it go away. It made it larger. But she kept pushing a few more times until my cheeks were hot.

"Stay still," she said again, firmly enough that I obeyed, soft enough that I felt loved. I did as I was told and kept my body limp. Eventually, she reached for some spare clothes and dressed me in clothes that were surprisingly well-fitting and easy to put on, unlike those darned overalls.

I began to look forward to worship days. It meant I got to be with Pastor Vandna and play with the bubbles. These daycare times would always end with me getting undressed out of wet clothes, her pushing away my erection, me staying still so she could finish. Soon, the pushing times were the main feature of my visits. Ma did not notice. She was happy that we got to keep all these free clothes that happened to fit me so well. When Ma began bringing home cardboard boxes of donated food, her devotions became our daily routine.

"What's that for?" I asked, pointing to the envelope Ma was stuffing with a check. I was still small enough that my chin rested on the surface of the kitchen table while Ma licked the envelope closed.

"It's my tithing."

"What's that?"

She did not answer. She never did, no matter how many times I asked her. I was a child then, though. And children can piece together truth whether it is told to them or not. The envelopes were issued during service just after my mother was paid by the Edelson family. These clothes, the boxes of food, and daycare weren't free after all.

One Saturday afternoon when Pastor Vandna was pushing into me, the congregation upstairs applauded at the same time I experienced my first ejaculation. A rim of sweat had developed just above Pastor's lip.

"You peed" is what she said before a custodian wheeled his bucket and mop into the change room and gasped. There was a brief silence I did not understand. Then Pastor Vandna quickly dressed me into clean clothes. She didn't look at me. She just dressed me. I knew to stay quiet as she ushered me past the custodian.

"Where is Pastor Vandna?" I asked the new caregiver the following day, this time an elderly Black woman.

"She won't be here anymore," she said with the widest smile I had ever seen on an adult. I went to the water table and began splashing any child who dared come near me.

The first time I saw an intervention was when I was ten years old. By that time, I was old enough to not go to the daycare and I was expected to attend various youth fellowships such as Bible study, Friendship Camp, and Next Generation choir. On my way to choir practice, I passed the daycare and saw a circle of women. On the floor beneath them was Andrew, a five-year-old boy whose mother was a cashier at the nearby No Frills and a former addict seeking salvation.

Andrew was wearing one of the princess costumes from the dress-up center. This was wrong. He was supposed to choose the fireman hat or the policeman uniform. He was not supposed to be a princess. And his mother, pledging allegiance to her new way of living, her new church, straddled her own son and beat this belief into him.

"'Do not be deceived!'" She broke down the Corinthians verse with every strike. "'Neither the sexually immoral! Nor idolaters! Nor adulterers! Nor men who have sex with men! Nor thieves nor the greedy nor drunkards nor slanderers nor swindlers will inherit the kingdom of God!'"

I wanted to stop them, but I froze. I knew that if I spoke up, the women would have to turn on me, for, surely, they could smell Andrew's disease on me too. Surely, they could see the bounce of my hips. Hear the lilt and delicate tone of my voice. See the movements of my slender hands. In my head, I heard the voice of Pastor Vandna. "Stay still, Keith. Stay still."

Andrew's mother did not stop until the circle of women were satisfied with her performance and held her back. She did not stop until Andrew lay motionless on the ground, his pleas too weak to continue. When she was done they held each other tightly, as if he was thankful for the teaching and she, thankful for this test.

"Freeze!" Andrew said to me the next day in the hallway as I was heading to Bible study. He was wearing the policeman uniform, and he pointed a Lego gun at me. I raised my hands up, surrendering to the understanding that princesses like us could never be who we are. There are consequences. I understood that, even later in life as a teenager in love. Even as I fantasized about Randell.

One night, I went to my *Lord of the Flies* book and couldn't find the photo. I thought perhaps it had fallen from the pages into my backpack and went to retrieve it from the hallway closet. But when I opened my bedroom door, I could see a group of six people I recognized from Winchester crowding our kitchen table. Pastor Michael sat in the bulk of his oversize suit, only this time it was powder blue with a yellow paisley tie. He gripped the edge of our table like he gripped the pulpit. I knew I was going to be spoken to, taught a few things. Ma held the photo and looked at me. She wiped her nose with a tissue and placed it in her sleeve alongside the evidence of my wrongdoings.

I'm ashamed to say it, Evan. I shudder wondering what you will think of me, reading my Whisper Letter. If you will think of me as a coward. I wish I could tell you I was brave. But I wasn't. Instead, I crossed my arms around my chest. It felt too feminine. I put one hand on my waist. It felt too feminine. I settled on my arms at my side, unsure, uneven, in the presence of these people.

Pastor Michael swept his overgrown salt-and-pepper mop to the side and gestured for me to stand before him. I did not.

"Good evening, Keith."

I hated the sound of my name. I hated the sound of this man saying my name. I hated the singsong quality of his voice.

"Please. Come here."

I did not. He exhaled. He had suspected I was far gone. "Your mother tells us that she has some suspicions that you are walking away from God."

Ma coughed out a sob, and her church folk rubbed her back in compassion. She buried her face in her hands and screamed, "Keith! Answer Pastor Michael!"

I hated my name.

"What was the question?!"

"The question is, are you walking away from God?"

"How would I be walking away from God? Is this about my hair? Is this about school? What did I do?"

"Are you walking away from God?"

"What do you mean? I'm not walking away from anything." I put on a confused face. "I went to all of my fellowships this past week, didn't I?" I did attend, staring out the window of the community center, wondering about where Randell was, the corners he loitered or the company he kept.

"Lying with a man as with a woman is an abomination." Pastor Michael referenced Leviticus to me as he struggled to stand up and round the kitchen table, slowly making his way to me.

Ma stood up, unsure of the pastor's next move.

"Hold your mother's hands." He gestured for Ma to come closer.

She held my hands. "Keith. You are not like other boys. I can see that," she said.

My hands were molten and moist. My jaw was locked. My eyes wide and preparing for the worst.

"You tell Mommy. Tell me. What are you doing? Who are you seeing? Who is this Randell?"

"That photo isn't mine."

"Then why do you have it?" Ma fished the photo from her sleeve. The tissue came out with it and fell to the floor. She held the photo up to my face, almost touching my forehead. "Why is he seeing you after school?"

"I stole the photo. I mean . . . I found the photo! It fell on the floor at school! It belongs to his girlfriend, Nadine! It's not mine! I meant to return it!"

"Why are you looking at this photo? Is Randell influencing you?" said Pastor Michael as he hiked up his pants.

"No! Randell doesn't even know me that well. We just have gym and social sciences together. His girlfriend dropped the photo and—"

"You're a liar." Ma's thumbs stroked the top of my hands gently, but her words were sharp. She cried as she would cry over a dying animal she was about to put out of its misery. "I can see you're lying to me, Keith."

The rest of her church friends rose from the kitchen table and approached me in the hallway slowly like an animal on the loose. What do I remember of them? One was a burly man in a white shirt with a red bank logo on it. One was a stocky woman with feathered brown hair pinned behind one ear. Another was a teenage boy, slightly older than me, whose determination carved two deep lines in his young forehead. Another was a tall woman who wrung her hands in worry. Ma backed into the kitchen as they proceeded to corner me. She cried over the sink.

"Ma? Maaaaaa!" I tried to move swiftly to the side and fool them, but just as Coach Smythe had said during gym class, I was "too much of a gaylord to be an athlete."

They surrounded me, and despite my most sincere protestations, I was dragged toward a chair in the kitchen. No. No, Evan. That did not happen. What happened? Wait. I remember now. There were no protestations. No. My body froze, Evan. My body was still. In my mind, I was dragged, but I was not. My body froze. It floated, compliant and limp, toward the chair in the kitchen. Slight pressure on my shoulders coaxed me to sit on it. My limbs were numb. A ringing in my ear. A swelling of my tongue. I stared at my hands, willing them to move. They never did. Red bank logo. Feathered hair with pin. Two deep lines in a young forehead. Wringing hands.

My mother, my own mother, filled a glass with water from the tap. My own mother did not look at me as they zip-tied my hands behind the chair, poked and prodded me. My own mother shut her face off, shut her body off, and spirited herself toward the apartment balcony. *Look at me. Look at me.* I prayed as they threw holy water on me. *Look at me. Look at me. Ma. Look at me.* I prayed as they shaved my hair and clipped my nails down to the nubs. Red bank logo. Feathered hair with pin. Two deep lines in a young forehead. Wringing hands. They screamed at me to repent, to change. Not until the sun rose in the morning did I finally, with my voice scratchy and weak from screaming, say the magic words.

"I admit it. I have been walking away from God. I am a Homosexual. I ask God for forgiveness. I am sorry. I will change." My body was limp. My lips numbly gave them what they wanted. I had soiled my pajamas. The exorcism, as they saw it, was complete. The burly man cut the zip tie, and my newly repentant body was free to leave. I walked out into the chill of the early morning. I walked and walked, past curious neighbors, through forests, under bridges, until I reached an old cemetery. I sat there among the dead until something deep inside reminded me it was time to join the living. I made my way to school.

"Hey! What happened to the knots I put in your hair?" Nadine passed by me in the school hallway and laughed. I was sitting on the floor near my locker, hugging my knees. I began to cry so hard that I drooled on my lap, unable to contain the water within. "Jesus! Are you okay?! Where's your uniform? What are you wearing?" She helped me to my feet and looked at the sad state of me in my pajamas from the night before. I explained what had happened. This was my coming-out moment. She was the first person I came out to. In my pajamas, in the hallway of our high school. Me crying into the hollow of Nadine's collarbones. Nadine tied her curly hair back, gathered up the sleeves of her Catholic school uniform, and wrote a note on a lined piece of paper.

PLEASE NOTE THAT MY SON, KEITH NOPUENTE, WILL BE ABSENT AFTER LUNCH PERIOD. SINCERELY, GABBY NOPUENTE.

She signed and dated it like an expert. Like a person who had done this many times before. I handed it in to the school office. I never returned home.

Nadine lived on the twenty-second floor of a high-rise in Crescent Town near the Victoria Park subway station. Since her parents were in the middle of a divorce involving extramarital affairs with younger people in international locations, Nadine reveled in perfectly quiet nights where she could invite over her boyfriend, Randell, or me, her newly outed Homosexual friend, Keith. On my first night living with her, still tender from the day's events, we sat on two plastic stools on her balcony, watching the subway trains head east and west.

"You can stay for as long as you want." My eyebrows rose. "No, really. My parents will do anything to please me right now. Each one wants me to love them more than the other. Plus, they're always away on business. They feel guilty, but not guilty enough to stay home or work things out with each other. So I get what I want. It makes me sick to my stomach." Nadine was half Black like me, but her dad was some dude from Australia whose work had him traveling often. I looked at the length of her legs pointing out from her cutoff jeans. The length of her curly hair, perfectly blond at the tips. Her breasts. Her makeup. She had grown in length and confidence since I drew her outline so many years ago. I ached looking at her, wondering what it would be like to be that confident in my body.

"Where did you get your name?" Nadine changed the subject suddenly.

"My dad. I never met him, though. Why?"

"You don't even look like a Keith."

"You don't look like a Nadine."

"What do you want your name to be?"

"Huh?"

"If you could change your name, what would it be?"

No one had ever asked me that before. My name was just the wish that was never granted, named after my father who disappeared.

"What about Kay? So like Keith, but just the first letter, and the first letter but like a girl?"

Kay. I liked that.

Nadine made a crown of twigs left over from an abandoned pigeon nest on the balcony. In the last light of that night, she raised the crown above her head, above the subway tracks, above the rustle of the forest and townhomes below, and said, "I now crown you, Queen Kay!" She placed the crown on my head. I became me. Me. The me-est me I have ever been. Me times a thousand. Me on full volume. The me you fell in love with.

3

It is midmorning three days after I last saw Liv. Dawn has passed. And still no Grand Caravan. Toronto has traded in rainstorms for sweltering heat, and it smells like mold everywhere. I traveled from Liv's house on Homewood Street westward toward Queen Street and Gladstone Avenue. The map of the city for me is different now that I have disappeared myself like the Others.

I remember once, well before the Renovation, I saw a meme on Facebook showing what the city of Toronto's transit system would look like if all the inaccessible spaces were deleted from it. Only thirty-four of the sixty-nine subway stops would exist, the map explained. As an able-bodied person, I remember being disappointed, clicking the angry-face button, and then, like a lot of able-bodied people, I did nothing about it. I probably watched a cat video right after. Maybe I posted a selfie. Something split screen with the before and after of my drag makeup. I would have gotten tons of likes.

Now that I have been Othered, I too have a limited map. And there is no one, alive or in hiding, that can angry-face button me out of this. No one has seen an image of me online in more than half a year. I can't post a selfie asking others to bear witness to this invisibility.

Because of Boots' checkpoints at major intersections where Others have been collected and sent to workhouses, we have traded in the main roads for parking lots and back alleys. As per Liv's instructions, I follow coded green-spray-painted shapes on brick walls. A simple drawing of a stick figure kicking a ball left or right acts as a flash, telling me which direction to go along the alleyway paths. The tail end of a swirl shows me where I can find hidden food. Concentric triangles show me there are back doors to abandoned businesses where I can hide and rest for the night. We traverse at late hours and early light, unaware of the time since most of us have had our phones destroyed or confiscated by the Boots. In the three-day journey to this address, I have traveled by foot, dodging passing streetcars, sneaking into garages during rainstorms, and raiding garden-grown raspberry bushes. I have stood perfectly still, with my gray hoodie on, in an alleyway while white folks, walking their dogs, greeted each other, unaware of my presence.

My sweet Evan. If you are reading my Whisper Letter while still in hiding, I must warn you. Things have changed in horrifying ways since the last time you and I walked the streets together.

Do you remember how we got used to being stopped for random ID checks, sometimes at gunpoint? Do you remember how our bodies developed a muscle memory until the cadence of starting and stopping became a dance, a wedding march toward our own erasure? In the six moons since I went into hiding, the Renovation has made animals of us, Evan, with saddles on our backs and bits forced between our teeth.

On my journey through the city these last few days, I have seen, through windows streaked with condensation, lines of Brown men wearing hairnets and connected by chains at the neck. In front of them, on a conveyor belt, traveled a never-ending supply of tiny dessert cakes which the men wrapped in cellophane packs and tied in small yellow ribbons. I salivated at the sight of the cakes and wept at the sight of the men but didn't dare risk being seen by the Boot on duty behind them.

I hid behind a fuse box near a converted school. Through a caged window I could see a gym below. White toddlers played and laughed while their Brown nannies observed their charges, silent and fearful. Despite two Boots pacing the perimeter of the gym, the nannies wore receiver collars that were triggered by a wireless fence. A child ran out of a designated play area, and when the nanny tried to retrieve him, an ear-piercing alarm erupted over the gym's speakers. It was loud enough that I too had to cover my ears. The nannies took their tearful children into the center, with eyes downcast and arms shaking.

One night, one fraction of the endless nights of hiding, I ran into six Others who were dodging a Boots checkpoint at Beverley and Dundas Streets in what was once Chinatown before the Renovation. Cylinders of light from the Boots' desperately seeking torches managed to chase us down a darkened laneway. A father and his child were apprehended, but the rest of us dispersed like the cockroaches they believed we were into every crevice of every run-down row house. I managed to find a spot in the construction zone of an old playground. Within the perimeter of the yellow caution tape, a dented metal slide lay sideways, detached from the graffiti-covered, pyramid-shaped climbing walls. It was tempting to consider the climbing walls as shelter for the night, but that place seemed too obvious to me, like slipping into a closet during a game of hide-and-go-seek. Also, judging by the whispers within, Others were already setting up camp inside. Blue tarps weighed down by bricks draped over a large pile of playground mulch. I decided to take cover there instead, burrowing into the moist, soft fibers of the mulch. I punched the surface of the tarp up slightly to create a crude window, large enough so that I could see around me and small enough to remain unseen.

About twenty minutes later, the four remaining Others—a mother and a toddler, and two young men—ran to the playground, straight toward the climbing wall. Without hesitation or remorse, they forced out two small children, who looked to be about three and five, from the coveted spot. The older child was a scrapper and attempted to reenter the shelter by punching with her wee fists and biting with her baby teeth. The mother, with her toddler still on her hip, emerged from the pyramid and towered over the child. The woman grabbed the child's face with her one hand and pushed with brute force, as though the child were a basketball, until she was flung onto my tarp. The woman reentered the climbing wall without a sound. This hiding and fighting for space to hide was always done in silence, with barely a whisper or grunt shared among us in fear of being found.

The two evicted children wasted no time in finding another spot. Adjacent to the playground was a blue metal dumpster full of blooms of black plastic garbage bags. At its base sat discarded furniture. The children appeared to be sisters, with a similar swell to their cheeks and gait to their walk. The Brown skin on their faces was covered in cuts and scrapes. Their long black hair hung to their waists, their wisps of bangs encrusted with filth. With an identical short-clipped scurry, they made their way to the furniture. They wordlessly assessed the potential of an overturned futon sofa by walking around it in their tiny running shoes. The wooden base of the sofa formed an A-frame and the mattress created a soggy two-foot-high tunnel above the cold pavement. The younger sister took a wooden chair, unscrewed one of its legs, and poked the center of the futon. Sure enough, a rat ran from the interior, its tail pink and its fur a slick brown. She nodded to her older sister. The older sister helped the younger one reach into the dumpster to grab several tin cans. I watched in wonder as they carefully placed the tin cans around the perimeter of the futon. I assumed it was a make-shift alarm system to alert them of Boots or rats. They slipped into the depths of the mattress, folding themselves like origami out of existence.

In fear for the children's safety, I attempted to keep my eyes open, lying to myself that I could ever protect them, but the delicious warmth of the soft mulch lulled me into slumber. I slept until I could hear rain tapping onto the surface of the tarp. I emerged into the cool of the darkness, passed the A-frame of the futon with a wordless prayer, and then continued my nighttime journey west along Dundas.

At first I was confused by this address: 32 Alma Lane. I wasn't sure what day it was, but I was concerned that if it was the weekend, I would be found by those frequenting the Gladstone Hotel, which was nearby. I knew that since the Renovation, the hotel had become a popular hangout for the Boots, a place to have a beer after the hard work of relocating the Others. The white hipsters who once made the hotel their headquarters for anything from poetry readings to dance parties, ended up fading into the background despite years of creating a reputation for "progressive thinking." Some joined the Boots. Some calmly witnessed what the Boots were doing and did nothing. But when the side window of the corner townhome unit slid open and a sandwich was placed on the ledge, I understood why I was told to come here.

My dirty hand reached out for the food with caution, and I caught the eye of a white woman pretending to do her dishes. This redheaded woman with baby bangs and black horn-rimmed glasses flashed me the fastest of smiles. Barely a smile. Her lips turned up for a fraction of a second. Then she was back to doing her pretend task, banging about cutlery in the sink, splashing water, when in fact she was feeding me. She filled a small watering can and placed it on the sill after I had taken the sandwich. When I reached out for the watering can, her hand briefly touched mine. It was purposeful, intentional. A moment of kindness. She never made eye contact again.

I hid behind this home's recycling bin and devoured my gifted sandwich. I downed the water from the watering can in one long stream into my mouth. Then I peed, dark yellow and hot, behind the lilac bushes.

That was yesterday, and the thought of that sandwich has my stomach aching for another meal. The kitchen window of this white woman's house has since gone dim and the curtains are shut tight. This makes me wonder if the woman's absence and caution are connected to why the van has not shown up. Around the perimeter of 32 Alma Lane is an uneven fence, protecting a small corner garden of tomatoes and zucchini. I press my face against the worn planks of wood to see a factory across Dufferin Street. Three cars are parked: a red Kia Rondo, a white Toyota Corolla, a blue Volkswagen Golf. No black Grand Caravan. I move my nose to another break in the fence planks. At the stop sign by 32 Alma Lane, a young white man in a suit clips on his helmet, unlocks his bicycle, and rides away.

"Hello!" A ball rolls toward the fence, and as the child comes to collect it, she peeks into the space between the wood.

"I see you!" The little girl has just grown out of toddlerhood, with baby fat still present in her ankles and wrists.

"Molly. No thank you. I saw you, young lady. Crossing the road without Mama is not nice."

Molly giggles.

"That's not funny, Molly. I'm serious. Please hold my hand."

Molly looks at me again through the fence. I shift just enough that she can't see me.

"Mama, look!"

"What is it?" Her mama reluctantly looks through the slit in the fence and sees nothing, since I hide from her glance, but I can tell by her silence that she senses me there. We are both quiet on either side of the fence. Me not breathing, the woman listening for my breath.

"Okay. We're going to go now," the mother says like an announcement, like she knows I am there. "Molly, take my hand, please."

They leave. I exhale. I peer through the slit again and see child and mother crossing the street, Molly with ball in hand.

I lean my head on the fence, looking through the opening, praying and praying for the van to come. My exhaustion and hunger make my eyes heavy, and I nod off. I turn my left cheek onto the warm wooden surface of the fence post, and I can easily imagine it as a soft pillow. I shake my head, forcing myself to pay attention. I cannot miss the van. *Don't miss the van*, I tell myself. But my eyes are so heavy, and the sound of my grumbling tummy is muted in my slumber.

In my dreams, I am six years old again. Ma came home with a new Sony stereo system. The Wright family was upgrading their sound system and donated the old one to her. I watched as she placed an album—also a donation from the Wright family—onto the platter of the turntable.

"You watch, ha? See this?" Ma pointed to the fine hair at the end of the tone arm. "This is the needle." When she lifted the tone arm, the platter automatically began to turn. She carefully and ceremoniously placed the stylus onto the record's first track. "Clair de Lune" filled the speakers. Filled our apartment. Filled my heart.

"Don't touch this, ha?" Ma said before heading to the kitchen to begin prepping dinner. I held the album cover in my hands. *Liberace Piano Gems* it read on the cardboard sleeve. On it was a picture of a man beaming from ear to ear and wearing a silver cape. On the side was a superimposed image of his graceful hands, covered in jewels and rings, on the piano keys. I had never seen a man look like that before: smiling so genuinely and wearing such lavish clothes. Still holding the album cover, I began dancing around the room. I could feel the swoosh of air past my ears with every flourish of my hands, every waltz step through the house. The music sounded like birds just about to take flight. It sounded like eyes slowly opening in the morning. It sounded like fog dissipating in the warmth of the sun. I danced and danced through the house, bracing myself on chairs to lift my legs up, rolling along the floor on my knees, reaching up to the sky at these sensations in my body.

"What is this?" My mother stood there, a plate of rice and beefsteak in each hand, staring at her child.

I awake to the sound of a black Grand Caravan rolling up to the stop sign at the corner of Dufferin and Alma. At first I am unsure. Is this the one? I see a white man inside unfold a map over the steering wheel. Maybe not. But when I see him briefly, ever so briefly, let his eyes stray from the map to look around, I know this is it.

I bolt from the fence to the van. The van's automatic door slowly slides open, and once I am inside it slowly slides shut.

"Get down," the white man says as he begins driving. He drives over a couple of potholes, and I bump my head on the ceiling of the van. "Head to the back. Get under a blanket. We should be there in five hours."

I do as I am told.

"Did anyone follow you?"

"I didn't see anyone."

"Good. Watch your head."

I crawl past two bucket seats laden with boxes to the back of the van, where the seats have been stowed down to hold several heavy gray blankets. I grab a blanket, and when I lift it up I see someone else lying there. They* look Queer too but younger. Head unevenly shaven. I can see from the barrel shape of their sweatshirt that their hefty chest is bound.

"The *other* one. Not this one," they say. I grab another blanket and cover myself. I feel the van move through stop-and-go traffic until I am asleep again, my face moist from my own breath.

When I wake, the road sounds smooth like one continuous hum. I lift up my blanket. From my position down below I can see blue skies from each of the van's windows. I catch the eyes of the white man in the rearview mirror.

"I'm not going to look back at you. I'm going to keep looking forward. Okay?"

"Okay."

"How are you doing? You all right?"

"Yes."

"My name is Beck. Did Liv give you something for me?"

I feel for the manila envelope under my shirt. "Yes."

"Good. I will need you to hand that to me at our next pit stop. As much as I want to tell you when we will stop, the truth is, we're never a hundred percent sure when it will be safe to do so. I might have to just fill up with gas and keep going, you understand?"

"Yes."

"Good."

After the sunlight shifts from the driver's side of the car to the other, we finally stop. The white man opens the door. We are unsure if we should still hide.

"Okay. We're in a safe zone, but I need you to run to the washrooms and run back. The gas station attendant is in with us. But we don't know who's watching. I will need you to be back inside this van as soon as I'm done filling up the tank."

The other person and I lift ourselves up from the back of the van and crawl forward. Our bodies are achy and sore. I hand the white man the manila envelope and he points us in the direction of the washrooms.

"What's your name?" I ask in the cramped stall.

"Bahadur," they tell me as they lift up their sweatshirt to clean themselves. There is no time for privacy between us. The binding around their chest smells musty and old. I imagine I mustn't smell any better.

"I'm Kay."

"Holy shit. This feels good." Bahadur splashes water on their face, neck, and arms. The sound of it all reminds me to pee. I face away from them and do my business.

"Wow. Sounds like you actually had access to water."

"I did. Some white lady gave me her watering can to drink."

"Jealous."

"No, I'm jealous. Looks like you had access to an electric clipper."

Bahadur's jaw drops in both laughter and shock. "Let me guess. You did drag."

"You bet."

"I can always tell when people were paid to throw shade." They wet their hair and armpits; what my ma would call a "cowboy shower," where everything gets splashed with water but no soap.

As we run back to the van, its automatic door slides open and we resume our positions. We see the white man in the driver's seat briefly leaf through the manila envelope's contents, then reseal it. He rolls down the window of the van and slides the envelope in between two jugs of windshield washer fluid. We drive away. The continuous hum.

"Pssst." Bahadur's hand taps my blanket.

We join blankets as if we are at a slumber party. Only we are not wearing pajamas. We are two smelly Queers wearing our runaway clothes, acting like teenagers whispering gossip with glee. It has been a long time since I have had a decent conversation. I pray that the odor between us will become bearable sometime soon.

"So? How did you get here?"

I tell them my story. I tell them about you. I tell them about Fanny and her dog. I tell them about Liv's basement and the lynching. I tell them about sandwiches on windowsills and children through fences.

They tell me their story.

One of the first signs that Bahadur was in trouble was during the processing of their refugee claim. They had a very clear case as a claimant having survived a gang rape involving two of their cousins who found out about their Queer identity. They endured repeated threats. They were ambushed in broad daylight.

"You should kill yourself!"

"You whore!"

"You disgusting piece of filth!"

With the help of the Transgender Assistance Center of Toronto, they filed the paperwork for a refugee claim.

"Now it's just a waiting game," said Bahadur's case worker, Firuzeh. "Be prepared. It may take some time. Especially with all the recent budget cuts to the center."

"Is your job in danger?" Bahadur asked.

"When is it not?" Firuzeh said sarcastically. "The center itself is owned by the city, and the programs are provincially funded. Between our asshole provincial premier and asshole mayor, not to mention our newly elected asshole prime minister, we're pretty much screwed. That's why I've stopped putting things up in my office." She gestured toward her desk calendar with pictures of Hawaii. "It's just this flip calendar and my laptop. That's all. But for now, we wait and hope for the best."

She smiled and winked at the same time, which made Bahadur's cheeks flush. Firuzeh presented them a gift bag. "I wanted to surprise you."

Bahadur's face was practically crimson.

"This week, we're expecting the first snowfall. It's coming early this year. I wanted you to be prepared." She took out a striped Blue Jays toque, a chunky winter coat, and a pair of boots that were two sizes too large.

"I look like a marshmallow."

Firuzeh stifled a laugh. "No! No. You don't look—"

"Yes, I do."

"Okay. Maybe a little." Firuzeh's laugh subsided into an affectionate smile. She held her face with her slender hands, then intertwined her fingers over her lap. She said with a sigh, "I'm proud of you, Bahadur. You've made it this far. Now you just have to make it through this winter."

Bahadur considered stepping forward and perhaps kissing her on the cheek, but thought better of it. Bahadur adored watching Firuzeh as she struggled to put her mess of curls into a ponytail. No elastic band was strong enough to keep it in place, and Bahadur would count down the minutes during their appointments until the elastic would inevitably loosen and let Firuzeh's golden-brown locks fall to her slight shoulders.

"Let's schedule you in next week, okay? We have to finalize your paperwork for your work permit, and I want to get that done sooner than later."

That Wednesday, according to plan, Bahadur made their way from their shelter at Jarvis and Shuter Streets to the center at Carlton and Sherbourne streets. The winter gear Firuzeh had given them was perfectly timed. Hail followed by freezing sleet came down in unforgiving sheets of painful granules. Unlike the sparkles that fell gracefully within a snow globe, the real hail fell sideways, which accumulated into the cuffs and collar of Bahadur's gifted coat. Perhaps this was why the streets felt empty and quiet. With their scarf covering their face, Bahadur marveled at the tracks they created while traveling north on Sherbourne. The street was wider than Shuter, and the wind picked up speed. Bahadur learned to lean into the gusts in order to move forward.

They finally made it to the doors of the center only to find it locked. Bahadur cupped their hands on the surface of the window, hoping for a glare-free view of the people inside. Normally, a security guard could open the door. Usually, a few people would be strolling about the front lobby, drinking coffee or perusing pamphlets by the community bulletin board. Bahadur walked to the other end of the center, where the walk-in clinic was oftentimes full to the brim. The doors were also locked and the waiting room was empty.

A familiar feeling of dread percolated into their stomach, but they shook it off. Perhaps Bahadur had come on the wrong day. Perhaps the weather had shut the center down.

The next day, Bahadur tried again. This time, the Transgender Assistance Center sign on the corner of Carlton and Sherbourne had been taken down. The week following that, Bahadur could see from a block away that the center had become lousy with soldiers in boots and leather jackets. Their armored trucks. Their unmarked boxes in and out of the center. Burly white men shaking hands, then heading inside.

With a scarf still covering their face in the early-winter flurries, Bahadur stood kitty-corner to the center watching this unfold. They could have asked someone what was happening, but they already knew. This place, this city, this country, was no longer safe. Maybe it never was.

Bahadur tried their luck at a recycling factory located on the industrial outskirts of town.

"Social Insurance Number, please?"

"I don't have one."

"Work permit?"

"No."

The middle-aged Black woman scratched her head through her beige industrial hair cap. Putting down her clipboard, she leaned in to Bahadur.

"Come with me." She led Bahadur down a long hallway with threadbare carpeting. She opened a fire door into a stairwell, then paused. "What's your name again?"

"Bahadur."

"Okay. So here's the thing. We're going to the lower-level factory where the majority of the recycling takes place."

"Recycling? I thought this was for loading. I'm very good at lifting and packing."

"I can see that. But that's the problem. People can see you. We don't want anyone to see you."

Bahadur looked at their winter boots from Firuzeh, now soaked from another snowstorm.

"I've been where you are. I know. I came here from Eritrea to this exact factory five years ago before my permit came in. These are jobs regular Canadians don't want. But new people, refugees, illegals, they all need them. They have families. They can't wait for paperwork. And I'm guessing you can't either."

Bahadur shook their head.

"I have to warn you, this job is dirty business. But trust me"—the woman leaned into Bahadur conspiratorially—"the way things are changing, these dirty jobs are the safest for folks like you and me. The less they want these jobs, the less likely they'll take them away anytime soon. Nice to fly under their radar, you know what I mean?"

Bahadur nodded.

"Good. Let's get you some steel-toe boots."

The people in the factory resembled ants. Dust-covered with goggles, Bahadur took their place among the masses.

"Stand here and watch." Isaac, Bahadur's training supervisor, began selecting certain items from the endless line of garbage. "I want you to just concentrate on electronics. Nothing else. Once you find something, you are to throw it into this bin here." Isaac tilted the bin to show various VHS tapes, remote controls, batteries.

Using thin rubberized work gloves that did not protect from moisture or filth, Bahadur picked electrical wires among piles of unfurled diapers. TV antennas from half-wrapped burgers teaming with maggots. Countless times a rat would jump from the detritus and attempt to hitch a ride onto the shoulders of one of the workers. It was typical to watch coworkers scream and dance about, striking their own bodies to rid their gear of vermin. No one could stop and assist. They all had to keep going. The only time they could stop was when the thirty-minute alarm went off to allow the workers to sit for a whopping two minutes. So all they did was watch and sort at the same time.

"If you see any of these, I want them." Ricky, the only white man in the factory, stood opposite Bahadur, leafing through an ancient copy of *Hustler*. Bahadur saw images of hairy crotches and large breasts gracing each page and almost vomited. The thought of nude bodies among the putrid landfill made their stomach turn. "You don't see chicks like this anymore. I love hairy pussies. See, this was beauty. Of course, these women are like, seventy years old now, but whatever."

Before heading to the cafeteria, the factory workers would go to the restrooms and try to wash their inflamed hands clean enough to eat, but rarely did the dispenser have enough soap. Knowing full well that they were in danger, Bahadur kept silent in the men's room so as not to reveal their higher voice. The men at the urinals began peering over their shoulders to stare at Bahadur as they washed up.

In the lunchroom, one worker removed his helmet and sat down among other men, equally curious about Bahadur. "Didn't I see you in the men's room?" he said loud enough so Bahadur could hear. "Why were you there?"

"Aren't you a woman?"

"Maybe she's a she-male."

"Really, are you?"

"Hey! Bahadur! Over here!" Ricky, the perverted white guy, invited Bahadur to his table with an eager swing of his arm. No one else sat with him. Bahadur made their way to Ricky's table and ate quietly, hoping for the conversation to end. "So how does that work anyway? You know . . . muffin bumping?" Ricky banged the back of his fists together, sincerely asking for a demonstration.

The next day, Bahadur tried to go to the women's washroom instead.

"We've had some complaints. Some of the women in the factory have said that they caught you looking at them while they were on the toilet." Isaac leaned his office chair back enough that Bahadur feared he would fall.

With their goggles strung around their neck, Bahadur shrugged.

"I can't see them. We all pee in stalls."

"So then, you're telling me you *have* tried to peek?"

Bahadur stopped using the washroom altogether. Trans bladder. Surely an eight-hour, no-pee shift wasn't going to kill them. After one week, they developed a urinary tract infection. With their crotch sore and throbbing, they waited for the thirty-minute alarm to go off and ran to the men's washroom to pee in one of the closed stalls. It was just a trickle. Bahadur banged their fist on the stall's walls. "Fuck!" They looked down. Two pairs of steel-toe boots stood outside the stall.

"Come on out, she-male." The two on the other side of the door laughed. Bahadur managed to escape the stall, but not without one of the workers cupping their chest to confirm the presence of breasts. "Don't ever come back here, you fucking freak!"

The next day, Bahadur allowed themselves to pee through their hazmat suit. It didn't matter anymore. They were covered in dirt anyway. The chemicals in the air had all the workers coughing. The moisture in the garbage had everyone's hands rotten. Pee didn't matter.

It was payday. Bahadur sorted garbage considering that envelope of illegal earnings. Enough to pay for rent at the shared housing, groceries, and maybe a fun trip to the dollar store to buy something frivolous or sweet. An alarm went off.

"That's weird." Ricky sat down on his stool across from Bahadur. "It's not time for the thirty-minute alarm. But I'll take it!" He took off his helmet and scratched his head. His face shifted seeing something from behind Bahadur. "Who the fuck are they?"

The Boots bled down the complicated steel stairwells in their leather jackets and boots. At first it was a spectacle, like a choreographed dance, all in sync and graceful in their movements. But when the workers saw Isaac with his hands above his head, everyone stood up off their stools. Isaac attempted to flee and was swiftly shot. Screams. All it takes is one person to be killed, to be humiliated, to be raped to make everyone compliant. They rounded up the Brown and Black folks without any further fight, shoved them into several cube trucks and drove off.

"Hello? Anyone there?" Ricky's voice echoed among the silent machinery of the empty factory. Or at least, he thought it was empty. Bahadur, at the first sight of the Boots, jumped into a pile of recycled clothes, covered themselves, and waited for quiet.

Months were spent braving cold nights beneath wooden stoops and escaping ice storms and floods under highway underpasses in an endless game of hide-and-go-seek. As the weather warmed, Bahadur managed to sneak into a condo parking garage, where they nestled into a corner of the building's storage room undetected. They slept between cages of surplus belongings with the hum of the electric lights ringing in their ear.

One night, when sneaking past security cameras to the condo's dumpster for food, Bahadur noticed a black Grand Caravan with the driver's window rolled down. A white man and woman sat in the front seats. It was trailing them. Bahadur ran. They bolted from the bin toward a line of bushes, but the van managed to circle around the bushes and drive directly into their path.

"Bahadur?" said the man from the driver's seat. Bahadur flinched at the sound of their name. "Are you Bahadur? Get in the van."

The automatic door closed and the man began driving. The woman looked back at Bahadur from the passenger seat.

"We've been searching everywhere for you. My name is Liv. I know Firuzeh."

4

I awake to find that Bahadur and I had fallen asleep holding hands, both of us supine under the weight of blankets. Our grip is less like romantic lovers and more like the kind of grasp you give to someone whom you're fishing out of the water, someone who doesn't know how to swim. Only we don't know who is saving whom, our hands are so tightly clasped around each other. I try to loosen my grasp, but they only hold me tighter. Bahadur's eyes race right and left under eyelids squeezed tight. Their square jaw is clenched, chewing at a scene I cannot see. Even the tendons of their stocky neck pulse at relived trauma. I wonder what they are dreaming about. I relax into this odd embrace with a stranger, in this moving car driven by another stranger heading to somewhere we do not know. I have not felt someone else beside me in so long that I realize my skin hungers and longs for you. I shake my head of your memory and squeeze my eyes of the sting.

The van's radio is shut off, and I can hear the wheels crunching along a dirt road now.

"Wake up, everyone. We're here." The white man rolls down the windows. The smell of chicken shit.

I lift the blankets aside and peek out the van's window. Two silos stand against the cooling amber of the afternoon sun. Beside the silos is a low open-air gray building. Across an expanse of coarse gravel is a two-story house with faded blue siding. Everything looks like it's standing on its last legs and with one push of a finger could collapse.

"Who are these people?" I say to Bahadur, pointing to an old man exiting the farmhouse. He is wearing worn jeans and a sad button-up shirt. At the sight of our van, he looks at our driver, confused for a moment, then settles his face into a grimace. He wipes his greased silver hair off his forehead and dabs the back of his sweaty neck using a handkerchief.

The van stops. Our driver exits. Slowly with a faint smile he says, "Hi, Dad." He rubs the blond stubble on his chin, unsure, uncertain.

The old man shifts his feet like a soldier standing at attention. A retired military man. There is a look of recognition. A confirmation in posture.

"It's me, Beck." His voice cracks at this attempt to be forthright.

"I don't know you." The old man maintains a look of solemn contempt.

"I know *you*, Dad."

"Don't call me that." They both look at their shoes. The stalemate is broken when the old man sees me and Bahadur peering at him from the van. "Who's in there? You brought people?! You brought Others over here?!"

"I need them to stay here for the next while."

"Hell no!"

"I have supplies for you and Mom."

"I don't want your supplies!"

"I know the floods hit McGregor's Bend hard, Dad. I know you need these supplies. I have food. I have clean water."

"I can get that at the Costco."

"Seventeen miles away in North London? Between the fuel cost and them gouging people because of the shortages, you can't afford that."

"Why didn't you come sooner, then?"

"I was still in service."

"You could have called! You're just here because you need something!"

The screen door creaks open, and an old woman braces herself against its frame.

"Just shut up, the two of you, and get inside!" Silence. The old woman waves her cane toward the van. Her clumsy gray coif reveals a sunburned scalp and thinning hairline. "And tell those Others in the van to clean up before we eat. They look filthy."

Beck leads me and Bahadur into the farmhouse, and I enter with caution. It feels like forever since I have interacted with white folks other than Liv, and I feel my body folding in on itself, making it as small, as inoffensive as possible. The old woman tells me to take off my shoes, but when I do so, she sees my socks are no cleaner than my sneakers, so I have to keep them on. Instead, I fastidiously wipe my soles on the mildewed welcome mat outside to ensure the pea-green shag carpet from the front entrance into the living room remains clean, even though it has been stained and tatted by moisture. With armfuls of supplies from the van, I enter and reenter the house again and again, feeling apologetic for my very presence. When the last of the water bottles are brought in, I stand by the bottom of the stairs, where dead-people pictures adorn the walls of a long hallway. I look closely at black-and-white images of babies in bonnets, men in overalls posing in front of a newly erected building, and plain women with intricate hairstyles smiling at the camera. The down on my forearms stands on end knowing these people most likely lived here once and all we have left of them are these creepy pictures. I scratch my arm skin to calm my goose bumps.

"Kay? Bahadur?" Beck says to us. I look to the side and see Bahadur has not moved an inch from the front door, and looks just as reticent as me. "You hungry?"

Beck opens four cans of corned beef using the attached key and divides it among all of us. Even with the congealed fat still waxy and yellow, layered between fibers of unknown meat, I bite my lip to keep myself from swallowing the plate whole.

We cautiously make our way to the kitchen, which is a sea of beige linoleum, and settle ourselves in the booth-like seats, side by side with these strangers. For a moment, all that can be heard among us is the ticking of a wooden clock sitting on the fireplace's mantel. Beck and his parents exchange soundless glances. Even when the old man and old woman motion for us to say grace before the meal, it is done in silence. Their hands automatically stretch out to join in a praying circle around the kitchen table, but they both realize it means they will have to actually touch us. They silently decide to just hold each other's hands in prayer. We sit awkwardly outside their grasp. The old woman closes her eyes.

Finally, she says, "Dear God. Thank you for this wonderful meal, for the hands that prepared it, and for the generosity of Beck to bring it here." The old man's lips purse. Beck sighs. The old woman opens her eyes and looks at us sideways. An afterthought. "And thank you for these . . . visitors. I hope they like McGregor's Bend as much as we do. Amen."

Bahadur and I share a look, then eat.

"You all seem hungry." The old woman daintily places a napkin on her lap and nibbles at her food in polite forkfuls. I am unsure if I should tell her that meals are a luxury after the Renovation, so thank you for letting us share your table, but before I can craft my sentence, she says, "My name is Hanna. I'm Beck's mother. And this is Peter . . . Beck's dad."

I open my mouth, about to say, "Thank you."

"Don't tell them our names!" A bit of congealed fat sits on the corners of Peter's mouth.

"Don't tell me what to say. They're here. They should know our names."

"Well they won't be here for long, I'll tell you that much. We don't want to be accessories to whatever this is." A gesture toward us before Peter scoops more corned beef into his mouth. He shakes his head.

"No. We won't be here for long. You don't have to worry about that. We'll be gone by the full moon." Beck downs the rest of his bottled water and looks at the bottle pensively. He heads to the kitchen sink and turns on the faucet. Nothing but a clanking sound followed by a putrid stream of liquid.

"Not a single clean drop since the flood. Unlike you city people, our wells have been left contaminated. Nothing fixed. Not yet. Not ever. We might as well be those Indians on the other side of the highway, drinking muddy water," says Peter, who thumbs the last of his food onto his fork and mouths it clean. "Not that you even care." He suddenly stands, pushes Beck aside, and slams his plate into the sink.

Bahadur and I watch Peter leave the kitchen in a huff, then continue eating in silence. A door slams somewhere down the hallway. Beck goes out the front door. From my seat in the kitchen I can see him inhale and exhale while looking at the darkening horizon. Unsure of what to do, I eat the last of the corned beef, even though all that remains is its stain on the plate. Hanna dabs the corners of her mouth, then throws the napkin onto the table.

"Well *that* went well." She looks down at her white knit cardigan and realizes that the buttons are not lined up, resulting in a small ripple just above her buxom chest. "Oh, for heaven's sake. Will you look at that?" She tries to redo her sweater, but her crooked arthritic fingers get in the way. "This is what happens when an old lady rushes to get dressed because of unexpected visitors, eh?" She chuckles.

"Do you need help?"

"Are you getting fresh with me, young man?" I hold my breath for a second, wondering if she's serious, then she laughs. I laugh. Bahadur laughs along nervously. We are all laughing. "I guess, that's not the case with you, is it?"

Another round of laughter, this time to push the sting of words away. I nod nervously. Hanna lifts her chin and consents to my touch. I redo the buttons. Each one is in the shape of a kitten's head. So small. So delicate.

"Excellent. Thank you, young man. Beck will show you to where you all can sleep."

Beck leads us outside to an adjoining cottage. He tells us this is where the farmhands once slept, back when this was a working farm. Four spring mattresses on simple metal frames sit in one long row in this small cottage between the farmhouse and the silos. Beck struggles to open the tiny windows to let the thick air break through, only to let in more chicken-shit smell from outside. But at least the air is moving. Whoever was here last left a long time ago.

He lights two kerosene lamps in the last of twilight.

"Can we all sit down for a moment and talk? You should know where you are and who you're with."

The day Beck signed up for military service was the day after he was discovered in the washroom with Finnegan Waters.

Unlike Beck's family, who farmed chickens, the Waterses were a well-to-do family by McGregor's Bend standards. They raised horses, and, according to Finnegan, his parents had earned and lost vast fortunes over their lifetimes, thanks to horses. "Or at least that's what my auntie said to me about why we moved to this shithole of a town." The two boys became as thick as thieves when they were paired up during hockey practice.

"Collins!" Coach Trent screamed at Beck. "Can you teach this faggot over here how to skate backward? Looks like the fancy-dancy Waters family doesn't think it's necessary to teach their eleven-year-old son how to play hockey."

Beck looked to the right and saw Finnegan teetering and unsure in his heavy gear. Finnegan's face was overrun by freckles, and when he looked at Beck he gave an eager smile. While the two runts engaged in peewee-level backward wall push-offs, the larger boys repeated backward crossover drills. It was humiliating, especially when that fucker Gary Tulle would come by and clothesline one of them. That asshole looked like he was thirty-five and had just escaped from jail, when he was actually eleven and had just ended a stint in juvie. The entire time, Finnegan wouldn't stop talking.

"I swear to God!" Finnegan's voice cracked.

"You're lying." Beck sniffed away a string of snot that pooled under his bulbous nose.

"But why would your dad put those magazines in the bathroom? Where everyone can see?"

"It was a mistake obviously!" Another crack in Finnegan's voice. The pair had moved onto practicing backward steps, this time off the wall. "My dad took a shit on the toilet and forgot his pile of dirty magazines there. He didn't mean for us to see it. Who would want their kids to see he was a pervert?"

"Your dad's a pervert?"

"Um, yeah."

"Why? What kind of stuff was in there? Like boobs and stuff?"

"Well, yeah, of course."

"Whoa."

"But there were dicks too."

"*What?*"

"There was one magazine called *Slick*. There were guys. Big guys. Black guys. Big, Black guys with their big Black dicks." Finnegan's eyes widened under his new helmet.

"So, it's true?"

"In that magazine it was."

Finnegan and Beck heard the sharp screech of the whistle, and Coach Trent waved them over to the group. "Okay, ladies. Once you're done with your knitting circle, maybe we can learn a thing or two?"

When Beck was invited over for a sleepover, Mrs. Waters asked him to wipe his shoes at the door.

"Mom!"

"Finnegan. I ask everyone to wipe their shoes at the door. Beck is no different."

She turned sharply and pointed at the top of her dress, where a hook-and-eye fastener remained undone. Finnegan clicked them together, looked at Beck, and made a face. Mrs. Waters was dressed like her outfit was a portal to somewhere much fancier than McGregor's Bend. As though somehow her soft lavender dress and outrageous puffed sleeves would transport her out of our chicken farming town to somewhere like the Hamptons. Her hair was styled like Paige Davis on that television show *Trading Spaces*, only spikier on the bottom and more voluminous at the top. Beck felt uneasy looking at her. Like his eyes were unsure where to rest: her sleeves or her towering hair. Beck settled on short bursts of smiles to show gratitude and then looking at his lap.

"Now go show Beck your room and get dressed for dinner. Your brother will be here any minute." She returned to taping the 'Welcome Home' banner on the fireplace while the boys ran up the grand spiral staircase. Beck was confused. Wasn't Finnegan dressed already?

Finnegan had a train set that traversed the perimeter of the room. With a sigh he said, "Go on. Turn on the switch. Everyone wants to try it out." Another roll of the eyes.

"You don't like trains?"

"I did. When I was like, five. I'm fucking eleven years old, which is only two years from being a teen, and I would really, really love it if my mom would stop decorating my room." Finnegan went into his walk-in closet and returned holding a small dinner jacket. Beck made his way to the window and brushed his overgrown mushroom hair-cut out of his eyes to see outside. He gasped.

"What's happening?"

From Finnegan's window, Beck could see the horse stables. In the clearing adjacent to the stables stood what appeared to be a gymnast's balance beam with four legs. A young woman with waist-length curly brown hair pulled a stallion from the barn, its coat a glistening brown.

"Oh, that? My mom says that she's dad's lover."

"*What?*"

"Yeah. That woman is Francesca. She's from Italy. They screw around sometimes. My dad fools around with everyone, and he thinks we don't know."

"But . . ." Thoroughly confused by the madness of this household, Beck pointed at the stallion mounting the balance beam as if the beam were a mare. "*What's that?*" A short balding man, who Beck assumed was Finnegan's father, slid a large tube over the stallion's genitals and collected a generous semen sample. With clinical efficiency, he capped the specimen and walked toward the stable, out of sight. The stallion was whisked away by Francesca, its hide soapy with perspiration.

"Oh that. My dad is a horse breeder. He's collecting his stallion's wet dream so that we can keep this house."

Beck's stomach churned.

"Mushroom soup?" Mrs. Waters asked Beck at the dinner table later that evening. Beck shook his head, but a bowl was poured for him anyway. He wanted to wretch at the sight of the creamy liquid, with the image of the semen sample still fresh in his mind. He picked at the next course, a dry chicken breast, and swallowed hard at the spit gathering in his throat. Across the table sat the guest of honor, Finnegan's brother Stewart, who had just returned from serving in Afghanistan. He too had a face overrun with freckles. He too picked at the chicken. He too wore a dinner jacket, although his fit much too small over the bulk of his new military muscle. The place setting for Mr. Waters remained vacant, as did the place setting for Francesca. Stewart picked at his food in silence.

"You can't tell me this food isn't a million times better than what you were eating in the mess halls." Despite the store-bought chicken and the canned soup, Mrs. Waters adjusted her apron in a way that begged for a compliment.

"Mom. There are excellent cooks in the army." His mother flinched at the insinuation. He backpedaled. "But this is . . . it's better. Yes. You didn't have to do all this, Mom. I know things are tight right now."

"Of course I did! My baby is home safe."

Stewart gave a tepid smile and changed the subject. "When is Dad coming?"

"Oh, you know your father. Always tinkering. If it's not a repair in the stables, it's a horse with an injury. He'll come to dinner when he wants. But that won't keep us from having our celebration, will it?"

Later, Mrs. Waters agreed to allow the boys to set up a tent in the field behind the house for the night. "I'm sure the sounds of the barn will help Beck feel more comfortable here on our estate," she said with pursed lips.

When Beck made one more trip to the washroom before returning to the tent, he spied Stewart smoking a cigarette on the stoop of the side entrance.

"You know it's rude to stare, right?"

Beck was startled. "I wasn't staring. It's just such a big house. I got confused which door I was supposed to use."

Stewart took another drag of his cigarette and exhaled smoke into the night air. "Whatever, kid. Stare all you want." A long pause dissipated as slowly as the smoke.

Beck twiddled his fingers and bit his lips. "Um. Did you kill anybody? When you were out there. In the war. Did you kill anybody?"

Even in the darkness, Beck could see Stewart's jawline tense. When Stewart turned his head to face Beck, what little light shone from the field lamp made a perfect halo around his puppy-cut hair. Stewart's silhouette stared back at Beck and said nothing, like he was letting the crickets' and grasshoppers' nighttime songs do the talking for him. Stewart threw his cigarette onto the grass, shut the door to the main house, and walked past Beck with a slight limp.

Beck found his way to the tent with his flashlight. When he unzipped it, he found Finnegan sitting inside with his arms crossed like a petulant child, stifling his tears with coughs.

"I thought you had left."

"Why would I do that?"

"Because my family is weird. It happens all the time. I don't even know where my dad and Francesca went. Well, I don't know, but I know." The dike that kept his sobs at bay broke and he wiped at his face with the bottom of his pajama shirt.

Beck didn't know what to say, so he put his hand on Finnegan's shoulder like he had seen his father do to his uncle Rodney at Grandpa's funeral. But instead of the wooden tap he once witnessed, his hand melted onto Finnegan's bony neck. It melted so warmly that Finnegan responded by snuggling down into his sleeping bag like a small child being coaxed into slumber with a bedtime story. When they woke, they were tightly spooning, watching the shadow of dew run off the tent's surface. Beck turned around and traced Finnegan's freckles. Finnegan took Beck's hands and inspected them.

"You bite your fingernails." Finnegan kissed each of Beck's stubby digits, then held his hand close to his heart. They both fell asleep until Mrs. Waters called them in for a breakfast of watery oatmeal and burned toast.

The boys grew older. Gary Tulle ended up in adult jail. Coach Trent graduated them from being pussies to being his star players, with Beck playing left defense and Finnegan as goalie. McGregor's Bend was still McGregor's Bend.

They never spooned again. The memory seemed so distant that Beck willed himself to believe it never actually happened. The only touch they shared was in a fleeting hug or a manly tap on the back.

"A toast to this ugly son of a bitch right here." Beck roped his arm around Coach Trent, now smaller than him, frailer than him. "Happy retirement, you punk!"

Everyone raised their Molson beers around the old man, and for the briefest of moments the only sound you could hear was the sizzle of the Costco burgers on the barbecue grill nearby.

Coach Trent managed to release himself from Beck's hold and raised his own beer. "I'd like to say a few things," he said, to which everyone responded, "Speech! Speech!"

"Oh God, no! I don't wanna give a speech, you assholes. I wanted to congratulate Finnegan here too."

Another brief moment of silence, this time a bit longer. All the players paused and shifted their focus to Finnegan, wiping his mouth of ketchup and waving his hand in faux humility. "Unlike you losers who will most likely be covered in chicken shit come the fall, this one here actually made something of himself. This one here is heading to university, and I'm proud of you. We're proud of you. So go, and please don't come back here to this shithole of a town." Everyone cheered. Finnegan's hair was tousled by his mates. Beck braced himself on the rattan patio chair and looked straight at him. Finnegan toasted Beck and awkwardly headed inside. Beck followed.

"You never told me you were heading out."

"Well . . . I graduated high school, Beck. That's what you do. You graduate, then you go to university. Where the hell is the bathroom here?" Finnegan searched Coach Trent's empty house. The endless hallway of shag carpet and textured wallpaper had door after door of bedrooms and storage closets but no bathroom. The sound of guests outside echoed along the textured wallpaper. Beck followed.

"Where? Where will you go?"

"U of T."

"Toronto?"

"Yes, Beck. That's the T in U of T. I'm going to Toronto." Finnegan finally found the door to the bathroom and stood facing Beck.

"Why? Why are you going so far away?" Beck surprised himself with the crack of his own voice. He suddenly remembered Finnegan's changing voice when they first met. Finnegan in his heavy hockey equipment, barely large enough to stand up. Finnegan crying in the tent. Spooning.

Finnegan was a man now. Standing in the doorway of a dark bathroom. "That way I can be who I am." Silence between them save for the boisterous laughter of people outside. Beck suddenly understood. It was who he was too. Beck took a chance and traced Finnegan's freckles. Finnegan closed his eyes for a moment, then looked at Beck's hands.

"You still bite your fingernails."

The kiss was brief. Much too brief. It was just long enough of a memory for Beck to form in his palm and place in his pocket like a treasured rock to admire in the future. But it was long enough for Coach Trent to walk in on them. He turned the light on to confirm what he was seeing.

"Get out of my house."

"Coach—"

"GET OUT!"

A countdown began in Beck's mind: How long until Coach Trent would tell everyone on the team? How long until his father would find out? How long until Finnegan would leave town?

The next day, Beck's plan was to drive back to Coach Trent's house to explain that it was Finnegan who initiated the kiss, that he wasn't a faggot. He had no idea what was happening. He wasn't responsible and what a faggot Finnegan was. How awful it was to have a faggot on their team the entire time. Maybe check with others to see if Finnegan was harassing anyone else. Right, Coach Trent? That would make things right.

The sentences were running through his head while he filled up on gas at the Spector Crossing strip plaza. As the numbers scrolled on the gas pump, Beck looked around, searching for signs that people in town knew. Two teen boys on skateboards were practicing their ollies in the parking lot of the plaza. Across the street at McGregor United Church, Pastor James was replacing the letters on the street sign that had been stolen last week. A mother and her small child exited the convenience store with a stash of lottery tickets and a box of smokes and headed toward her minivan. It would be only a matter of time before everyone knew.

From the parking lot, Beck watched a blond, middle-aged woman in duty uniform exit her sedan. The army officer saw Beck looking at her and nodded in his direction. A nice, tight, efficient nod with her nice, tight, efficient chignon, perfectly timed with the ding of the scrolling numbers at Beck's gas pump. He tapped the nozzle twice and watched her enter the station's store. Beck followed her. He followed her into the lineup in the store, watching her buy a pack of gum. He followed her as she drove to his high school, parked her car and got out, a pop-up banner under one arm, the other pulling a wheelie case of brochures.

"Can I help you with that?" Beck asked.

The officer smiled. "That would be lovely." Beck took the banner into his own arms and began walking with her into the school. She propped the front door open and looked at him. "I saw you at the gas station."

"Oh yeah. Yeah. I saw you too. What are you doing here at Sir John A. Macdonald Collegiate?"

"Career day."

"I've enlisted," Beck said as he entered the family living room. Peter and Hanna were on the couch, ready to confirm with him the news around town regarding Finnegan Waters and their only son. Peter said nothing. Hanna said nothing. Beck had managed to avoid any speech about bringing shame upon his family by offering service to his country.

Six weeks later, Beck was in basic training at Saint-Jean-sur-Richelieu. He left McGregor's Bend without any fanfare. No toast goodbye from Coach Trent. Time passed. Years passed. While his body bulked up, his mind widened to believe in the collective power of his infantry, in the collective importance of the team. They were one animal now, in step with one another. He was not one man now. He was of many men. And in this collective, he remembered nothing of himself. Through constant drills, he successfully removed the treasured rock of memory from his pocket—a memory of two boys in a tent, a memory of two men found together in a small town—and tossed it like a troublesome pebble found in his shoe.

Time passed. Years passed.

They collectively watched the inauguration news footage of a new

American president, named Colin Pryce, who used words like "animals" to describe illegal migrants and "pussies" to describe women. Medium close-up of his hand to his heart. Wide shots of mass protests. Clips caught on people's phones of protesters being run over by trucks. People screaming and running in every direction. News reports of mass raids. Photos of a migrant bent over a car, being searched by law enforcement while her small child cries before being taken away. Photos of migrants crowded into an outdoor chain-link cage, looking at the camera. Hot sun on their faces. Families lying on mats along the concrete ground, waiting for deportation.

They collectively watched the new Canadian prime minister, Alan Dunphy, come into power. The pretty boy won by a landslide, partly because of his charisma and good looks, partly because his election campaign used the word "vermin" to describe refugees and "cockroaches" to describe the Disabled on social assistance.

"We need to derail this gravy train and derail it fast!" Dunphy exclaimed over and over again on the campaign trail. "If the Disabled can wheel themselves to the welfare line, they can wheel themselves to a job."

In the aftermath of the floods, his predecessor, Marshall Pollack, had been too soft to use such words. But Alan Dunphy was no snake in the grass. One of his first actions in office was to establish a Zero Tolerance hotline to report terrorist and suspicious immigration activity. Within days, the hotline was saturated with messages from people snitching on their neighbors: too many Muslims convening in mosques, Black people hosting too many barbecues, Trans folks deceiving everyone around them with their gender identity. While white Canadians rejoiced in righteous indignation, Dunphy enjoyed photo ops near the shores of swollen bodies of water. He filled sandbags while cameras clicked, his handsome grin, wide. More photo ops near the charred remains of a home, devastated by yet another wildfire, shaking hands with first responders.

They collectively watched broadcast footage of a newly formed militia in Toronto patrolling flooded city streets in their helmets and leather uniforms. Extreme close-ups of the militia using their steel-toe boots to kick down doors in search of illegal immigrants siphoning resources. Those same resources being distributed among "True Canadians," who smile and give thumbs-up to the news cameras. The militia strong-arming protestors demanding equal access to shelter, food and water; the establishing of checkpoints at major intersections. Anchors referring to the militia as the Boots. Politicians and pundits referring to the Boots' actions as the Renovation, and the populations they seek to correct and control as the Others. Boots invading tent cities and evacuating the displaced and homeless. Wide shots of classrooms filled with Others reciting the creed of the Renovation. A photo of one of the children sitting in the lap of a Boot while being read to and fed. Video footage of the leagues of Boots marching in a parade toward the city hall. Cheers. Tiny white children clapping hands, sitting on the shoulders of their parents. Adults holding flags and pointing.

In the wave of this political change, Beck was sent to the rural town of Suffield, Alberta. Until recently, the region's part-time patrol group had been mostly manned by Indigenous officers, who facilitated evacuations from wildfires. Those soldiers were quietly dismissed in favor of people like Beck who would not question the disciplinary actions against a local First Nation that was protesting the construction for yet another oil pipeline that would go through their reservation.

Beck found himself part of the newly formed full-time Suffield Infantry, which was responsible for guarding the construction site and controlling large groups of protesters—Indigenous and non-Indigenous—who gathered from across the country and from around the world to try to block the pipeline. Still, in the cool of the spring thaw, the rolling landscape became dense with tents and trucks. Independent media crews dotted the perimeter. The instructions were to stand ground at the site of the new construction. Some days passed with Beck and his fellow officers in full riot gear while the protesters sang and prayed in their faces. Some days erupted in rubber bullets and tear gas. Some days were spent cutting off clean water supply and electricity, and deactivating telecommunication towers. Still, the protesters refused to back down. Months passed. Media attention dwindled to a few select units. When the media released videos of protesters being beaten, being hosed down, the world watched and did nothing. By the time the heat of the summer approached, Beck wondered if the wildfire evacuations would become priority once again and his unit would finally be free of this place.

In his collective thinking, this one-animal thinking, which honored and protected his infantry at all times, he was suddenly struck by the individuality of the protesters. He was like a lion confronting a pack of zebras, confused as to whether he was viewing one large mess of stripes or a series of beasts trying to fool him. To the hum of cicadas in the nearby brush, Beck would waver, closing one eye and then the other, seeing them all as a united power in his right eye, then as individual voices in his left.

"Charity. Hold Mama's hand, please," a mother said to her toddler one day as they moved about the encampment. The mother held a white lump in one hand, most likely a dirty diaper. Charity delighted in the fresh change of clothes and danced about to a song only she could hear. When the mother sensed Beck was looking in her direction, she scooped up her daughter and quickly entered their tent.

A group of teens took turns standing at the front line screaming their spoken-word poetry to the soldiers. An Indigenous teen stepped forward. He adjusted his dusty ball cap, and began.

"MIC CHECK!"

The protesters within twenty feet repeated after him. "MIC CHECK!" The phrase was repeated farther and farther away among the crowd.

"THIS IS A HUMAN MICROPHONE!" Again, the phrase traveled in ripples along the protesters. "WE AMPLIFY EACH OTHER'S

VOICES! SO THAT WE CAN HEAR ONE ANOTHER! SO THAT THESE SOLDIERS CAN HEAR US!" Waves of sound as the protesters repeated his phrases all the way to the horizon of the massive assembly. He continued with pauses in between to allow the human microphone to share his words.

He flattened the pages of his leather-bound notebook and read his poem.

We have been occupied
Papered
Carded
Listed
Interned
Torn
Ripped
Shorn
Walked
Blanketed

We have been occupied
Internalized
Assimilated
Bordered
Fenced
Reserved
Unrecognized
Colonized
Halved
Quartered

We have been occupied
Policed
Stripped

Searched
Patted down
Spotlighted
Assassinated
Imprisoned
Sentenced
Executed

We have been occupied
Whitewashed
Dyed
Bleached
Shaved
Starved
Sterilized
Stolen
Sold
Discarded

We have been occupied
Indebted
Unforgiven
Schemed
Played
Traded
Exported
Imported
Outsourced
Foreclosed

These are names they gave us
These are the ways they took from us
These are the ways they tried

But we are like the waters on this land
Slicing mountains in half

We have our own names
We did not lose everything
We survived them
We are more powerful than what hurt us

We will remember our ancestors

We will drum
We will sing
We will feed each other truth
We will look out for each other
We will come together
We will protect Mother Earth
We will speak for those who cannot
We will make way for our elders
We will listen to our youth
We will remember
We are memory
We will decolonize

There was no applause. Some snapped in agreement. Some nodded solemnly. Without any pomp or circumstance, other poets stepped up, one at a time, to recite their work, the human microphone amplifying their words.

Beck easily tuned out the protesters' songs and chants. But the poets stirred something in a place so deep within his body he could not locate it, so elusive he could not name it. One poet compared the image of the pipeline to her own tongue cut in half after losing her language. One poet spoke of wading knee-deep in the blood of his ancestors, trying to follow the current back to his own heart.

Another poet spoke of building false bridges made of bones arching over water filled with mercury, and the bodies of missing women acting as chevrons along the highway. No matter how hard Beck tried to hum or talk to himself, he was helplessly immersed in images of cut tongues, blood rivers, and bone bridges. He shook his head and coughed so hard he had to spit out the bile gathered in the back of his throat. Then their names, their many names began seeping into the spaces between his teeth, beyond the reach of his eager tongue to dislodge them. They would call out to each other during conversations that did not include him. Vera. Hope. Ronnie. Wayne. Then their faces, their many faces, bore holes into the hollows of his tear ducts. Jayme, the one who adjusts her glasses. Peter, the one with the cut on his lip. Tanja, the one with the starfish tattoo on her neck. He could not escape their faces.

When the media released videos of protesters and their poetic resistance, the world watched and did nothing.

Another day, Beck met eyes with a middle-aged Indigenous war veteran who served bottles of water to a row of elders sitting in camping chairs. The group began to break down into smaller recognizable molecules that Beck could not digest, could not swallow.

"I see you, son," said the veteran to Beck. "I know you see me. I know you're starting to see us." At the sound of his voice, Beck willed his vision to become soft and unfocused.

One evening, Prime Minister Alan Dunphy delivered a moving speech. To the flash of cameras, he said, "Canada has completed consultations with rights holders on this major project. And working with our Indigenous partners has been paramount. To date, forty First Nations have negotiated benefit agreements simply because the benefits are clear: jobs, housing, and financial gain," claiming the First Nation near Suffield was one of them. It was not. And due to the newly imposed media blackout at the site of the protests and disconnected telecommunications towers, no one could report on this false statement.

The morning after, instead of being handed a rubber-bullet gun, Beck was handed a flamethrower. Beck did as he was told and set the yellowing grass on fire. The flames did what they were supposed to do and forced the frontline protesters to retaliate in screams and coughs. But then, by command from Sergeant Sullivan, the soldiers began rounding the protesters' encampment until the rear of their settlement, once a modest stand of brush, was engulfed in flames. Beck did as he was told. He watched, through his face shield, as the mother ran the perimeter of the fire, her toddler on her hip, searching for a way out. She along with other protesters quickly hopped into the back of a pickup truck, which drove out of the pandemonium. Numerous other pickup trucks returned several times to pick up dozens more people. He watched, through his face shield, as the veteran, carrying an elder on his back, stared helplessly back at him, their clothes set alight. Screaming from the pain, the veteran managed to fireman-carry each of the elders into another vehicle, and they too drove off the site. Hundreds of people screamed, all at different pitches, different tempos in their pleas for help. Most escaped by foot, and once outside the circle of confusion, looked back at their tents engulfed in flames and coolers melting in the heat.

The world was told that wildfires had spread throughout the area, forcing the protesters to evacuate. But Beck knew those who escaped by foot were put into cube trucks and sent elsewhere. To where, he did not know.

A month later, still with the smell of burning plastic in his nostrils and mind, Beck submitted his memo requesting release from the military, claiming his aging father needed help on the family chicken farm. By the time Beck flew back to Toronto, the city was also in chaos.

"Can I help you with your bags, sir?" said one uniformed worker at the Pearson Airport arrivals area. Behind the worker, Beck could see a Muslim family being forced to kneel. A security guard began rifling through their suitcases.

"Get them off!"

The women of the family removed their hijabs.

"Now hands up!"

"Sir? Sir? Do you need help with your bags?"

Beck shook his head. He made his way to the exit to call for a taxi and saw a white woman standing by the automatic doors holding a sign that read, "BECK COLLINS."

His face betrayed his confusion. Who had scheduled a pick up for him?

Liv smiled. "Hello, Beck."

"How do you know my name?"

"From your memo requesting release from the military."

She slid the doors of a black Grand Caravan open. "Get in."

One of the kerosene lamps flickers, and Beck adjusts the knob to make the light brighter and steady. My eyes are heavy and lulled by the softness of these beds.

"I know you're both tired. But I need you to listen to what I'm saying now." Beck sits on one of the beds and makes eye contact with me and Bahadur. "You have absolute agency to leave. You are free to leave at any time. I'm not here to boss you around. I'm not your leader. I'm working every day to be your ally. Do you understand?"

We cautiously nod.

"I want you to know that what we saw in Toronto with the mass roundups and camps was just a pilot project. Because of its success, the federal government plans to make it a national initiative. There are people involved in a group that is fighting back, part of something called the Resistance that has been helping to hide you. They are now setting up training camps like this all over the country. People are learning to fight back. We're not the only ones. By no means are allies like me and Liv leading these camps. Instead, we are led by a network of Others who are heading the Resistance against the Boots. These

Others expect us to adhere to an allyship code of conduct and part of my allyship is teaching my skills in combat. As a gay man, I could no longer, in good conscience, serve in the military. But I can serve the Resistance. Here, I can teach you close-quarters combat and how to properly use your personal weapon."

"Why would we put ourselves in danger? We've been running on our own already." Bahadur looks at me, looks at Beck in confusion.

"Yes. You've been running, and it is a fucking miracle you both are even alive after the Renovation. But at some point, we have to stop running. What happens when we have nowhere to hide? What happens when we run out of allies? Out of food?"

"We?" Bahadur sneers.

"You're right." Beck backpedals and stutters. "I . . . It's not me. It's you. I have very little to lose."

"You have *nothing* to lose." Bahadur raises his chin slightly to meet Beck's eyes, and there is a pregnant pause.

I cross my legs tightly and look down at my mucky shoes.

"You think just because you're a gay man, you can guide us in the Resistance? No. You don't even have a clue what it's like to be us. You're gay. So what? You're not a feminine Black man, you're not an Iranian Trans person. All you'd have to do is act closeted, code-switch, and you'd be safe. Kay and I can't do that, can we?"

"You're right. I have nothing to lose. I'm sorry." Beck breathes deeply. "What I should have said is if you want to stop running and hiding, you will have to learn to fight back. And my job is to teach anyone willing to learn how to do exactly that. Each camp is being taught these skills to prepare them for the uprising happening on the full moon."

"*Uprising?*" I exclaim.

Beck continues in a calm measured cadence for maximum clarity. "Yes. On the day of the full moon, there'll be a Summit of Nations, where dozens of delegates from all over the world will travel to Toronto to witness the national launch of the Renovation. This may be our only chance to clearly state to the worldwide media that a genocide is taking place," Beck explains. "The UN is already watching Canada closely. Both Ireland and New Zealand have declined their invitations to the summit in protest of the Renovation. We need to show the world that these aren't workhouses, these are concentration camps. And people aren't resisting arrest, they're fleeing violence. The plan is to disrupt the summit by leading a procession up Yonge Street and in front of the international media, you will say your names."

"Why?" I ask quietly.

"Then it will be on international record what you have survived and that you are survivors."

Bahadur and I are frozen in an expression of bewilderment. At a loss for words, Beck gets up and grabs a kerosene lamp. He places it on the timber floor. He slides a bed to the side and uses his thumbnail to pluck up one of the planks. Underneath the slat of wood is a black vinyl hockey bag, covered in a layer of yellowed dust.

"Look." Beck lifts the hockey bag with a labored exhale and unzips it. Two rifles. Three handguns. Various boxes of bullets. Bahadur glares at me and my eyes widen.

"*What?* Why do you need weapons for a demonstration?!" cries Bahadur.

"It will be more than a demonstration. This will be one of many uprisings in the city happening at exactly the same time on July first."

"And ours will be the one that the media will be documenting?" I ask fearfully.

Beck nods and continues in his steady rhythm to ensure we understand. "Exactly. We'll need to hit them where it hurts. Your productivity. Make them unable to exploit you. Think about all the atrocities committed by the Boots in the Renovation in the name of profit and to advance ethnic cleansing. It's no secret what's happening here. There have been leaked images and videos of mass incarceration, slave labor, deportations, killings all over the internet. What will stop the Renovation is destroying their profit by destroying production, and white folks like me demonstrating that we're in allyship with that destruction. While we're on Yonge Street, with the majority of Boots surveilling the summit, the Resistance will be strategically bombing every workhouse in the city."

I think of the people who can be harmed. "What does that mean? 'Strategically'?"

"It means the Others inside these workhouses and undercover Boots are working strategically with the intention of escape and re-location to safety."

I wonder at the idea of safety, too afraid to consider the possibility of you being among the freed. My ears ring. Was this what Liv meant? A chance to never hide again? A chance to be reunited with you?

Beck continues. "Yes, that means we have to use force. Yes, that means we will use weapons. But know that our aim is evacuation for the Others, and pure offense on the part of the allies and undercover Boots."

"You sound like you're describing a football game," Bahadur scoffed.

"It's not a game to me, Bahadur. It was imperative to the leaders of the Resistance that any bloodshed will be on the hands of the allies against their own. The focus for the Others, everything I will teach you, is defense and escape."

"No. No way. No fucking way!" Bahadur begins pacing the room. "I *just* left a war-torn country. You Canadians want to play war? You want to play Cowboys and Indians? This isn't a game. War means begging for men to get off your body while they rape you. It means looking into the eyes of someone while you cut their throat open. Is this what you want, Beck?"

"No, that's not what I'm saying."

"Then what is it? You want us to just bow down and listen to some white boy's advice about how to keep ourselves safe when it's people like you who have gotten us into this shithole in the first place?"

"Maybe we should—"

"No, Kay!" Bahadur stops their pacing long enough to practically spit in my face. My cheeks flush, and I bow my head down. "Beck, what did Firuzeh arrange with you? Was the agreement for me to be part of this . . . this uprising?"

"Firuzeh arranged for you to be safe."

"And you call this safe? Is enlisting in a makeshift army safe?"

"I—"

Bahadur holds their hand up to stop Beck from speaking. "No. No. I don't want to hear your nonsense. I don't want to be polite about this any longer. I want to be frank. Can I be frank?"

Beck's face is red. He silently nods.

"Thank you." Bahadur continues. "I don't trust you. I don't trust you, or your racist parents. I don't trust that the world will somehow see our faces at this uprising and suddenly act on our behalf. Look at the Rohingya. There was solid evidence that there were atrocities committed against them by the Myanmar military, and the international community did nothing. Why? Because what did the international community have to gain from their freedom? Nothing. Did they have oil? Did they have any resources at all? No. It's the same with the Others, Beck. But instead, the international community gains so much from our incarceration. It gains free labor."

My head is down. I sense Bahadur looking my way, wondering if I will say something. I cross my legs tighter. My palms are buzzing and numb. I will them to move. I say nothing. I do nothing.

"And I love when you say shit like 'You have absolute agency to leave.' Are you fucking kidding me? Are you serious? What agency are you talking about? Can you imagine me and Kay walking off this farm, taking with us this agency you think we have, looking the way we do? Yes! Of course! Agency! We are dripping with agency. We have so much choice! Use your head, Beck. We're out here, and we're trapped. We go out there and one person sees us on the highway and we're dead. Anyway . . . Most of all I don't trust some ex-army soldier who was paid to basically shut out tribal members from a pipeline site."

Beck nods. I look away. Bahadur sits on the bed with a loud creak of the mattress springs, then silence.

Finally: "Listen. I don't know what has changed in you, all of a sudden you think you're our savior, but I can't go through with this. I'm not here to help you feel better about yourself."

"I understand." Beck looks at me. "Kay?"

I can't even look at anyone. I don't know what to say. I just stare at my muddy sneakers, considering why one set of shoelaces is double-knotted and the other is not. When was the last time I tied my shoelaces? When was the last time I walked around barefoot on clean floors?

"I understand. I . . . I hear you. You're welcome to stay here. But before the full moon, we have to evacuate." Beck makes his way to the front door of the cabin leaving one kerosene lamp for us, the other in his hand. "Good night."

5

"Check, please." Nadine gestured to our waiter.

Even though the Bridge Restaurant was a victim of its own success, its dessert selection made it our favorite place to meet. Sharing a triple-decker cream cheese French toast while catching up on each other's news had brought us back again and again throughout the years. We had finished eating and had been staring at our dirty plate for at least twenty minutes.

"Excuse me?" Nadine finally stood and raised her hand hoping to get the waiter's attention. The place was lousy with what seemed to be male models, all with expert fades and crisp black ties. Our waiter flashed his blue eyes in our direction and rushed to another table.

"This place is a joke. We'll never get out of here." Nadine leaned her elbows on the table and looked at me. "I guess this gives me more time to pry into your personal life."

I threw her a look of indignation.

"What? I'm allowed to pry!"

We share a laugh. She piled the cutlery onto the plate so she could reach over and cradle my hands. "Are you doing okay? How are your roommates? Are they legit?"

I pressed my lips and looked down at the table. "They're okay . . . I guess."

"I knew it. Kay, you always have a place to stay with me."

I didn't. Nadine's father was very clear about my being a burden in their household, even though he was on business trips most
of the year. But part of me could not endure the heartache of living with Nadine, watching her go to university each morning and
learn to be an adult, while I was left to stare all my barriers in the
face. Thanks to her, I did not live my teenage years homeless, but I
certainly had no roots under my feet, and I felt it, emotionally and
financially.

"Is it at least safer than the last place?" The last place was on Jarvis,
a single room among many, no windows, bedbugs.

"I'm fine. The place is fine." My most recent place was a town house
near Dufferin Mall, west of Toronto's downtown core, where the rent
was still manageable for poor Homos like me. Seven Queer artists,
dozens of windows, bedbugs. Two of my roommates were a couple
who spent their time either screaming at or fucking each other. One
of them stole money from my wallet. None of them washed dishes.
None of them flushed the toilet. "If it's yellow, let it mellow. If it's
brown, flush it down" read a paper sign in swirly, hand-drawn letters
by the toilet. But my roommates seemed to have conflicting views on
the spectrum of shades between yellow and brown.

"You promise? No one touches my Queen Kay. No one."

I smiled. She held my hands tighter.

That same week, I got a job washing dishes at a gay bar called Epic.
Everything about Epic was small. It was in an alleyway that had been
converted to an indoor space, like a thin slice of gayness on Church
Street. Six small tables, one small stage lit up by one sad LED. And
me, skinny and eager, washing dishes in the back kitchen over a tiny
sink, not large enough to fit five glasses in it at a time.

"It's not like we get a ton of customers eating here. It's more like a
place to grab a drink and watch a show," said Henry, Epic's owner. He
was an astonishingly tall white man with a long and discerning face.
"I would do the dishes myself but"—he held up his enormous paws—
"my hands are so dainty and soft."

I liked the way he held on to the vowels of his words before capping them with the tiny tap of a consonant. *Soooooooooft.*

My first Thursday I was gathering glasses from the bar and checking for watermarks. The bartender was put to task to paint over the giant "GAYLORDS!" and penis drawing that had been scribbled on our front door the night before.

"Payday!" Henry entered dressed in full drag holding a stack of envelopes. "Gerald." He handed a check to the bartender, who was still holding a paintbrush. "Bee." He handed a thicker envelope full of bills to the waitress, whose work permit had not yet arrived, so she was always paid in cash. "And you, young man"—Henry winked at me—"it's only day three for you. Just keep doing what you're doing and you'll get paid next payday, all riiiiiiiiiiiiiiiight?"

Henry had mistaken my awe of him for longing for pay. I stood there, unable to move at the sight of him. I had never seen a drag queen before. He caught a glimpse of himself in the mirror behind the bar.

"Fucking shit. My eyebrows." He turned his head right and left to confirm that they were indeed uneven. When he began making his way to his office behind the stage, I could not help but follow him.

He had left his office door open enough for me to see him wheel his chair closer to his desk and position a mirror in front of his face. He hummed to himself and began rifling through a large pink leather handbag. On the desk he placed a glue stick, a jar of powder, a large brush, and a tube of concealer. Using a tissue, he removed his painted-on brows. He clicked his tongue. A tragedy. A mess. He started over again. Glue stick along the fibers of his brows. Powder to set the glue. Concealer. Sable liner to make two perfect brow arches high on his forehead.

"You know, I don't pay you to stare at me while I do this."

I hid.

"No, no. Come in."

I froze.

"Kay. Come in. Really. I was just joking."

I tiptoed into his office. Four by six feet. The walls were covered with black-and-white photos of people smoking cigarettes and laughing. A woman flashing her breasts at the camera. Two men in an embrace sticking out their tongues. A line of men in tutus doing the cancan.

"Come sit." He slid out a small folding stool that was stored between his desk and the filing cabinet.

I cranked it open and sat. I wanted to cross my legs, but there was no room in that tiny office for me to do so.

"Where are you at with the dishes, Kay?"

"Almost done, sir."

"Oh God! Please don't call me sir. You know, I had to call my father 'sir'? My own father. What a fucking prick. Anyway . . . When I'm in drag, you may call me Clara McCleavaaaaaaaaaaaaaage."

I nodded.

I stared at Clara's reflection in the mirror. It was extraordinary.

"Hmmmm. I don't have your shade in my makeup case." He began looking through his bag. My heart skipped a beat. Was this Christmas? "But I think I have a spare set of lashes and tons of lipsticks for you to choose from."

He took out a bottle with a pointed tip. "Do you know what this is? Surely you know."

I shook my head.

"It's weave bond. Haven't you seen Black ladies use it to glue their extensions into place?" He circled his hand in my direction, assuming I could confirm this fact through an invisible network of "my people." I shook my head. A line of the adhesive was drawn along the length of a set of lashes. Clara placed them carefully along my eyeline. The wet along the rim of my lids felt tingly cold.

"Funny enough, we have weave bond on your eyelashes." He shifted his razor-sharp focus from the edges of my eyes to the pout of my mouth. "And lash glue on your lips." He pried open the plastic case of the lash set and a small tube fell onto his desk. The white liquid was applied, and its stickiness was used to adhere red sparkles on my lips. He reached into his handbag again and pulled out a lemon-yellow wig.

"Now, it's not a lace front. It's more like some opossum your dad ran over with the car. But it'll do for now." Clara made me tilt my head forward as he positioned the cap of the wig to hug the nape of my neck. I slowly sat up, and Clara used a rattail comb to smooth out my new tresses.

"You ready?" He positioned the mirror toward me, and I looked. "Oh! Sorry, hun. Looks like you're tearing up. Maybe I put too much glue?"

It wasn't the glue. I was crying. I looked so beautiful.

"That's . . . that's me."

"Yes. Yes, Kay. That's you."

Clara thought I was a quick study. At first, my job, in addition to washing dishes, was to pass the hat around the room for tips. Clara's numbers were too heavy with dramatic staging to allow for the distraction of grabbing bills from adoring fans while pulling puppets from her bra. Then my job expanded to include escorting hecklers out of the bar who entered just to call us faggots and throw things at us. It demanded a lot of finesse, not strong-arming people, but using humor and shade. The paying crowd played along and booed the hecklers out.

"Let's give them a soundtrack for their exit, shall we?" I would cheerfully say before we sang the "So Long, Farewell" song from *The Sound of Music*.

I wasn't the queen you knew right away, Evan. I had some growing up to do. Back then, only my face and wig were in drag. I began visiting Shoppers Drug Mart to spend what little income I had on my makeup kit. Clara made me return several times until I found the right shade of foundation. All makeup that was even close to my skin color was named after food. Cinnamon Roll. Chocolate Fudge. Caffe

Latte. As if we were meant to be eaten. Through clenched teeth, I settled for Hot Cocoa.

I pounded the pavement along Yonge Street's endless storefronts, past gelato bars and falafel counters, dodging pigeon poop and spit puddles to a hole-in-the-wall shop called Zenith. I stocked up on women's clothes in size ten to fit my length and coupled them with a belt to cinch my tiny waist. In another Yonge Street hole-in-the-wall called Hairy Jane's, I bought my first pair of heels. It was the only shop that the drag queens went to because they carried larger sizes. I bought a pair of red patent leather stilettos, size thirteen and a half. They fit like a dream. I was living a dream.

"Be careful in those. I wouldn't wear them in the streets if I was you," said the elderly clerk, squinting his eyes at me as I expertly transformed his dusty shop into my personal runway. I spied my legs in the shop's mirror and smiled. I was ready to perform.

Well . . . almost ready. Clara told me she had a gift for me. When I began jumping up and down in glee, she waved her hand trying to get me to heel like an excited puppy.

"It's not really a gift so much as a thank-you for not wasting my time. I can't tell you how many times someone wanted me to be their drag mama when all they can do is that boring-ass step-touch dance move. Not everyone can do this, you know?"

She texted me an address close to High Park where she would meet me. She refused to tell me any more. The 1950s apartment sat adjacent to the subway station and the expansive urban park. I spiraled up several flights of stairs until I made it to the suite listed in the directions. I knocked.

"One moooooooomeeeeeent!" a voice sang from the other side of the door. The vintage brass peephole swung open, and I heard another singsong, "Well, helloooooooo." A fat white Queer opened the door and posed. His face was still undone. His floral silk kimono curtained across the round of his belly. Judging by his hairlessness, I was catching him just after his shaving ritual. In one hand he held a roach clip with a soggy crooked roach letting loose a pathetic line of smoke into the already dusty apartment.

"My name is Korus, as in chorus girl." He waved his roach gesturing at all of the showgirl paraphernalia crowding the entryway behind him. "As you can see by my wardrobe, my drag acts fulfill my dream of becoming a Rockette, without risking losing my girlish figure." Korus framed his fat body with his newly shaven arms and curtsied.

"My name is Kay." I curtsied back, and he giggled.

"You are so damn cute!"

"Stop flirting and bring Kay in!" I heard Clara shout from some unknown place in the apartment.

"Hold your horses, you old cunt!" Korus screamed back, then looked at me and smiled. Korus began leading me through his tiny apartment as if it were a museum. Every square inch was covered with various costume pieces. Racks of clothes covered every window, so there was little to no natural light in the home and every bulb hung dim, waiting to be changed. Where "normal" people would put a television set sat a pile of hatboxes so crooked it threatened to fall at any moment. Where "normal" people would line up books on the shelf, Korus had lined up his footwear, from standard nude character shoes with their clunky heels and quick-release buckles to bedazzled boots.

"Don't mind the platform sneakers," he said, despite pointing right at them. "It was during the Spice Girls era. I thought I could be Sporty Spice, when I was more of a pumpkin. The left shoe squeaks, but I don't have the heart to get rid of it."

Korus led me to a kitchen-cum-dressing-room. Or at least I assumed it was a kitchen. A ballroom-dancing dress hung over the fridge, its sleeves half covered with twinkling cheap purple jewels. A silver tube of E6000 craft adhesive sat on the counter beside it with a tub of purple jewels waiting to be affixed to their new home. It was the brightest room in the house thanks to his vanity mirror with all twelve bulbs shining brightly in a golden glow. Sitting at the vanity was Clara with her hair in a head wrap and large sunglasses on.

"You look like a Warner Bros. star the day after her movie premiere!" I smiled at her, hoping she was impressed with my comparison. She did not smile back.

Korus put out his soggy roach in a weed box underneath a Styrofoam wig mannequin. He held the mannequin head under his arm while smashing the roach to bits in the debris of his past joints. Clara sat among dozens of mannequin heads, each with a different colored wig, each sitting on a wall of shelves that reached the ceiling and blocked any light from an adjacent patio. It appeared as though I was facing a jury of queens and wig heads.

"Korus?"

"Yes, Clara?"

"Suit this bitch up." I shuddered in anticipation. What was happening?

Korus opened what had been a cutlery drawer. Inside were dozens of tiny eyelash boxes grouped together in blue elastic bands. "Shit. Where is that thing?" Korus opened another drawer, where "normal" people would put serving spoons, this time with countless lipsticks. He opened another drawer, this one, deeper than the others, the type of drawer "normal" people would place Tupperware in, and found a large electrical saw among rolls of electrical tape and pantyhose.

"What's that?" I said, alarmed.

"What does it look like? It's an industrial cutter." Korus plugged the contraption in. I took a step back. The saw and each of its gleaming silver teeth looked large enough to cut someone's head off.

Clara pointed up and down at my sweatpants ensemble. "Take off your bottoms."

"Excuse me?"

"How is Korus going to do his work if he doesn't know what he's working with?" She waved her hands in frustration, then eventually landed them on her lap for emphasis.

I took off my pants.

"Now show Korus your bum."

I lifted the bottom of my hoodie. They both nodded.

"What do you imagine?"

Clara pinched the end of her chin in thought. "Obviously Kay doesn't need help in the back end, but he definitely needs help on the sides. We need to turn this triangle into an hourglass, stat!" Korus nodded, then left the kitchen/dressing room.

"What's going on?"

"You, my dear Kay," said Clara ceremoniously, "are getting a new ass and hips."

My eyes widened. If the blade of the saw weren't so close to me, I would've jumped for joy.

Korus returned with a block of solid foam and placed it on the kitchen table/vanity. He strapped on a pair of goggles, picked up the industrial cutter, and began carving an ass and hips.

After five minutes of foam pieces flying everywhere I exclaimed, "Wait a minute, wait a minute. Why do you own an industrial cutter?"

Korus froze. His goggled face was covered with foam bits. Clara stopped powdering her nose. Korus looked at Clara. Clara looked at Korus. They both looked back at me.

"I'd rather not say," said Korus.

"It's best we don't talk about it. Probably best you never know," Clara added while nervously looking side to side.

And that was that. Korus returned to carving, Clara returned to powdering, and I returned to sitting on a pile of Korus's dirty laundry still without my pants on.

When the carving was done, Korus instructed me to wrap the curvaceous foam creation around my hips before putting on four pairs of dark brown stockings to match my skin color.

"Thoughts?" Korus said to Clara, one hand still on the plugged-in industrial cutter.

"I won't know until I see her in swimwear."

I changed into a bathing suit and put on heels.

"Now?"

"Perfect, Korus." Clara finally smiled at the sight of me. She removed her sunglasses and I could see her right eye was swollen and bruised.

"Clara!" Korus exclaimed.

I stepped toward her. "What happened to your face? Who did that to you?"

"Shh shh shh shh shh," Clara said, placing her finger to her painted lips. "Please don't ruin this moment by reminding me of last night's misfortunes. You, Kay, are just perfect. Korus, show Kay what she looks like."

Korus opened up a tall cupboard door in the kitchen/dressing room, where "normal" people would put their canned goods, to reveal a long mirror and an image of a woman's curvaceous body looking back at me. Now I was truly ready to perform.

That night, I stood stage right waiting for my big moment. Clara Mc-Cleavage had just completed her ode to the horror movie *Carrie*, which ended with three audience members splattering blood onto her white dress using spray bottles. Out of breath, Clara took the microphone.

"I love being sprayed by complete strangers with questionable substances! It reminds me of last weekeeeeend."

Snickers. Clara made her way to a tall stool, where a tumbler of lemon water and a hand towel waited for her. She sipped on the water and then gently patted the sweat along her hairline and her upper lip.

"I just wish you sprayed me more. Look at me. Hardly any blood. I imagined complete carnage but this looks more like a papercut. These are dollar-store spray bottles. You have to pump them and mean it. You have to pump those cheap fuckers. This is an homage to a classic horror movie, people." Clara rolled her eyes, then gave a sly grin.

After the applause settled, Clara winked at me, then took a breath.

"Well, tonight I am one happy drag mama."

My heart grew two sizes.

"This is her first gig, so be prepared to catch her wig if she didn't pin it right. Put your hands together for Caramel Kay!"

The audience cheered. For a moment, I was thrown off. I had told her my name was Queen Kay. Suddenly, just like the foundation colors at the drug store, I too was fit for eating. I quickly tucked away my embarrassment into the sides of my forced smile. Shaking my hands awake, I exhaled to center myself and did one last check of all the props hidden in my pockets. *Don't fall in your heels. Don't fall in your heels*, I thought to myself.

An uncomfortable silence fell as Clara stepped off the stage and took a seat. She signaled the bar staff to press play. A slow and steady bass rhythm filled the room, and the audience applauded, recognizing "Giving Him Something He Can Feel," sung by En Vogue. Instead of the iconic red dresses worn by the group in their music video, I entered wearing a sexy nurse's outfit, which was tight enough to show off my new bum and hips, short enough to reveal my muscular legs. Cheers.

Determined to appear fearless and experienced despite being afraid and a rookie, I worked my way through the crowd, taking the vital signs of audience members in raunchy ways. I checked one person's pulse while placing their hand on my buxom bosom. I used a stethoscope on another person's crotch instead of their heart. With a more willing audience member, I took their temperature by making them suck a larger-than-life thermometer. In between each action, I would pass a patron who offered me a tip. I tried to remain casual and continue lip-syncing, but each crisp bill represented a meal, represented rent. By the end of the song, during the final chorus, I welcomed someone to reach under my skirt and reveal my Godzilla-size strap-on. The audience sang along while my fake phallus was stroked in rhythm with the bass guitar. The song faded in time with my exit. Standing ovation.

When the night was over, I sat in the office staring at the wad of cash I had earned, now damp from the folds of my fake titties. The adrenaline rush had yet to leave me, and I sat still, replaying the delicious details of my performance again and again. The faces of the audience. Each reaction. *I did it and I got a standing ovation.*

"You did it, guuuuurl!" said Clara, half out of costume. I smiled at her, unable to speak. I could feel the tresses of my wig painting my sweaty neck and the edges of my lashes fraying. Clara took one bill from her own chest of tips, slapped it onto the surface of the desk and said, "Now go buy yourself a hamburger. You deserve iiiit."

I became a regular feature at Epic along with regular guest queens such as Bitches of Madison County (specialty: housewife turned naughty scenarios) and Kamel Toe (specialty: foam body embellishments showcasing maximum vulva). I enjoyed sharing space in the tiny office while we transformed our faces. Our backstage exchanges with each other, both catty and endearing, translated onstage into my being hotter on the mic for insults and comebacks. This came in handy when we hosted Royal Travesty, whose shtick involved lip-syncing to eighties British punk wearing floral-printed dresses fit for Elizabeth II.

On the night she was scheduled, I greeted her at the entrance to Epic with my fervent hand extended. "I'm Queen Kay. We're performing together tonight. It's great to meet—"

She pushed past me with her large rolling suitcase trailing behind her. She wore extra-large sunglasses to hide her undone face. With lips pursed she said in a surprisingly deep, raspy voice, "If you see a drag queen walking with her suitcase, don't bother her," before passing me and heading to the office/dressing room.

I was slated to perform after Royal Travesty. Eager to learn some new skills, I waited in the wings and watched. During her number, the Sex Pistols played on full blast, while she waved her cupped hand hello to the audience. Everyone cheered.

Clara and Royal exchanged some witty repartee before introducing me. "Oh, look, there was a sale at Goodwill." Clara dryly eyed Royal Travesty up and down. She returned the gesture by inspecting Clara's blue organza extravaganza.

"Will you give the audience a twirl?" Royal Travesty said. She gestured toward Clara, then turned to the audience with expert timing. "Don't you just *love* estate sales?"

The audience winced.

"Nothing like stealing a dress off a dead lady."

Clara chuckled, then changed the subject. "Before we kill each other onstage, I think it's time to introduce our next performer. Is everyone ready for Caramel Kay?" Hurrahs from the audience. My name was said wrong again. I forced myself to smile, shake it off.

"Tell me about Caramel Kay."

"She's new on the scene, and she is quickly becoming one of Epic's favorites. I taught her everything she knows about drag. I am so proud of her!"

Royal Travesty put her hands on her hips, readying the audience for another joke. "But did you teach her how to get a job?"

Some of the audience members coughed in shock. Most of them laughed. The smile on my face wilted.

"Do you know this joke?" Royal Travesty raised her hand as if she were conducting an orchestra, orchestrating my demise. "What is the difference between a Black guy and a large pizza?"

Clara awkwardly guffawed, then managed to spit out, "I don't know. What is the difference, Royal?"

"The large pizza can feed a family of four!"

The white people in the audience laughed and laughed. An Asian couple shifted in their seats uncomfortably. My ears were ringing.

"Oh, come here, Caramel Kay."

The audience laughed again. I did as I was told. My arms were numb. I walked toward her feeling like my heels were stilts and my ensemble was rags. I smiled.

"You know I'm joking, right? You thought what I said was funny, right?" She smiled a devilish smile at me. Pleading. Forcing. There was a long pause. I knew this was my opportunity to make things right, to break the ice. But when I saw an audience member covering her mouth in shock, I decided to throw shade instead.

"I'm sorry, what?"

Royal Travesty looked at the audience, looked at Clara, then at me. A wider smile. "It's all in good fun, hun."

"Sorry, I don't understand what you're saying. I don't speak Asshole." The audience gasped. They choked. Royal Travesty stepped forward, her bottom lip heavy, trying desperately to craft a comeback. She was either going to spit at me or kick me offstage. I was the younger, less-experienced queen after all. Despite having crossed a line, I happily stood on the other side of it, delighting in the mess I made of her emotions. I had never felt this sense of authority before, fueled by the laughter in the audience. So drunk was I on this unfamiliar power trip, that the width of my grin felt like it was going to break my face in half. Clara quickly intercepted Royal Travesty and signaled to the bar staff to begin my music, which was a mashup of songs from the musical *Fame*.

Wearing a 1980s leotard and tights, I began lip-syncing to a recording of Debbie Allen's infamous lecture about working "your little tights off" to become a dancer. Laughter. I moved about the audience, waving a teacher's cane in their faces and preaching that it didn't matter how big their dreams were, fame costs, and here was where they had to start paying. The cheap sound system suddenly blared my badly edited audio track of the signature *Fame* disco downbeat. The crowd went wild. Buoyed by their reaction, I pranced about onstage doing faux jazz choreography while lip-syncing to Irene Cara's lyrics. By midsong, everyone was clapping in rhythm to the music. I pushed the audience into hysterics by miming the electric guitar solos using my own leg. Peals of laughter. I struck my final pose, and I enjoyed yet another standing ovation. As I walked off the stage I looked straight at Royal Travesty and gave her my most aristocratic wave.

Upstairs Clara and Royal Travesty finished their set of performances. I sat in the office/dressing room waiting for them. Down the stairs they stomped, both of them out of breath.

"Where is that fucking bitch?! Who the hell does he think he is, shaming me in front of everyone?"

Clara pleaded with Royal Travesty, "Come on. Kay is new. Maybe he took it too personally. He just needs some fineeeeeeesse."

"I don't give a flying fuck if he took it personally. This is a drag show, not art therapy."

The door of the office/dressing room slammed open. Both Clara and Royal Travesty were drenched in sweat. Their made-up faces had melted onto the surface of their necks. At that moment, Clara was Long-Faced Henry. Royal Travesty was Old-Man Arthur. Only, both of them happened to be wearing dresses with wigs askew. The magic spell was over.

With the same rage she had displayed onstage, Royal Travesty glared at me, then glared at the steaming-hot large pepperoni pizza sitting on the desk. Three clean paper plates and three cold cans of cola sat next to the box. The rage shifted to confusion.

"I'm sorry to have hurt your feelings, Royal," I said while delivering the deepest of bows. "Pizza is on me." It was worth sneaking through the back door of Epic to Pizza Pizza in my full costume to see the look on her face. She warily grabbed a piece of pizza and took a bite, as if the flavor of the slice would confirm whether it was a gesture of humility or yet another insult. I exited the room and dressed back into my street clothes just outside the office. While stepping out of my tights, I watched through the crack in the door as they devoured the pizza like pigs at a trough. I felt a thrilling combination of amusement and satisfaction at hearing nothing save for their breathy bites through the crust and the occasional belch. Sure, it wasn't a family of four, but feeding two angry queens felt just as triumphant.

Years later, during yet another dinner at the Bridge Restaurant, Nadine gestured to the waiter. "Is this asshole going to give us our check or what?" She kissed her teeth in frustration. She piled the cutlery onto the plate, now stained with maple syrup and icing sugar so she could reach over and cradle my hands. "Are you doing okay?"

"Yes." I actually was. My newest place was a second-floor walk-up in the gay village. It was a small apartment just above the Pizza Pizza at Church and Wellesley. I shared it with two other queens named Fanny and Nolan. I explained to Nadine that I had first met Fanny during the 20-Minute Drag Workout, where a dozen of the city's most renowned drag queens guided spectators in high-heeled eighties aerobics during Pride. I was just a baby queen back then, so I watched on the sidelines in full costume and awe. It was all fun and games until someone in the crowd threw an egg at Fanny and called her a tranny ho. The front of her leotard was covered in yolk.

"No!" Nadine covered her mouth in disbelief.

"Yes. I had to think quick. She was about to cry. It was so humiliating. I stepped forward, removed my own dress, and gave it to her. I happened to be wearing this Donna Summer wrap dress, so it was easy to take off, it was easy for her to put it on over the mess, and she still blended in with the rest of the queens. Even though I was out there in my skivvies, the crowd cheered for us. Next thing I know, I'm over at her place while she's cleaning herself off, she's letting me search through her wardrobe for something else to wear, and she tells me she's looking for a roommate."

"Okay, how easy was that?" Nadine said with an absent smile while still looking for a waiter to give us our check.

"Well, finding our third roommate wasn't as easy, let me tell you. We had a whole whack of jokers messaging us on Facebook saying they had seen our ad. Because of how desperate everyone is nowadays, lots of them didn't have jobs. Some smelled funny. Some of them, you wanted to disinfect the house after they came by for their interview."

"Nasty." Nadine waved at another waiter. He looked right at her and walked on by. She sighed.

"It was. Then I met Nolan. He was doing drag at Throb Nightclub, performing his famous *Miss Saigon* number with a tiny helicopter. I watched him work the room. Girl, he would earn his tips by hitting audience members with his red fans and demanding they cough up some crisp bills. I knew he would never be short on rent."

"But are they treating you okay? No more stolen money? Or fighting?"

I explained to Nadine that there was always body hair on the floor of the washroom, at least three ruined razors in the wastebasket every Friday, but there weren't any bedbugs. I gave her the impression that living in the heart of Toronto's gay village was a dream. I told Nadine about the topless gender Queer youth who wore the Pride flag like a cape and ran down the street screaming, "Check out my top-surgery scars, motherfuckers!" and I told her about watching the Wednesday night American Sign Language class through the windows of the 519 community center. I did not tell her that Epic had been vandalized yet again, that I had watched Henry sweep up the destruction one dust bin at a time, his dejected reflection shining off endless pieces of shattered bar mirror or about Clara McCleavage's dwindling audiences. I did not tell her how we all avoided darkened alleyways at night, the rumors of our disappearances. I did not tell Nadine about the woman who was walking down the street, going from stranger to stranger showing them a photo, asking if they had seen her Trans sister who had gone missing the week before. Instead, I told her it all felt like magic to me, living where I felt safe, despite being down the road from where I was assaulted by my mother's church folk. I could see from Nadine's face that her life was not so magical either. I had to shift the conversation and unlock the mystery of her faraway looks.

"How's your mom doing?"

Nadine raised her eyebrows, and the edges of her lips twitched away a deeper emotion than she was allowing me to see. "She's okay. Her new boyfriend couldn't handle the breast cancer thing, so he's history. Probably for the best."

"And your dad?"

"The usual. Traveling constantly. Might see him having breakfast when he's in town. But he spends his time ignoring me."

"I'm sorry."

"I'm not. I'm fine by myself in that house. Once I pay off my student loans, I'll be ready to move somewhere else. Maybe closer to my Kay."

In a rushed flurry toward another table, a waiter finally placed the black check folder in front of Nadine.

"Uh, thanks! Finally." Nadine rolled her eyes. The waiter rushed off before she had the chance to pass her credit card to him. "Jesus Christ. I swear this city is getting shittier by the minute."

I shrugged. I was finally feeling more like myself in ways I never thought possible.

"For reals? You don't think so?" Nadine looked around her conspiratorially. "Like, I noticed things shifting around here. Like, people are getting more and more brazen with their actions."

"What do you mean? Who is getting brazen?"

Nadine looked around again. "White people."

"Not all white people . . ."

"Yeah, yeah, yeah. I really don't want to hear it."

"You're half white."

"Yes. I know. I see my white dad when he comes home. I know my dad is white. It's not like he's *not* part of the problem. He's become more brazen too. After everything that happened during the flood, you can't tell me things didn't get fucked up and they didn't show their true colors."

Of course I could agree with her. I just didn't want to say it out loud.

"White people are happy to go on their social media and share quotes from Martin Luther King Jr. on MLK Day. But as soon as they have their back up against a wall, as soon as they're about to lose something, or in the case of the floods, when things get scarce, they're quick to mark their territory."

I looked around us, worried people would hear.

"You're getting paranoid."

"Like, look at this place. At first I thought it was just bad service or something. But, man, we've been coming here for years. They're serving everyone else. I think it's us. We might find spit in our food one day."

"Come on, Nadine! We just ate."

At long last, the waiter made his way to our table with a wireless credit card terminal to process Nadine's payment. His face was cold and unmoving. "Your card was declined."

Nadine's face twisted. "That's impossible."

"It was declined."

Nadine and I accompanied the waiter to the point-of-sale desk and tried her debit card instead.

"Declined," the waiter said, righteously handing back her card.

Nadine snatched it out of his hands. "I heard you. Do you need to say it so loud so you can embarrass me, you punk?"

I touched her arm, worried about the possibility of an altercation.

"No, Kay. This is ridiculous!"

I quickly reached into my pocket and sifted through a wad of bills from last night's show. I paid the waiter, and he did not say thank you.

Under yet another downpour, we shared an umbrella and walked to a nearby bank to check Nadine's debit card. Two ATMs sat in the foyer of the bank, with its accordion doors dividing its locked main section after hours. Nadine slid her debit card into one of the machines, only to hear a crunching sound deep within. She slammed it.

"What the hell?!"

"It's okay, Nadine. I'm sure it's just a glitch." I slid my own bank card into the other machine next to her to confirm that the malfunction was unique to that particular ATM. Then it ate my card too.

"Shit! No!" I screamed into the slot like I could call the plastic card back to us. I banged the surface of the machine and shook my head.

Two ultra-femme gay white boys came into the bank foyer and took off their raincoat hoods. One of them drunkenly pulled his bank card from his back pocket.

"Oh, fuck. I don't know if I'm sober enough to remember my PIN. Goddamn it."

"Oliver, come on. Lucas just texted saying they're already at Throb. Hurry the hell up!"

Nadine and I stood quietly and watched Oliver slide his card into the ATM and retrieve five crisp, green twenty-dollar bills. They replaced their hoods, then the two danced and swayed themselves out of the bank foyer. At a distance from us, we could hear them singing a song by Lizzo, but we remained silent.

I looked at Nadine as we began to make our way along Church Street. She seemed to be foggy, as if in a trance. I followed her. We walked speechlessly into a corner store a block away. We entered and made our way to the refrigerated section. Nadine reached for a bottle of water and froze. I followed her gaze to the quarter-dome safety mirror in the upper corner of the store. A Black woman was arguing with the cashier.

"Try my card again. I know I have cash in my account!"

"You're holding up the line, man. Move along!"

"I'm not a man!"

"Could have fooled me."

Nadine stood there, immovable, her arm still outstretched, her hand still grasping at the bottle, marked by the heat of her touch.

"Hey! You with the Afro puff!" the cashier shouted toward Nadine. "Close the fridge. I'm not paying to cool the entire store."

Nadine shook her head awake, and we left, empty-handed.

I returned to work the next day, prepared to ask Henry to issue me my payment in cash. I found Henry at the bar, clearing bottles of booze to make way for a large espresso machine. He looked at the instruction handbook and at the machine quizzically.

"Good morning." I had a sad feeling in my stomach. Nadine was right. Things were changing.

"Good morning, Keith." I hated the sound of that name. Why did he use it? Henry adjusted the spectacles on his long nose. He was wearing a surprisingly butch ensemble that day, full of somber neutrals. He could have been mistaken for a suburban dad with his golf T-shirt and khakis. He leaned on the bar closer to me, but not so close as to be intimate.

"Keith, we've made some changes around here."

I looked around. The stage riser had been dismantled and several more tables stood in its place. The LED had been cut from its wire. Henry's vowels were clipped short in neat suburban dialect. "I'm afraid you can no longer work here. Epic is now a café."

"I can still wash dishes at a café."

"I will have to ask you to leave."

"*What?* But—"

"Leave. I do not know you."

Nadine texted me, urgently asking to meet her at the same bank where we had lost our cards two nights before. A queue of people overflowed past the exterior doors. All of them Others. When I approached her, she didn't even hug me or greet me hello.

"You are not going to believe this, Kay. I went back to this branch wanting to get a replacement debit card. There's this huge lineup. I'm waiting for forever. I finally get to the front of the line, and the teller checks my ID and hands me this several-page document for me to sign. I had to put my name down, my Social Insurance Number, date of birth, name of my parents. It was detailed. I laughed and was like, 'Lady, am I applying for a passport here?' and she says, 'You'll need to fill this out to confirm you've received your Verification Card.'"

"What's *that*?"

Nadine reached inside her leather wallet and pulled out a plastic card. The letters of her name were punched into the surface of the card in official blocks. Underneath was a number. "And then she tells me that instead of using a debit card, I can use this to deposit or withdraw funds from my account. I'm all confused because . . . I don't know . . . is this a form of identification or is this a way for me to pay for things? And she says, 'It's both. It's a streamlining of our system to make things easier for you.' I'm feeling all uneasy but accept it for what it is. She smiles and asks me, 'Is there anything else I can do for you today?' and I ask for one hundred dollars from my account. She hands me the money and a receipt of the transaction."

Nadine's head looked left and right, suspiciously, then at me. "Kay, I had half the funds I originally had. I watch that account like a hawk! I know something's fucking us up, Kay. I know something's happening. Look at everyone in the queue. I'm not imagining things."

I looked at the lineup, this obvious cross section of citizens. Deep in my belly, I knew too that something was happening, but residing beside that big something was a muscular reaction, a contraction in the fibers of my being telling me that this was impossible. Surely this was a dream. Surely we were imagining things. The use of these Verification Cards was just coincidence between people who happened to sit at the crossroads of race, gender, and identity. These things didn't happen here in Canada. These things happened elsewhere. These things didn't happen without folks stepping in and stopping it from happening. The pages of history told us to never forget, to never forget the atrocities of the past, yet here we were in a city that was actively forgetting. That is why I kept my reactions, the waves of shock, from Nadine's pleading eyes. My body was so stilled by this disbelief that we were unsafe that I could not even bring myself to put a loving hand on her shoulder. She searched my face, from my eyes to my tight jaw until she gave up and we began walking the city again, silently witnessing the city falling apart.

6

I awaken with a sharp inhale of air, Nadine's name still on my lips. The once familiar sight of her crown of curls had disappeared, and I see Bahadur asleep on the bed next to mine, frowning through a dream. I creak softly upward from the mattress and make my way to the window of our room.

My Evan. If you are still in hiding, if you are in a place where real things exist beyond a window, or an underpass, or a set of dark stairs, let me tell you about how beautiful this morning is.

Through the cloudy glass, I can see a heavy fog sitting like risen cream above the wilted crops of long ago. A black bird flies above and below the fog in a lonely game of peekaboo. I wrap my blanket around my body and find myself turning the knob on the cottage door carefully. I actually turn a doorknob, open a door, and move my body outside of a room, Evan. I am free, at this moment, to move my body from one place to another. And it feels good. I want to touch the fog myself. I head outside and the black bird flies out of sight. All insects stop their singing in fear of me, and I try to creep quietly among the reeds in the hopes that the insect songs will continue despite my presence. I fail. I can never be quiet enough for them to forgive me. Even the dew on the grass slips into the secret of the deep green as I pass.

In your mind's eye, take your shoes off with me. Undo the muddy laces and let your feet emerge into the world. Take off your soggy socks. Wipe your feet with me, along the dew of the grass. Feel each cool blade between your liberated toes.

I look at you. You are smiling. You are saying something to me, but your voice is replaced by the sound of rustling woods.

"What did you say, my love?" I ask.

I am alone in the reeds. I hear a rustling coming from the woods. I follow the sound. I feel foolish, like those people who go into the dark room in horror movies, but I can't help myself. It's been so long since I could walk through places and spaces. It feels so good to move my legs. I touch each cedar trunk as I make my way into the thick of the bush.

In a clearing of cedar, wading in a pool of fog, stands Beck in his undershirt and pajama bottoms facing away from me. He holds a long wooden staff and stands at attention like he is about to begin a phrase of martial arts movement. Just as I am crouching down, Bahadur appears beside me. I stifle a scream. Jesus Christ. Bahadur mouths out the word "sorry." I roll my eyes and hold my heavily beating heart in shock. We slowly shift our focus back to Beck. What the hell is he doing?

"*When I do not act, I am complicit!*" Beck says while simultaneously raising his staff above his head horizontally, one end in each hand. He takes a deep breath here, steps forward with a lunge, and strikes down his staff.

"*When I know wrong is happening, I act!*"

Bahadur and I flinch at this. It feels strange to observe Beck instead of receiving the blow. Beck rocks back in his lunge as if receiving energy; his staff gracefully rocks with him.

"*When the oppressed tell me I am wrong, I open my heart and change!*"

With his back leg in a lunge, he kneels and raises the staff above his head.

"*When change is led by the oppressed, I move aside and uplift!*"

Bahadur and I look at each other, then back at Beck. He goes through the movements and phrases again and again until his undershirt is pasted on his torso with perspiration, until the fog of the morning dissipates.

"*When I do not act, I am complicit!*

"*When I know wrong is happening, I act!*

"*When the oppressed tell me I am wrong, I open my heart and change!*

"*When change is led by the oppressed, I move aside and uplift!*"

Arms raise, step forward, lunge back, kneel.

Beck finally sits on the corpse of a dead tree for a moment before closing his eyes and catching his breath. Bahadur shifts slightly, and Beck startles. He looks in our direction and wipes his face on his shirt.

"Sorry. Did I wake you?"

We quietly follow Beck back to the cottage. He sees a hose running from the side of the cottage. He turns the tap on just out of curiosity and sure enough, only mud sputters out a snake of filth. He sits himself on the porch and looks at us.

"Can we talk for a second?" Beck asks. Bahadur and I sit on the porch with him. In the heat of the rising sun, I adjust my blanket to my waist and listen.

"You didn't wake us up. We were just watching," I say. I look over at Bahadur, but they avoid eye contact with me and begin to pick at the crumbling siding along the cottage's exterior.

"It's just . . . It's not for show. It's for me. For people like me. For white folks. You know the creed of the Renovation, right? '*Through our work, our nation prospers. Through our unity, we end conflict,*' and all that nonsense? The Others who led the Resistance knew we had to come up with a response to that creed. The Resistance challenged us allies to train ourselves out of this behavior just as someone might train for a marathon or learn new dance steps. It had to be embodied the way white supremacy is embodied. It wasn't meant for you to witness. It's more like a prayer for change, but in movement." Beck looks out at the black bird returning to the wilted crops, this time with a companion. Up and down through the reeds.

"Bahadur, you were right about what you said yesterday. I followed orders. I am responsible for what happened. I didn't ask questions. I have blood on my hands too."

I shift uncomfortably under my blanket.

"I'm not asking you to forgive me. I'm not asking you to help me feel better about what I've done. I know those demons are inside me. When I was in training for the Resistance, there was something the leaders said that really stuck with me. You know when someone says something important to you that just ruins you? That feels like it tears you apart and you have to put yourself together again? Anyway . . . part of our training was understanding that we are not these white saviors because a liberation from the Renovation isn't just a liberation for the Others. It would mean white people could be liberated from maintaining the status quo."

He shakes out his arms and looks at them pensively. "Even that word affects me now. 'Liberation.' I thought about it a long time, and I realized how much of a price my body has had to pay. Every day, my body works to keep itself separate from and above the Others. My body forces me to fear, to see threat in the joy of the Others. To buy all the things, to display all the objects to show how much better I am than you. It's empty. It's so empty. I can't tell you how liberating it feels to work through this emptiness and allow myself to be soft, to be wrong and vulnerable. If I survive the uprising, I want to teach other white people to know this feeling. It feels like . . . like . . . taking off your backpack after wearing it for a lifetime."

Beck looks at us directly. "In the military, I was trained to do things. To protect my body, to fight. You're not obligated to fight alongside me. Not at all. If it were my choice, it would be us allies fighting for your safety while you all were on a beach somewhere enjoying piña coladas."

Bahadur stifles a laugh and looks at me, trying to figure out what I am thinking of this strange testimony.

"But I would love to share how you can protect yourself. And if you do decide to fight with me, to learn to protect yourselves, I would be honored. It will take a bit of hard work, but I can show you what I know."

"What if we don't want to do anything? Can we stay here?" Bahadur avoids eye contact with Beck and continues picking at the cottage's siding. The particle board is rotten and moldy.

"Yes. You can stay here. But the supplies will only last so long. And there aren't many allies around. I can't trust that my parents will not betray you. And I can't trust I will return after the uprising."

"Why won't you return?" I ask.

"Knowing there are rebels like you won't be a major surprise to the Boots," Beck says while dusting off the top of his brush cut. "But finding out that we allies have used this last year to double-cross them will be a huge betrayal. I might not get out alive. You might not get out alive. That's always a possibility when it comes to war."

By the afternoon, Beck is digging a trench while his father watches. Bahadur and I sit on the porch of the cottage still considering our options. Peter stands at attention, wishing and willing his body from old age to the bottom of that trench.

"Dad. Go ahead and sit down. I can handle this. No problem."

"I never asked you to do this. We don't need this."

"Yes, you do. Those carcasses are festering. You might not be able to smell it, but we could down the road."

Peter's chest wilts at the weight of his emasculation.

"It's not your fault, Dad. I just wish you had asked someone close by for help."

"I couldn't ask for help."

"Why?"

"No one . . . no one wants to speak to us because of . . . well. They know what you are. *That* I know is not my fault."

"Yes, Dad. I know. It's mine."

Beck and his father look at their feet in silence. This is my opportunity to speak.

"Can I help?" I offer, hoping I have the strength to actually do so.

"I suggest you find something to cover your mouth and nose," Beck says while resting his arm on the handle of his shovel.

Beck makes his way to the silo beside the cottage. Peter follows, his usual grimace growing more sour with every step. Despite all of us having covered our faces with old shirts, the smell of death sits unmoving along our path. While Beck inches his way up the ladder, Peter calls out to him, part apology, but mostly an accusation.

"I didn't know where to put them all!" Peter says as Beck peers into the silo.

Hundreds of dead, festering chicken carcasses. I can see Beck stifling his vomit. I feel like purging too just at the sight of his reaction.

Peter is ashamed. He can't even look at me as he says, "First they couldn't drink the water, then there was no water to give them. We weren't even allowed to burn them because of the wildfires. We weren't allowed to eat them because of the contamination. I couldn't bury them because . . . because I'm too . . . because I was alone. This was the only place we could put them."

We realize that we need the holes to be located farther away from the cottage. Beck and I dig four trenches in total. When I ask Beck if putting the dead chickens into the trenches may be an environmental hazard he tells me the entire town is an environmental hazard. We create a system where Beck descends into the depths of the silo on the internal ladder, scoops putrid soft chicken corpses onto an old shower curtain, gathers the corners together, then hands me the makeshift sack. I then descend the silo's external ladder, open the sack, and allow its contents to plop into our ditches to be buried. We do this one shower curtain surface at a time. We do this as I gag, as Beck gags and reassures his father he is not a failure. We do this. We finish the work. We cover the shame of the carcasses with neutral smelling sandy soil. We don't have water with which to wash out the silo, but Beck pours three industrial-size bottles of bleach into its depths hoping to kill the stench. But we know it will do nothing. Once we are done, I use my face covering to wipe the mess off my arms and pants. Just as I am about to pinch the last feather off my forearms, I wretch into a bush. I wish we had water for a shower. I long for Liv's bathtub. I decide to use sand instead, like those pigeons I watched at Moss Park with my mother near my old apartment. They would clean themselves using dirt. I find a reserve of dry sand and begin using fistfuls to cover my body. The sand dries my sweat, dries the muck of the chicken, and I brush it off. I continue to do this until my body is dusty but somewhat clean. I stop only when I realize the sand reserve is from ant hills. Some ants remain angry on my scalp and arms. I shoo away their bites. But I am clean.

I rubbed the coconut oil until it softened and melted into the surface of my skin, highlighting the sinew of my shoulders. I admired my reflection in Nolan's mirror, willing myself to leave the house.

It was Scorpio season. Nolan and I had planned to head to a joint birthday bash at some lesbian bar. There was a small cover fee to raise funds for someone's top surgery happening later in November.

"Who's getting the surgery?" I asked Nolan while he straight-ironed his hair into perfectly silky sections. Smoke from his hair product filled the air and made me cough.

"Cole. Ex-lover. Long story."

Nolan gave this suffix to many people in the LGBTQ2S community: "Ex-lover. Long story." This description meant many things, ranging from having to change directions at the Trans march to holding Nolan's hand while he laughed loudly to give the impression that he had moved on with his life. When Nolan asked me, "Is that what you're wearing?" I knew my job was to attend the party and appear to be his next lover and long story.

"Yes. I'm already wearing it."

He finished pulling his straightened hair into a high ponytail, then attended to my fashion choices.

"Listen, handsome. I know you wanted to wear that mesh top to show off your six-pack, but I want Cole to understand how my tastes have matured. That's why I need you to wear this Victorian puff-sleeve blouse with this top hat."

I cocked my hip and pursed my lips. Nolan pleaded. "It's like up-scale fag meets high-paid banker!" He went through his Rolodex of comparisons. "You'll look like Queen Victoria . . . on the day of her coronation."

I raised my arms and permitted him to continue fussing over me. In truth, I wouldn't have done anything. I would have stayed home alone. And it was my birthday, after all, and I hated my birthday.

"Bitch, what?!"

"Yeah."

"It's your birthday? Like today?"

"Yeah. I guess."

"Girl, I would have never thought you were a Scorpio."

I didn't know what being a Scorpio meant, so I nodded in befuddlement. I knew little about astrology as a whole and often wondered if I should return my Queer membership card until I at least knew my sun, moon, and rising signs, which Fanny once said were essential.

"Well . . . we will just have to celebrate tonight, won't we?" Nolan said while pinning a brooch to my lapel. "There! What do you think?"

I looked into Nolan's long mirror. A tiny top hat sat sassily off one side of my head. The sleeves of the blouse were extraordinarily voluminous.

"I look like Queen Victoria after she discovered the open bar at a wedding."

Instead of Nolan's usual music playlist, our low-rent television broadcast a low-volume soundtrack to our club preparation time. He began his contouring regimen as he watched a news program in which American president Colin Pryce addressed a news reporter's questions about mass deportation.

"You know what? If they come in illegally, they have to go out. These people are felons. These people are convicted of crimes. Next week, we will begin the process of removing millions of illegal aliens who have illicitly found their way into the United States. They will be removed as fast as they came in."

A cut to Canadian prime minister Alan Dunphy addressing media on Parliament Hill with a superimposed caption on the bottom of the screen reading "Two Nations, One Vision campaign launched by Dunphy."

"As Canadians, as neighbors, we will work alongside the United States in our endeavor to rid this land of invasive forces. Two Nations, One Vision is our joint strategy to target any threats to the values, to all we hold dear, which we have woven into the fabric of our collective societies."

"Shit. If Pryce doesn't watch out, he's gonna get his ass killed." Nolan began powdering aggressively, unable to peel his eyes from the screen.

"Maybe that's a good thing," I said, pinning my small top hat onto my hair so it sat askew.

"Hell no. That's not a good thing. You know what happens when a white supremacist gets killed? They become a martyr. Last thing I need is for a bunch of KKK bedsheets to have a patron saint of hatred. You heard about his last executive order banning the use of hijabs? Fucking hell. You might as well go back to forcing people to wear Stars of David." Nolan moved on to painting his eyebrows. He took a deep breath to calm down and steadied his hand. As he drew arches across his forehead he added, "We're in some critical times, my friend. I can feel it in my belly button. And I don't have just any belly button." He lifted his blouse to show me the peculiar pucker on his stomach.

"You see this? I was born with my intestines outside my body."

"What? No way."

"Yes, bitch. If my parents were still in Cambodia, I would have been long gone. It took two months for my insides to go back into my body. Then the surgeon gave me this off-center piece-of-shit belly button." He looked down at it, caressed it with his acrylics, and looked at me with fire in his eyes. "But I'm telling you: every time I get a bad feeling in this fake belly button, the thing I think is gonna happen, happens."

"What's it saying now?"

"That something bad is gonna happen. Like, really bad. Beyond anything we can ever imagine. Pryce is gonna burn things to the ground, and we're gonna be the first to burn with it."

"Us? Here? But we're in Canada."

"Are you kidding me? That shit's been happening already with the Indigenous people here for hundreds of years. It still is happening. Why would we be surprised? The Homos, the Trans folks, the freaks, the Brown people, the Black people, the Disabled, the old folks. They're picking us up and shipping us out, one by one." He began lining his lips with a blood-orange pencil.

"That can't happen."

"And why the hell not? It's happened so many times in history. Why not now? Why not here?" He pressed his lips into a tissue and assessed his work. He seemed satisfied but uneasy. "And that, my friend, is why I live every day as drag as I can, as Brown as I can, as loud as I can. We aren't safe. Not now. Not ever. Our days are numbered, Kay."

The news program cut to two Black women addressing an audience. "Identical twins Adea and Amana graced the stage at Yonge-Dundas Square stage today in a concert in downtown Toronto."

"Whoa! Who are they?" I asked Nolan.

"You don't know Adea and Amana? They are Queer as fuck. I love them. They travel the world doing anti-oppression work, teaching people how to be woke," Nolan said before pointing frantically at the television screen. "Oh my gah, look at those dresses! They always have these larger-than-life skirts that are joined together. You can fit an entire town under them." The fabric featured twinkling lights while the twins sang a song of resistance.

> *From scar tissue we are born*
> *From bones we rise*
> *Everything you fear*
> *Everything you despise*
> *We are the Others*
> *Other from you*
> *But same with the land*
> *We are the Others*
> *The change we need*
> *The change we demand*

Their braids cascaded down their backs in infinite patterns of knots, crisscrosses, and jewels. The crowd of Others cheered, some of them cried, some of them watched with their hands at their hearts, trying to hold on to the magic they were seeing onstage. Shots of police officers standing along the perimeter of the crowd, suspicious and poised for action.

The segment cut to the twins speaking to a reporter. "In the face of a dramatic increase in hate crimes, our duty is to travel from city to city to educate as many people as possible," Amana said.

Adea chimed in, seamlessly, the way twins often do: "We want safety for everyone, no matter what your religion. No matter what your gender identity. No matter what your skin color. We want peace."

Now that Nolan was in full drag, I could read him and his emotions easily. As we arrived at Wet Bar, he was already casing the joint looking for familiar faces. I had to remind him to pay his cover charge, he was that distracted. Across the crowded dance floor stood Cole with two big electric tape Xs on their* sweatshirt where the surgery was going to take place. Their asymmetrical haircut bobbed side to side and they did a nonchalant step-touch to a bass heavy R & B song. With that same amount of giving zero fucks, they nodded in Nolan's direction. That was Nolan's cue to begin the ruse.

"Kay! Not here!" With a faux chuckle, Nolan playfully slapped me and her chunky Lalique ring got caught on the Chantilly lace on my sleeve. "Fuck." He continued his laughter as he pulled. He decided to cut his losses. He whispered conspiratorially into my ear, "Just leave it there and I'll cut it out later."

All was well once a dance hall song came on. It gave Nolan the perfect opportunity to show off his moves. During the climax of the song, he descended to the floor on all fours ass-clapping to the beat. When the song shifted to some trance, he composed himself and whispered again to me.

"Here's the deal, handsome. I'll give you a wink if I decide to go off and do my thing. Otherwise, let's stick together, okay? I need you!" It didn't take long for me to receive the wink signal. A couple of songs, max. Some muscle head with a mesh shirt, the same mesh shirt I was going to wear that night, caught Nolan's eye, and he was off. His high ponytail disappeared among the pumping fists and slamming bodies. I sighed and looked around.

I moved past the dancing bodies to the side to assess my sad situation. Two hipsters stood beside me, leaning against the wall and staring at the bright lights.

"Fuck, man. Your dealer hooks it up."

"I know, right? He doesn't play."

"Like . . . my dealer charges twice as much and I don't feel this fucked-up."

I rolled my eyes and sighed hard. There were worse birthdays, for sure. But this night was giving some stiff competition. I decided to tuck myself away in the corner of the lounge beside a long corridor to the back of the bar so that the darkened shadows could obscure my pouting. I made a mental note to commemorate all future birthdays in complete isolation. For the rest of my days, I planned to brood in level-ten sulking all alone without anyone to bother me.

The lighting changed. A spotlight dragged itself across the sweaty crowd to the stage, where a femme with a 1920s bob haircut entered. It wasn't so much a stage as a raised flat of particle board atop two moldy skids. A nineties tune blared through the speakers and the crowd roared in recognition. She sat on a chair and took out a bowl of raspberries. In time with the music, she put one raspberry on each finger on her right hand, then naughtily sucked each finger's raspberry into her mouth. The crowd went wild in anticipation of every lick. As the song faded, she made her way through the crowd, sexily slinking her way past me, down the corridor, to the back of Wet Bar. One person whose shoulder she touched in her journey swooned and held their* heart. What a hot show.

Her titillating walk slowly switched into a tired gait the farther she got from the stage. As soon as she was out of sight of the audience, she removed her heels and sighed before entering the dressing room. Just as I was about to approach her and tell her what a stunning performance she had given, I felt someone brushing past me.

It was you, Evan.

In the dim club lights, I saw you holding a large sheet cake while fumbling with a lighter to touch it to the tips of a dozen birthday candles.

"Can I help you?" I offered.

"Yes, please!" I heard your voice for the first time. Deep and rich. I quickly held the bottom of the cake. A few flicks of your thumb along the spark wheel of the lighter and it became obvious the safety guard was confusing you.

"Would you like me to try?" I offered again.

We switched positions. You holding the cake. Me sparking the lighter. Our heads inches apart as I lit each of the birthday candles. The soft light from below catching your gaze upon me.

"It's—" Something caught in my throat and my voice squeaked out of nervousness. "It's my birthday today too." You smiled, watching me finish the last few candles.

"Then I guess you'll have to join us." You took the cake from me and ceremoniously walked down the corridor to the dressing room. The muffled sound of performers prepping went to full volume once you opened the door.

"Happy birthday to you . . . ," you began and everyone joined in with you. "Happy birthday, happy birthday, happy birthday to youuuuuuu!"

It was obvious by the look of things that the dressing room was actually the bar's office during the week. With the performers present, a strip of bare bulbs screwed into the wall lit up two greasy mirrors. The ambiance of the lighting helped us ignore the administrative elements of dusty photocopiers, posted staff schedules, and laminated inspirational posters. The dressing room was larger than the one at Epic, but with the dancers doing their makeup sitting on office chairs and their kits sitting atop mail inboxes, it was just as sad.

"Where are all the Scorpios?" you asked. "Inez, Kiley, Sandra! Blow out these candles before my arm gives out. This cake is huge." The three performers stepped forward as if they had won something. "And you, birthday boy. Sorry . . . what's your name?"

My face got hot. "Kay."

"It's Kay's birthday today too," you said with a grin. I cautiously joined the Scorpios and we blew out the candles. Smoke filled the air.

One dancer approached me wearing only one tassel while she fanned the other nipple's adhesive dry with a folded computer mouse pad. She gave me a peck on the cheek. "Happy Scorpio season, Kay." She kissed you on the cheek next. "Thank you, Evan. This is amazing." Another dancer approached me with a bong.

"Take a hit first so that it tastes like one of those artisanal cupcakes you get from a hipster pastry shop." I obliged and with eyes dry, I dug into the cheap chocolatey goodness.

"I wanted to pop in to see you all and let you know that thanks to your performances, we made our goal for Cole's surgery." Everyone cheered. I gulped.

What do I remember of you that night? Oh yes. Your suit was well tailored. I had never seen craftsmanship like that in real life. I had to fight myself not to touch the fabric. The deep gray wool with the most modest lines of pinstripes sat well on your wide chest and brought out the sleek texture of your black skin. The light of the bare bulbs caught your eyes and reflected back to me as the color red. I shook my head wondering if it was an optical illusion but when you stepped forward and extended your hand, your eyes went back to the most delicious shade of brown. Fuck. I admit, I was so stoned. It took every last calorie in me to not touch the perfect bald fade on the nape of your neck, not to trace the exact lines of your beard edging, not to offer you the lip balm in my pocket in case your lips needed moisturizing. Instead I stood there, in my ridiculous Queen Victoria ensemble and curtsied. You put your hand away and bowed deeply.

"Thank you for your help, your majesty," you said. I fell in love. It was you who had organized the joint Scorpio birthday party in support of Cole's top surgery. It was you who took me by the hand and led me outside for our first kiss. It was you who paid for the cab that drove us to my humble apartment where we made love for the first time.

"Who put you in this outfit?"

"My roommate, Nolan."

"Queen Victoria?"

"Yes."

"Nice. Take it off."

We made love like lions, growing skinny with the passage of time and sex. We took a selfie of us under the low canopy of my bedsheets, you biting my ear.

"You know when I post this on Instagram, it's official, right?"

"I do," you said while kissing the backs of my hands. We received dozens of well-wishes from friends who commented on our post. We were too busy making love to care about the comments from trolls telling us we were abominations and deserved to die.

I ran out of groceries and you went out to get supplies using your Verification Card. Like all of us, you too had mysteriously dwindling funds in your account.

"I had to use what little cash I had in my pocket. You okay with Pop-Tarts for dinner?"

"As long as I can have you for dessert."

We strolled around Yonge Street, window-shopping in the freezing rain. We held hands until we saw two cops doing a random check on a Black boy of about seventeen years old, arresting him for not having his Verification Card on his person.

"Let's go into this store until they move on down the street."

"Sounds like a plan, babes. I hope they leave soon."

Time passed. You called your mother to tell her the good news of our partnership.

"Put him on the phone. I need to hear his voice," she said.

"Hello, Mrs. King."

"Hello, Kay. When can I expect you two for dinner?"

I enter the cottage looking for Bahadur, assuming they ducked out of digging ditches and transporting dead chickens but they aren't to be found. I proceed into the main farmhouse with the screen door creaking behind me.

"Is that you, Peter?" Hanna calls out.

"No, ma'am. It's me. Kay."

"Come on in, young man."

I wipe off my shoes, walk past the hallway of dead-people pictures and into the living room. Hanna and Bahadur are sitting on the couch together looking at old photo albums. An entire pile stands in a toppled-over mess atop a multicolored crocheted couch cover.

"We've been at this for a while, but you're welcome to catch up," Hanna says, motioning for me to sit down in the nearby corduroy reclining chair. I am surprised she even wants me to touch anything. I am covered head to toe in sand. When I sit my butt down, I sink into the soft comfort of its cushion. I feel weary and weak.

Bahadur looks at me with a forced smile, stressing each word to ensure I understand the torture they have just endured. "Hanna has shown me each and every one of these albums." Blink. Blink.

"We got a bit sidetracked. Bahadur here was helping me sort out the last of our canned preserves. So many jars shattered in the floods. Next thing I know, I'm cracking open the spines of these old things, showing pictures of Beck during his hockey days."

Bahadur and I share a glance. The album she holds has a soggy bottom, but the photos in the upper half remain intact, albeit discolored. Hanna turns another creaky page of the album and uses her crooked fingers to pry open the adhesive sleeve. With one of her fingernails, she manages to lift up the corner of one photo, peel it off, and hand it to me.

"Can you believe how handsome he was?" Hanna says wistfully. She leans her head on the tops of her knobby knuckles. In the photo, Beck wears full hockey gear, the blade of his stick extended in a staged slapshot. He has that awkward teen smile, where the grin is present but the lips do not want to betray the line of braces underneath. Even then, you can see a longing in his eyes. "When he was a toddler, I can't tell you how many times people would stop me wondering why on earth I would dye my child's hair. I'd try to explain that that was in fact his natural color. He was blessed with the reddest of hair. It faded a bit to more of a strawberry blond when he became a teen. It broke my heart when he enlisted and had to get that darned puppy cut." She sits for a moment, looking to the right, as if imagining what could have happened had Beck remained in town, then looking to the left at the trajectory of what happened following that life-changing haircut, wincing a bit.

"You, young lady," Hanna says, grabbing Bahadur's knee with what is meant to be a loving and firm gesture. "I hope *you* never forget who you are." And with that, the old woman uses her cane to get up from the couch and heads to the kitchen to continue inspection of the canned goods.

Bahadur throws me a look so horrified I think their eyes are going to fall out of their sockets.

At the kitchen table, with all of us eating a modest dinner of pickled beets, Ritz crackers, and jam, we hear a vehicle approaching the farmhouse. The sound of wheels over pea gravel. The sight of headlights through the front curtains. Peter tells me and Bahadur to hide in the attic. Quick as lightning Beck pulls this seemingly magic ladder from the ceiling over the hallway and tells us to ascend. Before he lifts the ladder into place, he looks at me and puts his fingers to his lips.

Bahadur and I crouch in complete darkness. We both are feeling with our hands, as silently as possible, for a place to hide. My toe jams on a heavy box and I stifle a scream. I paw around until I can get behind the box. I crouch down further and make myself as small as possible.

From downstairs, we hear the screen door open and close. We hear Hanna's cane poke the ground before her toward the front of the farmhouse, then silence. A few muffled sentences.

The screen door slams open, and we can hear Beck shouting orders. Beck suddenly pulls down the attic ladder and calls out to us.

"Kay! Bahadur! Come down! Quick!"

We carefully inch our way down the ladder cautious of the scene below. It's Liv. It's fucking Liv! It's her. She wears a leather jacket like the Boots. Her hair is in a tight ponytail. She looks at me and smiles, but when she sees Bahadur her jaw and lips begin to tremble; her eyes pooling and wet.

"She made it here. She's safe."

Bahadur stops in their tracks. Liv takes their hand and guides them to the kitchen table. Huddled on a chair is someone wrapped in a blanket, wilted and weak. Bahadur almost loses their balance. I grab them at the elbows, but they propel themselves forward into an embrace.

"*Firuzeh?* Is that you?" Bahadur lifts the blanket to confirm. Her head is shaven. Her face is swollen and bruised. Her breathing labored. But it's her. She attempts to stand at the sight of Bahadur, then collapses.

"Firuzeh! Fuck! Firuuuuuzeeeeeh!" Bahadur manages to brace her fall and sits her back down. All of us watch with our hands over our mouths as Bahadur weeps, gently rocking her in a pained embrace. "Look at you . . . Firuzeh . . . Oh . . . What have they done to you? Oh no! I'm so sorry!"

Beck shakes his head out of his stupor and leaves the kitchen and returns with a first aid kit and a bottle of water.

Liv touches the surface of Firuzeh's neck, checking her temperature. "Once we got to the country roads, we were able to move her out of the trunk of the car. By then she was looking pretty weary. She's been having a hard time keeping any water down."

Beck and Liv work together to get Firuzeh to drink, even a little. She takes in small sips, although most of it dribbles down her cut chin. I hold Firuzeh's torso upright while Bahadur gently wipes her bloody body using an old shirt dipped into bottled water Hanna has warmed up over the stove. I notice that Firuzeh's fingernails are missing, but I say nothing.

"We're going to clean you all up, okay?" Bahadur says between sobs.

Peter leaves to cry in the living room in private.

Once Firuzeh is clean, Beck carries her to the cottage and sets her up on a bed. Bahadur sits beside the bed to watch for any progress.

"Did you want me to move your bed next to hers so you can rest?" I ask them.

"No. I won't rest. I can't rest. Not until I know she's okay."

From my bed, I spy Bahadur's silhouette over Firuzeh's sleeping body until they become a shadow in the darkness. In the middle of the night, I hear the cottage door creak open. It's Hanna. Bahadur and I startle at her arrival.

"It's just me."

She shuffles and pokes her cane on the floor until she is beside Bahadur. She sits on the bed beside Firuzeh and shakes her head. "What a poor and awful sight." Bahadur remains still.

"I'm guessing you knew her? Were you close to her?"

Bahadur cries quietly into their elbow.

"Shhhhhh. Shhhhhh," Hanna says lovingly. "You need to rest." Hanna begins a rhythmic stroke down Bahadur's back. "Whatever she's gone through, it's going to take a while for her to heal from. You need to rest so that when she wakes up, she sees a familiar face. You understand?"

Bahadur nods wearily and succumbs to the stroke of Hanna's hands. Once Bahadur is snoring softly, Hanna quietly makes her way out of the cottage and back to the farmhouse under the light of a half-moon.

7

In my sleep, I dream about meeting your mother, holding my pillow, and willing the dream to last forever. Perhaps if we work together we can both imagine the pieces of her well enough that we can conjure up her whole self.

We emerged onto the street level outside King subway station to yet another political demonstration. We waited to catch a streetcar to head west toward Parkdale, but the throngs of protesters kept the vehicle stalled at Victoria Street. Hundreds of people stood in three distinct columns, the rainwater from the night before splashing at everyone's feet. The center column's folks held eight-foot-long posts with red dresses flapping like flags at the ends. The outside column's folks held smoke grenades, each one emitting a cloud of various colors. They passed in intentional silence. My eyes widened at the arresting image.

You threw up your arms in frustration. "I guess we have to walk all the way to Dufferin Street."

After an hour of walking through the soggy streets, we arrived at an old brownstone storefront sandwiched between two monstrous condos. We could hear Mrs. King's voice crackle on the old intercom. "You finally made it."

Her tiny apartment sat above a sewing supply shop. In the storefront's window, a headless mannequin stood, wearing a patchwork of featured fabrics on sale, with a measuring tape artfully cinching its waist. When the door to her second-floor walk-up opened, we had to back up on the narrow stairwell to accommodate its outward swing. Mrs. King stood there with black dye still processing on her scalp and eyebrows. A stained towel protected her shoulders from the dark trickles down the nape of her neck.

"Hello, Mother." You kissed her weathered jowls carefully, avoiding the line of ink-like liquid dripping near her ears.

Before I could greet her, Mrs. King took me by my wrist and forced me to stand in front of her. "Let me have a good look at you. Come closer. Yes. I can't wear my glasses until I rinse my hair, so you have to stand about here. Very nice." Her arthritic hands squeezed the muscles from my forearms to my biceps to evaluate me. Two deep brown irises encircled by the blue of a ripe cataract studied every inch of me. The perimeter of my mouth. The balance between my right and left foot. The tiny protrusion of my belly button through my sweater. Then my hair. I gulped, suddenly recalling the sensation of my hair passing through a fine-tooth comb, my own mother pulling and pulling at her mistake manifested in my mane.

"Aren't you ever handsome." Mrs. King smiled. She looked at you and playfully squeezed your hand. "Be good to this one. The other one before made me want to scream with his gum chewing. But this one is a good one."

You sighed dramatically. "Mother, please don't start."

"First there was the one boy who was always on a diet. Then the one after that who was hungry all the time, but was a . . . what do you call it? What is it called, Evan?"

"A vegan."

"Yes. A vegan. Kay, tell me. Are you a vegan?"

"No, ma'am."

"Thank goddess."

I bit the inside of my cheeks to keep my emotions at bay. I was thankful when a kitchen timer dinged and she broke eye contact with me.

Without discussion, you pulled a chair from the adjacent living room to the kitchen sink, your mother sat down, and you gently rinsed her hair. How did this come to be, Evan? This graceful way between you and your mother? How did love become a language? Become a dance?

I looked around the small space and decided to rest on a depression in the mid-century chesterfield's upholstery, most likely your mother's favorite spot. When I felt springs poke through the frame into my buttocks, though, I changed position to the less-worn wooden step stool in the corner.

"I'm sorry we took so long. Those damn protesters got in our way."

"Nothing wrong with a little protesting," Mrs. King shouted over the sound of the running water. She wiped moisture away from her eyes with one of her crooked fingers.

"I'm fine with it, as long as it doesn't get in my way."

"Evan, dear. They're not going to give you the heads-up. They're not going to work around your schedule. They want to disrupt. They want to get your attention that it's no longer safe to be an Other. That's why it's called civil disobedience."

You expertly wrapped your mother's head in the stained towel. She used the corner of the towel to absorb water that poured into her ear before tucking the tail into the nape of her neck.

"You kids nowadays don't even know when your world is falling apart, and you don't even know when it's necessary to take a stand." She gestured for you to help her back up to standing. She slowly made her way to the kitchen cabinets and got three floral-printed glasses.

"Back when I was young, it was as plain as the nose on your face when you were being wronged. Take this place," she said to me while pointing to the four corners of her humble apartment. "I raised my son here. It was the only place I could find where the landlord was willing to rent to us. My husband, God bless his soul, said to the landlord, 'Mr. Willems, I am willing to give you five months' rent if you will let us stay here.' He said yes. It didn't stop him from pretending we'd only given four months' rent, but we finally had a place to stay. So when we would march way back then, it was clear what we were fighting for." She walked to the refrigerator, opened it, took out a bottle of ginger ale and a jug of orange juice. "Today, it's not so obvious. But you know it's there. People pretend more. Smile like it's not a problem, when they still believe the same things about me and my son. I think it's even more dangerous. Take Mr. Varela next door, for example. Lived above what was a Seven-Eleven back in the day. Stayed my neighbor for thirty-two years. The man had to be wheeled out on a stretcher and taken by ambulance to the hospital. Heat stroke. I almost passed out myself last summer. Good thing we're on the second floor. The floods didn't affect us much other than some power outages. And I'm familiar with a can opener and a can of beans. I am not a fussy woman. I can live on very little. But the heat wave was unbearable. No one thinks about why those things happen, other than climate change this and climate change that. But it's also because Mr. Varela is—or was, I don't know if he made it or not—a Venezuelan man, a Brown man, who was poor enough to live above a corner store with no AC. It's so complicated no one is able to see the bigger picture, and how it's connected to the Two Nations, One Vision campaign. They think it's two separate things. It's not. But when we marched back in the day, we never marched for people to be polite to us. It was clear as day what we marched for. We marched because we deserved to live."

She poured a bit of ginger ale and orange juice in each glass, then handed it to us. The intense sweetness of the beverage could not drown the sinking, complicated truth of what she was saying, that was growing in my stomach. I took several more gulps and still the feeling remained.

"Tell me, Kay. Tell me all about yourself."

"He's a performer, Mother."

"Did I ask you, Evan?"

Your knees clamped together at the sound of your mother's discipline.

"Go on, Kay. Pardon my son and his rudeness. He always fancied himself an expert in everything. Can you believe this fool had the audacity to suggest I redecorate my home? Please, Kay. You tell me about yourself."

I looked at the blue of her cataracts and held my breath before saying, "It's true. I'm a performer."

"How exciting. And do you like performing?"

"Yes, ma'am."

"I can see it in your eyes. The hunch of your shoulders. The way you look down at your feet. The smallness of you transforming onstage to be as big as you want to be. Am I correct?"

"Yes."

"I am happy you know where your heart is. Not everyone in their lifetime will be so blessed."

She simply pointed to the refrigerator and you knew to take roast chicken and side dishes from the shelves, heat it up in the microwave, and divide it among three melamine plates. Our hearty eating was punctuated every now and then with you giving your mother a tender kiss on the cheek. I could see the beginnings of you, the roots of you, and my heart was singing.

"We'll try to be back next week, okay?" you said to her as we made our way to the door. The late autumn sun had already set, leaving the home in sudden darkness. You enveloped your mother in an embrace. I stepped forward wondering if she would allow me to do the same.

She surprised me by cradling my face. "Look at me."

I tried, but in the twilight of the hour, Mrs. King's face had faded away into a shadow, already a memory.

"Be as big as you want to be, Kay," said the silhouette.

I nodded. Even though darkness had obscured my features, I knew she could feel my tears dampening her hands.

* * *

Time passed. The weather got colder. You and I fucked on the day of the first frost. We bit each other's lips into the holiday season. We experimented with who was going to be the big spoon each evening, trying to keep each other warm. Outside the door of my room, the world was changing. Random pat-downs from the police. Random raids of nightclubs we once frequented, or stores we once visited. Corner-store staff on their knees with their elbows spread wide, their hands on the tops of their heads, while authorities shook down their tills, toppled over shelves. Sikh men escorted by security out of a subway train during rush hour.

We shrugged our shoulders each time a restaurant refused us service, delightfully held hands and tried our luck elsewhere.

We wove through countless protest marches and political demonstrations to catch a movie, only to be told in not so many words that we were no longer allowed in such spaces, so we would shrug our shoulders again, head home, and make love.

We made love after finding out you had lost your job as a graphic designer. We made love each night another one of my drag gigs was canceled, our audiences dwindling to no one. The world was falling apart, and the one thing we knew we had to do was remind each other who we were.

On the night of the winter solstice, you and I had made plans for you to finally meet Nadine in Kensington Market for the night parade. She was my chosen sister, after all.

"Did you try her again?" you asked, blowing warm air into your fists.

"I texted her. I called her and left her a voice mail message. She's usually the one on time." I tried my luck again. I jumped from foot to foot to bring life to my freezing thighs while I scrolled through my messages from the inside of my jacket. I didn't want my phone shutting down in the cold. I looked through Facebook and Instagram for clues as to where she was, but her profile was gone. Did she block me? Impossible. Maybe she deactivated her account after yet another breakup. I took my mitten off my warm hand and placed it on your cheeks at the site of frostbite.

"Let's join the procession. She'll text me when she arrives."

We marched on Augusta Avenue, holding hands alongside the large crowd of painted faces and makeshift instruments, our free hands holding homemade lanterns. The air was like a bitter slap, and I looked forward to the end of the procession when the effigy would be burned in celebration of the year's longest night. Last year it was a giant star. The year before it was the word "Glow." I wondered what it would be this year. The crowd began to form a circle around what was once a concrete wading pool and waited for the big moment. Crude recycled instruments like yogurt-container drums and coffee-can shakers were banged in a monotonous beat as a red-nosed clown approached the effigy and set it alight. The crowd cheered. Some children cried. Many took pictures with their phones. While my numb lips thawed at the sight of the flames, my throat grew hot at the sight of the effigy's shape. Hay and twine burned brightly in the shape of twenty-foot-tall people joined at the hands. As the flames licked ever higher, the symbol of unity became animated into running, as though fleeing from immolation. I swallowed hard and shook my tingling arms.

Suddenly, I noticed people scurrying away, some people frantically scanning their phones and some talking furiously in clusters. You looked around, suspicious. You grabbed your phone.

"Damn it. My battery has died." I too looked at my phone. It had frozen in the cold and shut down.

I approached a white guy who had looked at his phone, scooped up his screaming toddler, and begun walking away.

"Excuse me, sir?"

He did not respond.

"What's going on?" You couldn't get an answer.

I looked around. The effigy was burning, but no one was watching. In clusters people left. They left in a hurry. People swiftly snuffed out homemade lanterns and dropped them to the ground.

In the midst of the confusion, I felt a hand on my shoulder.

"Where were you?" I asked Nadine. She was frazzled. No hat. No gloves. Her hair was unkept and untied. I hugged her and her arms were wooden. Her face was paler than usual, her lips chapped. I tried to continue as if I didn't notice. "Nadine, this is Evan."

Nadine was out of breath.

"Evan this is—"

Nadine stopped my hand as it gestured toward her in my introductions.

"Stop. Stop," she half whispered. She looked at both of us, her curly eyelashes catching the light of the burning effigy. "President Pryce has just been assassinated." The breath from her mouth made clouds around her face so thick, I was certain we had heard her wrong.

"What?"

"I need you to hide."

"What's going on?" You were as confused as me. Both of us leaned into her face and turned our ears to her mouth hoping for clarity. "President Pryce did what?"

"I can't explain everything right now, but my dad asked me to pack my bags. I'm leaving for Melbourne tomorrow morning."

"I don't understand." My lips were so numb I could barely speak. "Why would we need to hide if he's dead? We're in Canada."

"That doesn't matter! Not with the Two Nations, One Vision campaign. We're not safe, Kay. None of us are safe. This assassination, the protests . . . The more we fight back against everything that president stood for, the more excuses they have to control us. We're dangerous to them. Do you understand? They've been rounding up people like you and me. There are workhouses set up on Ward's Island already. My dad, through his work, found out about them and he sent me packing."

"Hold on, if—" You tried to reason with Nadine, whose eyes were as wide as saucers.

"Do you have a place to hide?" she interjected.

You and I looked at each other. Was this a trick question? "My apartment? Your apartment?" I answered half-heartedly.

"No. Not a place you call home. A place where no one will know you're there. You can't hide at my place anymore. It's not safe. People know you in the building."

"But why—"

"Do you have a place to hide?!"

"No." I looked at you.

We both looked back at Nadine and shook our heads.

"My dad has a connection with someone who can help you. I told him he had to set it up for you or I wouldn't go to Melbourne with him."

I smiled briefly hearing that.

"Listen to me," she said. Every word was precious. "I need you to remember this address: Seventy-Two Homewood Street."

You took out your phone to make a memo and remembered that your battery had died.

"Do not write anything down. I need you to repeat what I just said. Seventy-Two Homewood Street."

You and I looked at each other again. Was she just being hysterical?

"Do it!" she spat at us in a stage whisper. We flinched. We repeated the address. She continued.

"When you are ready to hide, you will meet someone by the name of Liv there. Can you remember her name?"

I jumped to answer. "Liv. Meet Liv at Seventy-Two Homewood Street."

"If she's not home, she said you need to let yourself into the back-yard and hide among the recycling bins. Do you understand?"

We nodded in disbelief. She reached out and melted into my embrace.

"I love you, Queen Kay. Do you hear me? Do you understand how much I love you?"

If I had known it was the last time I would ever see her, I would have said, "I love you too." I would have said, "Thank you for housing me. Thank you for forging that note. Thank you for naming me." Instead, I watched her run toward a Lincoln Continental waiting for her just beyond a set of yellow metal barriers left behind from the parade. The car drove away and we were left dumbfounded by the exchange.

I couldn't feel my face in the cold of Nadine's sudden and confounding departure. You and I cautiously walked toward a streetcar stop heading eastbound on Dundas. Had that conversation actually happened? When the streetcar arrived, we tried to get on, but the driver closed the doors in our faces. We waited for another streetcar. Same thing. No admittance.

In the bitter cold, we walked east toward home, occasionally warming our hands in heated bank ATM lobbies. We also tried our luck at each machine hoping to retrieve some funds using our Verification Cards. Nothing but error messages.

By the time we hit Yonge Street, yet another political march was in full swing. This time, it was almost impenetrable, with Black and Brown folks linking arms. It was hardly a march since the crowd could barely move.

"Jesus. How are we going to get home through this?" You stood on your tiptoes and looked over the growing crowds. "I'm freezing."

I shook my head at the commotion.

"I mean . . . we're all fighting for the same things, but I wish they'd at least create a path for people to get by," you said, trying to speak despite your lips being numb.

We had to push past one group banging on pots and pans and screaming, "FUCK THE FASCIST GOVERNMENT! FUCK THE FASCIST GOVERNMENT!"

A Black woman with forearm crutches spoke as the crowd attempted to march past, her friend helping her be heard by holding a megaphone to her mouth. "Random raids! Denial of access to basic services! Mass deportations! If you're like me, and have been issued a

Verification Card, ask yourself: When was the last time I was able to enter the store and buy food? When was the last time I was treated by a doctor?"

I covered my ears at the piercing treble of the megaphone's speaker.

In the alcove of one store, a white reporter, lit by a bright light on a stand, held a microphone and attempted to deliver to the camera despite the racket. "Following the assassination of US President Pryce, an estimated six thousand protesters are present here today to march against what some are calling martial law, right here in Toronto."

We wove through the crowd, past a large banner reading, "Two Nations, One Vision: Excuse for Apartheid in Canada." Two Indigenous women wavered under the weight of its poles while one spoke on a megaphone, shouting, "Genocide since 1492: Forced sterilization! Land theft! No access to water!"

One protester's sign was a photo of the Canadian prime minister and the American president shaking hands with red paint splattered over it to look like blood. A series of Brown women held signs with the words "The Far Right on Both Sides of the Border." A grouping of Black men wearing red targets on their jackets held up their arms.

You told me to look up. Above us, cops in riot gear stood at the edges of store roofs with their guns at the ready.

"Come on! Let's go!" I grabbed your arm and led us down an alleyway just as we saw a banner being set aflame. I could hear glass breaking from the store windows. We ran through a maze of cars in a parking lot, with the muted sound of chanting transforming into screams not far behind us.

"Figures. All these people protesting violence by using violence. It's absurd," you said.

When we arrived back at my apartment, we found Nolan positioning the rabbit ears on his television to get a clear picture of a press conference being held at the White House. We all sat down on Nolan's bed to watch.

Pryce had been shot. An assassination. Most likely a Black extremist group based in Detroit, founded after the water crisis. Several threats from this group in the last six months. Details to follow. Riots in Washington, New York, San Francisco, Toronto, Montreal, and other cities against the rise of a violent right wing.

Nolan changed the channel to Canadian news. Prime Minister Dunphy began his speech.

"We Canadians do not stand by terrorist groups who believe that bullets will justify their cause . . ."

Fanny picked up Sedgewick and began pacing. "Do you think shit will go down here too?" She walked to my bedroom, opened the window, and looked out at Church Street.

"Girl, things are already going down! Can't you hear them on Yonge Street?" Nolan said while putting tin foil on the antennae. You and I hadn't even removed our jackets or hats. We stood waiting for the best time to tell them what Nadine had told us. "That president represented all the hate white people have spent decades pretending isn't there. Now that he's dead, there's no pretending anymore."

I looked outside the window. "Compared to Yonge it's quiet out there. Too quiet." Fanny joined me at the sill to confirm my observation. Nothing but the buzz of the Pizza Pizza sign below. No one cruising. No blaring music from the clubs. No one lining up to wait for entrance to events. No one walking their dogs.

You and I didn't have the heart to tell them what Nadine had told us. We didn't believe it ourselves. Not yet. We still didn't believe it even as the curfew was put into place.

"We are declaring a state of emergency," said Premier Ogilvy at a press conference. "When day after day of demonstrations have left a scar on our beloved province, we must take action. When looting occurs under the guise of marches, we must intervene. When protests are no longer peaceful, we need to employ the help of peacekeepers."

"Please let me pass," you said to a Boot at the Wellesley and Yonge checkpoint early one morning. You held out your Verification Card like an obedient boy, displaying last night's homework. "I need to make my way to my mother's house in Parkdale. I'll be back before curfew." I stood beside you, fearful and tongue-tied.

"No. Stand back." The Boot did not make eye contact, rather, he scanned the barriers on all four sides of the intersection, while blocking your way with his rifle.

"Evan, please. Let's go."

"I will. If you let me pass now, I'll be back before eight. That's the rule. I'm following the rules."

"The rule is, you do what I say. Now go."

"Listen, sir. I'm not a protestor. I'm just a normal man trying to make my way to Parkdale to see my elderly mother. I mean no harm. I just need to pass."

"Evan," I whispered.

"Where in Parkdale?" The Boot's posture changed.

"Excuse me?"

"What is her address in Parkdale?"

"What? Why do you—"

"Why don't we pay your elderly mother a visit?"

You opened your mouth, but you knew not what to say. I tugged on your jacket sleeve, pulling you away from the exchange.

"Both of you pansy n_ _ _ _rs get out of my face and off the street."

You think I didn't notice but I did. And I do not judge you for that, Evan. The Boot barely had to raise his voice. He stated each word nonchalantly as if he were teaching two dogs to sit. I watched you, unable to form the words in your mouth. You couldn't even step forward in protest. You just rocked slightly on the soles of your winter boots unable to bridge the gap between your self-image as a respectable citizen and the image of a disobedient Black man, which you had avoided all your life. We made our way back to my apartment, and you spent the rest of the day staring blankly at the wall in my bedroom.

What went on in your mind that day, Evan? What helped you continue to pretend along with me? How did we continue our disbelief?

We didn't believe we were in danger when the so-called peace-keeping cops began their rounds along each street to ensure people were not gathering for another demonstration. In every house, shelves were being knocked over, televisions, computers, and phone screens were being shattered. Cupboards were left empty. We didn't believe we were in danger when the cops came into our apartment. Two cops were patting us down aggressively when another white man came in. His laced black boots were shiny enough that I could see the silhouette of my body, face flat against the kitchen wall, on its surface. Instead of riot gear, he wore a black bomber jacket with a heavy-duty zipper. Even as he barked orders to the cops, he was slick. Graceful.

"Where is their circuit-breaker box?"

"In the stairwell, sir."

"Good. Cut off their power."

Sedgewick fell out of Fanny's arms and began yapping to protect us.

"Sedgewick, come here!" Fanny cried.

The Boot kicked Sedgewick into a corner, where he whimpered and shook.

The Boot slowly paced along the line of us, our hands on the wall, four queens fearing for our lives. You and I looked at each other, our cheeks flat against the surface of the wallpaper. What were you saying to me in your head, that day, Evan? Our pressed palms were only an inch apart. If I could turn back time and touch your pinky with mine, I would.

"Where are your cell phones?"

Before we could choke out our answer, another cop returned from the bedrooms with all four of our cell phones, placed them on the ground before him. He stomped them into LEGO pieces. With every stomp of his foot, I could feel this version of myself, this version of me, who once took selfies, who once posted statuses, who once promoted my drag shows online, who once had proof of my existence, shatter onto the floor under his boot. Photos. Stomp. Passwords. Stomp. Profiles. Stomp. Text messages. Stomp. Phone numbers. My phone. A phone to call someone. *To call Nadine. To call someone. Anyone. I have no phone.*

We didn't believe we were in danger when the curfew then became a restriction on leaving the house at all.

"To buy food," I said to a Boot when he asked me why Nolan and I were visiting No Frills on Parliament Street.

"You don't have money," he said confidently as he pointed to a long lineup near a bank ATM where none of the Others could access their funds. Nolan showed him the handful of loonies and toonies that you, Nolan, Fanny, and I had scavenged for in every nook and cranny of the apartment. Enough to buy a loaf of bread, some peanut butter, and a package of beef jerky was the plan. Anything that didn't need refrigeration or heating. The Boot slapped Nolan's palm with the tip of his gun, and the change fell to the ground, rolling in perfect starburst lines from his feet.

"See? I told you, faggot. You don't have money. Move along."

Nolan moved to reach out for the change, but the gun blocked him. "I said move along." Nolan's jaw tightened in humiliation. We walked away from the cop, past two other cops tasing an Asian man off his bicycle, and I counted my blessings. My stomach grumbled on the walk home.

Nolan stopped at the sight of a large garbage bin and kicked a burned muffin tin still covered in overcooked crust. He picked up the tin, stared at it for a moment, then picked off some of the crust and ate it. He offered the tin to me, and I joined in the feast. We paused. We both looked around for a brief moment of shame, then dug in deeper to a pile of plastic bags left beside the bin full of other people's trash. We returned to you all with two unfinished water bottles, a half-eaten hot dog, and a bag full of cherry pits with meat still hanging on one side of the seed.

Yet again that night, in the freezing cold and deafening quiet, all four of us gathered under several blankets and coats and tried to sleep. We lay widthwise on Nolan's bed so that all of us could fit. I tried to make circles with my breath in the air. Fanny shifted constantly. Nolan suggested we sing songs together. We felt too weak to join in. You snored softly. We fought over who could hold Sedgewick, since his tiny body held so much heat and petting him made us all less anxious about the things to come.

"Do you remember that ice storm that happened back in 2013?" said Fanny.

We groaned, we shivered.

"I remember breaking up with some loser who refused to wear condoms. I sent him and his dirty dick out into the slippery glass of the night, and I locked the door. Felt good to let him slide and fumble his way home."

We laughed quietly.

Sedgewick was in my lap. I placed my hands on his warm fur and could hear his tummy grumbling. That's when I felt the words finally come to my mouth. In my hunger, in Sedgewick's hunger, I finally believed what Nadine had said.

"My loves . . ." I felt the void of silence. I measured the silence's width, length, and depth. I measured the words I was going to place in that void, unsure if they would fit.

"What is it, Kay?" Nolan said impatiently while tucking the edges of a blanket under his feet.

Your soft snoring stopped and you came to.

I told them about our encounter with Nadine. What Nadine's father knew. Seventy-Two Homewood. This person named Liv. I told them that at some point you and I were going to run and hide. I told them they needed to come with us, or they wouldn't be safe. We were in real danger, and we could be in danger for a very long time.

"No." Nolan suddenly left the bed, and the blankets became two degrees cooler.

"What do you mean?" I asked.

The remaining three humans and dog all shuffled together again to accumulate body heat. Nolan shivered toward his closet door.

"I mean, no. No, I will not hide. I will not hide. I will not hide. I will not hide." He said it so many times it almost became a song.

"Nolan, please—" Fanny cried.

"NO! I have been told to hide my entire life. I. Will. Not. Hide." He opened his closet door and began rummaging through his things.

"What are you doing?"

"What does it look like I'm doing, Kay? I'm going out."

"Don't be a fool, Nolan." Fanny held the top edge of the blanket under her chin in two fists. "You're gonna get yourself killed." Sedgewick whimpered under the covers in protest of the conflict between us.

"You know who's the fool, Fanny? You, for keeping a dog in here, when we don't have the means to feed it and we can't even walk the damn dog in the night! Who the hell lets a dog shit and piss in the corner of a house?"

"I don't have a choice! We can't leave the house past nine at night, and I clean up the mess when we have water."

I added cautiously, "Yeah, Fanny. If we have to run, the reality is, we can't bring Sedgewick."

"And why not?!" Fanny scooped her dog, and held him firmly.

"We'll be in hiding, not at the Holiday Inn. We can't risk the barking. We can't risk having another being to take care of. We need to travel light."

"He's my baby, not a piece of luggage!" she screamed back at me.

"Fuck this conversation!" Nolan threw his hands up in exasperation. He slipped on two thigh-high boots and a short fur coat to finish his look.

You chimed in. "The streetlights aren't even on, Nolan. Who knows who's out there waiting for you?"

"Exactly. I guess I won't know until I'm out there."

"You're going to get yourself killed." You rushed up and tried to block Nolan at the doorframe. "I told you what happened when I tried to cross that checkpoint the other day. No one is getting through. There's no escape."

"You don't even know what that means. You don't know what it means to run. But you know who does? My parents. You think keeping silent, doing what they were told to do in the work camps kept them alive? It didn't. I was raised by two Cambodian zombies, Evan. Two walking skeletons who lived in fear. Doing shit like that may keep you breathing, but you're not alive. Hiding is like a death. This is me. I am proud to be me. I'm not hiding, Evan." Nolan choked back a sob. He snapped his fingers trying to place a memory. It was hard to remember things these days, when all around us things were changing. "What was her name? Our drag sister who died during the Pulse Nightclub shooting?"

"Glorious." I inhaled deeply at the thought of her. She was a big name in Oakland. She just happened to be in Orlando for a gig at the gay club's Latino night. A shooter opened fire on the attendees, killing forty-nine of them.

"Yes. Glorious. Do you remember her dance number? The one with the bananas on her head and the bikini?" We all laughed wistfully. "Can you imagine the horror of that gunman entering the premises and just spraying bullets into people? The people rushing into the bathrooms trying to hide? The piles of dead bodies? Supposedly an inch of blood covered the floor. That's how bad it was." We listened with tight jaws. Nolan softly brushed the tears off his face and wiped the wet onto his pants. "Glorious was . . . she was glorious to the very end. She died in costume, with her stilettos still on. She died . . . being herself."

"But what about those people who hid? They are alive today and able to be who they are because of it," I added, hoping to change the tide.

"Kay. Those people, in this new world, are probably still hiding, or worse. I can't chance that. I can't hide. I will not hide."

Nolan's voice quavered. He wiped his nose, then composed his proud face. I watched you step aside. It must have been so hard, my love. But you did. You stepped aside and let him go. We all listened to the front door of our suite slam closed. Nolan stormed out into the blackness of the night. We listened to his heels clicking across the pavement until we heard nothing but silence.

We waited for him all night. The next day we watched the windows like they were televisions. He did not come back. The days passed. I'm unsure how many days it was. It was long enough that white folks began frequenting Church Street again. All the white Homos were much less extravagant, much less frilly. All of them walking like straight folks, pretending things were right as rain.

"I guess the curfew isn't for them," Fanny said, while Sedgewick pooped in the living room corner. "It was meant for us." It was a sobering reminder: We aren't white boys who can take off the gay like a coat, hang it up in a closet, then lock ourselves in that closet. People like us didn't have a choice. You can't take off the skin. You can't take off the femme.

On New Year's Eve, Church Street was full of revelers, wearing party hats and blowing on party favors. In the early evening you, Fanny, and I wrapped ourselves in blankets and sat on chairs right next to the window in my bedroom to watch a straight white couple eat pasta in the restaurant across the street. Fanny lit a candle. I handed us all a set of cutlery, and we pretended to twirl our fettucine before putting our empty forks into our mouths and savoring nothing. I wiped the corners of my mouth and poured all of us a glass of air. We toasted.

"To a new year." Your eyes watered. I swallowed back a sob.

"To a new year." A silent clink between each of us.

I waved my hands through the space between us to obliterate our imagined table setting and held your hands in mine.

"We can't leave each other."

"What are you talking about, Kay? Who says I would ever leave you? I love you."

"No one says you'll leave. But history is happening. And sometimes history means people get separated. People get lost. People make difficult decisions. People die." I wept into my blanket. You opened the wingspan of your comforter and enveloped me in your warmth. I shivered nonetheless.

"I wish we could wash this off! Our skin, our gay. I wish we could just pretend!" I sniveled into the hollow of your neck.

Sedgewick whimpered, and Fanny held him tighter. Partly to stave off the cold, partly to stave off the truth I was speaking.

"And lose one minute of loving you?" You forced me to look at you. It was so dark without the lights on, I felt like I was looking into the night sky. "Do you know the joy of risking our lives to be us? So many people in this world will never know what it means to truly love someone. To truly be themselves. I am proud to say I have been me. I would never wash this off. I will never stop loving you. I will never stop."

We held each other and cried. When I caught my breath I looked at you again, into the dark night sky of your face.

"What do we do? What happens tomorrow? And the day after that? What if you try to find your mom and we get separated forever?" I asked you.

"Pray. If the universe loved us enough to make us, then the universe will love us enough to keep us together. And if either one of us dies . . ." You choked on your words. "If either one of us dies, that doesn't mean anything. The universe still loves us. It just means we will be together in another way." You opened the width of your comforter again so that Fanny and Sedgewick could join in and add to the warmth. We all embraced. On the last night of that year, the three of us slept side by side, Sedgewick being the smallest spoon.

In the morning, I woke to the sound of something outside. You were asleep beside me despite a fitful night. I heard the sound again. Someone shouting.

"Babes. You okay?" you said, wiping your eyes. "What is it?"

Fanny stirred when I got up from the bed.

I opened the window. Church Street. The buzz of the Pizza Pizza sign below us. Softly falling snow. Nothing. I watched for a bit. Waited for the sound. Again. Someone shouting. From the horizon south on Church Street, I could see someone walking north along the yellow line in the middle of the street. Clumsy. Wavering.

"What do you see?" Fanny said groggily.

I squinted my eyes. When I confirmed what I was seeing, I held my mouth and screamed silently. It was Nolan. Nolan was naked, save for his high-heeled boots. His head was shaved. His face was bloody. Teeter tottering on his heels he hobbled north on an empty Church Street screaming something I could barely understand. Fluid gurgling in his throat, blood down his neck.

"Ruuuuuuuuuuuuuun!" he screamed.

You peered out the window. "Fuck! It's Nolan! What is he doing?! We have to get him."

I put my hand on your chest. Something was about to happen.

"WAAAAAKE UUUUP! RUUUUUUN! EVERYBODY RU-UUUUUUUN!"

Fanny scooped Sedgewick into her arms. "What happened to Nolan?!"

Sedgewick barked.

"Somebody has to go get him."

"Do not go outside, Fanny!" I said. Fanny ran to another window to get a better view of Nolan.

From the horizon an armored truck slowly wheeled itself along Church Street until it was twenty feet away from Nolan. I held my breath. I remember you squeezing my hand. We watched Nolan try to hobble away faster, just as a Boot aimed his gun and shot Nolan in the throat. His screams were only gurgles. Another shot to Nolan's head.

Chaos.

We watched silently as seven more armored trucks made their

way along Church Street. The Boots began crashing the butt of their guns into each store window. Broken glass. Fire. Screams. A line of people with their hands above their heads solemnly walked to the orders of another Boot. They were made to kneel in front of the Baskin-Robbins ice cream shop. One was shot. Screams. The others were put into another truck and driven away. One tried to run, but a bullet sent her head snapping back and her body collapsed on the pavement. I shut the window.

"WHAT'S HAPPENING?! SHIT! WHAT DO WE DO?" Fanny was pacing the hallway.

"Fanny. You gotta come with us," I pleaded.

"I can't!"

"Leave the dog and run! Come on!"

"I can't! I can't leave Sedgewick. I have to hide here."

I gave Fanny a hug that I wished lasted longer. You and I did as we had planned: we grabbed our small backpacks, got dressed, and headed to the staircase. You grabbed my arm.

"Kay. You ready?"

"Yes."

"You remember the plan?"

"You'll find your way to Parkdale, get your mom, then find me."

"You remember the address, Kay?"

"Yes."

We kissed. We kissed. We kissed one last time. I watched you run into a back alley and disappear. Then I ran in the other direction down another back alley thinking, *72 Homewood. 72 Homewood. 72 Homewood. 72 Homewood. 72 Homewood. 72 Homewood. 72 Homewood. 72 Homewood. 72 Homewood. 72 Homewood. 72 Homewood.*

8

We march with Beck and Liv toward a clearing. Slung over Beck's shoulder is a hockey bag, which he places carefully by a picnic table. Liv gestures for me and Bahadur to sit. Beck opens the bag and places two handguns onto the table in front of us like he is serving us dinner. Bahadur looks back at the cottage where Firuzeh is still resting and takes a deep breath. A reminder of why we are doing this. Beck reaches into the bag again and places boxes of ammunition onto the table.

I remember Fanny opening her costume bag and placing various tools from her arsenal before me. Razors. Bottles. Brushes. Liquids. Creams. I had begged her, as a fellow Black queen, to show me how to do my makeup. Wearing a pink velour jumpsuit, and holding a cup of coffee, she too told me to sit down. Fanny took one more sip of her coffee then said, "First we shave."

"These are Glock 40s." Beck encourages us to pick them up. "Go on. Feel it in your hand."

I take one in my hand. It is heavier than I thought it would be. I have never held a real gun before. The closest I ever got to purchasing a gun was in the toy aisle at the dollar store when Nolan wanted us to dress as Bonnie and Clyde for Halloween. My fake pistol was made of purple plastic and came with a spinning wheel of caps that made an ear-piercing snap with each pull of the trigger. Beck takes the weapon from me and shows us a firm grip. "When you hold it, don't be afraid. Hold it confidently."

"Drag isn't just about looking like any lady heading to her accounting job on Bay Street. It's about fantasy," Fanny said, both of us crowding her vanity mirror, both of our eyebrows glued over. "Even our contouring game isn't natural. But who wants to be natural? We are *supernatural,* darling." A base color was applied, this time perfectly matched with my skin. Using a large palette of nude tones, a perfect science of light and dark illusion played on my cheekbones. Fanny assured me that in time, it would take only an hour to put my makeup on rather than three. "Now press that powder on. Don't brush. Press."

"What you're going to do is press the bullets into the magazine like this." Liv shows us how to load the bullets into the compartment. She hands the magazine to Bahadur and they accidentally drop a bullet onto the pea gravel. They nervously apologize and pick it up. They try again.

"Now I've seen your numbers." Fanny taught me in her bedroom. It was like drag queen university, only the school was a three-by-three-foot clearing in her room where there were no shoes or clothes. "I mean . . . one thing you've got going is, your lip sync is bang on. Bang fucking on. *But . . .*" Fanny picked up a round hairbrush and placed it in my hands. "It's so much more than lip syncing. Any closeted gay boy from the suburbs can lip sync. This is drag, remember? Fantasy." She struck a pose, her eyes full of images and wonder. "Where are you right now? Are you in Fanny's bedroom? Wrong. When you come out onstage, I want you to imagine a five-hundred-seat theater complete with a lighting rig, dry ice, and a fucking trapdoor. You have to imagine it for the audience even though they're all just sitting in some nasty-ass dive of a bar with five sticky tables."

Beck leaves us for a few minutes and returns with two wooden posts and supplies. Using a metal fence-post driver, he positions the posts upright and three feet apart. He then nails a large piece of cardboard to join the two posts and draws the outline of a head and torso.

Liv instructs me to slap the magazine in and pull the slide. I can barely hear her with my shooting earmuffs on.

"Now your gun is loaded."

I can feel it. I can feel the power of every bullet in my hand.

"Watch your finger. Always think of your finger discipline." She shows me how to keep my right pointer finger straight to avoid a misfire. She corrects my grasp of the gun so that my hands are hugging the weapon, my thumbs lie, one above the other, in a snug embrace.

"Look at your feet."

I looked down at my feet doing a clumsy step touch to the tune of Paula Abdul.

"Girl, you have gorgeous legs, but you need to be aware of how your body takes up space. Women learn from a young age to be small. But now we all have the freedom to play with that smallness and make it large. Pull your feet together and cock your hip. Now lean on the wall. Lean on things. Press into them. Play with your space."

I press into the wall and trace my knee along the surface coyly.

"Yes, bitch. Yes. There you go. You're almost there."

"Widen your stance. Good." I do as I am told. Beck shows me how to aim by aligning my front and rear sights. I thought the sight would look like a cross, but instead it looks like I have to line up a point in the front end of my gun with an open square on the back end of my gun. I line it up and can see the drawn-on shape of a person about twenty feet away. "Now, the trick is to press the fingers of your right hand into the palm of your left hand to create tension. That will help with the kickback. Now exhale and slowly pull the trigger."

I shoot. A thunderbolt of energy rushes through my body. A lightning current creates a ripple through the muscles from my forearm to my deltoids. A deafening crack. I hear a muffled cheer. Beck gestures to me to point my gun down and be mindful of my finger discipline. He walks to the target and points proudly to where I shot the target right in the head.

"You okay?" Liv asks.

I realize that I'm shaking.

"I want you to think of a story. You're not some two-dollar performer up there singing along to some song asking for pittance. You are the queen of the stage. Do you have a crush on a cute boy in the audience? Are you on the run from the cops? Do you not fit in anywhere? What is the story?"

I press play on another song, this time by SWV and begin to experiment with feeling heartbroken. Fanny nods her head and does a slow clap.

"There you go. You're helpless around him. You don't know what to do without him. Yup. Keep going."

Bahadur tries their hand at shooting but they aren't as successful. Tiny clouds of dust explode at random close to the target but not close enough. "Sorry! Maybe I'm not getting this right." They speak louder than they need to on account of their earmuffs.

"Oh gosh, don't even worry about it. You've got a good stance. So you're ahead of the game compared to most people," Beck says to

Bahadur, who giggles sheepishly. "Everyone makes mistakes, and as long as we're safe, we will learn along the way."

"But what if my wig falls?" I said to Fanny while she rounded my newly shaven head with duct tape.

"Everyone's wig falls at least once," Fanny said while pinning my new lace front from the weave of the wig to the tape attached to my head. "That's called a drag queen baptism. If your wig doesn't fall off you don't get to go to heaven." She laughed. "Just kidding. But really, everyone experiences it. No harm done. Make it part of your act. Start holding it in your arms like a baby. Make it your ex-boyfriend. Whatever."

Beck takes a rifle out of the hockey bag. "This is an AR15."

Bahadur and I take a step back at the size of it.

"I will need you to learn this weapon because these will be carried by the Boots."

I wave at Firuzeh, who is walking toward us, perhaps to watch us train. She does not wave back. Over the last few days her face has been, as expected, motionless and catatonic.

"Here, give it a try."

I cautiously take the rifle. This gun is different. Rather than front and rear sights, it has a scope through which I can see a pin-size red dot. With the ergonomic butt of the gun against my shoulder, I aim, I exhale, I fire. I hear muffled cheers from Beck and Bahadur.

"Look! I got it again in the head!" I say. Suddenly I feel my grip on the AR15 loosen as Firuzeh takes it from me. "Shit, no!"

"NO!" Liv screams. We collectively imagine Firuzeh pointing the gun to her own head, pulling the trigger, scattering pieces of herself onto our faces, the reverberation of her last moments echoing among the trees, anything to erase the horrors she witnessed.

Instead, Firuzeh shoulders the gun, aims and shoots at the target several times until she hears the empty click of a used-up magazine. She screams. She drops the weapon and runs to the target, ripping it to shreds with her own bare hands.

"FUCK YOU! FUCK YOU! FUCK ALL OF YOU!" She collapses on the ground in a solid heap, wisps of cardboard littered around her tiny frame. Long, agonizing sobs. We stand witness to this opening, this tear in her fabric. We witness it until she is silent, her voice hoarse and raw.

9

In the main house's living room, Liv and I sit on either side of Firuzeh and hold her hands. Hanna sits on the edge of the lumpy recliner and Beck leans on the doorframe, both of them uneasy.

"How's this?" Bahadur tucks a blanket over Firuzeh's lap, then sits at her feet to listen.

"It's good. Thank you."

"Are you sure you feel ready to share? It's like what you told me when we first met: 'Feel *what* you want to feel. Feel *when* you want to feel,'" Bahadur gently says.

"Yes. I'm ready. I will stop if I need to. Thank you, *aziz-am*. I need to say all of this out loud. It's like telling someone your nightmares so that they don't come true. If I tell you this now, I know it will be in the past far behind me."

"I wanted to surprise you," Firuzeh said to Bahadur before giving them a gift bag. "Today is supposed to be the first snowfall. I wanted you to be prepared." Inside the bag were a striped Blue Jays toque she had found at the corner store, and some spare winter gear she had sourced from one of her Facebook friends.

"I look like a marshmallow." Firuzeh laughed.

"No! No. You don't look—"

"Yes, I do."

"Okay. Maybe a little."

"Let's schedule you in next week, okay? We have to finalize your paperwork for your work permit, and I want to get that done sooner than later."

She giggled watching Bahadur exit the Transgender Assistance Center, trying to make sense of the oversize winter boots with each awkward step.

It was Friday again. Firuzeh made her way to the cafeteria and heated up her leftovers from yesterday's loving-kindness dinner. According to her research on YouTube, the idea was to craft a loving-kindness meal meant for herself and no one else as an act of self-care in the wake of her recent breakup. She got to choose the menu, not her ex, who happened to be a critically acclaimed chef at a critically acclaimed restaurant. She did not need her ex to dictate menu choices or remind Firuzeh that her calorie intake was high. She did not need her ex to bicker with at the grocery store over organic or nonorganic. The meal was just for her. And, since Firuzeh was not a critically acclaimed chef, the meal she had created tasted horrible. Firuzeh's mother always said, "When you're in love, make a feast. When you're heartbroken, eat out." But since she had to shoulder the entire rent after her ex moved out, eating out was not an option. She watched the bland quinoa rotate in the microwave and considered her options for yet another evening practicing painful autonomy and liberation from codependence.

"Hey, are you coming to the party tonight?" her coworker Kyle asked, holding a Tupperware of cheesy lasagna.

"What party?"

"Drew's Queer anti-holiday party."

"Who's Drew again?"

"Remember Drew, who hosted that anti-Valentine's party?"

"I can't. Too many past clients in that room."

Kyle nodded his head in agreement, knowing the usual conflicts of interest frontline workers face in the LGBTQ2S community.

Firuzeh explained, "I'm facilitating the Trans elders' mindfulness group, then heading home."

Kyle nodded. "Cool." He adjusted his suspenders over his unicorn T-shirt and sat himself down to eat.

"Yeah. Just trying to be independent. Know myself. Be *with* myself. I'm trying to be the person I want in a partnership, you know?" The microwave dinged. Firuzeh opened the sticky door to the 1980s contraption and looked at the steaming bowl of beige grains and withered cucumbers. She smiled weakly at Kyle.

"Cool." Kyle took another bite of lasagna and opened a magazine to read. Firuzeh understood his signal and gave up trying to start a conversation.

The recreation room still smelled like cleaning products when Firuzeh entered. She sighed and opened the window to help the smell dissipate. She'd told the custodian again and again to use vinegar and water since several of the participants had scent sensitivities, but he refused to listen. She laid out fifteen yoga mats in perfect lines facing one wall and placed chairs behind each mat in case of mobility issues. She used to arrange them in a large circle to encourage conversation, but the elders became confused over their right and left depending on where they sat in the circle. She then shuffled the curtain over the mirror to avoid any confusion over directions.

"If you find your mind wandering, just guide yourself back to the breath. No judgment. Just watch your thoughts like they are clouds in the sky." As part of the exercise, each elder pointed at their distracting thoughts, imagining them passing over their head. Firuzeh found it ironic that she was teaching these folks to meditate when her own thoughts crowded her emotional brain. She thought of her ex surprising her at work with flowers. She thought of her ex dancing with her under a bridge while a train passed overhead. She thought of her ex painting her toes on a lazy Sunday morning.

"Great work," she told the elders. "Follow your breath from your nostrils into your lungs and back out again."

After most of the participants had left and Firuzeh had put away all the mats, she noticed one elder struggling with his jacket. It was Said, one of her favorites, although she would never admit to having favorites. She adored how in class he would assist Firuzeh by showing his fellow classmates his version of various poses and encourage them, sometimes a bit too aggressively, to follow along.

"Hey, Said! Did you need help with that?" Firuzeh rushed to his side.

"If you don't mind." When she reached out to bring the sleeve closer to his arm, she noticed a scabbed-over scar running down his forearm.

"What happened? Are you okay?"

"My neighbors. They jumped out at me in the stairwell. All my groceries fell to the ground." He closed his tired eyes and shook his head before enduring the last push of his arm through the fabric of his sleeve. He groaned.

"*What?* Why did they do that?"

Said smirked in contempt. "Why do any of them do what they do?"

"I'm so sorry, Said. I know you were just placed there recently."

"Housing for people like me is hard to come by. I'm not complaining about the bedbugs. Not complaining about the constant noise. I just want to be safe."

"Did you see the doctor? Do you need stitches?"

"No. Doctor told me to go home." He managed to get his other arm into the sleeve and winced in pain. "The doctors keep turning me away. First it was my prescriptions. The doctor refused to fill them. Told me I had an addiction problem. Now this. They told me to go home and sleep it off. How can you sleep off a wound? Glad it has scabbed, though."

Firuzeh's throat grew warm. This wasn't the first time she had heard of this happening to the Others. It was why the walk-in clinic at the center was constantly full. With dry pursed lips, Said kissed both Firuzeh's cheeks goodbye.

She closed up the recreation room, waved goodbye to Quin, the night security guard at the front desk, and headed home into the crisp winter air. Her head was full of worry about clients such as Said and Bahadur. *How fragile safety is,* she thought to herself.

Yet another Boots checkpoint was situated at the closest intersection to the center. Firuzeh sighed and decided to take an alternate route home. Anything to avoid yet another pat-down by the Boots.

By the time the streetcar approached her home, Firuzeh had decided that despite the cold, it was warm enough for her to sit at Riverdale Park and contemplate her new single status. She had a lot of time for this kind of reflection these days. She sat on a park bench next to another on which a couple was locked in a heated embrace, kneading their faces into each other. At the basin of the park, framed by a baseball diamond, Firuzeh could see another tent city alive with activity. Laundry hung on makeshift lines. Groups encircled smoky fires. Out of one of the tents, a Black woman emerged from the zippered door and braced herself against the brisk breeze. Ragged and weary, she made her way up the hill toward the public washroom with a tray full of dirty dishes and a half-empty bottle of dish soap. Firuzeh closed her eyes at the sight of the woman. These tent cities were becoming more common with no solution in sight.

She took out the joint she kept in an eyeglass case in her bag. With each exhale, the smoke blurred the skyline. The CN Tower was changing colors from blue to red to green. Laser beams shot out from some event in the heart of downtown, an exciting event that did not include her.

How fragile life is.

Firuzeh walked up the lonely staircase to her third-floor 1950s apartment, made a beeline to her bed and cried herself to sleep.

The next day, Firuzeh packed what was thankfully the last of that dreadful loving-kindness meal and headed to work. A Boots checkpoint was set up at the intersection outside her apartment building. She casually waited in line with the Others. Raised her arms for a pat-down.

As per usual, the Boot opened her purse for inspection.

"And what is this?"

"It's my lunch."

The Boot winced at the container's smell.

"Verification Card, please."

The streetcar was delightfully less crowded than usual. She entered Transgender Assistance Center. She said hello to Justine, the daytime security guard at the front desk. Took the elevator to the third floor. Nodded in Kyle's direction. Pumped some hand sanitizer from the dispenser on the wall and rubbed it dry. Sat at her desk and checked emails. Deciding that checking her emails would go better with coffee, she got up from her desk and headed to the hospitality station across the hall. She poured ground coffee into the filter and heard a noise. She peeked her head around the corner and saw seven Boots with leather jackets and shiny boots making their way down the corridor, aiming their guns left and right. They were like an arrow. Swift. Graceful. They wore matching helmets and held matching rifles.

"Excuse me, sir?" said Jesse, the second-floor front-desk administrator to the man at the front of the pack. "Can I help you?"

From far away Firuzeh could see one of the Boots in the back of the pack intercept Jesse, preventing her from following any farther. Firuzeh couldn't hear what was said but could see that it was a threat. Jesse's hands went up, and she stopped in her tracks; her face was red, and she helplessly looked down the corridor. For a brief moment, she locked eyes with Firuzeh in a look of terror.

Firuzeh ducked back into the station and tried to put the filter back into the machine, but for some reason it wouldn't fit despite her attempts to jam it in again and again. She could hear their footsteps getting closer. Firuzeh just knew in her heart the feeling of impending disaster. She had felt it many times. She knew what it meant to run for your life. So she did. She dropped the filter and the coffee grounds spilled like soil onto the floor. She ran to her office.

Through the wall, she could hear the Boots speaking to Kyle. They sounded calm. Quiet. Smooth. Barely discernible. But Kyle was pleading.

"I just work here . . . I don't know! Please!" The sound of an overturned table. Or chairs? A slam against the wall. Another smoothly delivered sentence. Moaning. A cabinet opened. Paper being scattered. Shattered glass.

Firuzeh frantically searched for her cell phone; it always slipped to the bottom of her purse. She started a live video on Facebook and aimed it at herself hiding behind her desk.

The video caught the sound of a doorknob turning. Firuzeh covered her mouth and shut her eyes, willing the nightmare to end. Two legs from the knees down could be seen rounding the desk. A Boot crushing the phone into static, into a memory.

With Firuzeh's hands up in submission, the Boots pulled the landline phone from its socket. All of Firuzeh's files were tossed to the floor, rummaged through and confiscated.

At gunpoint, the Boots gathered all the staff together in the cafeteria on the ground floor. Jesse could not stop whimpering. Her makeup had streaked across her cheeks. Daniel, the custodian, was so stunned he could barely obey orders.

"Sit there. Look down. Sit there!"

Daniel's body froze.

"Did you hear me, freak?! Sit your ass down, or I will make you sit down." One Boot made him sit down by slamming the butt of his gun into Daniel's forehead. Screams. Now forced into a seated position, Daniel calmly touched his head, looked at his blood-covered hand, and stared out into the distance.

Time passed. Maybe two hours. It was all a blur. Firuzeh needed desperately to go to the washroom but didn't want to risk punishment. She heard the sound of the sirens, and two cops in full riot gear coolly entered. They walked up to one of the Boots and shook hands.

At the sight of this exchange a ringing stung her ears. Firuzeh looked at her coworkers. *What kind of partnership was this?*

"You got this covered?" said one of the cops to the Boot. It was difficult to discern between one person and the other. They all looked and acted the same. Even their gestures and voices seemed identical.

The Boots escorted the staff toward the front door of the center, where a large armored truck was waiting for them. Just as Firuzeh was about to step outside, she looked back and saw a pool of blood at the floor of the front desk; the security guard Justine's hand rounded the corner of the desk, unmoving. Firuzeh did not scream. They were all beyond screaming. They silently got into the truck and obeyed orders to sit side by side.

In queues several blocks long, every visible Other you could imagine:— Brown, Black, Muslim, Sikh, Hindu, Trans, Queer;—were standing alongside the harborfront. Some were elders. Some were children. Some were crying. Some were listless. So many Others. Everyone, including Firuzeh, was shuffled onto a series of ferries, coming and going. One boatload at a time. Gusts of wind scraped across everyone's faces as they stood waiting and waiting and waiting. But for what? Firuzeh didn't even have her winter jacket, since the Boots had forced her out of her office. To battle the cold, she danced on the spot and closed her eyes against the downpour of ice pellets from overhead.

"Where are we going?"

"You can't do this to us!"

"Please! Help us! She's just a baby!"

The Boots responded to nothing. They simply paced back and forth, save for moments of discipline when people protested.

To the right of Firuzeh, a pile of canes, walkers, and wheelchairs sat precariously by the edge of the dock. Through half-closed eyes, bracing against the unforgiving sleet, she looked around frantically, wondering about the owners of those mobility aids. Firuzeh swallowed hard, realizing that everyone in the endless queues was able-bodied. Icy waves crashed against the complicated lattice of metal and wood until some of the mobility aids fell into the lake. A Boot came by and with one swift kick, he managed to toss the rest of the equipment into the water. Simultaneously, armored trucks drove off along Queens Quay West, with the sound of muffled shrieks within.

A Boot standing to the left of Firuzeh sprayed a crackle of gunfire into the sky, and people in her queue ducked for cover with their palms over their ears. Screams. One woman ahead of Firuzeh ducked a fraction of a second later, looking around in delayed fear. Confused, she got up and began pacing the dock.

"Get in line!" the Boot demanded. The woman reentered, but from the end of the line. "I said to get in line! Not there! Where you were before!"

The woman tried to enter the line from the end again.

"Are you fucking kidding me?! Get in the fucking line!" Firuzeh surmised that the woman was Deaf. She weighed her options, wondering if informing the Boot of this woman's disability would risk the woman being shipped off to some unknown location like the Others in the trucks. The Boot poised the butt of his rifle to discipline her, and Firuzeh stepped out of line with her arms waving.

"Stop!" Firuzeh shouted. Firuzeh waved her hand at the woman and signed, "Are you Deaf?"

The woman affirmed Firuzeh's suspicion.

Firuzeh turned to the Boot and said, "She can stay next to me. Please! I can interpret for her."

What felt like a lifetime passed as the Boot looked back and forth between the two women, snow accumulating on his eyelashes like sand in an hourglass. The Boot filed both of them into the line. "Get her to follow instructions or she's in the trucks like the rest of them." He began patrolling the other lines. Exhales.

"What is happening?" the woman struggled to sign with her frost-bitten hands.

"I don't know. But I need you to stay with me."

At the front of each queue were small canopies, wavering in the wind. In the shelter of each canopy sat a Boot at a small desk.

"Next, step forward!" said the Boot at the front of Firuzeh's line. This Boot was a woman with ruddy cheeks and lips that enunciated clumsily in the cold air. She wore a black parka over her standard leather jacket. Upon closer inspection, seeing the Boot's light brown skin and hearing the sound of her vowels, Firuzeh could tell she was also of Iranian heritage. They shared a split second of recognition, as though Firuzeh had interrupted her playing dress-up in Boots regalia.

"I said, 'NEXT!'" the Boot shouted away the shame, still looking at Firuzeh. Her chin raised in defiance.

"No! One at a time, please," the Boot shouted at the woman beside Firuzeh.

"She's Deaf. I can interpret for her." Firuzeh gestured toward her line mate.

"Fine. I need your Verification Cards. Both of you. Get them out. Now."

Firuzeh interpreted. They frantically pinched their cards from within their wallets, the frigid wind making it an almost impossible task. The woman finally produced her card with her name: Emma Singh. They both placed their cards on the desk.

The Boot struggled with the ink in her pen. She blew warm air onto its nib until the ink flowed once again in scribbles at the top of a page. She adjusted her clipboard and began entering the information from the Verification Cards in small fields, adding Emma's and Firuzeh's names to the columns upon columns of Others. Another clipboard had a spreadsheet of numbers. The Boot cross-referenced the spreadsheet, finding Emma's Verification Card number of 2437 and crossing it out with a straight line using a ruler and her pen. She crossed out Firuzeh's number of 1722. Ruler. Straight line. The

Boot took off her glove and reached into an inside jacket pocket for her phone.

"Stand here, please." The Boot pointed to a blue X taped to the dock, adjacent to the desk. The Boot used the camera on her phone to take photos of each of them separately, holding a dry-erase board with their Verification Card numbers. Flash. Flash.

Shaking violently with cold, Firuzeh and Emma boarded one of the ferries hours after the sky had turned lavender, squeezing in between a pregnant woman and a vomiting child. They encountered more lineups once they arrived at Ward's Island, just south of Toronto's skyline. The icy waves crashed along the shore as the arrivals were shuffled into more lines and given placements around the island based on their physical strength and their obedience.

"Raise your arms. Open your mouth. Turn around."

"You two! Come with me," said one of the Boots to Firuzeh and Emma.

They joined a group of twenty other women and followed him down the road.

"Mama! Maaaaamaaaaaa!" a child screamed in their direction.

Firuzeh could not tell who this child's parent was since they all kept their heads down, to avoid a beating. To avoid the child being beaten.

"Maaaaamaaaaaa!"

Emma tugged at Firuzeh's sleeve to encourage her to look forward and continue marching.

Around them were the old homes of Ward's. The island was once the most desired location in the city to live since the quiet and calm of the islands was a short ferry ride from the hustle and bustle of downtown. Oftentimes people passed the deeds to their houses down from generation to generation in an effort to keep the sought-after community tight-knit. Then the flooding began happening every spring. The homes became mold-ridden, and what was once a charming and quaint haven for the wealthy and artistic, soon became a ghost town. Firuzeh could see that the homes were tragically damaged. Each one leaned to one side or the other, unable to stand on its own rotten base, spotted with black mildew. Despite the cold, the air was thick with the smell of decay as they finally made their way to a wide bungalow.

The Boot opened the door and entered. They all followed, thankful for the warmth. Sniffles. Stifled crying. They walked down a long hallway with its walls covered with art installations, now soggy from the damp. A saturated photo of the lake had a Black woman smoking a cigarette in the foreground, a curious shape from the smoke emerging from her exhale. The woman's face had been crossed out with a black indelible marker. By a vandal? Or the artist themselves? Firuzeh couldn't tell. A large textile drooped heavily on the wall, smelling like garbage. When passing the fabric, one could see it was made of the fibers of newspaper headlines, woven together to spell the phrase "The End." Firuzeh realized this had been some type of artist's residency center before the floods. This was a public space.

The Boot introduced the Others to a cohort of four Asian women in purple scrubs, each of them holding a nightstick and wearing a look of determination.

"Line up! Line up! Line up! Line up! Line up! Line up! Line up!" They screamed at the Others, poking them randomly and aggressively with the nightsticks. Like sheep, the arrivals were ushered down another set of hallways where there were dozens of small bedrooms with two beds each. Emma and Firuzeh bunked together. The Purple Scrub women slept in four separate large bedrooms, which were set at intervals between the smaller rooms, so that they could surveil the Others. While passing one of the large rooms, Firuzeh could see a group of the children, presumably belonging to the Purple Scrub women, playing a game of Monopoly.

"You didn't count the money right! Count it again!" said a small child, trying to fan out her Monopoly money with her tiny hands. One boy had tossed the dice too hard and was searching for the missing pieces under the bed. Another boy was jumping squares along the gameboard, whispering numbers under his breath.

"Mooooom! Sebastian didn't count the money right." The little girl poked her head out of the room and called to the Purple Scrub woman, leading the Others at the front of the line. Without looking her mother screamed something in Cantonese.

The little girl exhaled and shut the door. They turned the corner of the hallway. A cafeteria. Then a great hall with expansive windows facing the frigid lake. A sorrowful shadow of mold crept up the walls to where the water line once was.

It was in this great hall, under the dim light of the hanging lamps, where Firuzeh's head was shaved. Where they were all shaved down regularly by the Purple Scrub women while the Boots stood aside and watched. Unevenly. Haphazardly. Aggressively. Like sheep they had become. Firuzeh sat opposite Emma, whose eyes were like a buoy in this sea of confusion. *Look at me,* her eyes said. *Don't let go. I'm here.*

It was in this great hall that they were forced to sweep their own hair into terrifying heaps and bag each of their identities before trashing them in the refuse container outside. They were each given an oatmeal-colored long-sleeved scrub as a uniform. It was in this great hall that they were instructed at gunpoint to sew various items including jeans, parachutes, plush toys, and the uniforms for the Boots. With Emma always stationed beside her, Firuzeh stitched heavy-duty zippers onto the fronts of jackets wondering who would wear them, if a person wearing them would harm someone like her one day. It was in this great hall where, on occasion, a random beating would take place, for asking to pee, for sloppy workmanship, for passing out.

Each day, one of the Purple Scrub women paced between their sewing stations, all of her subjects silent.

"Stand! Stand! Stand!" the woman would say before the workers obeyed and recited the creed.

Through our work, our nation prospers.
Through our unity, we end conflict.
Through our leader, we find peace.
Through order we find tranquility.

After long days, Emma would invite Firuzeh to sit on her bed close to the window, to watch the moon thicken and thin across the night sky. It was the closest they could get to binge-watching television. Sometimes they would tell each other stories. Sometimes they would look at this physical, astrological manifestation of time passing, in complete stillness. Sometimes they would lean on each other and weep. It felt good to communicate with each other in silence, without the patrolling Purple Scrub women interrupting them with their screamed instructions.

"I used to call this kind of moon a fingernail moon, but then I visited El Salvador and my host told me that in Spanish it's called *luna sonrisa*. A smile." Emma's face was wistful and glowing at this memory. "Fuck. I miss traveling alone. I miss being alone. My parents used to feel so sorry for me, thinking I would be this sad single woman all my life. I tried to convince them that I loved solitude, but they didn't get it. They didn't get me, ever."

"Did you ever have roommates?" Firuzeh asked.

"Never!" Emma made Firuzeh giggle, slicing the air forward with a grimace. "Do you know how delicious it is to leave your dirty underwear on the floor? To watch television and eat chicken wings in your bed, buck naked? Being alone was awesome. No offense."

Firuzeh responded with an eye roll, followed by a smile.

"Maybe you should add '*When I am alone, I get naked*' to this Renovation creed," Firuzeh signed before pushing Emma's shoulder.

Emma smiled, then signed, "I feel sorry for you each time you have to recite it. I just mouth along and tune out." There was a pause. "I wish we could come up with a creed for the Others." They both thought for a moment.

Firuzeh struggled with the signs in her head, then figured it out. *"Through rest, I allow myself to be more than what I produce."*

Emma fluttered her flat palms in the air, her fingers splayed out in ASL applause. "Yay!" before she added more.

Through fighting, I celebrate my will to survive.
Through hiding, I celebrate my ability to navigate my own safety.
Through choice, I celebrate my body's freedom.
Through pleasure, I celebrate my resistance.

At this last sentence, Emma signed, "Roll up your sleeves." Firuzeh obeyed with her face twisted in curiosity. Emma leaned the round of her shoulder against Firuzeh's, then continued to watch the *luna sonrisa* sail across stars in slow motion. Firuzeh could feel soft down covering Emma's warm skin. The gesture was not sexual. It was simply a reminder that two human beings, two people who cared about each other sat side by side. In this room, in this six-by-eight-foot room, there was peace.

Firuzeh floated. That's how she describes it to us, using her forearms in a wavelike movement to illustrate her disassociation. She floated through time, standing under endless rains/hail/sleet, making sandbags to protect the muddy shoreline. She floated through months of seeing fabric pass under the presser foot of her sewing machine. She floated past images of armored trucks patrolling along the narrow roadways of the island, the same roadways that had hosted sandal-footed beachcombers not so long ago. She floated through nights of wailing in every room of the residence, of women crying for their children, of the residence becoming more and more crowded with Others as the Renovation moved into full swing. She floated past piles of burning books. Piles of burning picture frames. Piles of burning clothes. Piles of dead Others. Emma and Firuzeh returned from morning snow-removal duty to see a mound of lifeless bodies near the dumpster beside the residence. Gentle, white flakes of snow accumulated on every limb, in every open mouth. Emma stood for a moment, lost in thought.

Firuzeh shook Emma's arm and signed, "It's cold. I'm going in. Come on."

Emma followed.

One night, Emma tugged Firuzeh's sleeve, interrupting her dream of choosing which ice cream flavor she wanted at a shop with endless options. Firuzeh groaned.

Emma persisted, shaking Firuzeh until she awoke. The wind howled outside the glass of their bedroom window. Despite the dim light, Firuzeh slowly gained focus on Emma's signing.

"Remember the bodies yesterday?" Emma signed.

Firuzeh's eyes opened suddenly. A heat across her throat. She nodded slowly.

"There's a doctor on the island. He's an Other like us, forced to work here. He gave them something. I saw it. Outside the cafeteria. At night. They welcomed me to join, but I wasn't ready. They all stood in a circle, swallowed the pills, and said goodbye." Emma's signs were quick and aggressive.

Firuzeh was terrified by these words. And even more terrified by her own reaction. *Could this be a way out? Could I just swallow a pill and be done with this nightmare?*

"I think . . . I think I want out."

Firuzeh couldn't speak. They looked at each other in the darkness, long enough that they both wondered if the signs had even been made.

"This is my choice," Emma signed, pointing middle and index fingers up and using the other hand to pick at each fingertip with determination. "This is my body, but every day, they show us how much our bodies are not ours. Every day they show us how they are in control. But this one thing, this one tiny thing. It's mine. I want my body back."

Firuzeh stared back, feeling nothing but betrayal. "But what about the creed we created?" Firuzeh signed the sentence. *"Through fighting, I celebrate my will to survive."*

"This is fighting back," Emma said. *"Through rest, I allow myself to be more than what I produce.* I am ready to rest. *Through choice, I celebrate my body's freedom.* The Purple Scrub women made a choice to work alongside the Boots so they could keep their children. Saying goodbye to this world, this pain, is my choice."

Emma took Firuzeh's hands into hers for a moment, then signed, "Firuzeh. That's your name. My name is Emma Singh." She signed it with certainty, like she was confirming what once was. Even in the dark, Emma's smile was wide, her signs swinging and sweet. "I was once a photographer. Like, a real one who had exhibits and had double-page spreads in magazines. My parents, Ravi and Ishita, were Indian from Tanzania. That's who I am. I need you to remember me. Can you do that? Can you remember my name?"

Firuzeh angrily collapsed Emma's signs with her own two hands, like she was popping a balloon in silence. "Don't ever wake me again," Firuzeh signed before whipping her body around and pulling her blanket over her head.

Two nights later, photographer Emma Singh, daughter of Ravi and Ishita Singh, joined the dead by choice. Emma's corpse lay faceup with her back bent over the swollen abdomen of another underneath her. Emma Singh got her body back. Firuzeh looked at Emma longingly, aching for that kind of rest.

Firuzeh witnessed countless rapes. Witnessed obedient children get their heads shaven. Witnessed the Boots remove her fingernails for sport. She kept floating.

One morning the rains subsided and Firuzeh woke to the sound of birds in the bush outside her room window. They were tiny chickadees all screeching at once, saying nothing in particular. She reached out and touched a green leaf emerging from the knobby elbows and knees of this bush and the chickadees flew. Springtime was coming. Her tender fingers plucked the green leaf and placed it in her mouth.

A gash near her lip stung from her moving her jaw, but she managed to get it onto her tongue. The leaf was bitter but fresh. Fibrous but real. Her loving-kindness meal of the day.

A month or so later, with the heat of the spring rising, with windows wide open in the great hall, the women were to complete a batch of dress shirts that had been commissioned just the week before. Yara and her crew were to do sleeves. Farrah and her crew were to fashion the torso. Firuzeh's crew was in charge of buttons. She completed the task with a final ironing of the shirt before handing it to packaging, which was located at what had been the schoolhouse.

Close to the deadline, an entourage of Boots came in, with a white woman strolling in behind them, also wearing a leather jacket. Since she did not wear a helmet, Firuzeh could see how clean her hair was in its ponytail. How soft the skin on her face looked. Firuzeh wondered at her clean smell.

"As you can see, Liv, the Gibraltar Point has been converted from an artist residency to an around-the-clock manufacturing shop," said one of the Boots.

Her name is Liv, Firuzeh noted.

Liv looked around the room and cheerfully waved at everyone at the sewing machines. Then, for a brief moment, she looked at Firuzeh at the ironing table. Firuzeh's heart sped up-tempo as Liv approached her.

"And what are you doing?"

Firuzeh cowered.

"Are you ironing the finished prod—" Liv touched the iron and it fell on Firuzeh's hand, on the nubs where her fingernails once were.

"Ahhh!" At the sound of Firuzeh's pain, one of the Boots aimed his gun at her.

"No! Guns down. It was my fault. I'm so sorry!" Liv said, making meaningful eye contact with Firuzeh again. "This looks *very* bad."

"She'll be fine. These shirts need to get done," said the Boot, his gun still aimed at Firuzeh.

"I insist. She's burned herself pretty badly. You don't want any markings on these shirts do you?"

A pause.

"We'll take her to the clinic. They can treat her there," said a Boot as he gestured to one of the other women to take Firuzeh's place.

"No, no. Just point me in the right direction, and I'll bring her there. I want to take a look at this clinic, make sure we're not wasting resources," Liv said with a nasty smile. A look was shared by the Boots. "Do I have to say it again? Go on!" Liv gave them a gesture and they left.

Out of the sides of their eyes, the sewing team watched as Liv escorted Firuzeh outside and down the road toward a line of run-down houses in an enclave facing the lake, rotten picket fences enclosing each yard.

"Mama? Mama?" said a small voice. In one of the yards, a young Brown girl in a white ankle-length dress capped her hands over the sharp edges of the fence posts, her bowl cut of black hair shining in the sun. When she confirmed that Firuzeh was not her mother, her plea transformed into a playful song, her body swinging from the posts, side to side, dancing. "Maaaaamaaaaa. Maaaaaaamaaaaaa." Behind her, other little girls in the same white uniforms played tag. A Purple Scrub woman approached and banged her nightstick on the fence until the little girl joined the others.

"I think this is where they told me to go," Liv said while guiding Firuzeh past the uneven steps of one of the homes. A South Asian man in a doctor's coat, but with one of his eyes bloodied and beaten, answered the door.

"This woman has been hurt." Firuzeh showed the doctor her burn, now weeping and inflamed. The doctor nodded and showed them to a treatment room where Firuzeh sat on the paperless examination table. He began to rummage through the random supplies strewn throughout the room.

"Actually . . . can you give us a minute, Doctor?" Liv said pointedly.

"I want to have a look at her myself." The doctor looked between Firu-zeh and Liv curiously, then obeyed orders and left the room. Silence.

Liv walked toward the window of the messy room and grabbed a bandage off the sill. "You know, Firuzeh . . . I saw you."

Firuzeh froze. How did this woman know her name?

"It was last month. I saw you reach out for a leaf outside your win-dow and put it in your mouth. We've been watching you for a while, and there was something about watching you eat that leaf that told me, this person, this special person has hope. She hasn't been beaten down yet." Silence. Liv positioned herself to face Firuzeh and began inspecting her hands.

"Where are your fingernails?"

Firuzeh held her breath at the question.

"Did this happen here?"

Firuzeh gave the smallest nod.

"Do you know how President Pryce was killed?"

"Excuse me?"

"The president of the United States."

"Last winter . . . He was . . . assassinated."

"Yes. That's what you may have heard. By that Black extremist group. That's what everybody heard." Liv took a tube of half-squeezed ointment from a cabinet and applied some to Firuzeh's hand. A sting, then relief. Liv stepped close enough to whisper in Firuzeh's ear. "But did you know he was already dying of cancer? That he actually died of cancer? There was no assassination? Or maybe you knew that al-ready."

Firuzeh withdrew her hand from Liv's grasp. This was a trick question. This was a setup.

"Firuzeh, would you like to leave here?"

Silence, save for the fluorescent lights humming above their heads.

"I know you're scared. But there's not a lot of time. I can help you."

Firuzeh got off the examination table and made for the door.

"I'm serious. I can get you out and to a place of safety. You're not the first one I've approached. I helped a man out of the workhouse in the Junction. I helped a mother reunite with her two children out of a workhouse in Scarborough. Both of them are now being trained to take part in an uprising. Firuzeh, we're going to fight back. I can help you, but we need your help too."

"I'm going to get in a lot of trouble."

"Will you be any less safe than being here at the workhouse? I know who you are Firuzeh. Firuzeh Pasdar. You worked at the Transgender Assistance Center of Toronto. I know you. I know your politics; I know you have the skills to lead people, to work within a group; I know you have supported people who have survived far worse than what you are surviving now. And we need someone like you to work with us, to fight with us. I need you to listen to me. Give me your hand." Liv began to bandage Firuzeh's hand, and Liv's voice became but a whisper. She leaned into Firuzeh's ear again. "There will be a work order for denim overalls next week. The following week will be bedsheets. The next week will be comforters. That week, when one of the Boots comes by to collect the work order, he will expect you to hide among the duvets before he wheels it toward packaging."

"A Boot?"

"Yes. There are a few more like him on the inside, helping others escape. The cart will not make its way to packaging, though. And I promise you, if you follow my instructions, if you tell no one, you will get out."

"But what about everyone else?"

"I can only help one person at a time. I need you to trust me. I will bring you to a safer place. I promise."

Liv made her way to the door nonchalantly.

"Wait!" Firuzeh pleaded. "There are others." Once a social worker, always a social worker.

"I can't take any of the other women. Only one at a time."

"No not here. I had clients. Please." Liv looked at her, confused.

"Please remember these names." Firuzeh struggled to remember the faces of her numerous clients and finally one came to her. "Said Damji! He's a Trans elder who lived off Shuter Street."

"Listen: If he's an elder the chances of his survival are slim. The Renovation tried to eliminate elders and those with disabilities first. We have relocated a few, but sadly we weren't able to rescue many."

"Bahadur Talebi!" Firuzeh begged. "They're a gender-Queer youth. They just got here from Iran a year ago. I know in my heart they ran. They're a fighter. They're probably hiding somewhere. I know it. Please."

"You're certain?" Liv's lips tightened.

"Absolutely. I know it. I know they would have figured out a way to hide. Please find them a place where they can be safe. Please."

Liv nodded in agreement, then she placed a finger over her lips before opening the door. Liv escorted Firuzeh back to the sewing shop, with the bandage on her hand, and she began counting down the weeks. Denim overalls. Bedsheets. Comforters. Freedom.

Rolls of fabric and cotton batting arrived the day the work order came in for the comforters. The fabric featured the most unattractive scene of a bloodhound, an American cocker spaniel, and a sheepdog playing in a rural setting. It was hideous and hard to believe anyone would buy it. Still, there were one thousand of them that needed to be made by the end of the week. Firuzeh looked around at the Boots who delivered the supplies, wondering which one was in cahoots with Liv. None of them made eye contact. All of them moved the same way. Maybe Liv was a liar. Maybe no one would come to save her. Maybe she had betrayed Bahadur and put a target on their chest, now that she'd revealed their possible survival to a Boot. She would shake her head at these thoughts, choosing to believe that Liv's promises would unfold as planned. After Emma's passing, she had nothing to lose. Emma made one choice. Now this was Firuzeh's.

The week passed. Yara and her crew were to cut and size the fabric and batting. Farrah and her crew were on assembly. Firuzeh's crew did the final quilting pattern of alternating hourglass swirls across the fabric to ensure the batting wouldn't shift. She remembered what Liv had said, which was to not tell a soul about her escape. But with the completion of each duvet, she looked around the room wishing she could take each one of the women with her.

The deadline for the completion of the work order had arrived. Firuzeh opened up the window of her room and saw that the bush was completely full of both birds and leaves. She plucked one leaf from the bush and placed it in her mouth. The taste had changed. Not as bitter and much more tender. She savored the slight crunch of the leaf before heading to the cafeteria for the usual white bread with an economical smear of peanut butter and one glass of powdered milk. She looked around at the Boots who patrolled the cafeteria; all of them looked identical. No suspicious movements.

Firuzeh watched as the final comforter was assembled. The batting was tucked into the two sections of fabric and sewn together in a flawless seam. She watched the fabric pass under the presser foot to create the wave patterns to quilt the comforter. Her coworkers were already stretching their legs when she pulled the final piece from the machine and cut its thread. Night had fallen. One of the Boots blew a whistle. Dinnertime. Two Boots escorted her coworkers to the cafeteria. Firuzeh stayed behind to stretch her back and looked around. She was to place the final piece into a large cart full of other comforters, manned by one of the Boots who would wheel it to packaging.

"Get in," the Boot said. They all looked the same. Sounded the same. Firuzeh remembered Liv's instructions and did as she was told. The Boot calmly hoisted her into the cart, covered her with the duvets and began wheeling the cart down the hallway.

"What in the world is this?" said another Boot through the muffle of the batting.

The cart stopped. So did Firuzeh's heart. *This is it. This is the end. A pile of bodies.*

"Who the hell would buy this?"

"I know, right?"

"What is on the fabric? Is that a cocker spaniel?"

"I think."

"Fucking hell. That is ugly."

"I know."

"You're off to packaging for that?"

"Yeah."

"It's that way."

"Oh yeah."

"I mean, it's a tiny island. You can't get lost here." A shared laugh. The Boot turned the cart around. The squeaking of wheels. A beep. A door opening. Cool night air. The cart stopped. The smell of cigarette smoke. The cart turned in the other direction again and the pace was quickened. Another beep. Smoother floors.

"Where are you off to with that?" The cart kept wheeling.

"Delivering supplies."

"They're almost done serving dinner in the mess hall."

"Yeah I know. I'm just behind. See ya."

"Are those dogs on those comforters?"

"Ugly right?"

"Fucking ugly. Who would buy them?" The voice was fading away.

"Who knows?"

A door opened and closed.

"Okay. Get out." Firuzeh cautiously emerged from the blankets and found herself in a luxurious sitting room. A lavender chaise longue sat at the base of silver-gray drapery, which covered the windows. A long tan leather sectional filled the corner. A crystal chandelier hung from the high ceiling. A large kitchen was adjacent to the sitting room, with white cabinets and tiled floors. Despite its opulence, the same line of mold crept up the walls of the house to the water line from the floods. A slight damp smell.

The Boot opened the door to a pantry. "Get in." Calm. Graceful.

Firuzeh obeyed. She sat herself down on the floor of the pantry and folded her knees in to her chest. The Boot nodded and closed the door of the pantry. He left the room, closing the door behind him. Time passed. Was she supposed to escape from here? Was she supposed to run while the room was empty? She sat, her heart pounding, confused and conflicted as to what to do next. After what seemed like hours, she could hear voices down the hall. The room's door opened. Firuzeh watched through a narrow opening in the pantry. The room lights turned on and people entered.

"Can I get you more champagne?"

"No, Charles. I'm very close to making a fool out of myself," Liv said to a Boot who wore a well-trimmed beard.

More voices.

"Dinner was excellent."

"I rarely like lamb, but this was exceptional."

"Champagne? Can I top you up?"

"Yes, please. Please do."

Firuzeh could distinguish about four different people in the room. Since they had just eaten, they did not have their headgear on. From her vantage point, Firuzeh could see Liv lounging with the bearded man, Charles. Two other Boots, one with a strong cleft chin, and another with a handsome mustache, occupied the room. They downed their champagne over more frivolous conversation, and then Firuzeh could hear the clinking of ice into tumblers. They were moving onto more serious topics with more serious drinks. The smell of cigar smoke.

"This is smooth."

"Did Charles ever tell you we met at a bar? Yeah. I was serving back then. So if you all behave, I may mix you a drink later."

Firuzeh nervously moved her head right and left to see what was happening. While Firuzeh was drenched in sweat, Liv acted as cool as a cucumber. Did she even know Firuzeh was there? Liv's familiarity with Charles made her even more nervous. The image of her playfully rubbing his thigh had Firuzeh thinking this was all a setup. She bit her lip and searched her mind for a possible plan B or C or D for escape, none of them sensible. She willed herself to breathe, albeit silently.

"Shall we bring them in?" Charles said, his arms wide across the sectional. He looked in Liv's direction.

"I'm not leaving."

"I didn't ask you to leave. It's up to you if you want to stay, Liv. It's just shop talk. I don't want to bore you, is all."

"Well, where am I gonna go? Have a walk along the beach? Look into the windows of each of the workhouses? That sounds like fun."

A few laughs.

"Where's my cigar, by the way?"

Charles obliged and lit her up. Liv took several puffs like a pro. Charles forcefully pinched her chin between his forefinger and thumb and gave her a kiss.

"Okay. Liam. Go get them, please."

A door opening and closing. The sound of shuffling along the hallway.

"Here they are!" Charles exclaimed. At first, Firuzeh could see only fabric. Then she could see that the beautiful graphics of gold and black and red on a large skirt were worn by two Black women. Firuzeh covered her mouth in shock at the sight of them. It was Adea and Amana, the Queer twins who had traveled the world, promoting peace leading up to the Renovation. *Of course they were captured*, Firuzeh thought to herself. *Peacekeepers are always the most dangerous ones in a time of revolution.*

Their skirts, as always, were wide enough to be parachutes and seamed together at the hips like they were conjoined through tulle. Their arms were tattooed from their fingertips to their neckline. Indiscernible messages from a lifetime ago. The Boot with the cleft chin nudged the two sisters and they began to recite the creed as the Boots watched silently.

Through our work, our nation prospers.
Through our unity, we end conflict.
Through our leader, we find peace.
Through order, we find tranquility.

"Excellent," said Charles. "Adea and Amana. My name is Charles. You already met Liam. And this is Carl. And this is Liv. Everyone, these are the twins." Rumblings of introductions. The twins nodded silently and held hands, fearful.

Charles gestured toward the chaise longue. "Why don't you two have a seat?" They both stood still, unsure of what to do. "No really. Please. I insist."

With reticence, Adea and Amana slowly made their way to the chaise longue and sat down in unison. Their skirts cascaded a printed waterfall along the curve of the couch. Firuzeh's heart ached to see their beauty. It had been so long since she had seen racialized people clean and in the clothes of their choice. They were both the kind of femmes whose self-adornment was their magic. Every placement of every jewel, every choice in earring, of tattoo was a form of expression and resistance. But their unevenly shaved heads told the story of capture.

"Would you like a drink? The booze and cigars aren't for you, but would you like water? A juice box?" Charles started making his way to the pantry, and Firuzeh held her breath. The twins looked to the pantry, made direct eye contact with Firuzeh through the crack of the door and said, "No. That's fine. We were taken care of already." Charles made his way back to Liv's side and his cigar.

Charles dragged an accent chair closer to the twins' chaise until they were practically touching at the knees. "I'm so glad you've been taken care of. I imagine it's quite different from where we found you. I mean . . . how long were you in hiding? Four months? Five months?" The twins held their grasp on each other. "It must have been quite the struggle without power or food in that community center you hid in. I mean . . . when we busted down those doors . . . you remember, right, Liam?"

The one with the cleft chin nodded.

"It smelled pretty dank in there, right?" Liam nodded. "There you were among dozens of Others, hiding like cockroaches. I'm glad to have you both here where you are safe." Charles toked on his cigar. The twins were unmoved.

"It was extremely important to me that I met with you face-to-face. While I know my men are quite capable of getting a message across, this message is different. Do you know why you're here?"

The twins shook their heads cautiously at Charles.

"July first will be the Summit of Nations, and it's taking place right here, in Toronto. Delegates from all over the world will be coming to the city to discuss everything from climate change to AIDS to trade agreements. Lots of lunches, photo ops, politicians shaking hands, blah, blah, blah. This is our chance to show the world the glory of our Renovation and its launch as a federal initiative, led by me and my team. You can imagine the last time we had such an event, the entire country was trying to rebuild itself, no thanks to riots inspired by people like you. Now that things have changed for the better, now that the Others are finally putting what little skills they have to good use and we're finally at peace, it's very important that we make a good impression. Even Prime Minister Dunphy will be there. Now, I know you haven't seen any television for a while . . ." Charles looked at Liam and Carl with a smile. "So let me bring you up to speed. It seems the UN has some concerns over our tactics to ensure that people like you across Canada are put to work. Seems they have issues with cleaning up a place. Of course, from the inside, it's pretty clear how incredibly things have changed in such a short time. We need to give them that perspective. That's where you two step in."

Adea and Amana looked at each other knowingly, then back at Charles.

"During the summit, all officials will report to the main stage, which will be set up at Yonge-Dundas Square, the same place you two held your concert before the Renovation. But this time, the world will be watching you, listening to all the details of how you have been cared for, hearing your story of being rescued from hunger."

The twins looked at each other confused.

"Rescued?" Adea asked fearfully.

There was a pause. The pause was long enough that Firuzeh could hear the waves crashing on the shore outside. Long enough for her eyes to widen. Long enough to cover her mouth to keep herself from screaming inside the pantry.

Charles abruptly grabbed the back of Adea's neck and forced her head down in her own lap. Amana shrieked.

"Amana, can you please explain to your sister why you were rescued?"

"Because, because . . . ," Amana scrambled.

"Because?" Charles held Adea's head down with increased force, and Amana covered her ears, struggling with the words.

"Because . . . we were rescued and brought here to safety!"

Charles loosened his grasp. The twins held each other close, quivering with fear.

Charles stood over them, his tone suddenly a quiet bedtime story. "You will be delivering a speech about how the Renovation has created prosperous change. About the safety of the Others. That they've all found jobs. That the country has improved. Do you understand now?"

The twins nodded quickly.

"You don't even have to write the fucking thing. We'll write it for you. You just have to deliver it perfectly and believe it. And if you don't—" Charles pointed his cigar toward Amana's face, and she shook in fear.

Liv stood up.

"Hey. Leave it to me." Liv took the cigar away from Charles and kissed him on the cheek. "Go on. I'll meet you in the foyer after I'm done. I'm sure the truck is ready to take us to the ferry dock."

Charles passed his cigar to Liv.

"Thanks." Liv laughed. "Now go on." The Boots left. Silence.

"Firuzeh? Are you still there?"

Firuzeh slowly emerged from the pantry, her legs cramping.

The twins approached Firuzeh.

"Are you okay?" Amana asked.

Firuzeh wasn't sure what to say.

"You can trust Liv. You can trust us."

Firuzeh exhaled and the entire group of women embraced.

"That man, Charles. He held your head down. Are you all right?" Firuzeh asked.

Adea nodded. "I was more scared than hurt. My heart was in my throat!" They embraced tighter.

Liv loosened herself from the circle and said, "All right. We don't have a lot of time. Adea and Amana: let's go over the plan."

Amana started. "When we hit the stage, and once I get the signal from you, we will deliver the alternate speech." Adea continued. "Allies will subdue the Boots, and we will lead a procession of Others north on Yonge Street. At the same time, the workhouses will be bombed. But what if we are attacked? What if they turn off our microphones?"

"We have allies throughout the crowd whose job it will be to protect you. The Others with you have been trained to defend themselves. And the media will follow the story. They'll capture all the audio they need as we do the procession."

"But what will happen after the procession?" Firuzeh asked.

"That's a big question, Firuzeh. And I wish I had solid answers for you. I'm not going to lie to you. The international community may do nothing. The last step in any genocidal campaign is denial. We saw this with the residential school system here in Canada. But I can promise you that the allies will do everything in our power to relocate the Others to several strongholds outside of Toronto and using our privilege, negotiate your freedom under the guidance of the Resistance leaders." Liv glanced at the door. "We should get out of here pretty soon. The truck should be here by now. Are you ready?"

The twins nodded in unison. They took the cigar from Liv's hands, and Adea toked on it until the embers turned orange. Amana closed her eyes and readied herself before Adea placed the burning cigar on her sister's face.

"YAAAAAAAOOOOOOOOW!" Amana screamed. Amana took the cigar and did the same on Adea. Another scream.

Firuzeh's jaw dropped in confusion. Liv touched her arm.

"As for you. Let's talk about the most immediate plans."

All of us are leaning into Firuzeh, wondering what happened next. I want to give her enough time to wipe her face with tissues after recalling the events she has endured, but the agony of suspense is gnawing at me.

Finally, Bahadur pleads, "I'm dying to know: How did you get out of that room?"

Firuzeh looks at Liv, and they share a weak laugh. "Do you want to explain this? I mean . . . I could barely see. And it's so unbelievable to describe it, even now."

"I'll try," says Liv. "Yes, it may seem far-fetched. But in history, the most preposterous ideas are usually the ones that work the best."

The twins screamed from the cigar burns. Liv opened the doors of the sitting room to the foyer where Charles, Liam, and Carl stood waiting. Charles was grinning from ear to ear. Proud. Liv emerged triumphantly with the twins behind her, each of the twins shaken, holding hands tightly. A perfect red circle marked where Liv had burned each of them.

"There you go," said Liv.

"All good?" inquired Charles.

"I'm pretty sure my message was clear," Liv said before moving behind the twins and forcing them to walk forward. The Boots led the pack, but Charles couldn't help but look back at the women.

"Jeez, Liv. What did you do to them? These twins are walking funny," he said with a laugh.

Liv smiled in a smug way, despite knowing Firuzeh was hiding and crawling forward under the twins' immense skirts.

In history, the most preposterous ideas are usually the ones that work the best, Liv thought to herself, willing success as she nervously watched the twins make their way to the ferry dock. Safe passage to freedom was sung behind the backs of slave owners. Sharing self-defense techniques against colonizers has been disguised as dancing. Outlawed Indigenous storytelling survived by being woven as code into textiles. *Firuzeh is going to make it*, Liv believed. *She is going to escape.*

It feels like a lifetime since Firuzeh's story has ended. But my body is doing that thing it does when time does not matter, when my limbs are not screwed on right and my eyes are looking to the upper right corner of my vision, where all the bad memories sit like misbehaved children. They all sit here on time-out, waiting to be triggered and cued into place for me to relive again and again. Only, this time, I'm contemplating the shape and form of my Whisper Letter to you and I need your help, Evan. You see, when I was still in Liv's basement, I could divine with absolute clarity the transmittance of my messages to you. I could, without a doubt, envision you somewhere, in your respective hiding place, grasping my words from the ether and stuffing them into whatever you lay your head on at night.

Now . . . after hearing the horrors of Firuzeh's experiences, I fear you're not in hiding at all. I know now the likelihood of your capture. The commodification of your body. The subdividing of your most exquisite parts into the cogs of the Renovation's machine. The urge to fight back met with gruesome force.

Is this why I sense you beside me between the physical and spiritual realms? Is this why I feel you holding my hand or laughing at my thoughts?

I suddenly hear the sound of crickets. It is night. I am sitting on my bed. I squeeze my eyes shut after fixating on the frame of the cottage's window. I look around the room. You're nowhere to be seen but I can sense you. Feel you.

Firuzeh stirs in her sleep, then sits up and coughs herself into waking. She looks at me. I cannot see her face, but I can see her piecing together her surroundings.

"Are you okay?"

She shakes her head silently. I slowly walk past Bahadur's bed and approach Firuzeh slowly.

"I'm not okay either."

Firuzeh clears space for me to sit beside her on the bed. I try to do so without it creaking, but the springs are too old for it to obey the slowness of my descent. Bahadur turns over on their bed and resumes snoring. We cover our mouths in a soundless chuckle.

Outside the moon waxes across the sky, fatter than the night before. We watch. Without words, Firuzeh rolls up the right sleeve of her shirt, and I do the same with my left. We touch shoulders. Warm. Soft. I wonder about the quality of my shoulder compared to Emma Singh's. I imagine the spirit of Emma sitting on the other side of Firuzeh, joining in on this moment of care.

And then it happens. I sense the spirit of you, on the other side of me, rolling up your sleeve connecting with my right shoulder. I know now. The past tense of you.

We continue our training.

"You ready?" Beck asks Firuzeh, who nods solemnly and joins us. She has changed into one of Beck's high school tracksuits, and she rolls up her sleeves.

Beck draws lines in the soil beside the cottage's porch with a brittle birch branch to illustrate the plan of attack. I follow the doodles of his instructions along every grain of sand trying desperately to understand. Two lines representing Yonge Street. Squares. Xs. Arrows. Every scribble a movement, our movements, using our own bodies, using our own weapons. He makes us stand in formation. He demands that we act out every possibility, from best- to worst-case scenario. He says that for each one of us, the first action will be to disarm a Boot and use his weapon against him.

Days pass. The moon waxes. We continue the drills of four moves to disarm. Deflect end of rifle with left palm. Punch with right fist to the chin or kick to stomach. Butt of the gun to the face. Take the weapon. It is a clunky dance for me and Bahadur. Something stops the full breadth of our extensions, a forced passivity in a world that thrived on our inaction.

In response to this, Beck shows us another exercise. He demonstrates on me. He asks me to lie on my back; he straddles over me and Liv hands him punch mitts to wear.

"You ready? I want you to punch me from where you are. Keep punching and don't stop." I look at him. I notice I am holding my breath. My arms are at my side, frozen. He is suddenly my ma.

"Keith. You are not like other boys. I can see that," she says.

"Kay? Kay? Feel the ground underneath you. Can you feel it?" I nod. I hear Beck's firm voice in the present. I begin to feel the rocks and sand on my tailbone. I feel the sun on my face. I can see the silhouettes of people above me. "Good. Breathe. Can you look around you? It's me, Beck." I see him. "Look around. Take your time. Can you see things that are blue? Can you find at least three things that are blue?"

Firuzeh's sweatpants. Beck's eyes. Liv's shirt. The sky.

"Good. Keep breathing. Now I want you to be here. I want you to be here, seeing everything around you, but I want you to punch back at me. Can you do that?"

I nod. I punch at Beck standing above me. It is a half-hearted punch, as I am still slowly coming back into myself.

"Can you use your breath each time you punch? Can you make a *ssss* sound when you punch this time?"

I try. The exhale tightens my core and the punch is stronger. The colors around me are more vibrant. Beck's voice is clear. I am more in my body.

"Again. Again. Again."

Firuzeh, Liv, and Bahadur clap for me and the sound of their applause is crisp. My breathing is deep. My arms are warm.

"Kay? How are you doing?" Beck searches my face.

I give an affirmative nod from my position on the ground. "This time, I want you to punch left right again and again, nonstop and I will back off when I feel your energy push me back. Does that make sense? Can you do that?"

I shake my head unsure of myself.

Beck looks right at me, although I am uncertain if I am looking back at him. "Kay? I need you to remember why you're doing this. Remember how these actions are connecting all of us. I want you to feel that power running through your body."

I take a deep breath and begin. I punch, again and again. *Ssss. Sssss. Sssss. Ssss. Ssss. Ssss. Ssss.*

"Lying with a man as with a woman is an abomination," Ma says as she brushes out my curls, my scalp bleeding.

"*Ssss! Sssss! Sssss! Ssss! Ssss! Ssss! Ssss!*" says the little boy with every punch.

"'Do not be deceived. Neither the sexually immoral, nor idolaters, nor adulterers, nor men who have sex with men, nor thieves nor the greedy nor drunkards nor slanderers nor swindlers will inherit the kingdom of God.'"

"*Ssss! Sssss! Sssss! Ssss! Ssss! Ssss! Ssss!*"

Soap bubbles bursting. Soap souls going to heaven. The sound of applause in the congregation upstairs.

"*SSSS!*" the boy exhales, extends a punch, and the daycare washroom collapses in a pile of dust.

Ma covers her ears at the deafening sound.

"*SSSS!*"

A soundtrack of Liberace plays on full volume. Thousands of fairy costumes fly through the air and a kaleidoscope of scripture passages explode into beautiful fireflies protecting his tiny body.

"*SSSS!*"

Another final punch and the lattice of the Winchester church implodes. The steel framing melts. Every wall hiding every secret crumbles into shadows. Ma, in tiny pixels, becomes grains of sand. She watches in pain as her body is wished away by wind, by time, by my own breath.

Applause. I hear applause. Firuzeh and Liv embrace me. I am crying. Bahadur squats beside my supine body, crying too. Beck is covered in sweat. He tosses the punch mitts and extends a hand to help me up. I stand. I hold Beck and continue bawling, fully trusting. Fully in my body.

Firuzeh looks at me and ceremoniously rolls up the sleeve of my T-shirt. I tearfully do the same. We touch shoulders. Liv, Beck, and Bahadur join in, rolling up the sleeves of their shirts and touching deltoids. A circle. Joy.

As the days pass, our drills become more graceful, become muscle memory. Some days Beck holds us each at the waist, guiding us sideways as we shoot three targets using an AR15. Some days Liv has us practice loading ammunition in the dark. Some days we review the plan of attack. Each day ends with us dirty, covered in dust and watching the waxing of the moon.

While we train, Bahadur and I witness another curriculum that does not include us. Every morning, Liv and Beck make their way to a clearing and practice the embodiment of their resistance, complete with corresponding movements and words said out loud:

When I do not act, I am complicit!
When I know wrong is happening, I act!
When the oppressed tell me I am wrong, I open my heart and change!
When change is led by the oppressed, I move aside and uplift!

And each morning, Bahadur and I have followed them to the clearing, overwhelmed with curiosity. At first, we experienced the same discomfort we would feel when witnessing white folks taking up too much space with their guilty tears or their complete denial. Each morning we waited for the shoe to drop, for their ritual to suddenly become performative. It was obvious to us that it had taken years for them both to arrive at this level of awareness because their chants were said in a whisper, their movements delivered with authenticity. There was something about their efforts having nothing to do with us, that their unlearning and undoing was not leaning on our labor of explanation nor our praise, that made this a ritual for us too. It forced Bahadur and me into a place of ease, of witnessing, of relaxing while folks processed their allyship. It felt foreign to us to not have to bear this burden. Foreign and delicious. It became our daily morning event without Liv or Beck even knowing of our presence.

One morning Bahadur and I watched Hanna make her way to Beck and Liv in the clearing.

"Where are you going?" shouted Peter from inside the house.

Without turning, Hanna shouted back, "Where does it look like I'm going? I'm off to spend some time with our son!"

Once she got to the clearing, she stood there with her cane bearing her weight and asked questions.

"So you do this every day?"

"Yes, Mom." Beck wiped sweat from his brow.

"But why every day?"

"Because we have to unlearn every day." Beck went down on his haunches and retied the shoelaces on his combat boots. He looked back at his mother, whose face was twisted in confusion.

Liv chimed in, hoping to clarify things. "Oppressing others is learned from the minute we're born, Hanna. It's like trying to sink a beach ball in the water. It pops up every now and then, whether we want it to or not."

"And when it pops up, we either pretend it's not there or we ask oppressed people to help us keep it down, or we ask them to praise us for sinking it." Beck tentatively held his mother's hand. Hanna shuddered at his touch. Her face and neck were red. "For me, the most challenging part is not crying. It's hard to not feel shame, to not feel guilty for having this much privilege. But shame or guilt doesn't help anyone."

The rest of the day unfolded, with Hanna unable to look us in the eyes. Over dinner, she quietly crunched away at crackers, her eyes focused on some unknown point on the horizon. When she rose from the table to leave, the crumbs that had gathered at her waist fell to the floor and she absentmindedly wandered back into her bedroom for the night.

"I'm really sorry you have to watch my mom struggle through all this," Beck said to us awkwardly once she was out of earshot.

"No, no. We're all accustomed to this type of discomfort," said Firuzeh, smiling eyes meeting mine, then Bahadur's.

Miraculously, Hanna returned to the clearing the next day. Her eyes were swollen from crying.

"When are you making breakfast, Hanna?" Peter called from the house.

"You're perfectly capable of opening a can of cocktail wieners," she answered as she made her way to the clearing.

"Hi, Mom. Are you ready?"

Hanna nodded wearily. She proceeded to learn the set of movements and the set of chants and adjusted them to suit her level of mobility.

Some days, she argued with Liv, her left hand flapping in the air as if to dispel any of Liv's truth into the ether of their collective shame. "I gave them all a place to stay, didn't I?"

During these times, Liv would hold her palms up as if to calm a wild animal she had cornered with truth. "Yes, you did give them a place to stay. But we need to dig deeper than that. What makes us believe we are better than them, that we are entitled to certain privileges? That's what has led us here."

Hanna would storm off, pushing past branches and brush toward the house. On these difficult days, she would intersect me in the hallway of the farmhouse and say, "I'm a good person!" then make her way to her room to cry some more. I would force my arms to my side, willing myself not to assist her in her process. I have done enough of that in my lifetime.

Some days, Hanna would change her tactics. "Why do you and Liv need to lead this fight? Why can't we leave this uprising to them?"

"It's different, Mom." Beck would hold his mother's shoulders and stare deep into her eyes. "We're not leading it. What we're doing has been planned by activists who have fought their entire lives just to live, to work, to love. Everything from what we're saying in our chant, to how we're moving when we say that chant has been guided by them. They have done that work. And believe me, Mom. They had to do a lot of work on me to get me where I am now. I will continue to do that work, on myself and those around me, for the rest of my life. And you know what? It feels good. It feels good to wake up and stop pretending. It feels good not to be afraid, not to set myself apart, not to defend what wasn't mine in the first place."

Hanna looked around helplessly. "But why *my* son? Why do you have to fight? What if you die? What will happen then?! You might not have a life to live!" She attempted to embrace Beck to soften his approach, but he held firm.

"Mom, I need you to understand that, for me, even having a choice to fight is a gift. People right now are being raped, killed, taken away from their children, being forced into workhouses. I will not let that continue. I choose to fight."

Hanna shook her head wildly to keep Beck's words from sticking. "Not my son! I'm not one of those evil Boots! I'm a good person!"

Liv had had enough. She approached Hanna, until they were face-to-face, Liv's glare demanding connection, willing eye contact.

"Look at me right now, Hanna. I don't give a shit if you think you're a good person." Liv was seething.

Bahadur and I looked at each other with mouths agape, then turned back to the trio, wondering if this exchange would transform from peaceful conversation to a rowdy episode of *The Ricki Lake Show*.

"How dare you. You watch your tone with me."

"No."

"*Excuse me?*"

"I said no. I will not watch my tone. I won't. We're trying to enact change, Hanna. We're not here to make you feel better."

Liv wiped the hair from her face and retied her ponytail, as perspiration surfaced on her blushing skin. "I was once like you. I once believed that a few good deeds were a job well done. I thought I was one of the good white people. I wasn't like my family who lived in small-town Ontario all their lives, who could trace their English lineage all the way back to colonial times, who would collect the arrowheads found in the garden and place them on the mantel like prizes they'd won. Surely, I didn't benefit from the land they took away. Surely, I was not complicit in their actions. As long as I looked at my great-grandfather with shame for his slave ownership, his penchant for Black women, as long as I recited the Indigenous land acknowledgment every morning to my fifth graders, then I was doing the work, right? Oh, and even better, to show everyone how progressive I am, I could be Queer! Hell, I could shack up with a Mohawk woman!

Save her by having her live with me in my fancy home in Hamilton. Yeah! I'm not a slave owner. I'm me. I'm a good person." She shouted toward the tops of the trees, pacing. Hanna cowered, trying her best to maintain her grimace.

"Erin didn't deserve that. She didn't deserve to be my little experiment, my statement, my cause. But she stuck with me. I shudder to think of how many times I put her in a position of explaining herself, to be paraded around to my family and friends and at my school, to deal with my fetishizing her, using her to assuage my own guilt. My great-grandfather had his arrowheads. I had Erin. It was . . . it is disgraceful. Everything I did with her was to prove that I was a good white person.

"Next thing on my agenda was to have a child together. Of course, it could have been me who got pregnant first, but no, I really wanted, deep down, a Brown baby, so I could parade it around too. Another arrowhead. I still remember us driving an hour east to our donor in downtown Toronto, two separate hotel rooms, running the sample into ours, and Erin propping her legs up on the wall after inserting the semen. She was like, 'Wow. Isn't this romantic?'" Liv stopped pacing and sat on a tree stump. She paused and swallowed back the sweetness of this memory. Her tone softened.

"I watched Erin grow. I loved seeing her get out of the shower. I would pretend to brush my teeth but really, I was looking at her. She would towel off her tummy and I would wonder how I got so lucky." Liv looked up at the treetops for a moment. The hum of cicadas. "When labor started, we drove to the hospital. We were so excited. Between contractions, Erin was on her phone telling her grandmother and her aunties to start heading over from Six Nations to see her. I can still hear them all on the other end cheering, even though it was three in the morning. They must have been waiting for news from us. The labor went faster than we expected. We got in there, and they checked Erin's dilation, and they were like, 'She's ready to push.' Baby Myles was on an express train out. Once he arrived, he let out this healthy cry, and Erin and I laughed and laughed. We were so happy. I didn't know you could smile that wide, ever.

"I thought the nurses were supposed to clean him up, then place him on Erin's chest, but they wheeled him out of the room in his little bassinet instead. I thought, well, they're medical staff, they know what they're doing. I was still kissing Erin's face and thanking her for giving me this beautiful gift. Then, just after Erin gave birth to the placenta, a nurse comes walking over to us all official and stern.

"Erin asked, 'Where's our baby?' The nurse hands us this clipboard with a contract on it. She tells us that if we want to get our Myles back, we have to sign this contract for Erin to be sterilized. I lost my shit. They almost had to call security on me. I was hysterical. Erin was screaming for our baby. I was running down the hallways of the hospital searching for Myles, calling out his name as if he could call back. This was a nightmare. A horror story. This wasn't happening to us. I was going to change it. By the time I ran back into the room where Erin was, she was holding Myles, bawling her eyes out. She had signed the contract. She told me, 'I had to. I couldn't live without holding my baby.' I was so angry at her. I had the audacity to say, 'How could you? They don't have a right to do that!' and she looked at me and said, 'You don't know what it's like to not have rights.'

"She got a tubal ligation. We got our baby. And I got the wake-up call of my life. I was one of the many good white people who never believed that forced sterilization of Indigenous women could happen in Canada. It was just a news story of something vague and unproven. And once I saw it happening, right in front of me, I knew I had to name it for what it was, for me to change. I knew I had to call it genocide.

"Shortly after the tubal ligation, and after we heard of the supposed wildfires in Alberta, we knew we had to change things. We decided together that Erin and Myles would go into hiding. I would leave my teaching job, change my name, dissolve the house, and join the Resistance.

"And you know what is the most shameful thing about it all? It took the mutilation of my partner's body for me to understand what being an ally is. That's how deep it runs, Hanna. What will it take for you to wake the hell up? What are you willing to lose? What horrible thing are you willing to watch before you understand that you have to change first?"

Hanna reached out to Beck's body to stabilize her stance. Liv pivoted herself around to face the forest and cried silently. Hanna stepped forward with the instinct to apologize and console, but Beck held his arm out and gestured for them to give Liv some time alone.

The training continued. Despite Hanna's frustration that no one among us would coddle her, would lessen the blow of these lessons by affirming her or congratulating her, still she returned. Still she trained.

"I wonder what internal dialogue goes on inside that woman's brain to have her come back for more," Bahadur said one morning while wiping their face with their T-shirt.

I rolled my eyes. "I kind of don't care. Whatever it takes for her to learn and do the work is good for me." We chuckled.

In the time it took for Bahadur to finally figure out how to shoot a target, there was a shift in Hanna. When we first arrived at the farm, the tip of her nose pulled away from us; more like away and up, as if allowing her body to share the same spatial plane as us was too much of a risk. She began to share space easily with us. She began to ask us sincere questions that stemmed from sincere curiosity about our lives. She began sitting quietly to listen with her whole body, with her whole gaze while we spoke.

In the clearing one morning, Hanna said quietly, "Last night I had an idea." Excitement brimmed in her eyes. Liv and Beck looked at each other, then gathered near Hanna.

"You know how you said that being an ally is a verb and not a noun? That I had to ally every day? And I shouldn't ask for praise? I was thinking we could add another movement. Something to train us to never ask for praise. Something to keep the focus on them instead of us." There was a pause.

Liv nodded. "That's a great idea, Hanna. But is there a way we can do that without it being performative?"

"What do you mean?"

"Like . . . a lot of oppressed activists complain about how much space we take up congratulating ourselves for doing this work."

Beck chimed in. "That's tricky, right? We want to show prospective allies this important element but we need to do so without being showy."

We watched from afar as they experimented with the movements. Hanna finally showed them a promising gesture. She placed one hand firmly over her mouth and the other hand in the air. "No wait. Let me try again. That seems like I'm telling them to be silent. That's not what I'm trying to say. Wait a second." She thought for a moment, then performed another gesture. This time she used both hands to cover her mouth, then moved her hands to her heart in humility.

Beck hopped gently in place, buoyed by his inspiration. "Yes, and then we can pass the focus. So we put our hands to our mouth, hands to heart, then we can point one hand toward the oppressed party who needs to be seen and heard."

"I like it," Liv said, trying the gesture a few times. "It's performative as a way to get other allies to join us in the resistance, then it challenges us to shift focus to those who need the attention."

Tonight, we sit around the dinner table to eat canned artichoke hearts and beef jerky. When the conversation turns to the loved ones we have left behind, I tell the group about how you had planned to find your mother, then meet me at Liv's house.

"But now . . . after everything I have seen . . . I doubt very much we will find each other again. I doubt very much he is alive. No . . . I know he is not alive, and I have accepted that." This is the first time

I admit this out loud. As soon as I say it, I feel your forgiveness wash over me.

Peter rises from the table and heads to the living room to sit in his reclining chair. The awkward silence is broken by Hanna shifting in her seat.

"Evan. Evan." Hanna struggles with the words and we all hold our breath. Perhaps she will tell me loving you was wrong. Perhaps she will cry and apologize until I am forced to soothe her. Perhaps she will expect me to praise her for not being like the other folks who kept you away from me. "He sounds like a beautiful man. And you sound like a beautiful couple. I am so very sorry this happened. You both did not deserve this. I will work hard and pray that things will change." With the help of a gentle hand on my shoulder, she rises from the table quietly, tosses her beef jerky wrapper into the garbage bin, then makes her way to her bedroom.

When she closes the door, I look around in shock at Firuzeh, at Beck, at Bahadur and Liv. I silently say, "Whoa!"

Firuzeh covers her mouth to stop herself from giggling. Liv exhales. Bahadur shakes their head in wonder. Beck holds his hands up in a hallelujah. Change is possible.

10

"Look up," Firuzeh says to everyone as we set up camp outside the cabin.

The waxing moon hangs low enough above our heads that I'm tempted to reach up and grab it. I imagine putting it into my mouth and crunching it between my teeth like a crater-covered potato chip, along with the astronaut and the American flag. Crunch. It's Firuzeh's idea to sleep outside tonight.

"I want to feel what it's like to sleep with nothing but nature around me. No ceilings or walls."

We all agree. This may be the last time we will experience such things.

Beck builds a fire in the center of our gathering. He uses bunched-up newspaper at its base; their unhappy headlines going up in flames and ascending into a smoky memory above the trees. Soon, if all goes as planned, we too will be headlines on those same papers, and maybe, just maybe, we will make history.

"Do you think it'll matter? You know . . . us calling our names at the summit?" I say while we all unroll our sleeping bags for the night.

"*If* all goes as planned and *if* we're able to say our names at the summit." Bahadur looks into the center of the flames, their faraway gaze making black marbles of their eyes.

I turn to Liv and Beck, hoping for clarity. "I mean . . . our plan is to lead a procession up Yonge Street and say our names, and we've all been working hard to follow instructions and strategize the best way to do this without getting killed. But sometimes, I have to wonder what it's all for. The bombing of the workhouses makes sense to me. If the Renovation sees us as nothing more than producers and products, it makes sense to resist by ending our productivity. But saying our names . . . I don't know."

Liv and Beck nod their heads slowly, absorbing my words, one at a time.

"No. I don't doubt the importance of this." Firuzeh stands and says with conviction, "Do any of you remember those Palestinian children who broke the Guinness World Record by flying the most kites simultaneously? It was incredible, watching news footage of tens of thousands of kids in Gaza, flying their kites. Each kid had decorated their kite with their dream of what a life free of apartheid would look like." She illustrates with her hands so that we can all imagine the numerous kite lines and tails soaring along the shores of the Mediterranean Sea. "One can look back at that and say, 'So what? What did they accomplish?' But you see, what they achieved is so much more than a metaphor. These are children who were born in war and will most likely die in war. When they flew those kites, though, they became the kites. They flew beyond borders. When they flew those kites, they knew freedom." Firuzeh looks me in the eye. "When I say my name at the summit, I will be a kite." She reaches out to squeeze my hand and returns to setting up her sleeping bag.

The evening wears on. We're supposed to be resting, now that all of us are settled for the night, but we can't stop chatting.

I can tell by Beck's body, in its freedom of movement, that his parents are inside, keeping to themselves, not wanting to be feasted upon by the mosquitoes. Here, among us Others, he is comfortable in his gayness; his squat wide as he pokes at the embers.

"I wish we had marshmallows," says Liv wistfully.

"Shit, I wish we had a side of beef!" Beck says while rolling his sleeves up to showcase his defined deltoids. We all eat our crackers and wince at the familiar blandness of dry goods. "If the Renovation never happened, I'd probably be out, having a burger somewhere on a patio somewhere."

"I love that!" Liv exclaims. "Jeez. What would we be doing if the Renovation never happened?" She hums a bit and rubs her chin pensively. "Around this time, my wife, Erin, and I would probably be chasing down our son, Myles, trying to get him into the bath. What about you, Bahadur?"

Bahadur sits up and begins shyly making a pile of rocks in the triangle of their crossed legs. "I don't know."

"Come on! What's more boring than bath time?"

Bahadur exhales. "I . . . would . . . be . . . most likely . . . surfing porn." We all burst out laughing. I am rolling on the ground unable to control myself. "I had a roommate in the shelter who had data on their phone. I traded an hour of internet every week for doing their laundry. Hey . . . you'd watch porn too if you spent the day sorting garbage." We laugh even harder.

Bahadur raises an imaginary wineglass and we join them in a toast. "To porn. God, I miss porn." Everyone clinks imaginary glasses. Bahadur looks at Firuzeh and says, "Okay. Your turn."

Firuzeh laughs and almost spits out the cracker she is munching on. She waves her hands in embarrassment. We all egg her on.

"Okay, okay." She wipes her mouth and flicks crumbs from her lap. "Prepare to be underwhelmed, everyone. Okay. I would be home making a loving-kindness meal for myself." We all look confused. "It's because I was trying to heal from a really bad breakup that happened because of my codependence. So I had to learn to make a meal just for myself. I had to learn how to date myself. I had to learn how to love myself." A pregnant pause ensues, with everyone's faces slowly evolving from deep compassion to withheld laughter. We begin to spit out our guffaws. "See? I told you it was underwhelming!"

Liv adds more logs to the fire, and our faces get brighter. "It's not that it's underwhelming. It's more like, it's funny because of how hard Queer relationships are, and how much we worked at them and worked on ourselves. I miss those conversations. I miss processing." We laugh even harder.

Firuzeh adds longingly, "Perhaps something a bit more exciting would be the workshops. Back at the center I would head these workshops and sometimes they'd schedule them for Fridays, and then you're stuck in a room full of Trans youth who'd rather be at a club picking up than with you learning about writing theater scenes or learning movement. But then each of them would get up, turn on some music, dance to their favorite song and you could see how important these sessions were. It's as though performing in front of each other, being seen, is medicine. We're told by straight people that we're lying to ourselves, that we're not real. There's something about being onstage, using our imagination. Instead of being invisible we are the stars of the shows in our head. And that keeps us alive."

There is another pause, and my face gets hot with the weight of everyone's gaze on me.

Beck breaks the silence. "Kay. Queen Kay. What would you be doing tonight if the Renovation never happened?"

"Well . . . what day is it?" I sit on a log and cross my legs, longing for a pair of heels.

"It's Friday," says Beck.

I look up at the moon, this almost full moon and I imagine a spotlight. "I would be performing."

Everyone leans into me, curious.

"Where?" Beck asks.

"Probably the cabaret space at Buddies in Bad Times Theatre. That was my usual place on Friday and Saturday nights. Epic on its Thursday club night and Glad Day Bookshop for the drag brunch on Sunday mornings."

Everyone's eyes are full of wonder, full of memories.

"Around this time, I would be heading into the dressing room. The place would be lousy with queens. Beside me, Fanny, my old roommate, would be powdering down her face and bitching."

Bahadur stands and looks at me. It's a moment in which we can hear each other's thoughts. Just as Firuzeh said, performing in front of each other, being seen, is medicine. It is time to imagine. It is time to play. To be the stars of our own show in our heads. We nod in agreement.

Bahadur sits next to me and begins powdering their face, pretending to be Fanny. Everyone laughs, but it triggers something inside me. It's like Fanny is sitting right next to me. The gentle wind of the forest around me fades into the underground dressing room of Buddies in Bad Times Theatre. I am no longer sitting on a rotting log; I'm sitting on a rickety plastic chair with bras hanging over my backrest. I look down and I am no longer wearing my runaway clothes covered in chicken shit. I am wearing my signature red leather strapless pencil dress, the one I found for $14.99 at the Goodwill.

"Girl, tell me the truth. What is the difference between a sixty-five-dollar highlighting palette and two-dollar glittery eye shadow?" Fanny would say to me, her face framed by a halo of bulbs and a mirror.

I look at Bahadur and play along, my heart aching. "Nothing, I guess."

"That's right. Nothing. All you gotta do is use a big-ass blush brush and you're off to the races. Thank you, Dollar Store. No thank you, Sephora." As I am outlining my lips, Liv gets up from the fire and walks into our imaginary dressing room, turns one of the dead lightbulbs on our mirrors clockwise and it is alive again.

"Evening, ladies."

"That's 'Goddesses' to you," Fanny corrects her playfully.

"Well, Goddesses. You're up in five." Liv exits and heads upstairs.

"Thank you," I say, as I turn my head upside down and crown myself with my cherry-colored wig. Before I put my red evening gloves on, I help Fanny into her dress and zip her up. She does the same for me. We do one last pat-down of any sweat in our armpits and head up the two flights of stairs to the cabaret space. We can hear bass music pounding against the concrete walls. When we enter, the place is alive with shirtless men. Quartets of gender Queer folks book-ending each other and swaying to the beat of the music. A couple of leather dykes kiss in the corner. Three baby Queers wearing rainbow suspenders take selfies on the dance floor. We pass the bar. Beck gets up from the campfire and joins in on our improvisation. Behind the bar, he wipes down a glass and nods in our direction.

"Hey, Queen Kay! Hey, Fanny! Are you up soon? Have time for a shot?"

"We always have time for a shot!" says Fanny.

Beck pours us all tequila shots, including himself. We toast each other, down the golden liquid and suck on limes. Liv interrupts us before heading to the tech booth.

"Goddesses? Places, please." We wince at the strength of the tequila and nod at Liv at the same time. We head to the stage. The light changes and Fanny gets the mic. I take my place in the wings.

"Happy Pride, bitches!"

The crowd goes wild.

Fanny's face scowls and she assesses the crowd. The spotlight is so powerful she has to shield her eyes with her flat, gloved hand. "Uh-huh. Uh-huh."

People giggle.

Fanny spots a handsome bearded man in floral printed briefs. "Yes, please."

More giggles.

"And you, ma'am?"

Firuzeh gets up from the campfire and points to herself.

"Me?"

"Yes you," Bahadur reaches out their hand and brings her into the scene onstage.

Firuzeh is suddenly onstage with Fanny, nervously covering her face.

"What's wrong, darling?"

"I'm so nervous!" she says.

"Let me guess." Fanny puts her fingertips to her forehead like a psychic. "You have just been through a breakup."

Firuzeh nods and giggles. The audience laughs.

"And you're here to celebrate Pride and maybe . . . perhaps . . . if you're lucky . . . you're hoping to find a meaningful relationship?"

The crowd guffaws.

"I mean . . . that's where you find meaningful relationships, right? At Pride? That's where I find my meaningful relationships: during Pride; at the bathhouse."

More laughter. Firuzeh covers her face in playful embarrassment.

"What's your name, darling?"

"Firuzeh."

"Well, who here would like to help Firuzeh have a great Pride tonight?"

The crowd cheers.

"Who wants to bite her box?"

More cheers.

"Who wants to put a dog in her bun? Who wants to teach her the Big Finger Bang Theory?!"

The crowd goes wild.

"Well, beautiful Firuzeh, if I have my friend, Queen Kay, sing a song for you, would that help you get over your breakup?"

Firuzeh nods eagerly.

"Okay. You go ahead and have a seat among these good-looking people."

I wait in the wing of the cabaret space knowing my moment is coming. I go over the lyrics of the song in my head. I practice the hand movements.

"Now, who is ready for some show?"

Screams. Thunderous applause.

"Next up is the performer I know you've all been waiting for."

The audience goes silent. It's quiet enough that I can hear Fanny's hand rub against the handle of the microphone. I can hear her labored breathing.

"Let me tell you about her. You may know her as Queen Kay. But I know her as my sister. She told me to run. I didn't listen. And I know every day she thinks of me and wonders if I am safe."

I can't resist peeking my head around the curtain of the wing. I can see Fanny's stunning fat silhouette against the heat of the spotlight. It is a voluptuous shape achieved from our countless weed sessions and late-night poutines. My jaw drops at the sight of you in the front row, wearing the suit you wore when I met you. You are smiling from ear to ear. You sit proudly, awaiting my performance.

"And tonight, I want to tell her that no, I may not be alive. Her beau, Evan, may not be alive. But, girl, thanks to you, we lived."

Liv, Firuzeh, and Beck's eyes become misty, and they hold hands waiting for me to step onstage. "Everyone put your hands together for her royal highness. Queen Kaaaaaaay!"

The crowd cheers. Liv puts leaves on the campfire to create smoke. It diffuses the light of the moon above my head. I take my place, my back to the audience, taking hold of the wall.

In the mist and semidarkness, Liv cues a Deborah Cox song and starts the laser light show from the tech booth. Everyone is on their feet screaming and dancing to that familiar song with the endless intro. A side light bathes my silhouette in red. The light shifts to a crisp spotlight over my head. Applause at the sight of me. When the lyrics begin, I whip around and lip-synch, looking directly at Firuzeh. She shyly points to herself, and I nod my head in approval. I sing to her as if she is an unwanted romantic interest, someone I cannot resist despite having given up on love long ago. I hold on to the wall stifling my desire for her and the crowd howls. Firuzeh's face erupts into blushing.

In the audience, a bearded queen twirls her skirt, revealing her fat hairy legs. A lesbian elder dances as if it were her very own show, her audience in the corner of the bar. A Trans femme twirls a baton into the air and catches it. The beefcake in his floral briefs nods his head to the music.

As the song crescendos into a frenzy of bass beats, you begin dancing to the beat of the music, your arms conducting a staccato symphony of queerness. My eyes well up with tears. My beautiful Evan. My beautiful people. We are visible. We are dancing. We are fearless. We are fierce. Full length, width, and depth. Our bodies at full volume. Unfurled. Unhiding. Just as the song reaches its zenith, my lips quiver the sustained final note in mock vibrato, you toss a handful of golden sparkles into the air, and we all watch the sparkles fall.

The cabaret fades away. In its place, a meteor shower streaks the night sky. The sound of crickets singing among the reeds.

We hold hands, shaking, crying. The five of us Others. History makers. Soon to be dead. Soon to be free. Under the cosmic light show of our resilience.

11

When I awake, I sit up immediately to confirm the location of the moon. It has moved since last night. It now sits prettily in the sky to the west of us, just above the skeletal remains of a rotten cedar trunk. It is the full moon now. It is time.

Beck pours a bottle of water over the campfire's embers, and smoke sizzles up toward the cloudless blue above. Other than that, we are taciturn, considering our precious last tasks on the farm. We pack up our sleeping bags. We eat another humble meal of dry goods. Liv takes inventory of the weaponry and distributes it among us. I sit beside Firuzeh, and we load our magazines with bullets. Click. Click. Click. Each one a life we may take today. I notice Bahadur standing over the remains of the campfire with their eyes tightly closed.

"Hey, Bahadur," I say gently. "Are you okay?"

They smile weakly before picking up a stray cracker sleeve wrapper from the ground and wandering away from my concerned gaze.

Hanna stands on the porch, watching us carry supplies to and from the van. Back and forth. She cradles her big bosom like a bag of spoiled apples she no longer wants, her face sour with helplessness. Each time Beck passes her I can see words forming at the edges of her lips. And each time those words are about to spill I see her catch the eye of Peter, who is scowling as always and pretending not to care about our impending journey. Beck makes his way to the van again, this time with a case of bottled water. He almost falters in his grip, and Hanna steps forward. Another strong scowl from Peter and Hanna backs off, swallowing hard.

We all enter the van. Liv covers Bahadur and Firuzeh with a blanket and looks at me, ready to tuck me into hiding yet again. Before I join them I look back one more time at Hanna, choking on tears.

Beck places his jacket over the back of the driver's seat and makes his way to his mother. They stand about six feet apart. Hanna wrings her hands together in a continuous circle trying to make sense of this final exchange.

"Mom . . ."

"Please don't—"

"Hanna!" Peter shouts from the front door. He does not make eye contact with Beck. "Let them all go. They made a choice. They all made a choice. Let them do it."

"Beck."

"Hanna! Get inside the house. Now." Peter makes his way into the house and closes the screen door. A gesture. A symbol. A line. A border.

"Beck?"

Beck sobs. "Yes, Mom."

"Beck. Beck." Hanna feels the word in her mouth. Lets the word lift from her lips into the air. An experiment. "This is who you are."

"Hanna! Will you get inside?!"

Hanna turns to Peter with the look of the devil in her. Her face is red. "Shut up!"

Peter's mouth twists and he moves inside away from the door and out of sight. She turns back to Beck. Wipes her face. Starts again. Love.

"Beck. My son. My beautiful son. I love you. I love you. My beautiful Beck. I love you. Just the way you are. Just the way you are now. I love you. And I hope whatever shape you are in, whoever you turn out to be, one day you can love me back."

Beck's shoulders are pumping up and down. Hanna reaches out and holds him. Maybe even holds him up, he is shaking so hard. It is a full-body hug. She laces her fingers into his hair and covers his forehead with kisses as he whispers into her ear something that makes her release a single, vocal sob. It comes from deep in her belly, a place so deep, a place she hasn't touched since her first cry into this wicked world. Then she looks at him straight in the eyes and says, "Okay. You go and fight."

We drive. The dusty road is bumpy and unforgiving. It jostles about our silence like it jostles our supplies in the van. Before I go under the blankets with Bahadur and Firuzeh I see Liv considering whether to say something comforting. Instead, she holds her concern in her throat and between her eyebrows. Liv turns on the radio and scans for a station. Country music. White noise. Soft rock. White noise. A vague signal of a news program. White noise. She gives up and shuts off the radio.

We drive. The sound of the squeaking shocks is replaced by the constant hum of rocky asphalt. With the blanket covering only my legs, I lie back and run through our plans in my head the way I used to run through choreography before a performance. Thumbs, one above the other, in a snug embrace. Fit the point in the front end of the gun with the open square on the back end of the gun. Slowly squeeze the trigger. I catch myself imagining the paper target Beck created for us on the farm transforming into a Boot. A leather jacket. The zippers. His rifle pointed straight at me. A decision moving from my brain, down the length of my arm into the tip of my finger, to kill or be killed. My bullet flying out of my weapon and piercing the surface of his chest. I shake my head to douse the image burning in my mind. I wipe my face of the imagined blood sprayed from the Boots's wound. Your imagined touch on my arm calms me and I ex-hale. Evan. My beautiful Evan.

"Kay. The traffic is getting heavier. You need to get under the blan-ket before a truck sees you," says Liv.

I lift the blanket enough to see that beside me, Firuzeh is spooning Bahadur, who is shaking like a leaf. I break our silence.

"What's going on? Are you okay?" I motion to remove the blanket.

Bahadur stops me, as much as their shaking will allow. They try to spit words out, but I cannot understand.

"Do you need help? Do we need to stop?"

Firuzeh is behind them, trying to stifle their shakes.

"I . . . I can't! I can't! Please . . ."

"Shhhhh . . . Shhhhhh." I hold their hands together like two hands in a fisted prayer. Their knuckles are white in their tight grasp. Sweat. Drool. Tears.

"Breathe, Bahadur. Come on. Breathe with me." They take a breath, then another, then another. They finally slow down enough to speak, but every now and then they hiccup on their own tears.

"I . . . don't know if I can do this, Firuzeh. I am not a fighter like you. I'm a runner. I run. I know how to hide. I know how to make myself as small as possible so that no one can see me. Harm me. I know how to freeze and go somewhere else, go outside my body when bad things are happening to me. But I don't know how to fight."

"I saw you, Bahadur," Firuzeh says tenderly. "You can fight. We all have learned how to fight. We're capable."

"No. No. I can't!" Sweat. Drool. Tears. Firuzeh tries to will them to breathe again. I can see that she is working hard to contain Bahadur in her loving arms.

"Is everything okay back there?" I hear Liv call out from the passenger seat. Bahadur suddenly emerges from the blanket cover and unlocks the van door. Beck is forced to pull over on the country road as Bahadur tumbles out of the van. They collapse on the side of the road. We all huddle around them as they scream.

"What's going on?! We can't be out here. Everyone back into the van!" Beck demands in a stage whisper. He looks around frantically. The van is a black cube in a vast stretch of open field. Rows of corn stand low and green to the right of our vehicle. Rolling hills undulate softly in the distance. At the top of one knoll, a farmhouse sits beside a droopy willow tree, its windows framing the scene we are creating.

"Just wait!" Firuzeh says to Beck before she crouches down to Bahadur's reddened face. "Bahadur! Look at me. Look at me!" Firuzeh attempts to touch them, but Bahadur flinches.

Bahadur starts spitfire monologuing. "Firuzeh. What if this were a movie? What if we were all in a movie right now and all of us were characters? We would be as we are in real life: the first ones to get killed. The first ones to become invisible. Silenced. Disappeared. We're the ones. We're gonna die. We're all gonna die!"

"SHHHHH!" Beck spits at us. I look out at the farmhouse Beck has been eyeing, and we both see the curious homeowner open the front door.

A middle-aged man with a red golf shirt shifts right and left wondering what's going on behind our black minivan. He waves and says something inaudible. I hide. Firuzeh hides. Bahadur shakes. Their sobs transform into hysterical choking, as if fluid has gone down the wrong pipe. Their tongue hangs just outside their lips. Their face is beet red.

"You need a boost, young man?" the man repeats to Beck. Liv quickly emerges from the side of the van, pretending to wipe the front of her pants.

"Just a couple of sick kids, sir." Liv poses in pretend irritation and laughs.

"Boy, do I miss those long drives with kids!" the man says sarcastically. He gives a dismissive wave and goes back inside. The distant sound of a screen door closing.

Beck waves, then focuses on us with an alarmed glare. "Get in the car!"

Firuzeh holds Bahadur's face in her hands.

"We're gonna die!"

"No. Not today. Look at me, Bahadur! Not today!" Firuzeh screams, loud enough that my ears are ringing.

Everyone is silent, including Bahadur. Everyone is surprised by the sound of her voice.

"Look at me. Look at me!"

Bahadur obeys, their breathing still labored, spit gathering in the corners of their mouth.

Then quietly, calmly, "You will not die today. You are not that character. This is not that movie. You are not invisible. You will not be silenced. You will not disappear. You will not die. You will not die. You will not die. You will not die." She says it again and again, until I too believe it. Until she has little breath in her body. Firuzeh models a deep inhale and exhale until Bahadur's face slowly returns to its normal color and their breath slows.

We all crowd around Bahadur, silent in the wake of Firuzeh's words until Beck finally solemnly speaks up.

"We need to get into the van before somebody sees us."

We drive again. The sound of the rocky asphalt becomes the sound of city potholes. Under our blanket cover, Firuzeh continues to spoon Bahadur, who faces me, speaking prayers into our six inter-twined hands as we enter Toronto.

I close my eyes and consider all those who have come before me, who have prayed over the barrel of their own gun, before fighting for their own survival. What objects did they touch in the corners of their pockets to steady the beat of their hearts? What pictures did they kiss to remind them of their reason to fight? I touch two fingers to my own mouth imagining you kissing me good luck.

I close my eyes and remember that dreaded day I was exorcised. At dawn, after my mother's church folk released me, I walked, Evan. I walked for as long as my legs would allow me, my head unevenly shorn. In the light of dawn, I walked north on Parliament Street, away from my neighborhood of St. James Town, away from my mother, away from those who prayed over me. A storeowner cranked his awning open and shuddered at the sight of my humiliation. See-ing me in my soiled pajamas, a woman walking her dog avoided me and crossed the street. I kept walking. I descended a steep hill under a bridge into a ravine, hoping for quiet, away from the sound of the city and the repetition of scripture. I walked until there were no longer sidewalks, until the only people who passed me were joggers who assumed I too was on my morning run. I walked until I saw a white bridge towering above me and underneath it an old cemetery. I approached the weathered headstones, each leaning in different directions, each one moist with the morning dew. I felt nothing. I too was dead. Perhaps if I sat down among them, I would have something in common with someone else. Maybe I would belong. I ran my raw and newly clipped nails along the surface of the epitaphs. 1850–1911. 1872–1895. 1922–1963. I found one that read "Lord, we give you our littlest angel" for someone by the name of Beatrice Annabel Anderson who lived and died in the year 1937. It was a humble flat marker. I laid my head down onto its cold surface, outstretched my arms and legs, closed my eyes, and prayed to join her.

That's when I felt the sensation of being watched. I jolted upright and searched the forest and bridge for yet another person about to attack me. The crack of a branch breaking startled me again. From the grouping of headstones I saw a majestic doe. Her neck peeked from the grass she was eating and she looked me in the eyes. She chewed for a while and then swallowed, the grass going down her graceful neck. The fearful pounding of my heart slowed in the presence of her. As minutes (hours? lifetimes?) passed, the glow of the morning sun warmed the surface of her golden fur as it warmed the surface of my weeping face. What did she transmit through her gaze that day? What message did she have for me from beyond? I still cannot put into words what was communicated. Only images. In the reflections of her eyes I saw myself as a young child again, listening to the magic of a piano playing. Me spinning about the room as an LP turned on its table. Dancing like birds just about to take flight. Dancing like eyes slowly opening in the morning. Dancing like the fog dissipating in the warmth of the sun.

I knew then, being my true self now more than ever, I was a child of God. I stood, walked toward school, and never returned home.

12

"Do you know how to use this?" A sound technician holds a body microphone between his thumb and forefinger. Adea and Amana nod in unison. The technician wears a Boots uniform, albeit sadly. One can tell by its ill fit that underneath the leather jacket he is just a ninety-pound geek who serves the regime with his expertise, but not his heart.

"Do you need me to wire it up for you?" His voice cracks.

Adea and Amana look at each other knowingly, then look back at the technician who is quizzically inspecting their enormous skirts, bridged together as if they are conjoined twins in golden sparkles and pink tulle.

"No. We're good," they say in semi-convincing rounds.

"You sure?"

Liv interjects from her lounge chair in the dressing room. Rather than look at the diminutive technician to assert her authority she looks into the bulb-framed mirror and removes a smudge of lipstick from her two front teeth.

"They said they were good. Now leave." Liv shifts from one bum cheek to the other to deliver a sly grin at the technician, her black pantsuit in drastic contrast to the twins' skirts. "I want to have a conversation with these two young ladies before we start."

The technician looks at Adea and Amana, then leaves reluctantly, assuming that Liv will discipline them. The door shuts.

Liv hears white noise on her walkie-talkie and she picks it up. "Liv here."

"What's your ETA? The delegates are already in place and are waiting."

"We're just putting mics on the twins and then I'm escorting them out. Give me five."

"Five it is. Over." White noise. Liv shuts off her walkie-talkie.

The twins each quickly pinch a body mic onto their respective bone corsets and expertly thread the wire along the inside of its seams, then connect the wire to a receiver. They help each other clip the receiver to the back of their corsets, barely moving the parade float of a costume.

"Are the body mics off?" The twins check each other's receivers and nod at Liv. "Good. Everyone is in place. When I give you the signal, we will begin." They all hug as much as the skirts will allow, foreheads touching. The twins' faces have healed from the cigar burns, and their heads are evenly shaved now to appear intentional, fashionable, and not an act of humiliation. Just in time for this internationally observed event. Breathing heavily, their heads all meet in the center of this circle and their arms intertwine in a last embrace. Liv releases herself from the circle to meet eyes with the twins. She holds their hands in hers, the corners of her eyes gathering water. They embrace one more time. Looks of fear. Of ending. Everything final. Liv turns on the twins' mic receivers and places her forefinger to her mouth to alert the twins that people may be listening. The twins nod.

Liv walks to the double doors of the dressing room and opens them. They continue through a darkened theater, slowly walking past marble walls, empty box office windows, and dusty chandeliers toward the sound of a raucous crowd. Two Boots stand at the doors of the theater and open them for the procession.

Liv speaks into her walkie-talkie.

"This is Liv. We're about to exit the theater. Over."

"Copy that."

Liv leads Adea and Amana out into the hustle and bustle of the Summit of Nations. Cameras. Reporters. Microphones. The twins squint their eyes against the dazzlingly bright sunshine.

A tall brunette woman, wearing a pantsuit and a headset, approaches Liv.

"Hi, Liv. I'm Joan. Is everyone ready?"

"Yup. They'll stay right behind me."

Joan rushes toward the front of the procession, where a marching band awaits in their crisp red-and-white uniforms and gives a signal. A team of baton twirlers in maple-leaf-printed tracksuits wait patiently behind the marching band. A whistle is heard. A rhythmic percussive intro starts a rollicking rendition of "O Canada." The twins begin to step forward, and Joan rushes to intervene.

"Not yet," she says with her arm blocking them, looking at the marching band's progress down the street. "I don't want any bottle-necking. I want it to be nice and smooth." Joan talks into her headset, then another signal. "Baton twirlers . . . Go!"

The team obliges by dancing in the direction of the marching band.

Joan lifts her arm. "Okay. Twins. Go!"

Amid the noise, Amana looks at her sister and sends her a silent message through her eyes and the tight grasp of her hand. Adea looks back, her breath shaky and her eyes clear, confirming that the message is received. The twins gracefully step forward. Joan signals for three Boots to clear the path for Liv and the twins as they make their way from Victoria Street to Yonge Street, then to Yonge-Dundas Square. Joan waves goodbye and says, "Have fun!"

"And we're off to the races!" says one of two commentators sitting in an elevated platform overlooking the procession, their image broadcast on the giant screen in the square. One commentator with blond ringlets flashes a lipstick smile at the camera and the other's bushy mustache hovers over his handheld microphone. Both of them sport Canadian flag tees, and white straw hats.

"Well, Kelly, it looks like thousands of proud Canadians are gathering here today to kick off the Summit of Nations. Why, people are so rowdy, you'd think this was the Santa Claus parade!" says Mustache, buoyant and cheerful.

Kelly giggles and waves at the crowds. "Well, Paul. It's not Santa Claus, but we certainly celebrate our esteemed delegates from afar . . ."

The international media representatives do not don the same smiles. Instead, they each wear a face of determination.

A reporter in the crowd squeezes between several spectators holding Canadian flags to reach the twins. "Adea and Amana! What does your presence say to the world about the Renovation?" she asks in an Australian accent.

Other international reporters materialize and chime in.

"Are you being held captive?"

"Are all Others like you safe?"

"Do you believe the Renovation was beneficial to you?"

The media scrum that has appeared on the parade route is tight.

Another reporter manages to elbow her way between two cameramen. "Adea and Amana! Delegates from New Zealand and Ireland refused to attend today's summit after expressing concern that the Renovation is a sign of the rise of a fascist regime here in Canada. Do you agree?"

They move slowly in their immense skirts, observing the banners celebrating the Summit of Nations and Canada's birthday. Yonge Street is a sea of spectators wearing white straw hats with red bands, all fighting for a better view. Once they gain access to the front of the barriers, they gawk at the twins walking freely on the street and tainting the city. Some eyes are wide at the sight of them. Some laugh. Some take pictures. Some spit at them.

On the east side of the street, a vendor sells straw hats, Canadian flags, and popcorn. He catches the eye of the twins as he twists a plastic bag closed and hands it to a young couple. His glance is solemn and serious. Is it apologetic? Disgusted? It is unclear.

Farther south, a father carries his toddler on his hip and points at the twins. His older child jumps in front of him begging for a better look at the procession.

On the west side of the street a pair of women sandwich a Boot and take selfies. All three make the peace sign before taking several shots. "Yay!" the women exclaim.

Behind them a man sits atop a newspaper box. He watches the twins pass. His arms bookend his fat belly. When the twins make eye contact with him, he mouths the word "sorry" before descending from the box and disappearing among the masses.

The media continue to follow the sisters north on Yonge, both Adea and Amana seemingly calm, their faces neutral. The crowd begins to chant.

"REH! NOH! VAY! SHUN! REH! NOH! VAY! SHUN! REH! NOH! VAY! SHUN! REH! NOH! VAY! SHUN!"

Liv can feel the breath of the crowd pushing against her chest with each unified word punctuated with cartoonish war cries.

"REH! NOH! VAY! SHUN! REH! NOH! VAY! SHUN! REH! NOH! VAY! SHUN! REH! NOH! VAY! SHUN!"

Adea squeezes Amana's hand and gestures with her chin to look up. Boots pace along the edge of each building rooftop. Guns point at the twins' heads. Helicopters circle the sky. The twins interlace fingers to join their now-sweaty palms and continue their graceful procession.

As they approach Yonge-Dundas Square they see risers full of international delegates in their finery waiting, watching, with translators by their sides. A sea of more than three thousand white spectators in their straw hats parts, and the twins slowly ascend a wide ramp to the concrete stage, with two large speakers on either side.

Liv reaches her hand out to stop the twins momentarily as Prime Minister Dunphy begins his speech. He is even more handsome in person than he is on television, although slightly thinner in build under his charcoal-gray suit. His charismatic smile flashes at the audience of delegates and they can't help but smile back. Beside him stands Charles, smirking at Liv. Liv smiles back and stands guard over the twins. A quiet descends upon the crowd.

"Good afternoon, my fellow Canadians."

Cheers.

"Ladies and gentlemen, *mesdames et messieurs*. One year ago today, I stood on Parliament Hill doubting everything we were celebrating. We faced some of the greatest challenges our country has faced since its inception. Widespread floods followed by drought and wildfires left countless Canadians homeless and businesses out of commission. Leading a nation forward while its citizens were on their knees begging for mercy was no easy feat. But I was determined to lead nonetheless." Dunphy chokes up. He takes out a tissue and dabs his eyes at tears that do not exist. Cameras click. He continues. "In the wake of such turmoil, difficult decisions were made during difficult times including the Two Nations, One Vision campaign, which, along with our neighbors in the United States of America, worked to rid our lands of terror and tyranny. I can tell you that despite the madness of those times, the government of Canada never stopped believing in the power of democracy and the power of its people!"

Cheers.

"Here in Toronto, the pilot program, the Renovation, has created jobs and has helped feed families across the nation. The founding of seven strategically placed workhouses in this great city has transformed the manufacturing industry into a local operation, made for Canadians by Canadians. On these compounds live flourishing, healthy communities of Others who are given free housing and shelter. Within walking distance of each workhouse are schools ensuring the next generation of Others will receive an in-depth education in the skills they need to succeed in the future. It is with Canadians in mind that we assert the government of Canada's constitutional authority to expand this vital project as a federal initiative. It is with great excitement that we announce that on this day, on this nation's birthday, we launch Renovations in Vancouver, Calgary, Montreal, and Halifax. From sea to sea, this nation will see the glory of hard work, of unity and peace. This time in our lives is a time of great transformation, here in Canada and around the world. From climate change to the rise of extreme politics, we must fight against the forces that have the potential to pull us apart. The Renovation will help us weather these changes the way Canadians always do when faced with adversity: by pulling together!"

The crowd of straw hats lets out a thunderous cheer. Liv steps aside to stage right and the cheers die down. Adea and Amana make eye contact with Dunphy. Silence. The twins, still holding hands, bow ceremoniously, spreading the enormous tulle of their conjoined skirts into a pool of pink at the feet of the prime minister. He grins. The crowd roars. Submission.

"Adea and Amana. Internationally renowned heroines of the LGBTQ2S and Black community, it is with great honor that we welcome you to the stage to share with the world the beauty of change, the beauty of the Renovation."

Cheers.

The twins proceed to the microphone and the prime minister takes his seat among his entourage. Charles and the rest of the Boots cross to stage right where Liv stands. The delegates watch with bated breath. A media scrum pools at the foot of the stage. Reporters point their recording devices toward the twins and adjust their headphones for this momentous occasion.

When the sisters, still holding hands, assume their position, they see that two transparent teleprompters have been placed on either side of them, projecting the speech that Charles has prescribed them.

Amana starts as per the scrolling script. "Good afternoon, Summit of Nations." Her voice is even. Calm. Smooth. The audience is completely silent. "My name is Amana."

"And my name is Adea."

"We are here today to not only welcome the world to our wondrous nation, but to celebrate its birthday." Thunderous applause.

Adea continues. "This milestone is marked with revolutionary change helmed by our esteemed prime minister." The prime minister waves back at the twins, offers a small wave to the delegates and the crowd. A flash of that charismatic smile.

Amana reads, "Since its inception only seven months ago, the Renovation has created thousands of jobs across Toronto in manufacturing and distribution. In addition to making goods for Canadians by Canadians, all workers are entitled to housing for themselves and for their hardworking families. All Others like me and my sister have been put to task, living the creed of the Renovation: *Through our work, our nation prospers. Through our unity, we end conflict. Through our leader, we find peace. Through order, we find tranquility.*" Applause. Inquisitive looks from the media scrum, waiting.

Liv takes out a tube of lip balm from her pocket, applies it, and looks straight at the twins. The twins nod. They reposition themselves away from the teleprompter.

Adea continues, this time with conviction in her voice. "Perhaps this may all seem familiar to you. But they are lies. Because what our prime minister calls jobs, what he may call 'housing,' others call forced-labor camps." A collective gasp across the crowd of spectators.

Charles stands. Liv steps close and points a gun into his back, hidden from the crowd. He stops.

"Remember, Charles, the world is watching." Liv flashes a look at the prime minister, who glares back at her with surprised contempt.

The crowd waits, frozen.

"People of the world, international media, know this. What you are seeing is a ruse! And my and my sister's presence here is simply subterfuge to distract you from a greater tragedy! A continued tragic story spanning back to the genocide of this land's Indigenous people. We are not free! We are among millions of Others who have been forced either into camps or into hiding! We must liberate our fellow citizens from this tyranny. At this very moment, every workhouse in the city is being destroyed. The Renovation must be stopped!" The microphone is swiftly disconnected and Amana's speech can no longer be heard.

The spectators raise their voices in a collective uproar. The media scrum around the base of the stage goes into a frenzy, microphones pointing at the twins, hoping to catch audio.

We emerge from the tulle of the twins' conjoined skirts. Three of us at first. Firuzeh lets out a loud yelp. Hearing the signal, five more emerge from behind the speakers. From under the stage, another twenty. Us Others. Holding guns. A round of shots is fired, and one of the Boots is flung from the top of a building to his death. We look up and we see a Boot who has pushed another Boot to his death. He removes his helmet and lets out a yelp to reveal himself as an ally. We look around and see several like him, stepping to the side and turning on their own as part of the Resistance. They each remove their helmets so that we can identify our allies. Yelps of identification. The delegates and prime minister hit the deck. Screams among the crowd.

We follow our plan. Firuzeh and I each disarm a Boot. Deflect end of rifle with left palm. Punch with right fist to the chin or kick to stomach. Butt of the gun to the face. Take the weapon. Bahadur, given their height, struggles a bit. I hold my breath wondering if they have it in them to do as we were taught. Bahadur finally delivers a kick to the Boot's stomach and manages to disarm him. They hold the rifle in the air and scream away the fear, their eyes focused and their body full of adrenaline. As instructed, we holster our Glocks and shoulder our newly acquired rifles. I look through the scope at Liv speaking to Charles onstage, her gun aimed now at the back of his head.

"Stand down!"

Charles hesitates.

"Tell your men to stand down, Charles. NOW!"

Charles debates this in his head whether to obey Liv. His arms up. His masculinity fragile. He looks around, confused and enraged as he sees Boots pointing guns at their fellow officers in resistance.

"Every camera is on us right now, and at least half of your men have turned against you, Charles. Do it!"

Charles sees Prime Minister Dunphy, his security ushering him from the stage. Delegates balled up on the ground screaming. Liv steps back slightly and shoots. The bullet rips through Charles's ear. "Stand down or I won't miss next time."

Cameras shift from the twins to the mess of artillery pointing in various directions. Holding the bloody mess at the side of his head, as if the blood is music he does not want to hear, Charles gives a signal, and the remaining Boots reluctantly stand down.

Through the scope of my gun, I can see Charles making one last attempt to reach for his own weapon and, again, Liv shoots. She does not miss.

"Good boy," she says to the corpse beneath her. Looking at me, she nods.

We Others proceed to move about the crowd, taking the Boots' weapons, the guns still warm from their hands. We act as we were trained to, assessing danger at every level, every angle.

Two Others in wheelchairs—one with a frayed denim vest and the other with a series of piercings in their* ears—move swiftly among the fallen. They bulldoze past screaming spectators who move to the side at the last second, seeing the unapologetic determination in their eyes.

Denim Vest approaches a fallen Boot, still twitching and bleeding from a towering fall. They lean over to dislodge the rifle. After a few earnest pulls Denim Vest punches the air with rifle in hand, yelping at their acquisition. They continue their work of disarming the bloodied and still bodies of Boots.

The Other with piercings launches several multicolored smoke bombs, wheeling their chair in larger and larger circles to force the crowd to clear the way, bulldozing anyone who dares to block their path. They signal for us to move forward as planned, and we obey their orders.

The rest of the Others gather in a circle around the twins. Some of us wear our runaway clothes. These clothes we wore before we disappeared, now weathered and stained. Some still have their heads shaved. Some have mouths that end in frowning scars. We rush toward our circle. All of us have the look of terror in our eyes. One disarmed Boot attempts to infiltrate our circle, and another Boot shoots him in the neck. He collapses. The shooter removes his helmet and yelps to identify himself as an ally. More screams.

"Fucking n_ _ _ _rs!" One spectator throws a can of cola at my feet. My face gets hot at the sensation of the brown liquid pooling at my shoes. I feel my arms go still.

"Get to work, towel head!"

"Go to hell!"

"Die, you tranny whores!"

Debris begins to fly from every direction. The sounds of bullets whizzing through the air. My arms. My arms. They can't move. I look at Bahadur, their grip loose on their rifle. Their arms are droopy, succumbing to the humiliation.

"REH! NOH! VAY! SHUN! REH! NOH! VAY! SHUN! REH! NOH! VAY! SHUN! REH! NOH! VAY! SHUN!"

Onstage, Beck appears on top of one of the speakers and hollers out a high-pitched call to the audience. I witness a slight pause. A split second. A fraction of a fraction of a fraction of a moment where he doubts himself. Wonders if he is doing the right thing. It is the slightest shade of shame for betraying those like him. And then it lapses. He breathes in, he shakes his hands free, then, with the power of the flames he once set on that protest site years ago, he lights within himself the rage needed to let his voice be heard.

"*WHEN I DO NOT ACT, I AM COMPLICIT!*" Beck says while simultaneously raising his rifle above his head horizontally with an end in each hand. He takes a deep breath here, steps forward with a lunge, and moves in a downward motion with his rifle. Another fraction of a fraction of a fraction of a moment where he wonders who will join him. Suddenly, I see dozens of other white folks taking a step forward, executing the same gestures, with or without weapons. Some are in the crowd. Some are in the audience of delegates. Some are Boots.

They continue in unison. Their words filling my heart. Liv joins in, Charles's blood pooling at her feet.

When I do not act, I am complicit!

When I know wrong is happening, I act!

When the oppressed tell me I am wrong, I open my heart and change!

When change is led by the oppressed, I move aside and uplift!

Arms raise, step forward, lunge back, kneel. Finally, just as Hanna suggested, Beck leads the allies in covering their mouths, touching their hearts, and pointing toward us like a spotlight, this gathering of Others. When their phrase of movement is over, the white allies move through the incredulous crowds and encircle us Others. They join hands to create a barricade. Firuzeh looks at me and nods. We move forward as planned, slowly, as a unified body. Allies on the outskirts. Others within, protecting each other. We slowly proceed toward Yonge Street in silence. Spectators angrily glare at us as we move past a sea of straw hats.

I abide by Beck's instructions and prepare myself to begin saying our names. Prepare to say mine loud and clear so that the media will know we are real people who have survived a real genocide. My heart races, forming the words in my heart and allowing them to travel up my esophagus, piece by piece.

"Queen Kay." I see the memory of you, my beautiful Evan, standing before me. Your image is pixelated by every word I have written in every Whisper Letter I have sent. Standing at your side is your mother who clasps hands with you and smiles at me in wonder.

"Look at me," says Mrs. King, the blue of her cataracts flashing at me like a beacon. "Be as big as you want to be."

I feel the words exit my lips, as planned. I hear my voice loud and proud, echoing off the storefronts, knowing that in every workhouse in the city, there are Others saying the same thing while evacuating the premises. Through the smoke, under falling brick, over barbed wire fences; from the Don Valley to Ward's Island, from Scarborough to the Junction, people are saying their names. A declaration. We are kites, prayers flying in the sky, knowing freedom.

"MY NAME IS KAY! I AM THE SON OF GABBY NOPUENTE AND KEITH WATSON SMITH! AND I DESERVE TO LIVE!" I say it loud enough that the media scrum shifts its focus to me. Microphones. Flashing cameras.

Bahadur looks at me, tears welling in their eyes, then looks forward with bravery. "MY NAME IS BAHADUR TALEBI! I AM THE CHILD OF FATIMA TALEBI. AND I DESERVE TO LIVE!"

We continue north on Yonge Street. The media following us. The circle of allies unbreakable. The twins holding hands, crying. Each one of us calling out our names. Perhaps for the last time. Perhaps so that the world will know we existed. We call out our names.

"MY NAME IS ISABEL RODRIGUEZ! I AM THE DAUGHTER OF MARIA AND ISADORO RODRIGUEZ. AND I DESERVE TO LIVE!"

"MY NAME IS ALAN SCOTT! I AM THE CHILD OF VIRGINIA SCOTT. AND I DESERVE TO LIVE!"

"MY NAME IS FIRUZEH PASDAR!" Firuzeh's voice shakes, overwhelmed with emotion. "I AM THE DAUGHTER OF AYESHA AND MOSTAFA PASDAR." She swallows again. "AND I DESERVE TO LIVE!"

"MY NAME IS GRACE CARDINAL. I AM THE GRAND-DAUGHTER OF ELEANOR THUNDERCLOUD. AND WE ALL DESERVE TO LIVE!"

"MY NAME IS BENJAMIN HUXLEY! I AM THE GRANDSON OF TEDDY COOMBS. AND I DESERVE TO LIVE!"

"MY NAME IS MARTHA GREER! I AM THE MOTHER OF

ANTHONY AND JESSICA GREER, WHEREVER THEY ARE. WE ALL DESERVE TO LIVE!" Sobs.

"MY NAME IS ARTHUR YEBUGA! SON OF REGGIE AND SARAH YEBUGA. AND I DESERVE TO LIVE!"

"MY NAME IS GILBERT LEFRANCOIS! CHILD OF LOUIS AND MAUDE LEFRANCOIS! AND I DESERVE TO LIVE!"

"MY NAME IS ZAHRA MOHAMMED! MOTHER OF MY BABY ALI, WHEREVER HE IS. WE ALL DESERVE TO LIVE!"

"MY NAME IS CHASE KWAN! SON OF ELIZABETH AND RICKY KWAN. AND I DESERVE TO LIVE!"

We march to the horizon of asphalt, heat mirages snaking into the air, not knowing what awaits us. We march in our runaway clothes, our hiding clothes, our disappearing clothes, our working clothes. We march to the sound of our own names. We march for those who cannot march. Some of us without our families. All of us older. All of us surviving. We march north on Yonge Street, calling out our names to the sky.

ACKNOWLEDGMENTS

Maraming salamat po sa in'yong lahat.

I remember when I was first learning Diné Bizaad I had an especially difficult time learning the Navajo word for "thank you." I feel like the language is all about breath control: when to let the air push through tongue and teeth, and when to stop it dead in its tracks. In the time it took me to learn how to pronounce *ahe'hee* properly, I had learned the depth of that thank-you and what it meant to be thankful in my new family. I am glad it took that long to learn the word because, as I know from my days in theater, struggling through meaning is part of arriving at an understanding. Let me struggle through this thank-you. Let me try to express my thanks when all I want to do is cry and hold you all. We did this together.

Ahe'hee to my partner, Nazbah Tom, whose powerful poem "We Have Been Occupied" is read during the pipeline protest in this book. I am honored to have heard you read this poem and for your willingness to include your work in mine.

Donna-Michelle St. Bernard and lemonTree creations: those hours spent dramaturging the first manuscript will always hold a special place in my heart. I couldn't do this work without you, and I hope you know what a blessing you are in this world.

Carolyn Smart and Queen's University: thank you for the time, space, and funds to work on this novel. I spent my valuable residency writing under the watchful eyes of ghosts. Releasing these words just steps away from Sir John A. MacDonald's statue felt like the ultimate finger flip to the architect of the residential school system.

Canada Council for the Arts, Ontario Arts Council, House of Anansi Press, ChiZine Publications, and Book*hug Press: thank you for giving me the funds to be brave. My agent, Marilyn Biderman: thank you for hustling to ensure this book could be read by all. I am forever grateful to those who contributed their insights and experiences through anonymous interviews. I hope my words did your stories justice.

I assembled a team of artist colleagues who represent various communities including Disabled, Black, Brown, Indigenous, Muslim, Queer, Trans, and Deaf-identified folks. Onar Usar, Kusha Dadui, Rania El Mugammar, Sage Lovell, Falen Johnson, Syrus Marcus Ware, Rashi Khilnani, Anne Graham, L, HC and others: your generosity in correcting me when I could do better is something I will never forget.

Erin Brockobić, thank you for giving me a full scholarship to Drag Queen University. It means a lot that you—a being brought into this world between borders and bullets—were a part of this project. Katleya Maya Neri: my Carter kin. Thank you for your insights about life in the military. Thank you to my #CanLit *barkada*, who have helped me make some difficult decisions in my career leading up to the publishing of this book: David Chariandy, Carrianne Leung, Canisia Lubrin, Cherie Dimaline, Vivek Shraya. I'm just a Scarborough girl from the theater world, so your guidance was very much appreciated. You all are welcome to my house any day of the week, dinner included.

To my brother, Tyrone Tom: I love you, no matter what. Thank you for sharing with me the true price of war.

To Team Jacaranda: thank you for sharing my words across the pond.

Michelle Herrera Mulligan: Your energy and insights gave me the fuel to make it to the finish line. Much thanks to you and Atria for seeing the truth behind the Canadian fantasy.

Jennifer Mother-Effin Lambert: You are the real deal. I chose you to be my editor because I wanted to become a better writer. Thank you for your allyship, and thank you to Team HarperCollins Canada for this adventure.

To my two monkeys, Arden and Nazbah: I wrote this book wanting my beautiful Queer family to be safe. No matter what the future holds for people like us, know that I am honored to have loved you both.

MY NAME IS CATHERINE HERNANDEZ. I AM THE MOTHER OF ARDEN MCNEILLY AND WIFE OF NAZBAH TOM. WE ALL DESERVE TO LIVE.

CATHERINE HERNANDEZ is a proud Queer Brown woman, an award-winning author, and the outgoing artistic director of b current performing arts. She is of Filipino, Spanish, Chinese, and Indian heritage and married into the Navajo Nation. Catherine's first full-length novel, *Scarborough*, won the Jim Wong-Chu Emerging Writers Award; was shortlisted for the Toronto Book Awards, Edmund White Award for Debut Fiction, Forest of Reading Evergreen Award, and Trillium Book Award; and was longlisted for Canada Reads 2018. *Scarborough* made the Best of 2017 lists for the *Globe and Mail*, *National Post*, *Quill & Quire*, and CBC Books. She wrote the screenplay for the film adaptation of *Scarborough*, produced by Compy Films, Telefilm Canada, and Reel Asian International Film Festival. Catherine currently lives in the Scarborough area of Toronto with her brilliant daughter and loving partner.

THE 5IVE KEY HABITS OF SMART DADS

A Powerful Strategy for Successful Fathering

PAUL LEWIS

FAMILY UNIVERSITY™

ZondervanPublishingHouse
Grand Rapids, Michigan

A Division of HarperCollinsPublishers

To Billy L. Lewis—
my father, friend,
a very wise man,
and forever my dad.

To Leslie—
my wife, lover, best friend,
and the greatest compliment
I'll ever be paid.

To Shona, Jon, Shelley, David, and Kevin—
you are the arrows in my quiver
and my sacred assignment.
I am proud of you and humbled
to be your dad.

To every father
who feels awed by his role
or unsure about what to do.
You are not alone.

CONTENTS

Acknowledgments

I am fabulously wealthy yet deeply in debt. My wealth is my friends, and I am deeply indebted to them for their help in conceiving and writing this book.

Two summers ago Tim Vandenboss at Willow Creek Community Church near Chicago invited me to return for a second summer to Camp Paradise along the Tahquamenon River in Michigan's Upper Peninsula to speak to Chicago-area fathers and sons gathered there. For lodging he provided the White House, a small cabin about a quarter mile down river. It was there, hunched over a pad of paper at the kitchen table, gazing out the windows at a quiet river flowing lazily by, that my ideas jelled and the first sketch of the "Five Key Habits of Smart Dads" wheel took shape. Later that week, a table full of fathers surrendered their recreational time in order to critique my brainstorm. To those men who were part of that moment, this is my thank-you for your helpful and enthusiastic input.

My long-time friend Sealy Yates introduced the project to Scott Bolinder and the team at Zondervan. Both Sealy and Scott knew me through *Dads Only* (now *Smart Dads*) newsletter, which I write, edit, and publish. Their excitement for bringing these thoughts into book form and their commitment through delays along the way kept the window of opportunity open. Connie Neal set aside several weeks to help shape the first draft of the manuscript. Connie, you are a pro and more! And in the final analysis, a writer is no better than the editors who help make the ideas flow and the words sparkle: Sandy Vander Zicht and Tim McLaughlin, you have my highest praise.

My pastor, Harry Kiehl, gave time on more than one occasion to comment on what I was writing. A number of fathers attending Dads University courses in Oceanside, California, and Bellevue, Washington, also offered feedback on this book's premise. Those reality checks helped.

The taskmaster who most buoyed me, though, is Leslie—my wife, lover, companion for life. Sweetheart, you have given to me the gift of fatherhood five times. Without your tireless support and savvy, what I could have written worth reading would have made a small book indeed. I am looking forward to at least another twenty-seven years of family adventures with you.

Paul Lewis
December 1993

Introduction

While I was growing up, I don't recall ever seeing my father pull another dad aside for advice about being a good father. Maybe he did so discreetly, but I didn't notice it. He seemed to fulfill the role without much day-to-day coaching. What I observed during my childhood left me with the impression that fathering skills came naturally. In my birds-and-bees conversations with my father, he took care to explain how one *becomes* a father, but he never mentioned what it took to *be* a good father.

You may wonder why men today need to learn how to father well. Haven't previous generations of fathers succeeded at it, more or less? Yet life has taught me during my nearly fifty years that good fathering is not a matter of chance.

Learning to Father

One Sunday evening I was interviewed on a radio talk show about the Dads University courses I teach. The next morning I received a call at my office. "That fathering class you spoke about last night interests me," a man said. "I have a twenty-year-old daughter, and I'm not very happy about the way this whole thing has worked out. Could a Dads University class help me?" And before I could respond, he added, "Heck, no one teaches us men how to be dads."

The intensity of his voice echoed the emotion many men feel but seldom verbalize. Where does a father go these days to learn his craft? Should a man know intuitively how to be a good father? It seems to me that, beyond the fundamentals of protecting and providing for his children, whatever natural instincts a man has about fathering are used up about the time sperm meets ovum. Fathering, like most life skills, is learned and requires discipline.

Stop Leaving It to Chance

It was over lunch in 1977 with a friend that an intriguing idea surfaced: A newsletter of insider tips on how to be a good father. Didn't men read newsletters to keep up with careers, investments, and hobbies? Why not a newsletter on fathering? In assuming one of life's greatest assignments—a role that, more than any other, shapes a man's personal legacy—it made no sense to leave the outcome to chance and simply hope things would work.

So I conceptualized, created, and began publishing *Dads Only*—a newsletter that gave busy, fast-lane dads winning advice on building healthy relationships with their children and managing family roles well. Recently retitled *Smart Dads*, the bimonthly newsletter is read by thousands of fathers across America. It is eight tightly written pages of practical tips and insights. Twice a year a "Dad Talk" audio cassette is sent with *Smart Dads*. (See the announcement at the back of this book for more information.)

Throughout the 1980s the newsletter remained an engrossing hobby for me while I continued my career as a free-lance graphic designer and writer. But as 1990 rolled around, it became clear that—as one columnist phrased it—this would be the "Decade of the Dad." So in response to growing interest, I condensed thirteen years of study and effort in fathering into a curriculum known as Dads University.

In June of 1990 a church in East Lansing, Michigan, sponsored the first Dads University half-day course: "Secrets of Fast-Track Fathering." The feedback from those ninety-six fathers confirmed that the course filled a definite need. From that beginning, Dads University has traveled from one end of the U.S. to the other, from high school cafeterias, community centers, and church social halls to university classrooms, hotels, and corporate seminar rooms.

Experience Is a Superb Teacher

I've gathered and shared many resources about fathering. I have gleaned wisdom from thousands of dads from whom I have learned much of what I write on these pages. I have gained my best experience, however, by being a father.

If you have a child out of the nest—away at college or married—I can identify with you. My oldest daughter married four years ago. She's a fourth-grade teacher helping put her husband through his second year of law school. Typical of most firstborn children, Shona was fun-loving, always tried hard to please, and made fathering seem easy.

Which is probably why Jon came into my life. From day one Jon has been an adventurer and risk-taker. On his eighteenth birthday, the only present Jon wanted was to skydive. Fiercely independent, he challenged my directives throughout most of his first eighteen years. During the toughest two or three of those years, Jon abandoned what we had taught him and turned to drug abuse and other risky behaviors before coming to his senses. Now twenty-one,

INTRODUCTION

Jon lives on his own, employed as a locksmith while completing his last year of training to become fully certified. Once that is under his belt, he intends to return to college to earn a degree, perhaps in outdoor education, for he loves individual sports like rock climbing and surfing.

If you have a young teenager in the house, I can identify with you as well. My thirteen-year-old daughter, Shelley, is in middle school. When the phone rings these days, it's usually for her. She's a conscientious student who loves gymnastics and cheerleading. Friends and artistic endeavors run a close second. With a ready laugh and the competitive spirit of her father, she frequently wins the table games played around our house.

If you have a son or daughter in elementary school, I can still identify. My third-grader David is the sensitive one, who thinks deeply, who regularly hugs my neck with no prompting, who loves babies, books, videos, roller blading, Little League baseball, and climbing most anything.

And, if you have a toddler, preschooler, or kindergartner in the house, I can *still* relate to you. Six-year-old Kevin, our youngest, has unlimited energy and curiosity, aggressively taking on life from sun-up to sundown. He's most curious when he's thinking about how mechanical things work. If there's a repair to be done, he's right there to help me, and frustrated if he can't take part. To Kevin, real work is better than play. (I can't wait until he's old enough to mow the lawn by himself.)

These are my children. Each one is a unique challenge as I try to apply the habits of a smart dad. Each child gives me the opportunity to test, apply, and revise my fathering theories. Like you, I face the difficulties of fathering every day as I try to raise my children to become responsible adults.

One thing stands out in my conversations with dads over the years: Few things are more important to fathers than to know the deep love and respect of their children. Most of us really do want to be good fathers, even if fathering is only a frustrating fight at times. We want more depth to family relationships and a deeper connection to our children. We want our children to really know us. We want to wield our "father power" well.

I believe that most men today lack a clear picture of what a good father actually is. Without some simple guidelines to help them win at being dads, they lack the confidence that breeds success. But once a man gets a picture of what it takes to be a good father, he usually chooses to try to make that picture a reality.

FIVE KEY HABITS OF SMART DADS

In this book I will give you a picture, a model, that will help you envision and remember the five key habits of a smart dad. Over the past fifteen years, I have pondered the complexities of fathering. As with most life skills, there are a handful of key ideas that, if acted upon, yield great results. My quest has been to identify those key ideas and present them to you. The ideas you will encounter on these pages are intended to help you recognize and maximize the powerful position you occupy in the lives of your children.

1

Dad, Pop, My Ol' Man, Sir
On Being a Father

Nearing the end of his life, John Kingery was alone, abandoned by a grown daughter at an Idaho racetrack. This victim of Alzheimer's disease sat in his wheelchair, clutching a teddy bear. A note was pinned to his jacket; on his cap were the words "Proud to be an American."

When the story and photo hit the papers, Nancy Kingery Myatt—another grown daughter of the old man—discovered the father she had lost. Twenty-eight years earlier he had slipped away from his first five children, divorced their mother, and remarried. But over the years Nancy's longing for him never diminished. As far as she was concerned, he never stopped being her father.

When fifty-five-year-old Nancy greeted her eighty-two-year-old dad, he didn't recognize her, didn't know who she was, couldn't recall her name. But none of this stopped her tears when she finally saw and touched her long-lost father again.

"I didn't have a dad for all those years," she said. "Now I have one. The more I see him, the more I want to see him and talk to him."

"What my ear picked up in Nancy Myatt's words," wrote columnist Ellen Goodman, "was the simple endless hunger of a child of any age for the father who disappeared."[1]

This lost-and-found father illustrates the unquenchable power of fatherhood and the undying love of children—even adult children—for their own dads. In his condition John Kingery could do nothing for his daughter. Yet precisely because of his inability to do anything, he was reduced to the single fact of being this woman's father. And to Nancy Kingery Myatt, even that little bit of him was powerfully significant.

You are a father. You may be new at it, or you may have twelve kids. You may rate your current fathering performance as excellent, ordinary, mediocre, or poor. Whatever state you're in, you are light years ahead of Mr. Kingery in your ability to respond to your children. By merely being their father, you have tremendous power in their lives. That power does not come primarily from your fathering performance; much of it is simply inherent in the role. Your choice is not whether you will have power and potency as a father—you already do. The choice is whether you will unleash that power in constructive or destructive ways.

What Your Children Want and Need Most Is You

If you listen closely to your children they will tell you what they want from you: most important, you—then your approval, your interest, concern, guidance, and love.

Magic is in the air as I walk up the steps to my home and hear my sons inside: "Daddy's home!" How can children get so excited just because you're there? We can find it hard to believe that we matter so much to our children simply by being there. It's easier for us to think that we must perform in order to earn our child's love. There's some truth there, but only a bit. What your children want most is you.

Today at Kevin's soccer game, David told me he wanted me. He didn't say it in words, but his body language spoke it loudly: He walked up to me along the sidelines and wrapped his arms around my waist and just hung on for a while. Later he wanted me to watch his daring jump high into the air from a swing. All this mattered to David simply because I'm his father—a powerful figure in his life.

In *Father Power*, authors Henry Biller and Dennis Meredith observe that

> the principal danger to fatherhood today, and to the American family for that matter, is that fathers do not have the vital sense of father power that they have had in the past. Because of a host of pressures from society, the father has lost the confidence that he is

naturally important to his children—that he has the power to affect children, guide them, help them grow. He isn't confident that fatherhood is a basic part of being masculine and a legitimate focus of his life.[2]

Your active presence in the lives of your children is enormously powerful—probably more potent than you have imagined. No matter how nurturing, skillful, and committed a mother is, she cannot give her child a father's love. Only you can fill that void in your child's heart. It takes a father (or an effective surrogate father) to love his children with a father's love.

20th Century Fathering: A Unique Set of Challenges

Fathers at the turn of the twenty-first century face a unique predicament. Record numbers of fathers have abandoned, disowned, or otherwise given up on their children. Consciously or unconsciously, many have turned their attention and energy to arenas where success is more measurable, where men can count the rewards in dollars and cents. Our society is only beginning to tally the enormous price of fatherlessness, a price still to be paid in the currency of human lives and emotional turmoil.

Though you probably are not part of the problem (you obviously want to be a better father, or you wouldn't be reading this book), at times even you harbor mixed feelings about fathering. You're not alone. A national Gallup survey reflected such mixed feelings, concluding that "seven in ten respondents agree that the most significant family problem facing America is the physical absence of the father from the home." Virtually all adults (ninety-six percent) agree that fathers need to be more involved in their children's education. Yet only about three-quarters agree that "fathers do care enough about children's feelings" and that "most fathers are doing a good job in providing for their families financially."[3]

Even if you fully commit yourself to your children, there can be a gap between what you wish you could do and what you can actually manage. "I love my three kids more than life itself," a father told me. "I have sacrificed some very important dreams so that I can have a career that allows me to provide for my children. I have overcome substantial personal problems because I am

Smart Idea:
Mail a short note to each of your children's teachers. Express your appreciation for their dedication to education, and assure them of your support at home. The five minutes this takes will create more magic than you think.

determined to keep my marriage and family together. I am doing the best I know to do, but I am often frustrated. It takes so much work to stay competitive in my field, to provide financially, to coordinate schedules, to maintain a healthy relationship with my wife—that I never seem to have enough time with my kids. It's not a matter of wasting time on personal interests. I just don't have enough time with them, and it's not a matter of choice."

I frequently ask men what their greatest fathering frustrations are. Their most common answers are variations on their lack of time:

- **Not enough time with their children.**
- **Trying to get away from their jobs so they can have time with their kids.**
- **Finding a constructive way to use the small amount of time they have with their kids.**

In a national survey a friend and I commissioned on fathering practices, we asked dads to describe their feelings about fathering in word pictures. Here are some of their answers:

"I feel like a lone lion roaring in the jungle."

"I feel like a duck out of water."

"I feel like a loved teddy bear with all the fuzz rubbed off."

"I feel like the sun on a partly cloudy day, warm and nice when it's there, but not there quite as much as my children would like."

"I feel like a Dachshund running in deep snow."

"I feel like I'm swimming against a river of things that are demanding my time, struggling to get to the island where my children are waiting."

"I feel like water in the shower, which runs hot and cold depending on who is using water in other parts of the house."

Struggling to Find the Balance

So you're not the only father who loves his children, wants to be a good father, but is frustrated. When asked if they were stressed trying to balance home and family, seventy-two percent of men in a 1989 survey answered yes, compared with only twelve percent who answered yes in 1979.[4]

Economic Pressures

Yet economic pressures mean that men will only face greater problems as work and family commitments become more complex.

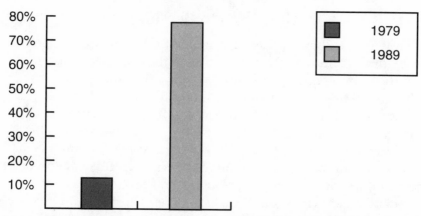

Percentage of men who answered yes to the question:
"Do you experience stress related to trying to balance work and home?"

Research shows that "since 1973, real earnings of men between 25 and 29 have declined more than twenty percent, leading some researchers to conclude that men flee family life—or are pushed out by women—because they are not reliable breadwinners."[5]

And there's the probability that serious fathering is a glass ceiling to a career—a phenomenon much discussed among women in the workplace, but now, *Time* reports, "it is the fathers who are beginning to ask themselves whether their careers will stall and their incomes stagnate, whether the glass ceiling will press down on them once they make public their commitment as parents, whether today's productivity pressures will force them to work even harder with that much less time to be with their kids."[6]

Your Fulfillment as a Father

You know the times you come home from work preoccupied or exhausted. And simply reminding yourself that the reason you go to work is to support your family doesn't automatically give you the energy to actually enjoy your time with them. You may even look for a retreat *from* your children—which is ironic, considering that they are the supposed pay-off for all your hard work. Sooner or later, every father wonders if this is all he is: Someone who works to provide for a family he doesn't have the time or energy to enjoy.

Smart Thought:
A hundred years from now the size of my bank account won't matter, nor the size or style house I lived in, nor the model car I drove. But the world may be different because I was deeply involved in the life of my children.

There Has to Be More

Recent years have witnessed a surge of interest among men to better understand who they are and how they can better connect with their children. The inadequate cultural images with which we've grown up—and which have shaped the role of father in our society—are, I believe, the driving force within the Men's Movement. It is not enough for men to see themselves—and be seen—as mere financial providers. While most men endure much emotional turmoil when they cannot provide the financial needs of their families, there is growing recognition that being a good provider isn't all a man wants out of the relationship. And it certainly isn't all his family members need from him.

If you have ever felt the indignation that says "Being a father has to include more than just providing a paycheck!" you are far more aware than society in general of who you are supposed to be as a father.

The Transformation of Fathering

How could generations of men get so far out of focus? A look at the transformation of fathering over the past two centuries can help you understand why the yearnings you feel, which tug you back to your kids, are legitimate.

In *The Third Wave* Alvin Toffler writes,

> The role system that held industrial civilization together is in crisis. This we see most dramatically in the struggle to redefine sex roles. In the Women's Movement, in the demands for the legalization of homosexuality, in the spread of unisex fashions, we see a continual blurring of traditional expectations for the sexes.[7]

Toffler maintains that the breakup of traditional roles through gender blending is one of several factors that "produce crisis in that most elemental and fragile of structures: the personality." Victims of that personality crisis, says Toffler, are anxious "to become what they are not. They work to change jobs, spouses, roles and responsibilities."

Men must resist some of the cultural changes that challenge their unique role in society. We cannot allow special-interest groups to tell us who we are, if their definition of us mars our children. I see how gender blending in our culture—as well as the demands of the Women's Movement—has confused some men about who they are and how to behave. And in their confusion, in their uncertainty about what is expected of them, they have failed to be a strong figure in their families. The result is a generation of children missing the strong paternal leadership they need.

Cultural Changes in the Role of Fathers

These powerful cultural and economic changes have us in their grip and, over the past several generations, have distanced us from our children. Yet if you understand how and why fathering has changed culturally, you can then choose whatever elements of fathering you want to reclaim as yours.

As the Industrial Revolution separated a man's home and work, fathers understandably disengaged themselves from the day-to-day routines of bringing up their children. Because their husbands relinquished these tasks, wives logically assumed them.

What emerged was what we have called "the traditional family" —Dad gone to work, and Mom keeping the home fires burning. A *Time* report states that "by the 1830s, child-rearing manuals, increasingly addressed to mothers, deplored the father's absence from the home. In 1900 one worried observer could describe 'the suburban husband and father' as 'almost entirely a Sunday institution.'"[8]

Societal Markers

If we could go back two hundred years, we would see clear social markers that defined a man's role as a father. A man in colonial America, for example, understood that he was responsible to—

- **Provide for his family's material needs.**
- **Model good citizenship by being politically informed and involved.**
- **Educate his children and teach them a trade.**
- **Understand theology and communicate absolute values to the next generation.**

Today? Fathers still feel obliged to contribute financially to the rearing of their children. They also understand that they need to contribute more than financially— but *how*, society doesn't spell out clearly. Society gives fathers mixed messages. Does

Smart Idea:
Create a "verbal sandwich" when talking with your teenager: Open with something personal, soft and gentle (the bread). Spread on some positive reinforcement (the mayonnaise). Address the problem (the lunch meat). Finish with more encouragement (another slice of bread). Tasty!

a father's masculinity bias or bless his children? Does his maleness make him less an inherent nurturer than a woman?

Fathers once gained their identity by being the sole breadwinner. But now most families depend on both mother and father to contribute financially, so a father's role as sole breadwinner is diminished. The government has also taken over the role of providing financial subsistence for low-income women and children. (It is here, in fact, that men find one of many mixed messages about their importance: one of the requirements for women to receive Aid for Dependent Children is that the father must be absent from the home. Society still recognizes the need for fathers—kind of.)

"The story we tell ourselves is a curiously old-fashioned story, that fatherhood equals economic support," contends David Blankenhorn, president of the Institute of American Values, a New York think tank that studies family issues. "But fatherhood is more than sending checks. And the consequences of fatherlessness are deep and profound and long-lasting."[9]

Beyond the duty of colonial American fathers to provide for their families' material needs, the remaining three paternal responsibilities—model informed citizenship, educate their children, and pass on absolute values—have been delegated by modern society to someone other than the father. Good citizenship and political awareness are now the domain of the public school system and the media. Education and career preparation have been turned over to public schools, colleges, and government. Theological truth is perceived by our culture as something to be kept within the church or synagogue. Whereas parents once took personal responsibility for their children's religious education, it has become the domain of the church school or other out-of-home religious institution.

Is it any wonder men in our society struggle with defining their role and measuring their success as fathers?

What Has Happened to the American Family?

"The structure of the family has been very stable over a long period of time, and it's only over the last generation that we've had this enormous change," wrote historian Christopher Lasch.[10] In a *Fortune* article entitled "The American Family, 1992," three cultural changes in the last thirty years were cited as working powerfully to restructure family life:

1. The sixties' quest for personal liberation and gratification, combined with rebellion against authority and convention, under-

mined stable family life and devalued lifelong family commitments.

2. The sexual revolution legitimized promiscuity. "The whole culture's glorification of the joy of sex without reference to marriage allowed married people to feel an unprecedented self-justification in the pursuit of sexual adventure, even if it broke up their marriages."

3. The "most vocal contingent of the Women's Movement . . . encouraged some women to see family life's inevitable constraints as an oppression from which they needed liberation. Moreover, it encouraged women to value themselves for their career achievements but not for motherhood."

The article concludes with a prescription: "Now we need to reflect on what we've learned: that children are important, that they don't grow up well unless we bring them up, that they need two parents, that our needs can't shoulder theirs aside, that commitments and responsibilities to others have to take precedence over personal gratification, that nothing is more gratifying than to see children flourish. What is our life for, if not for that?"[11]

Me-Firstism

For the last two centuries, social values have pushed a man away from putting family responsibilities first, and toward putting himself first.

"It was overwhelming," remembers a young dad about the moment he first laid eyes on his newborn. "I picked up this baby and thought, 'Here's my kid. I created him. But the money I'm going to spend on him, I could have spent on a Lamborghini.'"

The experts have their own terminology for this dad's way of thinking. Blankenhorn calls it "expressive individualism," our culture's emphasis on personal fulfillment and freedom at the expense of commitment to family and community. This "me-firstism," he argues, "dovetails with today's tendency to discount the role of fathers, to turn them into superfluous check-writers."[12]

If Patriarchy Is Passé, Who Am I as a Father?

Most men I talk with genuinely want to be good fathers to their children—but

Smart Idea:
If your child is off to college or on an extended trip, send along a special pillow case on which every family member has written (with permanent markers) words of love, respect, and encouragement. It's a great refuge at the end of a lonely day.

they are less sure about how to do it. In their uncertainty, many succumb to social pressures that make patriarchy passé. Our culture frequently treats fathers with a disregard or outright disrespect (in part because so many fathers have failed to meet the needs of their children). Society tells fathers in numerous ways that we are nearly unnecessary to the well-being of our children. Why else do so many fathers disengage with such apparent ease from their children? More than ninety percent of divorced dads are not in regular contact with their children a year later. Nineteen out of twenty single-parent families are headed by women.

• **Mr. Mom.** It does not surprise me that men have reacted in various ways against this disregard. One reaction is what I call the "Mr. Mom" approach: Dad takes on domestic duties, traditionally done by women, in an attempt to find himself as a father. It is humorous in movies—but when fathers are busy trying to be assistant mothers, who provides what only fathers can give their children? Mr. Mom simply isn't the answer, contends psychologist and author Jerrold Lee Shapiro. Fathers are more than pale imitations of mothers. "If you become Mr. Mom," he writes, "the family has a mother and an assistant mother. That isn't what good fathers are doing today."[13]

Not that a father should scorn housework. There needs to be an equitable division of labor to take care of the home and your children's needs. Merely helping out in domestic duties, however, does not fulfill your role as a father.

• **Mr. Money Bags.** Neither is the "Mr. Money Bags" reaction adequate. Such fathers act on the cultural mandate that, if nothing else, they must provide for their children. They define their fatherhood primarily in financial terms. After all, isn't it their duty to provide their children with the material possessions necessary to achieve the American Dream? So they pursue careers that give their children everything they "need"—and many of those professional or executive careers are notorious for denying fathers time with their family.

"After those at the bottom of society," believes Cornell University family expert Urie Bronfenbrenner, "the second most threatened group are those at the top, those who are supposed to be the leaders of the world—the college graduates who are having children at the start of their careers."[14] These children are left with "quality time," Myron Magnet writes in *Fortune*, "which means little time, from parents, and with what Amitai Etzioni calls 'quality phone calls': 'Honey, I won't be home. I love you.' Though not neglect in intent, this can turn out to be neglect in effect."[15]

Beyond what it doesn't do for your children, putting all your energy and time into the career basket can set you up for an identity crisis if your career is derailed. In the present economic climate, it's tough just to hold your ground, not to mention to stay on top of your career. Many who make long-term commitments to their companies, thinking thereby to cement themselves into a secure career, are devastated when their companies peel them off in corporate down-sizing. Decades of hard work and sacrifice for that coveted, supposedly tenured slot in middle management goes down the drain when such men find themselves out of a job. Some men go into a tailspin in these circumstances. If their identity is largely rooted in their careers, they experience an identity crisis as well as a financial crisis. And their frustration is doubled if they've sacrificed time with their families in hopes of acquiring security for them, only to lose on both counts. They end up with neither financial security nor the depth of relationship they really want with their kids.

Just as you would diversify a financial portfolio, you must balance your life choices to provide security and satisfaction in family relationships.

• **Mr. Outta Here.** A third reaction to society's disregard of fatherhood is "Mr. Outta Here," in which a father calls the bluff of the feminist philosophy. "You don't need me? Fine! Try getting along without me altogether." Such absentee fathers have proved their point, tragically, that children can't get along just fine without them.

More proof:

- **Fatherless daughters are 111 percent more likely to have children as teenagers.**
- **Fatherless daughters are 164 percent more likely to give birth to an illegitimate child.**
- **Fatherless daughters are ninety-two percent more likely to fail in their own marriages.**
- **Fatherless men are thirty-five percent more likely to experience marital failure.**
- **Fatherless children are twice as likely to drop out of high school.**
- **Fatherless children are failing school not because they are intellectually or physically impaired, but because they are emotionally incapacitated.**

Smart Idea:
On your next family car trip, give each child a responsibility to manage—purchasing gas, cleaning the windshield, throwing out trash, directing roadside stretching games, etc. Devote thirty minutes of each hour to a good book on tape.

- In schools across the nation, principals are reporting a dramatic rise in aggressive, acting-out behavior, especially among boys who live in single-parent homes.
- Fatherless children are fifty percent more likely to have learning disabilities.
- Fatherless children are from 100 to 200 percent more likely to have emotional and behavioral problems according to The National Center on Health Statistics.
- Fatherless young adults are twice as likely to need psychological help.
- Fatherless sons are 300 percent more likely to be incarcerated in state juvenile institutions.
- Seventy percent of all young men incarcerated in the U.S. come from fatherless homes.
- Fatherless daughters are fifty-three percent more likely to get married in their teenage years.
- The most reliable predictor of crime is neither poverty nor race, but growing up fatherless.
- More than seventy percent of all juveniles in state reform institutions come from fatherless homes.

"This trend of fatherlessness," says David Blankenhorn, founder of the Institute for American Values, "is the most socially consequential family trend of our generation."[16]

Creating a New Definition of Yourself as a Father

None of these reactions—Mr. Mom, Mr. Money Bags, or Mr. Outta Here—meet the needs of children or fulfill your own inner longing to father in a satisfying way. We must create our own definition of fathering that acknowledges cultural realities yet still allows us to regain whatever ground we've lost with our children.

I had been writing my fathering newsletter (then titled *Dads Only*) for several years when I thought one day, *I wonder what the word* father *means?* Among the variety of meanings *father* has, these two definitions leaped off the dictionary page: A father is "the source" and "that from which one derives significance."

A father is certainly a child's biological source, as is the mother, the moment sperm meets ovum. If you provided the source of life for a child, you are a father. Period. You no longer have the option to be or not to be a father. The only choice you have now is how you will manage your role and responsibility to your children.

A Father Gives Significance to His Child's Life

As the second definition of *father* suggests, children acquire their sense of significance largely from how their fathers (biological or adopted) respond to them. Particularly in our culture, mothers are expected to be deeply involved in their children's lives—with the result that children grow up with the cultural message that dads are *not* as deeply involved in a child's routine day as moms are. The social message is that a father's involvement with his children is much more optional than a mother's.

Yet this damaging cultural assumption actually works *for* fathers, because when a father gets involved with his child's school functions, for example, the perceived impact is stronger. Considering the social bias against significant fathering, a father's affirming remarks to his child—"You are valuable . . . You are a worthwhile person . . . I respect and appreciate these qualities about you"—hit home with added force. I've noticed that when kids use the phrase "My dad . . ." there is often a special pride in the inflection. And the older we grow, the more we value those things our fathers taught us, even above the skills or knowledge we learned from others.

On the other hand, I have never met individuals rejected or abandoned by their fathers who did not at sometime question their own worth or significance. One way or another, they all doubt that they could be special if their own fathers didn't see them as special.

Defying the Cultural Definitions

We are fathers in a society that loves to laud the flag, motherhood, and apple pie. Our culture esteems the successful businessman, although he may be a disaster as a father. On the other end of publicity, editors write headlines about deadbeat dads and make hard copy out of fathers who abuse their children.

Few kudos, however, are handed out to men who ran businesses, yet who excelled in fathering. The dad who puts his children ahead of his job may be quietly belittled or held back on a "daddy track," while colleagues are promoted who neglect the needs of their families

Smart Idea:

Here's how to put your child in the news when she wins an honor or does something interesting. Write a brief account of the event; then take it (with photo) to the feature, sports, business, or religion editor of your community paper. Even if the event wasn't spectacular, the boost in your child's self-esteem will be.

in order to put in long hours on the job. These are tough cultural values to resist.

You and I father in a culture whose dominant paternal images moved from "Father Knows Best" to Homer Simpson and Al Bundy, from "Ozzie and Harriet" to Ozzy Osbourne. Where once "Leave it to Beaver" children revered their fathers, sit-com characters—especially those of the seventies and eighties—publicly humiliated their dads. For thirty years or so now, fathers have been regularly portrayed in much of the broadcast media as inept, stupid, bumbling, vulgar, or harmlessly irrelevant (as former vice president Dan Quayle dared to condemn in his comments about the TV single-parent Murphy Brown).

Yet about the time this decade began, fathering became a hot topic in publishing, television, and movies. Fatherhood was the June 18, 1993, *Time* cover story. Not too long ago Bill Cosby's *Fatherhood* became one of the best-selling books of all time. Bookstore shelves are laden with books on fathering and men's issues. Before and after the seventies- and eighties-era TV programs with negative father images come reruns of Bill Cosby's character Cliff Huxtable. And then there is the critically and popularly acclaimed "Home Improvement," whose nineties' dad asserts his high-horse powered masculinity while also lovingly staying involved with his children. Movies such as *Hook, Field of Dreams, Boyz N the Hood,* and *A River Runs Through It* reflect the deep father-hunger of our generation. You also see paternal sacrifice and love displayed in distinct masculine terms in *Patriot Games,* in which a father risks his life to protect his wife and daughter.

In short, the pendulum appears to be swinging back toward acceptance if not outright applause of fathers.

Even outside the entertainment industry are positive changes. The Men's Movement gives us a forum for discussing and reclaiming our lost masculine influence on our children. Robert Bly, Sam Keen, and other prominent voices exalt fathering and encourage men to embrace their responsibilities to their children. A couple decades ago fathers began returning to the delivery room to be present at, and now assist in, the birth of their children. Now ninety percent of fathers are present at the birth of their children—instead of pacing in the waiting room, as their dads did in the fifties.[17] Birth participation is significant in that it creates a strong father-child bond early on. The jury's still out, though, on whether a father's presence at birth strengthens his commitment to the fathering task throughout the child's life.

The 1990s: The Decade of the Dad

A business friend in the office next to mine brought me a *Playboy* article entitled, "The Decade of the Dad." In this social commentary, Asa Baber offered his personal reaction to the way society has dishonored fathers.

> In our culture, the father has always been seen as a dispensable item. Portrayed as either a tyrant or a wimp, prejudiced against in divorce and child-custody actions, viewed in the media as an unnecessary appendage, considered unqualified to be included in the enormous question of abortion, available to be sent to war but rarely honored or accepted in times of peace, the father in America has been toyed with and excluded, endured and banished, mocked and misinterpreted.[18]

The heart of Baber's argument is this: Your dissatisfaction with the culture's restricting the scope of your fathering can be the fire in your belly that compels you to reclaim and deepen your fathering passions.

Once we decide to reject the images of fathering handed us by our culture, we can translate our sincere intentions into actions that play out in our decisions about career, lifestyle, and scheduling. In each decision we will lose in one area to gain in another; the fact is, we live in a society that forces us to choose between career advancement and deepening relationships with our children. So we manage this daily dilemma the best we can, trying to keep a healthy balance between work and our relationships with those who motivate us to work for their well-being.

What often energizes me to choose my kids instead of my work is the fact that I get only one shot at my kids. My kids will be two years old and six and ten and twelve only once in my lifetime. If I am not there to enjoy that moment, I miss forever the opportunity of shaping a memory. Sure, it's difficult to hang on to this perspective. But when I do, it empowers me to make more balanced decisions.

Answer Cultural Myths with Truth

The truth is this:

- **You are a father if you have given life to a child or if you have**

Smart Idea:
Write a letter to your soon-to-be-born child (or create an audio cassette). Express your joy, anticipation, and hopes for the child—and your commitment to fathering. Then tuck it away in your safe-deposit box to be pulled out and read again on the child's twelfth birthday.

assumed that responsibility through remarriage or adoption. As a father, your importance lies in your role and in your responsibility to each of your children.

- As a father, you have inherent power in the lives of each of your children. Your only choice is if you will use your power for good or ill.
- You powerfully and directly impact your children whenever you are absent from loving involvement in their lives. Although a mother can care for a child's needs, a mother cannot be a father. If you are not there for your kids, they will eventually pay a heavy toll for your absence.
- By far the most valuable thing you can give your children is a loving relationship with you, their father. The material possessions you provide are of secondary importance.
- It is *never* too late to do what is right.
- You can find success and fulfillment as a father.

You can design a winning strategy for fathering, even amid current cultural influences to the contrary. This book explains one way to simplify the demands of the job; it works for me, though I am no perfect father. As you grasp the five key habits of a smart dad, you can win at fathering—and your children win as well.

2

Cruise Control
The Power of Your Habits

"Dad, you're going the wrong way," a young voice said from the back seat. Sure enough, I was headed for the school, not toward the park for the morning's soccer practice.

"You're right, David. Force of habit, I guess." I felt a little foolish as I nosed back into the driveway to turn around.

I'm sure you've experienced lapses like this hundreds of times—moments when the force of habit prompts you to do or say the wrong thing.

Habit is a powerful force—and the key to success as a father. Habits are like cruise control: When properly set for the driving conditions, habits add ease and pleasure to the trip.

Furthermore, your habits inevitably drive you to whatever life destinations for which they've been set. So to become an effective and consistent father, any life changes I make must be made at the level of my habits. In fact, if you can make habits out of the five characteristics of smart fathering I will explore in this book, you will not have to continually struggle to be a good father. It will become second nature to you, as natural as reading the newspaper in the morning or turning on the car radio as you drive to work.

Making these five fathering habits part of your life will shape a legacy worth passing on to your children and grandchildren.

Habits: Life's Shorthand

Indeed, we are creatures of habit. When we get up in the morning, how we brush our teeth, even how we dry off after a shower—these and hundreds of other routines are prompted and guided by habit. Gratefully so. Life would be considerably more difficult if we had to decide anew every day about each of those mundane duties.

We even think in patterns laid down by habit. Researchers who study artificial intelligence (for the purpose of programming computers to think like people) have noted that we use hundreds of "scripts" as a basis for thinking. These scripts are a kind of generic story line we have composed in our heads that direct us into certain behavior in a particular situation.

No longer, for example, must you consciously think about appropriate behavior when you meet a stranger in a social situation. Somewhere along the line, you've probably programmed yourself to offer a handshake, introduce yourself, and attempt at least a little conversation of mutual interest. Such routines and internal scripts leave your mind free to grapple with matters of life that require fresh thought and decisive action.

Habits by definition are repetitive and cumulative. As you carry out an action in the same way day after day, you reap the cumulative effect of that habit. Habits of exercise and habits of eating prove this point. If you top off lunch every day with ice cream, the cumulative effect will eventually register on your bathroom scale. Similarly, the sure route to permanent, long-term weight loss is changing your eating or exercise habits. Drastic measures for short periods of time produce results of about the same duration. But dramatic changes in your health and weight can be effected by adopting a few good eating and exercise habits and repeating them until you see the cumulative effect. (Researchers say that if those who regularly drink two-percent milk switch to one-percent milk, they can lose ten pounds in a year—from that single change of habit.)

So take a careful look at your fathering habits and ask yourself if you need to adjust anything at this powerful level of habit. It's critical for obtaining long-term results. Even a single, small positive change of habit will reap its cumulative effect. It is your *habitual* fathering activities that impact your children most significantly, because they play out in your relationships over the many decades of your lifetime.

Anatomy of a Habit

Because habits are so powerful and indeed tough to change, let's look deeper. Every habit has four components: *desire, directions, diligence*, and *destination*. Understanding the interplay between these can help you evaluate habits that affect your fathering and guide you in making changes.

We may be creatures of habit, but we are *not* mere creatures. We are set apart from other animals by our ability to assess our lives, estimate the results of our decisions and actions, then choose what track to follow. With diligence, we can let habit take us along the track until we reach the destination we visualized in the first place. Desire, directions, diligence, and destination interact to form habits.

1. DESIRE →   → 4.DESTINATION
2. DIRECTIONS → 3. DILIGENCE

First, I will never form a habit unless I can connect it to something I *desire*. (This is why you fail when you try to change a habit to please someone else.) Once you have the desire, it takes accurate *directions* to lead you toward whatever *destination* you've chosen. You carry out the directions with *diligence*—sticking with them until the desired *destination* is reached.

Now, to make each step in this sequence work for us who want to become smart dads.

Desire

Desire lies at the heart of habit. Each of your habits, good and bad, satisfy some desire. Some children, for example, discover that begging usually guarantees getting what they want. (You may remember the procedure working in your favor during your own childhood.) Until their folks wise up, the tykes play out the pattern for all it's worth.

No parent teaches a child to beg, but somehow kids stumble onto the habit, probably from noticing other kids use the technique. And after some trial and error, begging can become a toddler's habit—an early way of getting what he or she desires.

Even habits we regard as bad are spawned by desire. A man begins drinking to deaden emotional pain. He probably didn't consider drinking a bad habit until the cumulative negative effects began piling

Smart Thought:
How long has it been since your child has heard you say you were wrong? That you failed? Communication is enhanced when you admit your faults and errors and seek forgiveness.

up: a DUI arrest, a lost job, a wife's ultimatum. Even then, because drinking medicates some inner pain, he will probably continue his habit until it becomes more painful to drink than not to.

Desires also reveal our ability to imagine our future, our destination. When we set our minds on a desire, we have a goal. To reach those goals, we develop habits. To achieve the goal of a college degree, for instance, you acquire and practice habits that equip you to take clear lecture notes, to pass finals, and to research, write, and turn in a paper on time.

Directions

These kinds of directions are internal road maps that guide us in making decisions. Like it or not, we live our lives by following directions (despite the fact that men are constantly chided for failing to stop and ask for them). Directions are the how-to guides we use whenever we choose to do or not do something. These directions regularly take one or more of the following forms:

• **Specific instructions about how to perform a particular task.** Just as you may get out the car manual and follow step-by-step directions for adjusting the timing, as a father you read a credible book about discipline when your children's behavior needs particular attention.

• **Regulations to follow in a particular setting.** Laws govern our fathering behavior—laws that range from the ancient Ten Commandments to your state's vehicle code about infant car seats and safety belts. Obeying these laws habitually affects your safety and your child's well-being.

• **Beliefs and values.** Your belief in the sanctity of marriage and the preservation of the family—and the values that support them— affect your commitments to your wife and children. If you value hard work, discipline, order, and cleanliness, then these values express themselves in the directions you follow and the way you work at passing these values on to your children. The values and beliefs we model inevitably play themselves out in our children's feelings and behavior.

• **Principles to apply in particular situations.** In a given situation, you honor and adhere to a set of ideas that govern the way you respond. For instance, parents who believe the axiom "Children should be seen and not heard" enforce behavior quite different from the parent or teacher who believes, to the contrary, that children should be given the same respect accorded any person.

• **Your worldview.** That model in your mind of the way life works helps you interpret life's events—and is a major element in shaping the relationship you craft with your children.

Sprint or Marathon?

Your worldview, for example, determines whether you picture fathering as a sprint or a marathon. If you think of it as a sprint, you'll give little thought to long-term conditioning. You'll prepare far differently for an eighteen-year fathering sprint than for a fathering marathon.

A sprinter knows he can push himself to the limit as needed for a short period of time and win the race. Fathering as a marathon, however, requires a vastly different approach to your role. You can't just wing it. You have to run smart, run with endurance, run for the long haul. The expectations you have of yourself and the excuses you accept from yourself are different because of how you view fathering.

As you've probably guessed, it's the marathon runner rather than the sprinter that best represents a successful father. And the five key habits of smart dads that this book explains will help develop in you a father's endurance.

Architect or Farmer?

Here's another helpful direction finder: Do you see fathering as the work of an architect or of a farmer?

• **The architect.** The architect father believes that his assignment is to shape his child into the individual he should be when he grows up. Such a father sets boundaries for what he wants his child to become, what experiences and talents he wants his child to develop, and what kind of person his child should marry. An architect father feels it is his responsibility to cut away anything that may derail his child from fulfilling the father's design. Heaven help the musically gifted son whose architect father has already designed him as a running back, or the C-minus student headed enthusiastically for cosmetology school—but whose father wants a college degree for her. Architects

Smart Idea:

If you leave in the morning before your kids are up, write your affection and good wishes on some Post-It notes. Stick 'em to their bedroom door, bathroom mirror, in their shoe—even on their sandwich in their lunch bag.

chisel, hammer, and discipline their children to conform them to the ideals their architect fathers have in mind.

You may remember the movie *Dead Poets Society*, in which a boy commits suicide—thanks to a classic architect father in action.

Architect fathering is as stark and unhealthy as it sounds—and we all lapse into it at times, usually motivated by the best of intentions. It can seem to be the easiest, most direct path to your child's success.

• **The farmer.** The man who imagines his fathering role as a farmer waters, nourishes, and tends his children as they grow. He studies them to see what is growing there, what natural bents are showing up unique to her nature. He does his best to remove weeds that steal critical nourishment. He fights off pests. And he waits patiently, knowing that you can't rush the process of raising children, who need time to mature.

A farmer father accepts his children for the individuals they are, celebrating the growth he sees. He is as enthusiastic about a son talented in writing as he is about the daughter on her way to an athletic scholarship, even if he was shaped in his youth by neither writing nor athletics. (And you know how difficult it is *not* to channel your kids into the same hobbies and jobs and GPAs that worked for you in your formative years.)

A final word about directions as an element of habit. The trouble with directions is that you may follow *bad* ones, all the time believing that you're on the road to good fathering. You'll end up, of course, at a different destination than you had intended.

Diligence

After desire and direction, diligence goes into the making of a habit. By diligence I mean your commitment to repeat the required thought or action continually until it becomes a habit.

Diligence is the hallmark of a good father, who heeds Winston Churchill's famous wartime words, "Never, never, never give up!"

Habits have the force of motion. When you are used to behaving in a certain way, even if that way no longer serves your purposes, it is easier to continue the habit than change. This is why, if you want to replace a bad habit with a good one—or even a good one with a better one—you need diligence; for without diligently repeating a new habit pattern, you cannot overcome the force of previous habits.

Those who study human behavior say that if one practices a new behavior for twenty-one days, the behavior will become a habit.

Launching a new behavior, then, takes thought and determined, diligent effort. Constantly remind yourself that you are improving yourself for the sake of your children. Once the debris of your old habits is shoveled out of the way, the road before you will smooth out. And remember that the tough initial diligence you need to *begin* a new habit is the toughest part; once your habit is formed, living this new way will be a lot easier.

Destination

Your destination as a father is the legacy you leave for your children after your lifetime. Legacies aren't built in a day, nor would you want them to be. Like a spreading oak, strong and large from steady growth year by year, your fathering legacy is built layer by layer, action by action. Your legacy is a by-product of the thousands of mundane decisions you make and habits you follow in your fathering.

Want to leave a worthwhile legacy? Then make sure your fathering habits are leading you toward, not away from, the destination you chose for yourself.

Don't berate yourself for not having given much thought to fathering habits. You are not alone. Mothers have nine months during which their habit patterns are disrupted and reformed. As they adjust to the changes in their bodies, they gradually change their lifestyles and habits in preparation for the birth of a child. Becoming a father, on the other hand, seems to happen overnight, usually before you change any of your habits. Men generally change their fathering habits as a matter of choice.

So think about them now, if you haven't before. Deliberately developing good fathering habits now ensures that you won't be disappointed later. Start by answering the following questions:

Desire	→ How badly do I want to be a good father?
Directions	→ Am I going in the right direction to reach my desired destination? If not, am I willing to change direction?
Diligence	→ Am I willing to diligently practice some new ways, according to good directions until they become habits?
Destination	→ Have I thought about my destination as a father? Are my habits currently taking me where I want to go?

Are you willing to change any fathering habits that don't check out?

Make the Power of Your Habits Work for You

Though you have the power to choose your habits, you do not have the power to choose their consequences. Consequences play out as though on cruise control. "Sow a thought, reap an action," says the maxim. "Sow an action, reap a habit. Sow a habit, reap a character. Sow a character, reap a destiny."

How you think as a father determines how you act. While reading this book, for starters, you can choose to consider new ideas about fathering—new ideas that can change your direction, your level of diligence, and your destination. It's up to only you whether your powerful habits will either work for you or against you as a dad.

Small Changes over Prolonged Time

One advantage of habits: Small changes create major impacts. Want to reshape a fathering habit? Then don't make your first change a major one. Make several smaller changes; they will do just as well to steer you in the right direction and to your desired destination. Changing your habits, even in small and simple ways, dramatically changes your relationship with your children, especially as that habit plays itself out over years. Like compounding interest on your money, small investments in fathering add up.

Smart Idea: Ten-minute chats are a great bedtime habit. Choose the topic from an assortment you've written in a small notebook. Try some of these ideas: My latest dream, a fear I felt today, what I'll be like when I'm older, the _____ thing I did today, etc. Date your child's answers.

After begetting a child, which may be a man's choice, our only choice is what kind of father we will be. Fathering is a daily and lifelong process, not an assignment you psych yourself up for and "do" once and be done with it. There are no shortcuts or magic formulas—only solid principles you must incorporate into your thinking, actions, habits, and character. In those dedicated to good fathering, these habits take root and shape relationships with your children.

When Rayna was seven, her dad delighted her with a bouquet of wildflowers in a soda can. He noticed the effect of this small act of kindness, and so regularly picked wildflower bouquets throughout each spring and summer. Whenever Rayna found a bouquet of wildflowers in a soda can in her room, she immediately knew that her dad was thinking of her. Rayna is a grown woman now, the mother of her own two teenagers. And guess what? Her aging daddy still leaves an unexpected wildflower bouquet on her doorstep or kitchen counter. She says it's still one of the most significant ways her father shows his love for her.

A small action that became a habit acquired a potency far beyond the mere act itself.

Don't try making big changes in your fathering tomorrow or even next week. Start with small changes—like the five key habits of a smart dad, discussed in the next chapter—and maintain them over time. In this way you can reap a lifetime of rewards.

3

The Five Key Habits
A Fathering Model

I worked my way through college as a free-lance graphic designer, creating more book covers, corporate logos, brochures, posters,
ads, and magazine page layouts than I care to remember. The projects I really loved, though, were not these flat graphics, but three-
dimensional projects—those calling for a box or display.

Leslie—my wife, my best client, and my most rigorous critic—
has a business in which she creates, mats, and frames under glass
one-of-a-kind, personalized statements of friendship and love. She
needed a point-of-sale display to test the response to these framed
messages in retail book and gift stores. So, box knife in hand, I set
out with a sheet of cardboard to mock up a display. The trick in creating a display is to visualize how the parts fold and where tabs are
needed to tuck into slots for adequate strength and good presenta-
tion. It took three tries just to correctly cut out a single flat sheet
with side panels, tabs, and a snap-on pocket for brochures. Yet once
I had a good working model as a template, it was a breeze to make
several tight-fitting displays of the same design.

That working model was a *paradigm*:

• A paradigm is a serviceable tool that can help you understand,
visualize, and internalize what it is you want to do.

• A paradigm represents a complex set of issues in a simple way so that you can work with them.

• A paradigm pictures something for you in a way that you can remember it, and then associate that picture with truths you can apply.

• A paradigm gives you handles with which you can grasp the information, recall it to memory, and use it whenever you find the need.

A few years ago I launched a study of fathering practices in America with Chuck Aycock, another fathering activist. Our questionnaire probed fathers for how they viewed their task, how they learned what to do as fathers, how they measured success, and much more. More than two thousand in-depth questionnaires were returned by fathers reached principally through churches and religious organizations—for here, Chuck and I assumed, would be found the most conscientious and deliberate fathers.

One of the short-answer questions we asked was, "What makes a father successful?" We wanted to discover whatever key ideas American dads used as they worked to succeed at fathering. When the answers to this question were analyzed, we were surprised to discover *no statistically significant clusters*. We could only conclude that, as a group, fathers today have no *dominant* models or ideas about fathering success to guide them in their efforts. Men apparently have no broadly held understanding of what a good father does to win. The ideas expressed about fathering success were all over the map.

So I began pondering what I could do to help men formulate a useful fathering model, a model that any man could relate to, one that linked the most important ideas and critical fathering practices with something familiar to most men. This paradigm would have to showcase the key habits that lead a dad from *desire* (to be a good father), to *directions* he needs to follow with *diligence*, so that he can arrive at his desired *destination*: A positive fathering legacy for his children.

My model is an ordinary automobile wheel—not fancy, but functional. With it I can explain five foundational fathering habits that will help you visualize your role so that you can move beyond where you are to where you want to go—which, of course, is exactly what good wheels on a car do for you.

Smart Idea:
List the names of the five best dads you know. Then create an opportunity (a note, phone call, lunch together, etc.) to ask each of them these two questions: What key ideas guide you as a father? What three family activities do you most enjoy?

Fathering does not have to be a regular fight with yourself. Fathering is fundamentally a natural function—once we understand this, all we need to do is act out our role in a habitual way. Solomon, reputedly the wisest man to walk the face of the earth, understood how one's inner world shaped one's outer practice. "As a man thinks in his heart," he said, "so is he." To reshape the way you father, then, you must reshape how you perceive fathering.

An Overview of the Five Key Habits of Smart Dads

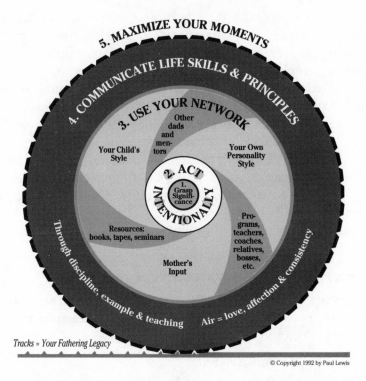

Five Key Habits of Smart Dads
FATHERING PARADIGM

5. MAXIMIZE YOUR MOMENTS

4. COMMUNICATE LIFE SKILLS & PRINCIPLES

3. USE YOUR NETWORK

Other dads and mentors

Your Child's Style

Your Own Personality Style

2. ACT INTENTIONALLY

1. Grasp Significance

Pro-grams, teachers, coaches, relatives, bosses, etc.

Resources: books, tapes, seminars

Mother's Input

Through discipline, example & teaching

Air = love, affection & consistency

Tracks = Your Fathering Legacy

© Copyright 1992 by Paul Lewis

There is a logical, inside-to-the-outside progression in this wheel model: axle, lug nuts, rim, tire, then tread. Even the *tracks* the tread leaves have significance, for they represent the fathering legacy you leave behind for your children.

Axle:
Grasping your significance as a father

The axle on which this wheel turns represents grasping your significance as a father. Any real fathering power, any clear sense of your objectives as a dad flow from this core realization. How you habitually think about fathering and yourself as a father reflects your grasp of a father's significance. If you do not perceive the inherent, intergenerational power in your role as a dad—or if your experience with your own father has distorted your sense of a father's importance—the resulting perceptions will unhealthily mark your fathering for a lifetime and beyond. All of the other habits emanate from and turn on the axle of how you grasp your significance as a father.

Lug Nuts:
Acting intentionally

The lug nuts represent your intentional actions as a father as you take responsibility for setting goals, for making commitments, for evaluating progress, for correcting your course as necessary, and for turning good intentions into actions. As lug nuts attach the wheel to the axle, so your intentional actions connect your understanding of your fathering role to what you *do* to keep your commitments to your children. The lug nuts represent being proactive as a father instead of reactive—that is, accepting your responsibility and choosing how you will father instead of merely reacting to family and fathering crises when they arise. Acting intentionally means putting yourself in a pivotal role in the home, pursuing purposeful goals, and continually evaluating where you are as a dad, making whatever corrections you need to make along the way.

Rim:
Using your primary and secondary networks

The rim represents your fathering network—specifically, primary and secondary networks. Your primary network is the human resources in your family:

- **Your own personality style.**
- **Your child's personality and abilities.**
- **The input of your child's mother.**

Your secondary network includes—

- **Other fathers and fathering mentors.**
- **Other individuals who interact with your child, such as teachers, coaches, relatives, bosses, friends, etc.**
- **Resources that strengthen your fathering insights and skills—books, tapes, seminars, etc.**

The components of this network are available to you; you simply need to use them. In the interplay of personalities in your family and among resources outside your family, there is much strength that encourages and shapes your work as a father.

Tire:
Communicating life skills and principles

Mounted on the rim sits the tire, which represents the critical life skills and principles your child must learn from you. Between birth and the time your child leaves home, your job is to raise that child to function maturely and productively in society. Your commission is to take a helpless infant and, a few short years later, release him or her to the world—grown, prepared, and functioning as a capable adult. The steel-belted plies of the tire represent your personal example and how you apply discipline—these support the life skills and principles you work to teach your children.

And just as any tire is useless unless inflated, your love, affection, and consistency is the air, which give your fathering buoyancy and a smooth ride.

Tread:
Maximizing your moments

The tire tread in this wheel paradigm represents maximizing your moments with your child. This is the element of time. The moments you spend with your children strongly impact them for life. A loving father makes his mark on sons and daughters as he spends time in relationship with them. Different tread patterns—in our analogy, different patterns of time spent with your kids—create different effects.

The amount and quality of time you spend with your child leaves its corresponding imprint. Little or no time available to a father-child relationship is like a bald tire with dangerously little grip and faint imprint.

Tire Tracks:
The fathering legacy
you leave with your child

The tracks that a tire's tread makes—memories of myriad moments spent with your child—represent the fathering legacy you leave behind. This imprint is largely shaped by the kind of life skills and

Smart Idea:
Take a poll tonight at dinner: "What's the most fun we've had as a family in the past month? In the past year? Ever?" Look for the reasons why and put a date on the calendar to do each again.

principles you select, and affected by whether these are communicated with love, affection, and consistency, whether you make good use of your network, whether you act intentionally, and how you grasp your own significance as a father.

(Beyond these fathering habits is the overarching issue of your worldview. As we'll explore more in chapter twelve, how you perceive the world works—that is, your life philosophy and religious views—will affect how you father. But more on this later.)

When these five habits are integrated and functioning together, you move down the road without having to think so much about the details of fathering. Good fathering will become for you a growing habit that influences your children's lives in an ongoing and cumulative manner.

To begin exploring the "fathering wheel" thoroughly, we must first consider the axle aspect: Your father's imprint on your life. Let's take a look . . .

4

Dad in the Rearview Mirror
Your Father's Imprint on Your Life

If you don't count high school, when watching my complexion and taking the zit count was a daily priority, I don't spend all that much time in front of mirrors. Approaching fifty as I am, I spend only the necessary minimum of time looking at myself—to shave, maybe blow dry and comb my hair, do a quick visual check of how my choice of attire really looks. Once in a while, though, I linger at the bathroom mirror, not checking for displaced hairs or overlooked patches of shaving cream, but studying my changing face and figure.

The other evening while channel surfing, I came across the Emmys—and there was Mr. Entertainment himself, Bob Hope. For ninety years old, Bob Hope looks great—but he *is* ninety. And even if you didn't notice that his gait is slow these days, you would detect those telltale changes in his posture, the subtle but unmistakable changes in the shape of his head and neck that come with aging.

It prompted me, an hour or so later, to linger in front of the hall mirror. Whipping around the corner, my youngest saw me just standing there. "What are you doing, Dad?"

I didn't know how to explain to him what I was doing. I don't entirely understand it myself. It's a jumble of vanity, self-talk, pity, pride, confusion, wonderment, and more than a little nonsense.

I can name one reason I mirror gaze like this: I'm assessing my father's legacy to me. There in the mirror I see my family's genetic heritage at work. When I'm in this frame of mind, after a long look in the mirror I can close my eyes and see the image of me as a young man and new dad—an image that bears a striking resemblance to the photo in our album downstairs of my father holding me, his new baby boy.

The baton is being passed. The legacy, both genetic and emotional, is being lived out.

Every father leaves a legacy. The imprint of your father is on your life, whether or not you think much about it. Your father left on you the marks of his tire tread, so to speak, whether positive or negative.

But what good does a knowledge of your father's legacy do for you? If your father was a good one, the imprint he left is a model for you to follow. In those ways that your dad was not what you wanted or needed—absent, for instance, just when you needed him most—you have a sterling opportunity to learn from his mistakes and father your children differently.

Recognizing your father's imprint on your life is the first step in grasping your own significance as a father. Understanding the natural power with which your father shaped your life will empower you to positively affect the life of your children.

Good, Bad, Indifferent

In 1992 the National Center for Fathering commissioned Gallup to conduct a national random sample of fathers across America. Among other questions, adults were asked what word best describes their relationship with their father. The resulting report, *The Role of Fathers in America: Attitudes and Behavior*, pointed out that seven out of ten described their relationship with their fathers in positive terms—"super," "great," "close," or "loving." Only seventeen percent described their relationship with their father in negative terms: "distant," "bad," or "nonexistent." Eight percent of those responding described their paternal relationship in neutral terms, such as "average" or "normal." Four percent did not answer.[1]

If you are one of the fortunate sons who could describe your relationship with your dad in positive terms, it's clear that your dad's good work as a father left on your life a positive fathering influence.

I think of when we lived in the Julian mountains behind San Diego, and of the tracks my Jeep Wagoneer left in new snow. If I were the first out on the road that morning, the perfect tracks revealed minute changes in the Wagoneer's direction, showed subtle changes in speed, and duplicated precisely the patterns of the tires' tread.

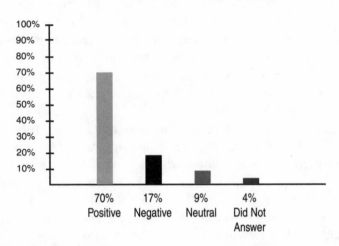

Relationship with Father
Summary of Responses By Type

70% Positive	17% Negative	9% Neutral	4% Did Not Answer

The distinct tread of an all-weather tire represents to me the influence of a father who was there for his children—an affectionate man, good role model, a man who conscientiously fulfilled his responsibilities. If this describes your father, you hardly have to think about what a good father does. You recall the moments and the feelings, and you rely on the prototype of your father.

Film actor and director Kevin Costner had this kind of relationship with his dad. In a *Parade* magazine interview, the star of *Field of Dreams* and *Dances with Wolves* says,

> Cindy and I talk a lot about raising those kids. I want them to like being with their family and doing things with us, like I did with my dad—hunting, fishing together. . . . I want them to have a dad they remember. What if I'm not around when they start learning how to drive, or not home to discipline them when they come in late? Or not home for dinner with them after work, like my dad always was? I've gotta be their parent. That's the most important thing. . . . I'm not responsible for their behavior for the

Smart Tip:
Take a tip from newlyweds. Celebrate "monthiversaries" (the day of your wedding each month) with a quiet walk together . . . renewal of your wedding vows . . . a love poem from a book . . . a sexy call from the office . . . a soda with two straws. Magic!

rest of their lives, but I have to be there for them now. To tell them when they please me and why.[2]

If you are one of the seventeen percent of this country's men who, as the Gallup poll suggests, characterizes his relationship with his father as negative, I would guess you are consciously trying hard not to pattern your life like your dad's. On some days you are pleased with your progress; other days you despair that you're caught in your father's web of inflicting pain on your kids. For some fathers, calling their dads' influence on them merely negative is putting it mildly; it's more accurate to say that their fathers ran them over, and the tread marks on their hearts are proof. No pristine, solitary tracks of a tire in new snow, but the dark skid marks of more than one hit-and-run.

The images you carry of your father may have simply made you numb. You may have no feeling and little clarity about how your father imprinted you. You acknowledge the man as your father; but once you outgrew childhood, you made your own life. Your dad's fathering style, you believe, affects you neither one way or the other.

These very feelings belonged to a successful executive whom I visited. His father left him when he was eight. Yes, he has seen his dad a few times over the years, but he got the distinct impression that the relationship means little to his father. The imprint shows in the hurt he still feels from being abandoned. Yet this dad created a new pattern of fathering to overcome the pattern of abandonment his father left him with, a pattern more noticeable the more he speaks of his own children. He has aggressively poured himself into his son and daughter, taking delight in their activities and achievements.

Men floundering in deep fathering waters, with few or no models, are not alone. This decade is witnessing what may be the first generation of Americans in which a substantial number of dads have grown up without fathers in their homes. Two years after a divorce, one study shows, more than eighty percent of the noncustodial parents—generally the fathers—have little or no steady pattern of visitation with the children.

Men learn best how to be a father by watching and imitating a good one. The most important model, of course, is their own dad. Without a good dad to guide them—and no matter how strong their desire to do a better job at fathering—boys usually grow up into fatherhood with much confusion.

So whether good, bad, or indifferent, your father left his imprint on you. His presence or absence contributed to how you see yourself and how you perform a father's role. Recognizing and dealing with your father's imprint on you, particularly if it has been negative, is a prerequisite to acquiring the five key habits of smart dads.

Then, by accentuating the positive in your father's relationship with you and processing the negative, you unleash a power and freedom in you for shaping your own fresh fathering style.

The Legacy of a Bent Axle

If, as my automobile-wheel analogy suggests, the axle represents your sense of significance as a father, a destructive relationship between you and your dad is like a bent axle.

Collisions can damage axles, although you may not know it at first. The worst thing you can do is assume the axle is okay and mount a new wheel on that axle. If the axle *is* bent, the car will never drive exactly right. The wheel and tire will endure extra stress because of the distortion. The tire and any or all parts of the wheel assembly will wear out far more quickly than normal.

If you were deeply wounded in relationship with your father, you have been damaged at the core of your being. Little builds a man's sense of his significance and establishes it more deeply than to be fully accepted and loved by his own father. If your childhood relationship with your father (or a stepfather or other father figure) was bent or distorted, and you simply get on with your own fathering without recognizing and undoing the damage, you might as well mount a new tire on a bent axle.

If you still doubt that your dad could influence your own fathering as much as I claim, consider these:

• **Your father (and mother) imprinted you genetically.** Research has left no doubt that heredity shapes us. Body type, height, weight, hair color, eye color, skin color, facial features, abilities, disabilities— they are all patterned directly after the genetic code given you by your biological father and mother. Your genetic code also determines some diseases, weaknesses, and susceptibility to certain conditions, such as depression or alcoholism.

• **Your relationship with family members, including your father, teaches you how to relate to others.** In other

Smart Idea:
"Monday Night Interviews" keep kids talking. Make a 20-minute recording of their answers to your reporter-style questions about weekend activities, the day at school, pets, hobbies, friends, dreams, latest fads, etc. Send a copy to grandparents, and archive the original.

words, heredity is only part of the story. As much as genetics, how you were raised can contribute to a pattern of behavior that carries to future generations. The relationships and family interaction of your childhood created a familial pattern that, if good, you can build on; if the pattern is unhealthy, on the other hand, you need to break that pattern. Although you are not *destined* to repeat a pattern you were raised with, you are *likely* to pass on to your kids familial patterns of relating—unless you take deliberate steps to break them.

  • **The relationship with your dad in particular affects how you react to your children—particularly during emotionally charged moments, when instinct takes over.** All fathers catch themselves doing, responding, or saying the very things they vowed they would never visit on their children.

Tired from an especially difficult day at the office, a dad I know of came home to the evening's first demand: a drink of water for his two-year-old daughter, who not only immediately spilled it, but fell down and hit her head, hard, on the kitchen floor. The four-year-old son, meanwhile, unaware of his sister's trauma, continued goofing around to get his father's attention. Emotionally worn before he walked in the door, standing in a puddle of water holding a toddler who was, for all he knew, seriously hurt—in the confusion and stress of the moment, he cut loose. "Stop acting like such an idiot!" he shouted at the boy—who dissolved into tears on the spot, then turned and ran to his room.

After the chaos subsided, the father reflected on his outburst. When he was a child, he remembered, his dad had routinely called him an idiot. He vowed he would never call any of his children an idiot. Yet, in a moment when his resistance was down, the words had tumbled out anyway.

  • **Unhealthy ways of relating tend to be repeated in generation after generation.** The Old Testament chronicles generations of family life, and it's fascinating to see what the prophets call the "sins of the fathers" consistently appearing in the next two and three generations—even as far as the tenth generation. It is common now to discuss the persistence of generational patterns in terms of dysfunctional family systems. The "sins" of alcoholism, drug addiction, and abuse—sexual, emotional, and physical—are characteristically repeated by the victims of such behavior.

Investigate the Legacy You've Inherited

Because your relationship with your father influences how you father your children, you need to examine your legacy. Here's one way to get a handle on your fathering circumstances:

• **Complete a family genogram with as much information about your family tree as you can get your hands on.** Emotional or behavioral patterns—alcoholism, depression, abandonment, divorce, abuse, suicides, raging tempers—among your ancestors affect your life, including your fathering. The appearance of such patterns in your family tree does not mean you are destined to repeat them, but only that the odds are greater that the trait will surface, in some form, in your family. By the same token, you can trace—and reinforce—the *positive* family strengths of your ancestors, virtues that you want to preserve and pass on to your children.

FAMILY GENOGRAM

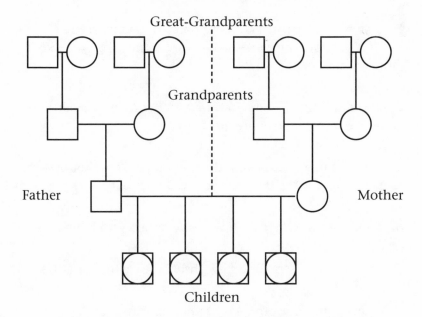

Fill in family names and shade the square or circle of any person who struggled with addiction.

• **Answer seven quick questions.** Men are generally most comfortable taking an intellectual approach to their father's impact on their lives. These seven questions may help get you out of your head and into your heart. You probably have deep feelings about your father, but you've found ways to distance yourself from your feelings. If you let yourself answer these questions honestly, you just may touch some feelings you haven't felt since childhood.

You may stir up some painful memories, but there's gold in this pain. Identifying powerful feelings from your childhood is the first step in dealing with them, which in turn can equip you with positive fathering habits for your own children.

So grab a pencil (really, get up and get one; your responses are more effective if you write them instead of merely answering in your head). Then write a brief, off-the-cuff response to the seven quick questions that follow.

Seven Quick Questions

1. How often have you and your father communicated during the last twelve months?

2. On a scale of 1 to 10 (1 being poor, 10 being excellent), rate your father's performance as a dad, compared to what you expected or wanted in a father.

3. By the same scale, rate your own fathering performance so far, compared to your fathering ideals.

4. Choose three words—or a three-word phrase—that best characterize the relationship between you and your dad.

5. Complete this sentence: "I wish my father would say to me—"

6. Complete this sentence: "I wish I could say to my father—"

7. What is your most frequent fathering frustration?

Among hundreds of confidential responses I have received to these questions, I see the following responses over and over again to the question, "Finish this statement: I wish my father would say to me—":

- You did a good job.
- You are doing well.
- Well done.
- I am proud of you.
- I respect you.
- I love you.
- I respect your life's work.
- I appreciate you.

Other responses, not so frequent, included these:

- Whatever you do, do it well. (Instead of "Do what I want you to do.")
- It's okay not to be perfect.
- Confidence counts. Don't be discouraged.
- I think these things really matter.
- I'm sorry about how things were at times.
- I wish our relationship had worked out better.
- I wish we had spent more time together.
- I want to do something with you.
- Let's try to get close.
- Let's pray together.
- I'll never drink again.
- Nothing.
- I'm back.
- I'm sorry I wasn't a good leader when you were young.
- I'm sorry for the pain.
- I don't get angry anymore.
- Let's talk.

Other men finished the statement "I wish my father would say to me—" a little differently. They talked:

- About their own problems growing up.
- About how much their parents mean to them.
- About their spiritual faith.

Clearly, father hunger is prevalent among men today. Acknowledging it is no

Smart Tip:
A "Saturday Box" will encourage kids to make a habit of putting things away. Agree that toys, clothes, and other items left laying around may be put in the Saturday Box— a big box in the garage or service porch—and cannot be retrieved until Saturday, no matter what. (The rule applies to you too, Dad!)

sign of weakness, either, but a positive and powerful move toward self-fulfillment and confidence in your manhood.

Alan is the eldest of three children; he has two sisters. His father was a hard-working career man in a large company. The family was well cared for, but Alan can't remember his dad ever taking much time to play ball, go fishing, or show up at his football games.

His dad helped Alan get through college, and the new graduate began a career in banking, landing eventually in mortgage lending. After fourteen years of being pushed around by corporate merger and downsizing games, Alan launched his own mortgage brokering company. It was both an economic move up and an opportunity to be his own boss.

It was on Thanksgiving that Alan's folks, now retired, visited him and his family. Sitting around the pool at the motel where his parents were staying, glass of iced tea in hand, Alan began giving his dad an update on the new business. As he talked, Alan noticed his dad nodding off—right in the middle of his son's explanations.

His dad could not have hurt Alan more if he had plunged a dagger into Alan's chest.

Over the next few months, Alan made occasional weekend trips to his parents' home in Phoenix, hoping to receive the honest expressions of approval and respect he deeply wanted from his dad. On the first two trips, the response was the same: As Alan reported the success of his business, more often than not his dad would counter by mentioning the superior successes of one of Alan's childhood friends. More and better was the inexorable quest of Alan's dad. When Alan pushed him, his dad only got frustrated. "What more do you want from me, Alan?" he said angrily. "I don't understand. I provided for you. You always had everything you needed. I got you through college. What's the problem? What do you want from me?"

On Alan's third trip home, he tried again. This time when he confronted his dad with his feelings, the dam broke, the tears and words of approval flowed, and their father-son relationship began healing.

If you uncover issues to resolve with your father, you aren't alone. To the contrary, you're in the majority. In a random survey conducted for the National Center for Fathering by the Gallup poll organization, three in five adults agreed that "most people have unresolved problems with their fathers."[3]

How to Resolve a Poor Childhood Relationship with Your Father

Once you recognize unresolved issues in your relationship with your father—issues that, in your mind, diminish your significance—you can begin to resolve them, even if your father is not available, has passed away, or is unwilling to work it out with you.

Here's how to start:

1. Recognize the Problem

It is not unusual for a child to create an idealized view of his father, especially in cases where abuse has occurred. The child learned to pretend that whatever his father requested of the child was okay; after all, to do otherwise was not allowed. Your idealized view of your father may have helped you cope as a child, but you are no longer a child. You now have the freedom and the power to be honest about your relationship with your dad.

So start by being honest about the history of events. What really happened in your relationship with your father? What are the facts? If these are not clear to you, ask your brothers or sisters or others who were there at the time to help you reconstruct what happened.

Next, be honest about your feelings. I suggest writing them out (the point of a pencil prods you to be clear and more precise than you would otherwise), putting phrases and stories down on paper so you can review your thoughts and sort out the emotions. What hurt you? What were your disappointments? What are the fears and emotional scars that remain from the hurts you received from your father? Start some sentences with "I am angry because—," "I am angry when—," "I feel angry when I recall—," and so on.

If you were forbidden in childhood to feel or express anger, it may be difficult for you to express it now. But today as an adult, if you feel angry, dare to be honest about it—and about whatever else you hold in your heart. Take time to write about any sadness or deep regrets for what did or didn't happen during your childhood.

"At first I wrote mainly about the present and the frustrations I felt with work and love," wrote Sam Osherson in his book *Finding Our Fathers*. "But then came memories and feelings about the past, about my childhood and adolescence, my

Smart Idea:
Take your appointment book to dinner tonight, show each family member your schedule for the next two weeks, and write in a date with each of them at the times you agree on. Then turn to the two weeks after that, and do it again.

mother and father. When my difficult and conflict-riddled relation-ship with my father came into focus, I realized that I had found the man I had been searching for, the father who, more by his absence than his presence, was the key to the sense of emptiness and vul-nerability in my life. The journal helped me to gradually expand and enliven my relationship with my father, and to appreciate the loving and caring sides of him that had been there all along."[4]

Consider even writing a letter to your dad. Whether or not you send the letter, it's still useful to write it.

After you are honest about events and about your feelings, then talk with someone you trust—a friend who is willing to listen and affirm your right to feel whatever you may feel. (This is especially useful if your father has died, or if you cannot talk with him.)

This brings us to the next step in the process of resolving your father's impact upon you.

2. See Your Father in a New Light

• **Consider the relationship your dad had with his own father.** Your grandfather's influence on your dad had a lot to do with how well or poorly your father related to you and your sib-lings. How much do you know about your grandfather's perfor-mance as a dad? Find out somehow—from conversations with your grandmother, uncles or aunts, even with your father himself—about your father's history with *his* father. Any similarities between how your father was treated and how he treated *you*?

Visualizing your father as a son can help you empathize with his behavior toward you. The father of a woman I know regularly hollered and even screamed at her as a child, and seldom spoke to her in a civil tone of voice. Her father's tirades, of course, troubled her throughout childhood and adolescence.

He rarely spoke of his own father, and she never thought to ask—until after her father died, when the woman began asking rela-tives about her father's childhood. When she discovered that he was raised by two deaf parents, she could objectively evaluate her father's difficulty monitoring his volume. She did not excuse his verbal abuse totally, but the uncovered context helped her see her father in a more positive light.

• **Presume your father once had high hopes for you and for himself as a father.** A child naturally tends to assume—wrongly—that any deficiency in his or her relationship with a parent is the child's own fault. So try to figure out what may have disillusioned your father or dashed the hopes most dads feel. If your father withdrew or distanced himself from you, chances are that the cause was not you but pressures in his own life. Do your best to uncover what it was during your childhood that overwhelmed him or made him feel unable to be the kind of father he once hoped he could be.

• **Empathize and understand what influenced your father's behavior.** A man told me he resented the time his father had spent away from the family during a long military career. One day the adult son asked his father why he had chosen a military career in the first place.

His dad's response was unexpected. "It was all I was sure I could do to provide for you all," he replied. He too regretted the years away from his family, he explained, but he felt that the military was the best choice, given his limited education and marketable skills.

When he put himself in his father's shoes, this son acquired an entirely new perspective of his dad. There was a connection between the two that had not been there before, for the adult son, too, was feeling the same tension between providing sufficient money for and sufficient time with his family. The son was also in a business that demanded much time away from his children, yet it provided adequate security for his family. Limited like his father in education and transferable skills, he reluctantly chose to stay in a job that kept him from his family more than he liked.

Only when he empathized with his father did this man finally recognize the tremendous love his father really had for him. For decades he had interpreted his father's absence as lack of love. Now as a man, he well understood the inner agonizing fathers endure as they are forced to choose how they will express their love for their children.

3. Presume Your Father Craved the Love and Respect of His Children

What man does not intuitively crave the love and respect of his children? Some men have disavowed this deep desire for some reason. One seventy-year-old man I know of has entirely lost contact with his children. He never speaks of them. I didn't even know he had children until a mutual friend mentioned that he had three grown children. After a brush with death, he was asked if he had contacted his children. He

Smart Idea:
Reminisce with your kids about your own childhood favorites: games, toys, teachers, playmates, foods, pets, clothes, candy, vacations, hobbies, subjects in school, adult friends, TV shows, rewards for good behavior, etc. Recall your least favorites, too.

instantly became defensive. "No, I don't care about them, and they wouldn't care about me." I don't believe a word of it. The man spent many years as an alcoholic and probably destroyed his relationship with those children. I suppose he is so certain they would reject him that he has tried to reject them first. I find it very sad to think that this man, and others may go to the grave without ever receiving the love and respect they so desperately crave.

4. You Can Give Your Father What He Will Not or Cannot Ask For

And that's forgiveness. Forgiveness cleans the slate and lets you start fresh as a father, regardless of what your father has done or failed to do for you. To forgive is to identify the wrongs done against you, recognize that they were wrong, and admit how hurt you really are.

Then you let go of what has become the burden of making your father pay for his wrongs or make it up to you. You draw a line between the past and the future; you stop using the past to excuse you from taking full responsibility for your life. Whatever the injury received from your father, you choose to leave vengeance in God's hands. A sincere apology from your dad would be wonderful—but even if your father cannot or will not see his errors or ask for your forgiveness, you can still forgive him.

And that forgiveness is your purchase order for a new axle.

His father's alcoholism ravaged his childhood, I heard a speaker recall for his audience. Before the man arrived home on payday, he had spent it all at the bar. It was no surprise when, after a childhood of shame and poverty, the son cut off all contact with his father as soon as he could. But years later someone warned him that, until he let go of the grudge he carried against his father, he would never be free. The friend suggested he recall one thing for which he could thank his father, and then express his love and gratitude for that one thing.

It took more than a few moments, but the adult son finally recalled one Christmas when his father saved enough money—he even worked a second job for a while—to buy his boy a bicycle he desperately wanted.

Later, doing his best to keep this and only this picture in his memory for at least a few minutes, the son wrote his dad a letter—not to rehearse his father's well-documented wrongs (they had covered that territory many times already), but to put aside his long list of grievances and instead express his love and appreciation for the only act of kindness he could remember from his father. He didn't know where his estranged father lived, so he mailed the letter to a relative he hoped would forward it.

It wasn't too long before the son got a phone call. His father was alone and terminally ill in the hospital—but he wanted to see his son. There at a hospital bedside, the boy received from his father the apology he had wanted, a weeping penitence for the mess the old man had made of his own life, for the wounds he had inflicted on his son. Much of what both of them had longed to say and longed to hear passed between them that day.

Shortly after that visit, the father died. His son has no regrets about his choice to forgive his dad—a choice that gave him power over his past.

Theirs was a happy ending. But there was no guarantee that the father would respond at all to his son's attempt to end the estrangement. You take similar risks when you try to resolve your relationship with your father; you know too well the hazards, perhaps, of merely communicating directly with him. So weigh the risks against the rewards before you bare your feelings to your father. If the risks seem too great to you, then wait a while until you feel comfortable to proceed.

What if you simply cannot find it in yourself to forgive your father? The freedom you will experience by forgiving him is worth seeking the professional help you may need to assist you. In any case, don't plow ahead before you take enough time to work through your own feelings first.

Most men carry inside them words they want desperately to say to their fathers, but can't for one reason or another. Men attending Dads University courses gave the following responses most often when asked to complete the sentence, "I wish I could say to my father—"

- I love you.
- I appreciate you.
- I am glad you are my dad.
- I am proud of you.
- Thanks.
- Thanks for all your work.

Other responses include these:

- I'm not always right.
- I understand how things were for you.

Smart Idea:
Preschoolers and grandkids love to wiggle through the holes you create when you lay on the floor and join your hands into a circle, raise your knees, bow your legs to join the bottoms of your feet, arch your back, etc. Add some traps and tickles.

- You've done a great job—keep it up.
- You taught me a lot.
- I wish I'd tried harder.
- I wish things could have been better between us.
- Good job, Dad. Thanks.
- Thanks for doing the best you knew how.
- What are your feelings about us, your family?
- I wish we weren't so competitive.
- Thanks for being you.
- I want to be like you, Dad.
- Thanks for having me.
- Let's pray together.
- I respect your life's work.
- I wish you had been there.
- I'm sorry.
- You need to get your life together.
- Nothing.
- I forgive you.
- Accept me for who I am.
- I need you.
- Wake up and smell the roses.
- Let's talk. I need your advice.
- I've got my own life.
- Let's go somewhere together.
- Please include me.
- Try to be a better grandparent than you were a father.

You cannot change what happened in the past, but you can go forward with your own children—beginning with your attempts to reconcile with or speak your heart to your father. You can't do anything about your ancestors, but you can do a lot about your descendants.

You can learn from your father's failures as well as from his achievements, and you can put experience, good or bad, to good use.

In our survey of fathers we asked, "What was the most significant thing your own father did with you?" We grouped the responses logically and added the headings.

The most significant thing my father did with me was—

Taught skills/values

- Taught me how to work.
- Taught me how to be honest with myself and others.

- Taught me responsibility and love.
- Taught me that the most important thing in life is one's relationship with God.

Affirmation/encouragement/support

- Supported me in activities and interests.
- He loved me and supported me in all that I did.
- Supported me in everything I did.
- Continually praised me and said how much he loved me.
- Was always available and stood by me.

Modeled a behavior/characteristic

- Set a good example.
- Set a proper example of fathering.
- Provided a model of leadership.

Shared activity

- Worked in the yard together and learned the names of plants, birds, etc.
- Spent time with me fishing and doing other things.
- Played ball with me when I was younger.
- Took time to do with me what I wanted to do.
- Spent time with me in my hobby.

Answer the question for yourself: What was the most significant thing your own father did with you? And consider how your children may one day answer this question. Their response will reflect the decisions you are making today.

A Fathering Legacy

As your father left you a legacy, you also will leave one for your children. When you recognize the imprint of your father on you, you now have a chance to choose your legacy.

Smart Idea:
Play Balloon Volleyball in the living room on a moment's notice. Lay a center line on the floor with masking tape, then two back lines—and maybe tape between two chair backs for a net. Blow up a balloon, review the rules, and play!

In one parenting program, the men are asked to write obituaries for themselves—as their children would write them.[5] This exercise cuts quickly to the bottom line—when all the fluff and glitter are stripped away, what *is* my personal bottom line? I, too, will occasionally ask a group of fathers, "What epitaph would you like to see on your tombstone?"

I hope my tombstone will read, "He was famous with his kids." What greater validation of my worth in life could there be than to have the respect of my children, who had lived with me for much of their lives and who knew me best?

It may be too late for your father to alter his legacy, but it's not too late for you. You choose and build your legacy one day at a time, one decision at a time. If you are determined to be a good dad—whether by following the good imprint your father left for you, by overcoming the negative effects of a bad relationship with your father, or by finding an effective model to follow because your father was absent—in any case, you can be a good dad.

Now for the five key habits of fathering that allow you to create the kind of legacy you want to leave for your children. It begins with another view of the axle, where fathering power begins.

5

Habit One:
Grasping Your Significance
The Axle

A crisp wind was at their backs, and a low afternoon sun flushed the white sails of the sloop as it heeled to starboard. Laughter and thumbs-up signals animated the interchange between six men and one thirteen-year-old son as they enjoyed an afternoon's coastal sail. No other boats were in the area, so it's anyone's guess what the boat struck. They heard a thud and felt a shudder—and then began to take on water. They came about, desperately wanting to make the distant shoreline, but it was soon apparent that they wouldn't; the boat was taking on water too fast. Their hope was reduced to life jackets and a long swim. It was every man for himself.

The boy could not keep up with the men, so his father held back to swim beside him. Up ahead in a pack, the men survived a strong current, large swells, and finally pounding surf—but each eventually dragged himself up onto the isolated beach.

Meanwhile, the boy was no match for waves, distance, and a strong undertow. Yet when his father took him in tow, he made no headway himself. At the point of exhaustion, the gut-wrenching moment came when this father realized that his boy wouldn't make it.

He could let his son drift away to his death, alone, as he swam to shore and preserved his own life. Or he could stay and die with the boy.

From the surf line, this man's anguished friends witnessed his last act on earth as he wrapped his arms around his son and stopped fighting. Several hours passed before the friends found help and could launch a search for the pair. They were never found.

Was it a father's supreme sacrifice, or did he waste his life needlessly? I don't know any more about this dad. I can't recall where I heard this story, but I've turned that father's horrendous dilemma over many times in my mind. Did he make the right decision? Was there a "right" decision? In any case, I deeply respect him for his choice. One thing is certain: This father knew how deeply significant he was to his son.

I wonder what I would do in such a crisis. Most fathers, I believe, are willing to die for their children if confronted with the stark choice. Yet we can also *live* for them as well, if we understand our enormous significance to them. Though most of us are gratefully spared the severe alternatives that the shipwrecked father had to

Five Key Habits of Smart Dads
FATHERING PARADIGM

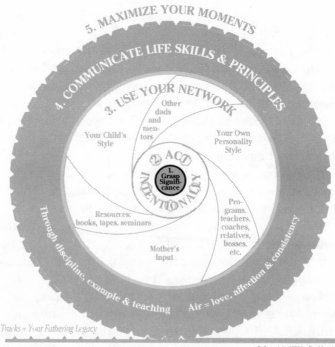

Tracks = Your Fathering Legacy

choose between, we do face everyday opportunities to make tough, love-saturated, even heroic choices that balance our lives in our kids' favor.

A car axle is the point of contact between the wheel assembly and the rest of the car. Similarly, comprehending your significance as a father is what connects your fathering to the rest of your life. The axle turns the wheel, and your grasp of your own significance gives the spin to the other aspects of fathering. The fathers who literally or emotionally distance themselves from their children, who can disconnect themselves from their children, who can strand their children—these are the fathers who have no understanding of their immense significance to their children.

During his career, a friend of mine has been president of two colleges. It's demanding, high-profile work. He's good at it and he loves the profession. Yet he is as committed to his relationship with his son as he is to his innovative role in college development. More than once this busy dad shelled out $500 just to fly home in the middle of a college business trip simply to see his son play ball.

Which is all nonsense if he didn't recognize his significance as a father. But this dad knew what dividends his sacrificial expenditure of time and money would return. He acted intentionally because he knew how significant he was to his son. Because, to my knowledge, he never said, "Sorry, son—can't make it to your game this time," he strengthened the bond between him and his son.

Understanding your significance to your children routinely affects how you use time and set priorities. If you know you are significant in your child's life, for instance, you schedule time to monitor her progress. You opt to attend a conference with your child's teacher instead of deferring to her mother—even if you have to rearrange your workday to do it. If your circumstances hamper good fathering habits, you look for alternatives that instead nurture your relationship with your children. I know men who would love to take up golf, or at least lower their handicap, but they decided against it—primarily because the time it takes to get good at golf would only eat into the already-too-few hours they have to relate with their children. They aren't perfect fathers, but they know their significance to their families.

Smart Idea:
On your business card, under your occupation or title, consider adding "Father of—" followed by the names of your children. The card will launch conversations as well as make your kids feel that they get equal billing with your career.

Children Need Their Father

If your ear is tuned to it, you can hear the anguish of this generation of children. It's a cry for their fathers, a soul-deep pain that mothers, no matter how skillful or conscientious, cannot soothe. When people articulate what it was like to grow up without a father, their words pierce you.

In an essay about boyhood written for a multicultural men's studies seminar, Everett Kline, a participant in the seminar, describes the difficult adjustment of growing up without a father to guide him.

> Family was a loving mother, a gentle grandmother, a fun aunt.
> I was loved. Life was free of concerns. It was a wonderful exciting adventure.
> Then things began to change.
> When other boys began to wear long pants, I was faced with the necessity of continuing with my uncle's discards—corduroys taken in and cut-off to achieve an approximate fit and remove the worn-out knees. The teasing began; the bully had his target. How was I supposed to respond?
> New games appeared—baseball, football, basketball, hunting, fishing. How did everyone learn to play?
> What happened to the fun? I became quieter.
> Why wasn't it still enough that I had the love and softness of those central people in my life—my mother, my grandmother, my aunts—those women?
> Why wasn't I being taught how to play hard, be strong, stand up for myself, be a man? Where were the men who could teach me? They weren't there.
> Angry, confused, ashamed, I spent more time in my room tending my tropical fish. I moved, between classes, eyes averted, head bowed, my right shoulder rubbing against the wall. I wanted to disappear.[1]

Unlike Kline, fatherless boys seldom give words to their pain. They find other ways to compensate for their paternal emptiness. A Los Angeles vice chief of police ties the soaring number of kids in street gangs directly to absent fathers. "A chief characteristic of boys who join street gangs was the absence of a father," he claims. "The gangs provided a sense of protection and commitment which the absent father did not."[2]

Across town, at the Dolores Mission Church of East Los Angeles, Father Greg Boyle agrees. Once, he said, he "listed the names of the first 100 gang members that came to mind and then jotted a family history next to each. All but five were no longer living with their biological fathers—if they ever had."[3]

The Power of Your Presence Shapes Gender Identity

The mere absence of a father's physical presence can mar a child's psychosexual or gender identity. Consider the evidence:

> Early research in the area of gender-identity development focused on the effects of father absence. These early studies dealt primarily with boys, since it was believed that the detrimental influence of a fatherless home should be particularly evident in young males. Early paternal deprivation has been linked to more feminine cognitive styles, lower masculinity, higher dependence, and either less aggression or exaggerated masculine behaviors.[4]

Fatherless boys have father fantasies that are more similar to those of girls than to those of boys with fathers present. Compared to boys from intact homes, boys with fathers absent are more likely to be perceived as effeminate by social workers familiar with the boys' case histories. As adults, males from fatherless homes display less successful heterosexual adjustment than their counterparts whose fathers are present. . . .

The observable effects of paternal deprivation can take quite different forms, depending on the age at which separation occurs. Separation during preadolescence is more likely to produce exaggerated masculine behaviors than when the child is an infant or preschooler at the time of separation from the father.[5]

Researchers Shasta L. Mead and George A. Rekers scrutinized the studies on the role of the father in normal psychosexual development. This was their conclusion:

> One of the more important functions that the father fulfills in the family is to promote appropriate sex-typing in his children. The father who is either physically or psychologically absent from the home can have a detrimental effect on the psycho-sexual development of his children. On the other hand, the father who is nurturant, dominant, and actively involved in child care is most likely to have masculine sons and feminine daughters. . . .
>
> The single most important variable related to appropriate sex-role identification in children is the paternal nurturance. Consequently, the father who is affectionate toward and actively involved with his children is the father who is most likely to foster masculinity in his sons. Mussen and

Smart Idea:
Strike a deal with another couple who have kids about the same ages as yours. Once or twice a year, keep their kids for a weekend while they get away for some special time alone. They will probably be more than happy to return the favor by keeping your kids.

67

Rutherford (1963) found that appropriate sex-role preference in boys . . . was correlated with father-son interactions which were characterized as warm, nurturant, and affectionate. In this study, high masculinity in boys was not related to explicit encouragement for masculine behaviors from their parents or to the degree of parental masculinity or femininity. . . .

This line of research tends to support the view that boys are more likely to identify with their fathers if their interactions with them are rewarding and affectionate. Like boys, sex-role preference in girls seems to be related to a warm, nurturant relationship with the same-sexed parent, that is, the mother. However, the fathers' influence on daughters is quite different. Feminine girls tend to have highly masculine fathers who encourage feminine behaviors in their daughters.[6]

The Psychological Impact of Fatherlessness

Your presence in your child's life does more than you realize. Research has documented that children without fathers more often have the following psychological handicaps:

- **Impaired psychological differentiation**
- **Deficits in social sensitivity**
- **Deficits in social role-taking skills**
- **Increased adjustment problems**
- **A poor self-concept**
- **Low self-esteem**
- **Lowered self-confidence**
- **Less sense of mastery**
- **Less self-assertiveness**
- **Delayed emotional and social maturity and internalization of morality**
- **Higher risk for psycho-sexual development problems**[7]

While a third of children from two-parent families rank as high achievers, the percentage drops to seventeen percent from single-parent homes.[8]

You are significant to your children in dramatic ways merely by being their father and remaining committed to them. Give your child the choice between having your presence or your presents, and they'll choose *you* any day of the week.

A Positive and Continuous Relationship

Although simply being present for your children is a good start, still better is a positive and continuous relationship through which you can meet your child's psychosocial needs—needs that only you can satisfy.

Many developmental and clinical studies of children have established that, in the vast majority of cases, a father's positive presence in the home is essential for normal family strength and child adjustment—specifically, for good self-concept, higher self-esteem, higher levels of confidence in personal and social interaction, higher moral maturity, reduced rates of unwed teen pregnancy, greater internal control, and higher career aspirations.[9]

Furthermore, when it comes to cultivating a healthy sense of masculinity in a son, the frequency of interactions he has with his father matters less than the quality of the father-son relationship. Studies show that when a boy has a positive, nurturing relationship with his parents—especially with his father—the son is less likely to experience gender confusion or other psychosexual difficulties.

Finally, the degree of leadership that you assume in your family affects your child's development. Being dominant without being domineering—active participation in making family decisions, for example, and fulfilling your role as head of the home—helps your child grow into a healthy, balanced individual.

A Father Brings a Unique Strength

Your strength and role as a father is no less essential to your child's development than is the child's mother. In the *Los Angeles Times Magazine* article "Life without Father," Nina J. Easton explains how

> social thinkers across the political spectrum are beginning to emphasize the role of fathers in building safe communities. Conservative sociologist James Q. Wilson contends that while "neighborhood standards are set by mothers, they are enforced by fathers. The absence of fathers deprives the community of those little platoons that effectively control boys on the street."[10]

Fathers are enforcers of socially acceptable behavior. They set the standards for a young child, back up the mother when the child challenges her authority, and discipline the child to teach him right from wrong. When the child of an absent father reaches adolescence, the mother faces the even more demanding job of raising socially responsible children. Without

Smart Idea:
The most productive fathering time of your day may be the five minutes you stop along your route home, close your eyes, and determine your family agenda for the evening— especially your first 30 minutes.

men around as role models, adolescent boys tend to create their own dubious rites of passage and code of morals.

More Than Substitute Mothers

Some researchers buck politically correct ideology, arguing

that fathers should be more than substitute mothers, that men parent differently than women and in ways that matter enormously. They say a mother's love is unconditional, a father's love is more qualified, more tied to performance; mothers are worried about the infant's survival, fathers about future success.[11]

In other words, says David Blankenhorn,

a father produces not just children but socially viable children. Fathers, more than mothers, are haunted by the fear that their children will turn out to be bums, largely because a father understands that his child's character is, in some sense, a measure of his character as well.[12]

Jerrold Lee Shapiro, who wrote *The Measure of the Man* as well as books on fatherhood, agrees.

Mothers discipline children on a moment-by-moment basis. They have this emotional umbilical cord that lets them read the child. Fathers discipline by rules. Kids learn from their moms how to be aware of their emotional side. From dad, they learn how to live in society.[13]

As children get older, notes William Maddox, director of research and policy at the Washington-based Family Research Council, fathers become crucial in children's physical and psychological development.

Go to a park and watch a father and mother next to a child on a jungle gym. The father encourages the child to challenge himself by climbing to the top; the mother tells him to be careful. What's most important is to have the balance of encouragement along with a warning.[14]

More than common sense tells you that a child needs both parents—there's hard research, too, to support this claim:

A vast National Center for Health Statistics study found that children from single-parent homes were 100 to 200 percent more likely than children from two-parent families to have emotional and behavioral problems and about fifty percent more likely to have learning disabilities. In the nation's hospitals, over eighty percent of adolescents admitted for psychiatric reasons come from single-parent families.[15]

Dangers in Divorce

As the divorce rate started soaring a quarter century ago, so did the popular belief that divorce did not damage children *that* much. Yet recent evidence suggests that kids are not as resilient as we thought they were. A surprising 1993 article in *The Atlantic Monthly* chronicled the effect of divorce on children.

Most experts believed that divorce was like a bad cold, as far as children were concerned. There was a phase of acute discomfort, followed by a short recovery phase. According to conventional wisdom, kids would be back on their feet in no time at all.

This proved not to be the case. In 1971, when researchers conducted clinical interviews with children immediately following a divorce, they were not surprised to find that the children were traumatized. When these children were interviewed a second time one year later, however, researcher Wallerstein was surprised to discover that there had been no miraculous recovery. The children, in fact, seemed to be doing worse.[16]

When Wallerstein's findings were made public, she recalls, in came the angry letters from therapists and lawyers saying the results were undoubtedly wrong. Wallerstein's cautionary words: "Divorce is deceptive. Legally it is a single event, but psychologically it is a chain. Sometimes a never-ending chain of events, leading to relocations and radically shifting relationships."

Here are just three of her findings, which anyone with children should be aware of:

- **Five years after divorce, more than a third of children studied were experiencing moderate to severe depression.**
- **Ten years after divorce, a significant number of children studied were troubled, drifting, and underachieving.**
- **Fifteen years later, the children as adults were struggling to establish strong relationships of their own. In a word, they were relationally crippled.**

All this evidence to say that your marriage is another critical molder of your children. If you are divorced and your children seem to be handling it well, consider yourself fortunate, and redouble your efforts to mitigate the downside, even if it hasn't yet appeared. I hope your child can buck the probabilities and sail through the trauma relatively untouched.

Smart Tip:
How would you finish the sentence: "One thing my dad always said was—" How will your children finish the sentence?

Yet I must be realistic enough to say that those children are the exception. Even loving them exceptionally well as their father does not erase the emotional hit they've taken.

I don't offer this information to condemn you if you are divorced. What's done is done. Your concern now is to manage the consequences as effectively as you can and to pray for the best. If, however, you are considering divorce, don't assume that your children will work through it just fine. Do everything you can to preserve your family and protect your children from the devastating effects of divorce.

Grasping Your Personal Significance

Down at your core, at the root of your fathering habits, is your self-concept. If you have a healthy self-esteem as a *man*, you will tend to have a healthy self-esteem as a *father*. Likewise, if your masculine self-esteem is low—if you doubt yourself or believe you lack inherent value as a man—it will be difficult to see yourself positively as a father.

You aren't alone if you feel inadequate as a father or are confused about the wide range of fatherhood's requirements. And what most dads were up against, we found out from our fathering research, were things in themselves. To the question "What are the two biggest barriers you face in wanting to be a good dad?" their answers commonly included these:

- Lack of patience.
- My own imperfections.
- Feelings of inadequacy.
- Selfishness.
- Laziness.
- I don't know what I need to know about my kids at each age/stage they live through.
- I am confused over what is right.
- I have a limited education.
- I am in poor health.
- I lack experience. This leads to a lack of self-confidence.[17]

You Are Significant as You Are

Starting at your core you have the power to change so as to enhance your self-esteem and your fathering. Remember that research points out that it is your *availability to* and *love for* your children that are central to their well-being. Whatever your limitations—personal problems you need to deal with, a sinking self-esteem that needs a boost—work through them. But in the meantime, don't miss the fact that you are significant to your child, exactly as you are this moment.

You Can Change—from the Inside Out

Genuine character development always flows from the core of who you are. So whatever change you want to make as a father, begin with an inner, core change. Here's how Stephen Covey describes this kind of change in his book *The Seven Habits of Highly Effective People*:

> This new level of thinking is . . . a principle-centered, character-based, "inside-out" approach to personal and interpersonal effectiveness. "Inside-out" means to start first with self; even more fundamentally, to start with the most inside part of self—with your paradigms, your character, and your motives.
>
> It says if you want to have a happy marriage, be the kind of person who generates positive energy and sidesteps negative energy rather than empowering it. If you want to have a more pleasant, cooperative teenager, be a more understanding, empathic, consistent, loving parent. . . .
>
> The inside-out approach says that private victories precede public victories, that making and keeping promises to ourselves precedes making and keeping promises to others. It says it is futile to put personality ahead of character, to try to improve relationships with others before improving ourselves.[18]

Fathering Success Is within Your Grasp

When we asked our survey group, "What makes a father successful?" many fathers in our survey cited personal qualities.

- **Humility and patience**
- **Ability to be real, genuine, and touchable—no macho image**
- **Ability to love truthfully**
- **Willingness to give of his time and affection**
- **Being a good role model**
- **Being a good example**[19]

Smart Idea:
Take photos of your kids doing things right—daily chores, cleaning their rooms, grooming a pet, doing homework, helping mom, dad, a sibling. Set aside special pages in the family album for these snapshots.

None of these are beyond your grasp. They begin every time with a deliberate choice. Sure, consistency may take a while, but with practice the growth of these qualities in you could be dramatic. You *can* practice humility and patience. You *can* honestly love your children. You *can* be real, genuine, and touchable. You *can* give your time and affection. You *can* be a good example and role model.

Want a place to start? In particular, you can make fairly quick progress as a father by giving your child your love, your approval, and your encouragement.

Your Child Needs Your Love

In *Psychology Today's* "Who Is the New Ideal Man?" reader survey, several respondents cited their own fathers as the ideal man. I noted that it was no extraordinary quality embodied in fathers that made them ideal to their children, but rather the simple love he gave them. "My father made me feel so loved and so important," one woman wrote, "that I feel ideal enough about myself to enjoy living and growing."[20]

Your Child Needs Your Approval

Listen to the words of two men, both well-known. One received the approval of his father; the other did not.

"I guess like every kid, what I most wanted was to please. I still care a lot what people think of me," remembers actor-director Kevin Costner. "I wanted to be liked by my dad most of all. I still do.

"As a kid, when my dad was coming home, my brother and I used to wait for him. He was a working guy, a lineman for Edison, and we used to race to undo the laces of his boots. My brother'd take the left boot, and I'd take the right, just really glad my dad was there. I wanted so much to please him."[21]

Singer B. J. Thomas, best known for his 1969 hit "Raindrops Keep Fallin' on My Head" and winner of five Grammy awards, grew up lacking what he most wanted to achieve through his music. His childhood seems to him now like one long search for ways to win his father's approval. Then the boy discovered that his father liked country and western music.

"Ultimately, Dad gave me music," Thomas says. "He was probably my first motivation to be a singer, so I love him for that. It was the only way I could get him to talk to me. I learned songs by Earnest Tubbs and Hank Williams, and I'd sing my tail off to him. And he'd just cry."[22]

Although B. J. Thomas succeeded on a grand scale financially and professionally, none of it could take the place of the approval he needed from his father—approval that was nearly impossible to get.

Your child needs massive and regular expressions of approval from you. And don't cheapen it by tossing casual, generic compliments in the general direction of your child. Instead praise what you can honestly praise about your child. Don't tell her the obvious exaggeration that she is the most beautiful girl in the world. She will trust your sincerity, however, if you're more inclined to say "Wow, your hair looks pretty braided that way."

Kevin Costner received a precious gift that laid the groundwork for a positive self-worth: the approval of his father. B. J. Thomas was deprived of his father's approval and has consequently struggled his entire life with his self-esteem.

What I found interesting about these two entertainment giants was that neither of their fathers achieved anything publicly notable. No grand talents or exploits. Just ordinary men with ordinary jobs and the ordinary personal shortcomings. Although the alcoholism of B. J. Thomas's father marred the family, I wonder if his dad understood that even with his alcoholism, his son needed his approval.

It is the mark of the male parent, I think, to fix our attention on whether we deserve our children's approval, while we ought to consider *their* hunger for approval from whatever kind of fathers we are, good, bad, or ugly.

Your Children Need Your Encouragement

All children need to know that someone is out there pulling for them, that someone in the stands is cheering them on. More important, children need to know that their *fathers* are there to encourage them. Because children look first and most to their parents for that encouragement, a cheerleading father helps his son discover his competence, helps his daughter perceive her ability to be successful, useful, self-actualized.

You see this phenomenon every weekend at athletic events and school plays. When Dad is on the sidelines encouraging his child, the child plays better. When Dad is in the audience, the child performs her

Smart Idea:
Tonight at the dinner table, switch places—everyone sits in someone else's customary chair—with this assignment: During the meal, they must behave like the family member whose chair they're sitting in. If you don't die of laughter first, you'll learn a lot.

best. A child may still excel without a father there to watch her, but the achievement is not as sweet.

"Bucky" Dent appeared on "Oprah" last summer. He plays shortstop for the Yankees. Raised by an aunt, he was nonetheless led to believe that the aunt was his mother. When he finally learned who his mother was, Bucky wanted the truth from her about his father, too. But his mom clammed up—and even forbade Bucky to make contact with him.

Although this void was sorely felt by Bucky, he still imagined during boyhood games that his father was there in the stands, just like the fathers of his teammates.

Only when Bucky became an adult did his mother finally relent and tell him who his father was. It turned out that this dad knew exactly who his son was—had followed Bucky's entire athletic career, in fact. He actually *had* attended football games and *had* cheered his son on, without Bucky ever realizing it. When Bucky heard this, a great need inside him was finally fulfilled.

Never Too Late to Start

As long as your children are alive, it is never too late to start developing habits of loving, approving, and encouraging your child—never too late to start cheering.

I have talked with dads who say they have failed with their first child. They mature, have another child, do better this time—but often dismiss their responsibilities to the first child. Yet he is the only biological father that first child will ever have, even if he was a flawed father.

In the case of Baby Jessica, you may remember, two sets of parents battled each other for months to gain custody of a little girl. Dan Schmidt, the baby's birth father, also had a thirteen-year-old daughter, Amanda—but Amanda he had not claimed or supported. She watched her father, the only father she had, fight tooth and nail to claim Baby Jessica while he did nothing to claim her. Before all the world, her dad demonstrated that he valued his new family far more than he valued Amanda.

In reality, Schmidt's negligence of Amanda probably stemmed more from a poor self-perception than from outright indifference toward his daughter. Because he is her father, however, no amount of explaining diminishes the devastation Amanda experienced.

Personal Effects of Grasping Your Significance as a Father

Let's admit it—men enjoy the feeling of our own power and significance. If you derive your significance from your work and career—if it is there that you feel important and highly esteemed—you will understandably feel motivated to work hard. Working in such a situation enhances your self-image. In short, you treasure your career.

"Where your treasure is," noted Jesus Christ, "there your heart will be also." If I find my significance—my treasure—primarily in my work, that's where my attention and my time will be focused. Yet when I have grasped my significance as a father, I will treasure *that* role and opportunity increasingly.

Recognizing your significance as a father elevates and invigorates even your ordinary tasks. Instead of merely "baby-sitting" your kids when their mom is out for an evening, you'll call it what it is—fathering! One man added these words to his business card, under his name and title: "Father of Steven and Carri." Clarity about who you are is the issue here.

No Plainer Words

You are significant by virtue of being the father of your children. Your presence and your family leadership is significant. You have exclusive abilities to meet your child's needs for love, approval, and encouragement. You are a massive power in the life of your child. You are absolutely crucial to their growth, wholeness, and well-being.

If you've got hold of your significance as a father, the engine is running, the transmission is engaged, the axle is turning in the right direction—now you're ready to tackle the second key habit of a smart dad.

Smart Idea:
If a kid on your block is receiving too little parental attention, include him in one of your family activities, even if it's just a short trip to the store or the park. Make it a point to tell his parents what good characteristic you observed in their child.

6

Habit Two: Acting Intentionally
The Lug Nuts

Too bad fathering isn't organized like football—players who are highly conditioned, safely equipped, and well-trained . . . an offensive unit, a defensive unit, and special teams for kickoffs, punt returns, field goals, on-side kicks.

If fathering were like football, we'd have everything from newborn fathering specialists to crisis-control specialists for fathering teenagers. The patient dads would help with homework and building science projects, while others would specialize at discipline, reasoning with toddlers, coaching soccer teams, and paying college bills.

On the other hand, we *do* parent like football—at least, how they *originally* played football. The same eleven played offense, defense, kick-off, punt return. There were no special teams. Every player did his best in any game situation.

When it comes to raising kids, the easiest half of the game to play is defense. At least that's what many dads spend most of their time doing. We respond. We answer questions when our kids ask them, not before. We step in to referee fights or dish out discipline when they harass their mom. Otherwise, we try to be a nice guy who minds his own business.

Defensive fathering is a wonderful fantasy. But it's fuzzy thinking like this that keeps us ineffective and out of the game until we're so far behind that catching up is nearly impossible.

Intentional action is what good fathering requires—and that's what the lug nuts represent in my analogy. Lug nuts secure the wheel to the axle. In fathering, your intentional actions (lug nuts) connect your understanding of your significance as a father (axle) to the living out of that understanding in your relationship with your children (the rim, tire, etc.).

Five Key Habits of Smart Dads
FATHERING PARADIGM

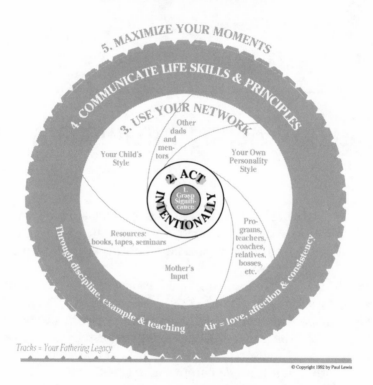

5. MAXIMIZE YOUR MOMENTS

4. COMMUNICATE LIFE SKILLS & PRINCIPLES

3. USE YOUR NETWORK

Other dads and mentors

Your Child's Style

Your Own Personality Style

2. ACT INTENTIONALLY

1. Grasp Significance

Pro-grams, teachers, coaches, relatives, bosses, etc.

Resources: books, tapes, seminars

Mother's Input

Through discipline, example & teaching

Air = love, affection & consistency

Tracks = Your Fathering Legacy

© Copyright 1992 by Paul Lewis

Two Companies

Intentional action, unfortunately, characterizes only one of the two companies in a man's life: the company he owns or works for, and the family or home company, of which he is supposedly the senior partner.

It's only reasonable to expect that, if your sense of significance comes primarily from your professional status and accomplishments, then it will be at the office where you will want to excel with goals, action plans, and other demonstrations of intentional action. Furthermore, if you do not understand your true significance at home as a father and husband, you simply won't look to home for satisfaction and payoffs. You'll charge hard all day in the work-place and arrive home tired, emotionally spent, and hoping your home and family will be a tranquilizer for you.

Now imagine this: How would you feel if, as you head out to work tomorrow morning, you knew that no one in your company had given any concrete thought to the company's mission? No writ-ten business plan, no goals, no quarterly projections, no one-year or five-year plan for growth, no one pouring over the sales figures and comparing them to projections. How secure would you feel about the future of your company and your job there?

In an economy like ours, we hear everywhere, only careful plan-ning, review, and course corrections by corporate management keep things moving forward and profitably. *A family needs the same care and consideration as a corporation.* Aren't the dynamics of your fami-ly's security, success, and future much the same as a company's? Don't family relationships deserve some of the same definition, planning, review, and energy you give to setting and reaching your business goals? When we realize that our homes and families yield benefits so enormously more important than any amount of corpo-rate ladder climbing can yield, we will treat our family relationships with more care and respect.

So what's stopping you from applying in your family the same intentional action you already practice at the office? Set goals, schedule production, do some evaluation and review, bring new ser-vices on line.

What Men Want at Home and Work— and What Women Want for Them

What men want in our jobs and companies is *growth*. We tend to be frustrated unless the company's going somewhere. For our families, however, we tend to value not growth, but *stability*. If I'm out slaying dragons all day in the field or the office, I don't want to walk in the front door of my home that evening to fight more dragons. I want the home front calm and stable.

Wives, to no one's surprise, often have very opposite agendas for their husbands. They want family life—the home corpora-tion—to be a growing enterprise, where

Smart Idea:
"Dear Abby" letters in your newspaper can spawn family dialogue. Read a letter—but not the printed advice, until family mem-bers have suggested their solution. Were yours even better than Abby's?

intimacy and relationships are consistently deepening, where every-thing is improving. Women tend to feel that it's reasonable to expect more love and joy *this* year than they observed in the house *last* year. Women want more fulfilling married love *this* quarter than *last* quarter.

Likewise, what your wife probably wants most for you at work is not growth, but stability. If you worry about job security, she knows, you'll have a difficult time cultivating growth at home. Even if she works forty hours in the field or the office, too, a wife and mother still tends to be more concerned about growth in the home corporation.

In short, *you* thought you left work to come home, relax, regroup. *She* thinks you left work to come home to go to work—as a father and husband. Is it any wonder conflicts often arise?

Yet there is common ground. Acting intentionally starts by accepting a role of leadership in your home and family. Evaluate your home life as though you had just been made the company's new president. Assess the organization's mission statement. What goals will lead your family toward the fulfillment of that mission?

When you realize your significance at home and begin to act intentionally there, your stability won't be diminished—it will actu-ally grow. For at home as well as in your corporation, people are your most important asset. When both employees and management are excited about what's happening—when production is up and everyone feels ownership in the process, the result is both growth *and* stability.

But consider this. If you ran your business affairs with the same amount of forethought and planning that you give to running your family, would you go out of business within six months? Too many of us play just defense in our families for years, simply expecting that things will work out fine at home without any particular plan in mind. Is it any wonder that marriages and families are either falling apart or are mediocre at best?

Simply put, your success as a father depends on your intentional actions.

The Five Lug Nuts

Each of these five lug nuts represents an aspect of acting inten-tionally. If one lug nut is loose or missing, you probably won't notice. The others carry the stress. Even if two are loose, you are still probably safe. But if three or more lug nuts are loose or missing,

Five Key Habits of Smart Dads
FATHERING PARADIGM

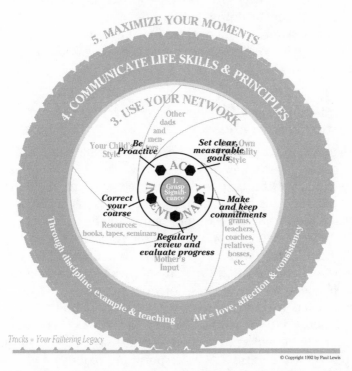

5. MAXIMIZE YOUR MOMENTS

4. COMMUNICATE LIFE SKILLS & PRINCIPLES

3. USE YOUR NETWORK

Other dads and men-

Your Child's Style

Be Proactive

Set clear, measurable goals

Own ability Style

ACT

Grasp Signifi-cance

Correct your course

INTENTIONALLY

Make and keep commitments

Resources: books, tapes, seminars

Regularly review and evaluate progress

grams, teachers, coaches, relatives, bosses, etc.

Mother's Input

Through discipline, example & teaching

Air = love, affection & consistency

Tracks = Your Fathering Legacy

© Copyright 1992 by Paul Lewis

you are in grave danger. Sooner or later—and no telling when—one of those stressed studs will snap and you lose a wheel. By the same token, you don't have to immediately master all five aspects of acting intentionally as a father. If you tighten down just *some* of these lug nuts, you can proceed with confidence.

It's as easy to check your lifestyle for whether you're practicing intentional actions as it is to pop the hubcaps off your car and check the lug nuts. As a rim would eventually rattle off the axle with loose lug nuts, so the best of fathering practices fall apart without intentional actions. Without intentional actions, sound principles of fathering are about as useful as an unmounted wheel. When you act intentionally, however, the rest of your fathering habits take off and you reach your destination.

Concluding the discussion below of each lug nut is a way to immediately start tightening down the lug nut. These aren't mere postscripts, but vital steps toward changing as a father. In his video *Hooked on Life*, Stephen Arterburn offers this rid-

Smart Thought:
I can't do anything about my ancestors, but I can do a lot about my descendants.

dle: Five birds are perched on a log. If one decides to fly away, how many birds are left sitting on the log?

The answer, says Arterburn, is five. For deciding to do something is not the same as doing it.

Here are the five lug nuts of intentional action: *proactivity, measurable goals, making and keeping commitments, evaluation,* and *course correction.*

Lug Nut 1
Be proactive—accept full responsibility for your fathering role.

Let me explain what *proactive* means by first explaining its opposite, *reactive.* A reactive dad sees himself ruled by what happens in his life. A reactive father perceives himself a victim of circumstance. By blaming his circumstances, he excuses his failure to be a better father and to have the kind of family life he idealizes.

For instance, a dad who was abused by *his* father may think, I can't help being rough with my children. My father abused me, and those who were abused often turn into abusers. By allowing himself to excuse his behavior on the basis of what happened to him, this dad merely reacts without exercising his power of choice.

The proactive father, on the other hand, realizes that while he has been affected by what happened to him—say, abuse from his father—he can still choose how to respond. A proactive dad realizes that some men, abused by their fathers, in turn abuse their own children. But a proactive dad chooses to respond differently. Even if he was abused himself as a child, he can begin therapy to heal the effects of the abuse. He can take parenting classes.

The proactive father refuses to let what happens (or happened) to him rule his life. He does not let either the present or the past dictate the future.

When you are a proactive father, you choose your response to problems so that you can fulfill your fathering responsibilities. You control your life for your purposes. Although you cannot control what comes your way in life, you can control how you let it affect you.

Suppose you accept full responsibility for being a good father. You also know how important it is to spend time with your children. Although you don't set your work schedule, because you are proactive, you use your creativity and power of choice to devise ways to spend time with your children.

This could mean, of course, not taking up golf until the last child leaves for college. But you accept this as a reasonable tradeoff. The proactive dad does not beg off with the excuse, "You know I'd *like* to spend time with my children, but with my schedule I just can't." Instead, you'll focus on the minutes you do have and make the most of them.

Proactive fathers speak a different language than reactive fathers. The reactive father's vocabulary is replete with "I can't . . . I have to . . . I can't help it . . . I must . . ." The proactive father, on the other hand, uses phrases like "I can . . . I want to . . . I will . . . I choose to . . . I am not doomed to repeat the past . . . No one can take away my power to choose my response . . . When opportunity doesn't knock, I will build a door . . . I may not be able to control what happens, but I can control how I manage around what happens."

It can seem easier to be reactive. You will always find someone to blame for your failures and frustrations. And being proactive—accepting full responsibility for your life—means you have to seriously ponder the effects your decisions have on others.

A proactive father shelves all the excuses, instead confronting challenges head on. He believes his true priorities will determine the course of his life, because he is tenaciously deciding to keep those priorities in line.

Granted, accepting full responsibility for your fathering can be intimidating—but it can free you, too. All the time I hear fathers say they feel trapped. "I want to be a good father," they complain, "but I just don't know what it takes. I wish I had more time [money, energy, whatever], but the pressures of daily life keep me from being the kind of dad my kids need."

He may be genuinely trapped in a despicable job at the moment, or engulfed in debt and unable to spend the time or money his children need. But he is a free man when he can say, "I may not have much money, education, or free time—but whatever I have, I will manage so that my kids are taken care of." Risking failure, he still tries, he still accepts the challenge of managing his own life and resources in a way that displays his love for his wife and children. This determination gives him power the reactive man will never have.

Now tighten down the lug nut of proactivity: Practice five-minute fathering.

You don't need large chunks of time. Lots of things can be done in just five minutes. In just five minutes, you can—

- **Have a wonderful discussion about your child's best and worst moments at school today.**

Smart Idea:
A big cardboard appliance box can be the most entertaining toy you've brought home in a long time. Drop by an appliance store on your way home and ask for one.

- Hug your child (hang on for a whole minute) and tell her how important she is to your family.
- Write a letter of appreciation to his teacher for taking special care with him in the classroom.
- Share a dish of ice cream.
- Wrestle.
- Have an impromptu pillow fight.
- Give your child a sincere compliment.
- Play freeze tag.
- Write and give your child a little note.
- Leave for work five minutes later and spend that time with your children.
- Dissect the values in a TV program or news report you've watched together.
- Read a picture book.
- Say a prayer for your child.
- Stop somewhere on your way home from work long enough
  to shift gears mentally and emotionally from
  work to your family.

You get the idea. Make a list on a three-by-five card of five-minute activities that appeal most to you. Carry the card with you, and during spare moments do one of them. If you make this a habit, over the course of a lifetime you will have created countless memories of a father's love.

Lug Nut 2
Set clear, measurable goals for fathering.

A proactive father naturally sets goals, because goals are the way he accomplishes anything he wants in life, whether in fathering, business, sports, finances, or whatever. When you realize you are responsible for what happens, you tend to make sure the *right things* happen. This is where measurable goals come in. You measure what is, measure what you want, and then take action to shorten the distance between the two.

In our survey of fathers, we asked what advice they would give a new father. A majority recommended goal setting, with responses like these:

- Set and achieve family goals.
- Be goal-directed and help kids set goals.
- Set goals, establish a plan, check your progress.

- **Set proper goals and work as though all things depended on those goals.**
- **Be goal oriented.**[1]

It's good advice. Clear and measurable goals enable you to better use what time you do have with your children. With clearly defined goals, you will seize opportunities you might otherwise miss. Just the act of setting goals can spur your creativity toward reaching them.

For example:

You want to set clear, measurable goals about conveying your family's values to your children. You give the subject some thought, then write down the values you want to communicate—hard work, honesty, education. Now you keep your eyes open for natural opportunities to highlight these values to your children. Daniel is working hard at his homework, you notice, so you praise him not only for his effort, but for his wisdom in recognizing the value of hard work. When you catch Kristi in a fib, instead of getting angry you take the opportunity to stress the importance of honesty in building trust in relationships. Sara is impressed with a newscast about the space shuttle, and you see your chance to explain that the astronauts' education has paved their career path for them into space.

Without clear goals for conveying particular values to your children, one easily overlooks such teachable moments.

But relationships don't lend themselves to goal setting, some fathers tell me—at least like more concrete and practical matters do, such as raising sales figures or saving money for a boat. So I have listed below some of the fathering goals our survey turned up. We asked dads, "What are the three most important goals you have for your relationship with your children?"

Interaction Goals

- **That they know I love them.**
- **That we can talk about everything.**
- **That we trust each other.**

Personal Goals as a Father

- **To always be there when they need me.**

> **Smart Idea:**
> On your next business trip, if you can't take one of the kids with you, tape record yourself reading a few bedtime stories for your children to listen to while you're gone. Leave the books with them, so they can follow along as they listen to your tape. Spice up your recorded readings by making a funny or unusual noise when it's time to turn the page.

- To be a good listener.
- To be a positive role model.
- To be a good father.

Personal Goals for my Children

- That they have good self-esteem.
- That they contribute significantly to society.
- That they become good citizens.
- That they be hard workers.

Spiritual Goals

- To help them make spiritual commitments.
- To help them understand and achieve God's will for their lives.
- To be a good spiritual leader in my home.
- To train my children for spiritual leadership.

Experiential Goals

- To have time to play what they want to play.
- To be able to share activities with them.
- To learn to play together and enjoy each others' interests.
- To enjoy doing things together.
- To share an interest in some fun activity.[2]

If you want your goals to be useful, make sure they are measurable. Actually, some of the above goals are wishes, not goals. (How will a dad know when he and his child "trust each other"?) If you must, go ahead and *start* with wishes—just make sure that you define them clearly in measurable terms. Then take that measurable goal and fit it into a time frame—a thirteen-week quarter or a year—so that you can anticipate what progress you will have made ninety days from now, or a year from now.

For example, take the goal "that we trust each other." You can clarify it and make it measurable by breaking it down this way:

- List each promise you have already made your child; then, setting calendar deadlines for each one, do your best to fulfill your promises.
- Commend your child whenever she keeps her word. Discipline her whenever she acts in an untrustworthy fashion. If you keep notes about these incidents over a quarter, you can look back and evaluate her progress.
- Make only those commitments you can realistically keep.

By clarifying your desires and making them measurable, you create fathering goals you can later evaluate.

This process works only if you write your goals on your regular to-do list and tie it to your schedule and calendar like your business goals. Set your measurable goals in a limited time frame: I suggest setting fathering goals for ninety days at a time. Ninety days, a quarter, thirteen weeks, the length of a season—I believe this is the ideal planning time for seeing results. A quarter is long enough to get an overview (a monthly view is usually too short to observe the rhythmic fluctuations of life), but short enough for you to identify specific actions and assign them to particular days and weekends during which you will act on them.

Now tighten down the lug nut of measurable goals: Write some. Now.

Start by writing your desires for fathering—then turn those desires into measurable goals. Think in terms of personal goals, goals about what you want to teach your children, family vacations you want to take before they leave home, and so on.

Pull your family in on your dreaming, too. Set aside an evening or a long dinner out in a relatively quiet corner booth at your favorite pizza place. Ask family members, one at a time, to list what they want to accomplish in the next twelve months. Dream together. Write down each of their goals, and discuss how the whole family can help each person reach his or her goals.

(Part of the rationale behind this pizza night is that sharing goals and dreams always brings a family closer together. It's no wonder that such commitment to one another, along with time spent together, are two of the most common characteristics researchers have consistently noted in strong families.)

Smart Idea:
Whatever your children's ages, they always enjoy back rubs and foot rubs—plus they create an excellent climate for honest communication (especially foot rubs, which allow eye contact during dialogue).

Now organize your goals by the calendar. Big goals may take one, five, or ten years to accomplish. Others can be reached within a week or two. In any case, the secret is to break down a goal into practical, manageable steps. Then write those onto your calendar, because only what's written on your calendar or to-do lists will you most likely accomplish. What is not written down tends to float and will never be accomplished.

Consider using ninety days—the length of a season—as your planning window. To get specific, ask yourself questions like this:

1. In what way do I want my relationship with my wife and each of my children to be different or better in ninety days from what it is today?

2. In what way do I want my fathering practices to change?

3. What are direct action steps I could take that would lead me toward these desires? On what actual calendar week and/or day will I take each of these steps?

Few things will sharpen your focus as a father more than writing down such answers on paper and then acting on your plan. On page 92 is a blank 90-Days Family Goals Sheet. A filled-in sample is also provided on page 93.

Now translate your ninety-day plan into weekly and daily activity calendars and to-do lists. On page 94 is a Weekly Plan Sheet that integrates family plans with your business and other time commitments.

As you lay out a week, first trace down the vertical shaded column for that week on your 90-Day Family Plan Sheet. Under the "Marriage/Family" heading in the lower left corner of the Weekly Plan Sheet, list the items you planned to include in that particular week.

Block out time for each activity in that week's plan so that other urgencies don't crowd out your family and fathering priorities. You've allotted the time, so now guard it as you do any other appointment.

When you have sketched out where your family fits in the week's plans, do one more thing: Take your appointment book to the dinner table tonight. Show each member of your family the unassigned times in your schedule over the next week or two, then write in their names at times you all agree upon. (Remember—it is not enough to make the commitment. It only counts if you keep the commitments you make.)

Smart Tip:
Read your high schooler's textbooks. You'll never be at a loss for a good conversation topic.

As you plan your day each morning or the evening before, again bring from your Weekly Plan Sheet the fathering and family activities that are scheduled for that day and slot them into the day as precisely as possible. The principle that daily moves the business world also works to your advantage in your family: only what you write on your calendar or "to do" lists will you consistently achieve.

Lug Nut 3
Make and keep commitments that help you fulfill fathering goals.

Commitments about your time, for example. The good Lord gives everyone on the planet 24 hours a day, 168 hours in the week. You are responsible for how you use your time. If you do not consciously choose how to spend your time, others will make the choices for you. One way or another, a choice is always made; because unless you die within the next 24 hours, you will use up the time allotted to you this day.

We commit time to work, to rest, to eating and sleeping, grooming and recreation—the essentials. Then there's discretionary time—and our use of it reflects our priorities and values. (The same holds true for discretionary money, energy, talents, patience, and so on.)

Without an intelligent plan for time management—and your *commitment* to it—you are merely drifting with the wind instead of steering yourself where you want to be as a father. And to drift in your fathering is to eventually face the consequences of not committing to a deliberate plan.

But I have no control over my schedule, protests the reactive man. Yet the proactive man sets goals and priorities, choosing to commit his time and resources toward achieving them. He may not reach half of them, but he will reach *some*—and steady though slight progress inevitably leads to the goal.

Here's one way to make clear fathering commitments: Set aside a regular time for previewing days and weeks. Plan your fathering week on Friday or Saturday or Sunday—whichever day is the eve of your "week." Similarly, plan each day that morning or—better yet—the evening before. You'll find that you control your time better by consistently giving it to those events that matter most to you. "To fail to plan is to plan to fail," goes the maxim—and it is as absolutely true in fathering as in most other arenas of life. You must direct your resources in advance to where you want them to go.

However simple the event you schedule with your children, put it on the calendar and guard it as you do other important dates. Don't trust to chance for communicating your love and support on a regular basis to your kids. *Schedule* opportunities to say or demonstrate your love for them. It's not as important what you do together as long as you commit the time, then guard it and spend it as you planned. "I wish earlier I would have learned to schedule time with

90-Day Family Goals

Goal	Steps to Fulfillment	Week of:
My fathering practices		
Relationship with *(wifes name)*		
Relationship with *(child's name)*		
Relationship with *(child's name)*		
Relationship with *(child's name)*		
Relationship with *(child's name)*		
Relationship with *(child's name)*		

90-Day Family Goals

Goal	Steps to Fulfillment	JAN 3	10	17	24	FEB 2	9	16	23	MAR 2	9	16	23	30
My fathering practices														
CONSISTENT PLANNING	Weekly 15 min review	～	～	～	～	～	～	～	～	～	～	～	→	
JOURNALING	Write down experiences	X	X	X	X	X	X							
TIME/CONTACT w/ DAD	Weekly phone + 2 visits		X	～	～	～	～	X	～	～	～	～	→	
Relationship with _(wifes name)_ KAREN														
Read 1 Book together	"Marriage passages"	～	～	～	～	～	～	～	～	～	～	～	→	
Sharpen tennis game	Clinic @ Community Center									X				
Plan anniversary getaway	Book hotel, arr. babysit	X											⊗	
Relationship with _(child's name)_ MEGAN														
TIGHTEN COMMUNICATION	Breakfast Tuesdays	～	～	～	～	～	～	～	～	～	～	～	→	
FOCUS ON LIFE GOALS	Start Notebook – 3 topics	X			(#1)			(#2)		(#3)				
Relationship with _(child's name)_ RICHARD														
SCOUTING TOGETHER	Select troop & enroll	～	～	→	X									
BUILD HOMEWORK SKILLS	Set-up place / tools	X	～	～	～	～	～	～	～	～	～	～	→	
Relationship with _(child's name)_ PETER														
READ FANTASY Books	C.S. Lewis – 3x week	～	～	～	～	～	～	～	～	～	～	～	→	
INVOLVE IN CHORES	Help w/ Fence repair / paint					X		→						
Relationship with _(child's name)_ JANET														
ENCOURAGE!	1 note / letter / card a week	～	～	～	～	～	～	～	～	～	～	→		
PLAN SUMMER TRIP	Clear calendars, get info					X	→	X						
Relationship with _(child's name)_ JON														
EST. FINANCIAL ORG.	Launch checking act.				X	～	～	→ Review						
DISCIPLE DISCUSS.	Bi-weekly breakfast.	X	X	X	X	X	X	X						

FIVE KEY HABITS OF SMART DADS

WEEKLY FOCUS

FAMILY 🏛 **UNIVERSITY**

Week of: ☐ to ☐

Month/Year _____

TIME	MONDAY	TUESDAY	WEDNESDAY	THURSDAY	FRIDAY	SATURDAY	SUNDAY
				SCHEDULED APPOINTMENTS & EVENTS			
5							
6							
7							
8							
9							
10							
11							
Noon							
1							
2							
3							
4							
5							
6							
7							
8							
9							

Weekly Personal & Family Focus

Spiritual

Personal Development

Marriage/Family

Social/Friends

Financial

Physical

Other

BUSINESS FOCUS

TO DO

TO PHONE/WRITE

my children," admits Josh McDowell in the video *Famous Fathers*. "If I don't schedule the time, I don't get it."

Without this lug nut firmly tightened down, you may not leave the imprint you want on your children's lives. When you learn the habit of making and keeping commitments to your children, you build in them a trust that will give them inner security throughout life.

WEEKLY FOCUS

FAMILY 🎓 UNIVERSITY

Week of: **24** to **31**
Month/Year **JAN**

SCHEDULED APPOINTMENTS & EVENTS

TIME	MONDAY	TUESDAY	WEDNESDAY	THURSDAY	FRIDAY	SATURDAY	SUNDAY
5							
6							
7		Bkfst-Began		Dept. mtg.		Fix bkfst	WK PLAN / JOURNAL
8	OFFICE	OFFICE	OFFICE		OFFICE	Karen shops!	
9							
10						Repair table table	CHURCH
11							
Noon	Calls Janet trip	Write letter to Janet	DADS TEAM		OFFICE		
1	OFFICE	OFFICE					
2		Qtr Review w/ Jack					FAMILY OUTING
3		2:30					
4				Megan's soccer gm.			
5	WORKOUT		WORKOUT	DINNER	WORKOUT		
6	Rich homewk	Talk scouts w/ Richard	Rich homewk	Family mt.	Dbl w/		
7					KAREN, SMITHS		
8	Read Peter				(Theater)		
9		Read w/ Karen					

Weekly Personal & Family Focus

Spiritual
- ☐○
- ☐○
- ☐○
- ☐○

Personal Development
- ☐○ 3 x Work-out/Jog.
- ☐○ DADS TM mtg. Wed
- ☐○ Plan + Journal
- ☐○

Marriage/Family
- ☐○ Prep Goal #1 - Megan
- ☐○ Ck Jon's checking
- ☐○ Dbl w/ Karen + Smiths
- ☐○ Read w/ Peter
- ☐○ Find topic for Jon bkfst.
- ☐○
- ☐○

Social/Friends
- ☐○
- ☐○
- ☐○
- ☐○

Financial
- ☐○
- ☐○
- ☐○

Physical
- ☐○
- ☐○

Other
- ☐○
- ☐○
- ☐○

BUSINESS FOCUS
- ○
- ○
- ○

TO DO
- ○
- ○
- ○
- ○

TO PHONE/WRITE
- ○ Letter to Janet
- ○ Call DAD - plan trip
- ○ Confirm Anniv. hotel res
- ○ Call Randn - re: Reunion

Now tighten down the lug nut of making and keeping commitments: Make some—now—and determine to keep them.

On the form on page 96 take five minutes to inventory your time spent. Add up your total, subtract it from 168 hours—the amount available to every one of us every week—and see what's left to distribute among your children in one-on-one, focused fathering time. If your total comes to more than 168 hours (as I've seen happen), you now know why you've been feeling so pinched for time. Look for where you want to cut your commitments, and then do the hard part: Act on it.

168 HOURS OF AVAILABLE FATHERING TIME

**Estimated
Hours
Per Week**

1. On the job, at the office, etc. ...._____

2. Commuting to and from work.._____

3. Drive times to other destinations......................................._____

4. Sleeping (avg. 7 hours per day) ...._____

5. Dressing, personal hygiene.._____

6. Church and community involvement (meetings, phone calls, practice, games, etc.)......................................_____

7. Home/lawn/car maintenance..._____

8. Errands, hobbies, sports and recreation, exercise, etc........_____

9. Time alone with wife (or serious relationships, if not married)..._____

10. Reading, bill paying, etc. ...._____

11. Misc. (TV viewing, business trips, etc.) ...._____

    Subtotal   _____

12. Maximum family/fathering time available per week........._____

    Divided by ____ children = ____hours per child per week

Lug Nut 4
Regularly review and evaluate your progress toward fathering goals.

By regularly checking your fathering, you can catch yourself if you get headed in a wrong direction. Even if you're being diligent, your approach may be off base. With the feedback you receive from evaluating your progress, you can correct your course.

If you regularly come up short on your objectives, something's wrong. Let these repeated failures prompt an investigation of *why* you are failing. Maybe you lack a particular fathering skill. Maybe you're overcommitted and should eliminate or rearrange elements in your schedule to make your objectives realistic. Maybe you're good at setting clear plans and objectives for your family, but your behavior doesn't follow your professed priorities.

Denial is the plague of honest evaluation. Be willing to admit that, in reality, your supposedly critical objectives may not actually be so critical to you. When you admit this, you can actually begin changing and doing what *is* critical to you. Make change a one-step-at-at-time process. Efforts at wholesale change usually fail.

As well as plan the next day and week ahead of time, I try to *review* my fathering goals week by week, too. What worked? What didn't work? Furthermore, I *revise* my fathering goals quarterly. (Again, a quarterly review gives me enough time to detect trends, but not so much lag time that attempts at course correction are too late.) Try planning your quarterly fathering reviews to coincide with the change of the seasons—if not according to the exact solstices and equinoxes, then maybe these more natural seasonal markers instead: the first day of your kids' school year; Thanksgiving; Easter or your kids' spring break; and the beginning of their summer vacation. Or follow your company's quarterly review schedule.

Visionary men especially need to evaluate their fathering, because although they're great goal setters, they're lousy at recognizing what it takes to reach those goals. I know—I'm one of them. If you're like me, you have to be particularly careful to set *realistic* goals. And you have to be equally careful and realistic in your self-evaluation.

Suppose you want to spend more time in meaningful conversation with each of your children. To make this a goal, you start by realistically measuring the time you now spend talking with them. I suggest getting an *objective* measure of the status quo—like noting each evening how much conversation you had that day. Then, with a realistic assessment in hand, you know what you're measuring against and if you're improving.

This is no throw-away issue. A Gallup survey conducted for the National Center for Fathering asked fathers, mothers, and their adult children how much time the fathers spent talking with their children each day. The fathers estimated 2.3 hours per day; mothers, 2.0 hours; and the adult children, 1.5 hours.[3] Other research suggests that most fathers spend far less time even than this in

> **Smart Idea:**
> Make a habit of taking your child to breakfast once a month. That adds up to 144 conversations over twelve years.

97

meaningful conversation with their children. The average father has 2.7 encounters with his six-year-old and younger children per day, each encounter lasting an average of fifteen seconds. That's an average of only forty seconds per child per day of meaningful conversation. As his kids grow up, another study suggests, fathers get better at talking with them—but not much better. From a statistically valid and anonymous survey of more than a thousand teenagers during the summer of 1987, it was found that the average teenager during a typical week spends less than *fifteen minutes* in meaningful conversation with his or her father.[4]

So start your evaluation process by objectively measuring if it's fifteen minutes a *day* or a *week* you're currently spending with your child. The revelation may alarm you, but only then can you set a realistic goal—and later celebrate your actual, instead of imagined, progress.

Now tighten down the lug nut of evaluation: Plan to review and evaluate your progress.

Examine your calendar. Identify four hours or so sometime about ninety days from today. Schedule a time and place where you can review and evaluate your progress without interruption. Guard this time as zealously as you would a corporate planning retreat. Although it is easy to get started with enthusiasm, you need a firm date and place reserved so that you will carry on as intended three months from now.

Lug Nut 5
Correct your course as necessary to reach fathering goals.

There are no perfect fathers, which is to say that even the best fathers constantly correct their courses along the way. Whether you're setting too many goals or unrealistic goals, course correction lets you compensate for this.

Smart Idea: Get some sleep even when a teenager is out late. Set your alarm for the curfew hour. If they get home before the deadline they can shut it off—and wake you, if you want. Otherwise the alarm will alert you to a missed curfew.

Several years ago I heard a successful, busy surgeon explain a routine that kept his marriage happy. He habitually spent the first twenty minutes at home each day in his rocking chair off the kitchen. When he was in that chair, he intentionally gave his wife his full attention while they discussed the personal and family issues on their minds that day.

When I heard that, I thought it was a smart idea. So I made it a goal of mine, too. The trouble was, I had younger children with their own ideas of what my agenda should be when I walked in the door at night—and it didn't include leaving Daddy alone for twenty minutes so he could sit in a chair and talk with their mom. It may have been a great plan for the doc, but despite repeated efforts, it soon became clear that it wouldn't work for me. I had to correct my course and move to a pattern of bedtime or early-morning chats with Leslie when the children were asleep. Someday I'd like to try the twenty-minute chats when I return home. The idea still appeals to me.

When I sail—which I love to do—I can point a sailboat directly where I want to go. But because I cannot control the wind, rarely do I get to sail a beeline to my destination. Instead, I have to tack, zig-zag fashion, to reach my mark.

Fathering is the same. Circumstances interfere with my perfect plans, making a straight course impossible to travel.

When you find yourself off course, says motivational speaker Zig Ziglar, "you don't change your decision to go. You change your direction to get there."

That's good fathering advice. When circumstances blow you off course, reaffirm your commitment to your children, refocus on your goals, and figure out how to get back on course.

Now tighten down the lug nut of course correction: Do it regularly and often.

Throughout each day, whenever you preview and review your week—and especially when you review your progress after ninety days—correct your course as necessary.

Holding It All Together

Acting intentionally empowers you to be the best dad you can be regardless of your current limitations. Acting intentionally allows you to dream of your fathering ideals and yet be realistic enough to consistently take small, simple, and steady steps toward your dreams.

A set of lug nuts doesn't make a wheel, and acting intentionally is only one of the five key habits of a smart dad. But the lug nuts of intentional action hold it all together.

Now let's look at the rim, and we'll identify more resources for making you a great father.

7

Habit Three: Using Your Network
The Rim

In a Calvin and Hobbes cartoon, the diminutive imp hands his father a document. "Here, Dad," he says. "I'd like you to sign this form and have it notarized."

His dad reads the paper: "I, the undersigned dad, attest that I have never parented before, and insofar as I have no experience in the job, I am liable for my mistakes and I agree to pay for any counseling, in perpetuity, Calvin may require as a result of my parental ineptitude."

In the final frame, a disgruntled Calvin sits on his bed, muttering, "I don't see how you're allowed to have a kid without signing one of those."

Whether or not Calvin's dad is as inept as his little gargoyle of a son thinks he is, fathers nevertheless worry about it. They have few reality checks against which to compare their fathering decisions or style. They generally work out their fathering issues, like most issues, in isolation—without good models, without strategies, without support. Until recently, it seems, men did not converse openly about how to be a good father. Most simply tried to do their best, without help from outside themselves. Though sometimes I lament (with tongue in cheek) that fathering couldn't be more like football—with special teams and players to cover every situation—good fathering actually does resemble football in this detail: fathering was meant to be a team effort, not an isolated struggle.

Why a Network?

If it is true that no man is an island, then it follows that no man should behave as an island if he wants to be a strong father. Island living is a sign of strength, some men believe. Yet it doesn't take too many years of fathering to realize that the job really wasn't designed to be done alone.

Consider how the creator designed human reproduction—it requires both a man and a woman, together, to create a child. This is at least an indication that raising children is a team effort from the get-go. Finding and using a support network for fathering will be easier for you, of course, if your job or pastime requires teamwork. If you work alone, on the other hand, it will take more getting used to.

In any case, a network is as necessary to your fathering as a strong rim is to your tire's performance.

Rugged individualism is a hallmark of American history and folklore. Although most men probably understand that they can benefit from a network, far too many cultural messages have sent us packing in the opposite direction. In *The Seven Habits of Highly Effective People*, Stephen Covey notes that the current social paradigm enthrones independence. It is the avowed goal of many individuals and social movements. Most of the self-improvement material puts independence on a pedestal, as though communication, teamwork, and cooperation were lesser values.

But much of our current emphasis on independence is a reaction to dependence—to having others control us, define us, use us, and manipulate us. The little-understood concept of interdependence appears to many to smack of dependence, and therefore, we find people, often for selfish reasons, leaving their marriages, abandoning their children, and forsaking all kinds of social responsibility—all in the name of independence.[1]

Smart Idea:
Next month cash your paycheck in one-dollar bills. When you get home, pile them on the table along with the month's bills to be paid. Ask each child to count out the mortgage payment, car payment, utility and phone bills, and amounts for food, gas, and clothes—just to graphically illustrate for your children that the family operates on finite funds.

Although cultural messages still applaud independence, it is nevertheless becoming more acceptable for men to reach out and ask for fathering advice—perhaps because a record proportion of this decade's fathers were raised at least part of their lives without live-in fathers. Common sense alone dictates that if a boy doesn't have a role model, he needs to find some as a man.

Five Key Habits of Smart Dads
FATHERING PARADIGM

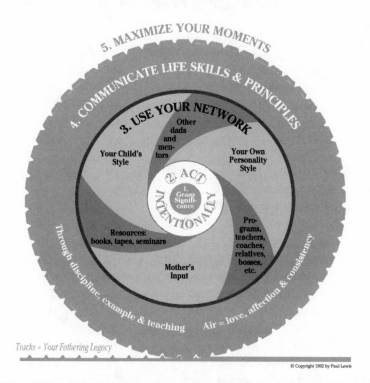

5. MAXIMIZE YOUR MOMENTS

4. COMMUNICATE LIFE SKILLS & PRINCIPLES

3. USE YOUR NETWORK

Other dads and mentors

Your Child's Style

Your Own Personality Style

2. ACT INTENTIONALLY

1. Grasp Significance

Resources: books, tapes, seminars

Programs, teachers, coaches, relatives, bosses, etc.

Mother's Input

Through discipline, example & teaching

Air = love, affection & consistency

Tracks = Your Fathering Legacy

© Copyright 1992 by Paul Lewis

Most dads in Dads University seminars already generally recognize their need for a network. After all, they *did* sign up to attend a fathering course. So when they are asked, "What would help you to be a better father?" their answers echo a need for network—either a primary network (the father, his child, and his wife or the child's mother) or a secondary network (other fathers, other significant adults, and inanimate resources).

"What would help you to be a better father?"

- **Knowing my children**
- **More time together with family**
- **More quality time together**
- **Being more direct in communicating with my teens**

- Developing a conflict-free marriage
- Being more considerate of others in my family
- Improving my relationship with others
- More help from my wife
- More time with my wife

"What help from resources outside your immediate family would you like?"

- Positive father role models to observe and talk with about fathering
- How other fathers have solved problems
- A peer support group of fathers
- Counseling with someone who has studied child psychology
- More information and input on fatherhood[2]

Using Your Network

Cultivate a network of support relationships for your fathering—one or two, four or five friends with whom you can exchange fathering discoveries and frustrations and questions, and from whom you can ask for advice when you need it—especially from a man who is a little ahead of you on the fathering road. Talking about adolescence with someone who has already fathered his way through his child's adolescence, for instance, can give you both moral support and insight into that season of parenting. Reading the findings of one who has studied discipline, sibling rivalry, or parenting styles can give you the knowledge you need to make wise decisions.

Start building your network with a simple phone call to a friend, or a conversation in the locker room or around the water cooler. "Jim, one thing I admire about you is the common sense you seem to apply to your family life—you know, just what you do as a dad. I'm not sure about some of the calls I've made in my family. Would you be interested in getting together from time to time to talk openly about scaling the walls I come up against trying to be a good dad? I know *I'd* sure benefit from that kind of interaction. Maybe Bill would be interested in joining in, too."

Set a time and place to meet, and start with the idea that you'll get together at least three times in the first five or six weeks for continuity and true support to take place in the relationships.

You can function at one of three levels, writes Stephen Covey in *The Seven Habits of Highly Effective People*—in dependence, independence, or interdependence. And he makes a strong case for interdependency:

> Dependent people need others to get what they want. Independent people can get what they want through their own efforts. Interdependent people combine their own efforts with the efforts of others to achieve their greatest success.[3]

When I function as an interdependent person, man, and father, I look for and regularly gain the opportunity to tap the vast experience, wisdom, and potential that is resident in the fathering pilgrimage of other men. I am less afraid and more motivated to reveal my inner self to other men—and, in return, be rewarded by deeper levels of friendship. A network allows me to create synergy with others for greater success as a father than I could achieve acting independently.

Your Primary Network

Three relationships intersect to form your primary fathering network, similar to the dominant spokes in a high-performance wheel rim:

Five Key Habits of Smart Dads
FATHERING PARADIGM

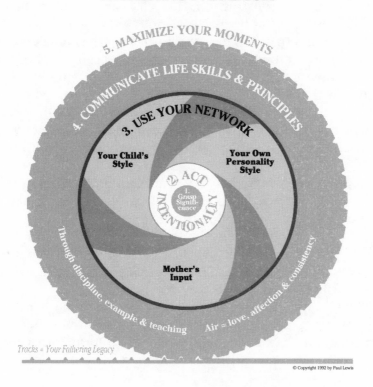

5. MAXIMIZE YOUR MOMENTS

4. COMMUNICATE LIFE SKILLS & PRINCIPLES

3. USE YOUR NETWORK

Your Child's Style

Your Own Personality Style

2. ACT INTENTIONALLY

1. Grasp Significance

Mother's Input

Through discipline, example & teaching

Air = love, affection & consistency

Tracks = Your Fathering Legacy

© Copyright 1992 by Paul Lewis

- **Your personality, style, and talents**
- **Your child's personality, style, talents, and development**
- **The child's mother's input and support**

The intersections of these personalities prompt various responses. Some of his children's traits, a father must realize, simply don't mesh with his. This apparent conflict doesn't mean that one personality is better than the other. The smart dad simply notes the differences, then finds ways to accommodate them—while still affirming the person his child was created to be.

Of my five children, Jon is least like me. He cares little about convention and what people think of him. As a youngster he never wanted me to show him how to do anything. Jon was always confident he could figure it out for himself. My fantasies of Norman Rockwell moments with him never came to pass. Jon didn't want to be taught woodworking. Before I could finish my little lecture about the safe use of the rotary sander, he'd grab it or else he'd walk away saying, "Okay, okay, I got it!" The difference between our personalities caused many tense moments over the years.

Yet I eventually learned to appreciate Jon's learning style, and he eventually learned woodworking in his own way. He spent some summers working in construction. He's a locksmith now, so he regularly works with wood as he installs various kinds of locks. His woodwork around the shop has even earned him the boss's praise.

If I had noticed sooner that Jon always had been ahead of others his age when it came to taking responsibility for himself, I could have saved myself a lot of frustration. I should have backed off and let Jon learn as he learns best.

The best parenting strategy is a difficult one: take note of your child's talents and adapt your training methods to mesh with the child's style.

After Jon moved out to his own apartment, I asked him if he wanted to meet for breakfast once a week to talk. Now over pancakes or oatmeal, our love and mutual respect for one another has deepened more as adult friends than as father and son. With the passing of only a couple years, our freedom to comment about each other's lives and to swap advice has changed completely. It was a matter of letting Jon be Jon.

A wise dad also listens to the input of the child's mother. A woman can often read a child's emotional condition more readily, or be more aware of what is typical behavior—if for no other reason than spending more time with her child than a father typically does. Leslie has abundant intuition when it comes to our children. She naturally has a different perspective of her children than I do—a maternal view that is an asset to me when I listen to her insight.

This primary network is dynamic; that is, it exists in motion, not at rest. At the office, on the other hand, relationships and boundaries and interactions tend to be more static. You typically have a designated work space, clear job expectations, and well-worn paths of communication with those above and below you in corporate hierarchy.

At home, however, boundaries tend to be fuzzy. Yet men tend to continue operating at home the way they did at the office, especially if they do not know themselves well. Such fathers run over other family members without respecting their differences. They don't recognize their blind spots.

Only when you respect your child and the mother as much as yourself can you take what each personality brings to your domestic mix, and from it help shape a pattern of mutual support.

Your Personality, Style, and Talents

It is in their work that men tend to express their personality, style, and talents most intensely. Although fathering is primarily relational, most men see it, too, as a job. So when you consider how you handle most jobs, you can see how your personality carries over into your fathering style as well.

Some guys are hands-on managers, some like to delegate, some are naturally strong leaders, others are naturally strong background and support people. How you father will reveal your management style—and don't be surprised if your management style doesn't mesh with all of your children.

Suppose you're a take-charge leader with two kids, for instance—one is naturally docile, a follower. The other child is just like you, a born leader. As sure as your eyes are reading these words, your take-charge style will go head to head with whichever child inherited your personality. So you need to understand the styles of you and all your children; in this way you can manage and reduce conflicts. You will avoid approving the docile child simply because he does what you want without asking any questions, and you will find

Smart Idea:
Next holiday when the grandfolks visit, videotape an interview with them, during which each of them reminisces about their childhood experiences, their own parents, what their best and worst choices were, etc. The video will become an instant family heirloom.

ways to affirm your other child's grit while teaching him how to submit to authority.

"Fathering Confidence: Shaping Your Own Style" is the title of a Dads University half-day course, in which I teach a personal-assessment approach I call *historical intelligence*. It doesn't plot you on a preconceived axis or grid of personality types based on how you score compared to a set of standardized norms. It runs contrary to the feeling we've grown up with, that measurement and evaluation highlight only our mistakes—what we do wrong. With historical intelligence, we begin by assuming that everyone is born with a unique matrix of drives, gifts, and abilities. It is these we want to discover by evaluating the content of stories they select from a life of significant and satisfying achievements. Historical intelligence looks only to what we do well or right to form an assessment.

What Are Your Strengths?

Your natural abilities shine most at the times you've achieved the best in your life. Your interests and achievements tend to flow from your deepest natural ability, something you naturally focus on and do very well. These *inborn* talents and *natural* abilities differ from the skills you have *learned* and may, in fact, be very good at.

To assess your strengths using the historical-intelligence method, you analyze the content of your achievement stories—five to ten episodes and experiences in your life from childhood to the present that you remember fondly as your best and most satisfying moments. Even if the stories are different and disconnected, you will find that common threads run through them all. Dads University participants select and tell stories of past personal achievements. These stories we examine for the tell-tale signs of natural drives and abilities:

- **What are the central two or three dynamics that motivate a father most?**
- **What kind of stage (that is, circumstances) does this man prefer to play on?**
- **What kind of supporting cast does he prefer to have around him?**
- **What kind of applause does he enjoy most? Financial? Praise? Status?**
- **What pace does he tend to work at?**

Then we compare these findings (a father's natural abilities) to the requirements of fathering (the five key habits) and see exactly what he does naturally that is also smart fathering.

Just as you will probably be stressed out in a job that requires talents you *don't* have, yet has no use for qualities you possess in abundance—so fathering will be much easier if you know your personality, your style, and your natural abilities and subsequently play to your strengths. What you don't do well, you can fill in from your network (mother of child, other fathers, outside resources). You accentuate the positive and compensate for the negative. You play smarter, not harder.

When his twin daughters were old enough to eat solid food, Noel Paul Stookey (Paul of the folk-singing group Peter, Paul, and Mary) unsuccessfully tried to get the baby food from the jar and into the girls' mouths, which they clamped shut at the sight of a spoonful of Gerber's. Attached to one of the high-chair trays Paul noticed a rattle, wobbling on its suction-cup base. He pulled it off, stuck it on his forehead, and got the silly thing dancing wildly. Of course, his girls were so captivated by the gyrating rattle projecting out of their father's head (or so it seemed) that their mouths dropped open—which gave him time enough to spoon the meal into their mouths.

Stookey did no more than what you can do. He simply used his own personality style to accomplish his particular fathering challenges. And you can do it your way, with your style and your natural abilities.

Your Child's Personality, Style, Talents, and Development

As you make the most of your own natural style and abilities in leading your family, do the same for your children. Become a student of each of your children—really noticing what is unique to each one—so that you can make affirming comments every time your child does something well. This habit fosters healthy self-esteem in any child.

Plus you have to consider some other facets of your children.

Smart Idea:
After dinner one night this week, haul out the photo albums or video tapes and relive your best family vacation. Before you get too far into the vacation's photos or video, hold hands in a circle and —with eyes closed—try to storytell your way through each day in sequence.

• **Developmental stages.** Children grow through predictable stages of physical, mental, emotional, and moral development. If you know what stage a child is in, you won't inadvertently demand behavior of which the child is simply incapable. You don't ask a two-year-old to carry a forty-pound suitcase upstairs—which is akin to what we unfairly require sometimes in ways other than physical.

In children younger than two or so, for example, normal cognitive development has not progressed far enough to let them project *what might happen* to them—which is why, up to about this age, they are perfectly content to sleep in a pitch-dark room. As the brain develops, however, and the child grows into the next cognitive level, she begins to project *what might happen* to her in the dark. Almost overnight, it seems, she becomes afraid of the dark and begins squawking for a night light. Nor will it do any good to point out to her that just yesterday she was content sleeping in a dark room.

When you know your child's developmental stage, you can make better decisions about your child.

So open your calendar right now and schedule a forty-five minute visit to the library soon. Get your hands on some child-psychology books with developmental charts. Photocopy one or two you feel will be useful, and put them where you can refer to them every two or three months—or whenever a child does or says something that makes you wonder about just where he is developmentally.

• **Learning styles.** Like you, children also have individual learning styles. Some learn best by *hearing* information; others, by *seeing* it; still others, by getting their hands on it and working with it. Determine how your child prefers to learn—especially if she has a learning difficulty—for then you can present material in the manner she can best assimilate it.

My nine-year-old is strongly auditory. If you want David to do a list of chores, tell him—don't leave a note. He'll remember what you tell him, but he'll forget to check a list I've written out for him. In his schoolwork, reading a book is a less effective way of learning for David than listening to a teacher explain the same information—which is exactly the opposite of his sister's learning style.

When I cooperate with the different learning styles of my children, I get more results as a dad.[4]

The Child's Mother

Her role in your child's life is inestimable. You are wise to cooperate with her. Even if you and she do not live together, it is vital that you work together in the best interest of your child. If you *are* married to the child's mother, of course, this aspect of your network will be easier.

If you don't regularly do this, start now asking your child's mother for insight into your child's personality, style, and talents. Use questions such as, "What's the best way I can encourage Kim? At this time, what does she need most from me? Is there an immediate goal you are working on for which I can provide support? Can I help you by coming in from a different angle?"

Take it a step further: Ask her for her perspective of your own personality, style, and abilities as they relate to your fathering. Let her encourage and support you in your fathering. The feedback of someone who loves your child as much as you do is a resource you neglect only to your own detriment.

The Secondary Network

Your secondary network consists of other fathers, other players in your child's life, and outside resources that can be used to enhance your fathering.

Five Key Habits of Smart Dads
FATHERING PARADIGM

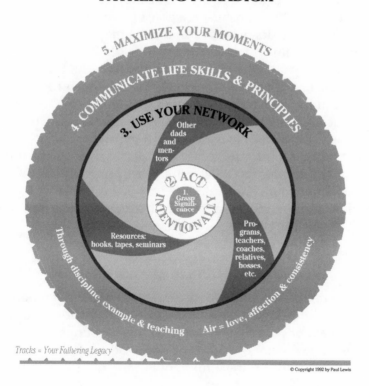

5. MAXIMIZE YOUR MOMENTS

4. COMMUNICATE LIFE SKILLS & PRINCIPLES

3. USE YOUR NETWORK

Other dads and mentors

2. ACT INTENTIONALLY

1. Grasp Significance

Resources: books, tapes, seminars

Programs, teachers, coaches, relatives, bosses, etc.

Through discipline, example & teaching

Air = love, affection & consistency

Tracks = Your Fathering Legacy

You need relationships with other fathers and mentors for your moral support, encouragement, and accountability. Mentors can also be a role model for *you*—something you may not have had as a child. Contact with other players in your child's life—teachers, coaches, club leaders—allows you to draw from their insight, knowledge, and awareness of your child as well as to monitor their influence on your child. Then there are resources outside your routine—material as well as people—than can fill in the fathering blanks.

A lot of divorced or separated fathers are in anguish when custody battles and unfriendly courts make contact with their children difficult or even impossible. There are no easy answers or solutions to this problem. The best advice I can give you is this:

• Call family-law attorneys, friends, psychologists—anyone you can think of for a referral to a fathers'-rights support group in your community. Discover whatever network they have of legal advice and resources.

• Let you child's mom know that, past history notwithstanding, you have no intention of giving up on having a good relationship with your child. As evidence, let her know that you are reading this book. Send her a copy, or at least photocopy for her a few pages from chapter five where you've underlined or highlighted the negative impact of children who don't have a regular relationship with their father. Appeal to her natural desire to give your child the best chance in life.

• When direct lines of communication with your child's mother are impossible, try tactfully staying in touch with the grandparents on either side, or with some other relative with which the child's mom communicates. Word of your love as a father can filter back.

• Patience is a crucial weapon. I've spoken with many fathers who quickly became discouraged and still remain angry. It's a natural reaction when you care so deeply and all the courts seem interested in is your child-support dollars. But time is on your side; if you will demonstrate your concern in any way you can, one day your child will begin thinking for himself or herself and will want to see you. Your dedication will be rewarded.

Other Fathers and Mentors

Want to double your fathering confidence and cut your anxieties in half? Get in the habit of meeting regularly with a small group of other dads to talk about fathering. For fourteen years now I've written a newsletter on fathering. I've read extensively about marriage, families, parenting, children. But the most valuable time

I've spent becoming a confident dad was in my weekly meetings with two other friends and fathers for an hour or two discussing our fathering skills and problems. At first we put a spin on our stories so we'd look good. But we quickly realized that omitting our ugly little details did no one any good. So to encourage each other to be honest, we agreed that any time one of us sensed the whole story wasn't being told, he had standing authorization to call the wife and get *her* version of the incident.

That took care of pretense.

We give each other freedom to ask hard questions of us—but that also help us become better fathers. In these discussions we've helped each other through daughters' boyfriends we didn't like, through children struggling to manage sexual values in school, media influences, poor attitudes, and problems about marital compatibility. We've watched each other's kids grow, and we've celebrated the victories along the way.

We don't meet as often now, but we still share a warmth and freedom on the phone or in person with each other that I don't easily have with other men. I wouldn't trade those hours for anything—sitting in a car, around a table in a mall restaurant, walking the trails at a nearby park. There's fathering power and safety in those relationships.

Every dad needs a group of men committed to his support. It creates a source of encouragement and feedback essential to maintaining the five key habits of smart dads.

Consider these ground rules for such a group:

• *Keep confidences*. What is said won't be repeated even to spouses, without explicit permission. Trust is impossible without confidentiality.

• *Don't gossip*. Be especially careful not to talk about group members in their absence.

• *Attend regularly*. How strictly you define "regular attendance" is up to your group. But keep in mind that casual attendance delays the development of the group and can frustrate more committed members. If you've asked for a commitment to a limited number of meetings—maybe six or eight—then regular attendance should be a reasonable expectation.

> **Smart Idea:**
> Collect in a folder, shoe box, or notebook all the quotes, clippings, anecdotes, and stories that best express your beliefs and favorite axioms. Label it "Ideas I Want My Kids to Remember," and organize the material as a going-away gift when they leave home.

• *Participate, but don't dominate.* Everyone has something to contribute, and no one has all the answers.

• *Accept disagreement.* Your purpose is not to see everything alike. You agree simply to disagree courteously.

Start your own fathering support group in two steps:

Step 1. Make a short list of dads with whom you enjoy talking—and who are committed to being good dads. Give each a call and, either on the phone or over lunch, explain what you're thinking about:

• You want to turn in a strong fathering performance, but you're not always sure what to do. As in other endeavors and business, you've found wisdom and strength in asking questions and getting wise counsel.

• You're looking for two or three or four fathers who would meet every week or two for ninety days to talk openly about fathering, family, and how to win the day-to-day fight to keep life in balance. You're looking for guys who could give and receive advice and hold each other accountable for carrying out plans the discussions might unfold.

• Ask for a commitment of six to eight weeks to see what value might unfold. Explain that you'll come prepared each time with a little agenda and some fathering information that can kick off a useful discussion. (Men are seldom motivated to carve out valuable time for a meeting with no agenda and no one in charge.)

Step 2. At your first get together, break the ice by asking each man to describe the differences between each of his children (their personality bents, interests, which parent they're most like, etc.). You go first, to demonstrate the detail and honesty you're expecting from each man.

Pass out photocopies of a short article about kids, families, or fathering you've found that raises good questions or offers advice. Read it together and talk about how it does or doesn't apply to each of your situations.

Assign simple homework for everybody based on conclusions you reached. Create a short list of topics you want to discuss next time. Review the ground rules for your group.

Once you're past a couple of meetings, close the group to new members so that you can build on the intimacy you've launched. You can invite others in when you restart the group or form a different group after a break from meeting.

A 24-page *Dads University Trax Team Captain's Guide,* available for $3.50 from Family University, offers numerous suggestions for launching and sustaining small fathering groups, curriculum sugges-tions, and a great selection of ice-breaker questions and activities. (See the Dads University notice on page 190 to order).

Other Players in Your Child's Life

As great a father as you might be, your child will not be raised by you alone—and that is fortunate. Gone are "Little House on the Prairie" days, when a father had supreme control over everyone who came in contact with his children. Today your child is proba-bly under the care of others, whether in day-care or school. She is influenced by radio, television, music, newspapers, videos, and movies. As he grows older, he will spend increasing amounts of time at work, on sports teams, in social organizations, and with friends.

So part of your job as a committed father is monitoring the impact these other players make in your child's life—and making the most of their involvement. Teachers, counselors, youth leaders, coaches, and neighbors can make a big contribution. They parent your kids when you aren't around. Expressing appreciation to these adults only enhances their attitude toward your child. Esteem them and their efforts in your child's behalf. Encourage them by volun-teering in your child's classroom, by chaperoning field trips or par-ties; by so doing you inspire them to keep up the good work and increase their level of connection with your child.

Other significant adults in your child's life give you a fresh per-spective of child. For instance, talk to your daughter's teacher to find out how she relates to a group. Talk to your son's employer to discover what life skills and principles he's good at or how you need to help him develop. Talk to your child's friends to see what kinds of kids he associates with. These interactions yield a wealth of information you can use to understand your child and learn how best to father him.

Unfortunately, you must also protect your children from people who can hurt them. Educate each child about appropriate and inap-propriate behavior by other adults. Be aware of who your child hangs out with, and limit the contact if it is in the best interest of the child. Equip your children in advance for circumstances they will encounter.

Think ahead. You can't keep your chil-dren sheltered their entire lives from out-

Smart Idea:
Secretly tape record your family's breakfast-table conversation next Saturday or Sunday morning. Then play it back that night as a dinner surprise.

side influences, but you can stay ahead of the game by anticipating influences they will encounter and by going on the offensive.

Using Outside Resources

Although I believe every father can be strengthened by the insight and instruction he can gain from outside resources, some men are too busy, they don't tend to read about fathering and family issues, or they simply don't feel the need to look outside their own intuition or family circle for help.

Aerobics guru Dr. Kenneth Cooper admitted how difficult it was for him to accept the fact that he needed help from an outside resource for his then-young daughter, who had a learning disability that made learning to read very difficult. Cooper's first response was to tutor her himself. Many hours of trying to teach his daughter to read only frustrated him and discouraged his daughter.

Then he used his network. He contacted reading specialists and educators experienced in teaching children with his daughter's learning difficulty. Shedding that job was the best thing to do as a father, under the circumstances. The professionals succeeded at teaching his daughter to read. Cooper's willingness to use outside resources empowered his daughter to learn and greatly enhanced her self-esteem.

Many excellent fathering resources are available—books, tapes, videos, seminars, classes. Family University recommends these:

• **Smart Dads.** A bimonthly subscription newsletter with a wealth of practical tips, ideas, and insights for fathering toddlers through teenagers. Published six times a year. Each year's subscription includes two semi-annual "Dad Talk" audio cassettes. (See page 190 for subscription information.)

• **Dads University.** A curriculum of half-day fathering courses that can be hosted in your city by community groups, churches, or corporations. Each course is taught by a trained and certified Family University instructor.

• **Dad Trax.** A series of hour-long audio cassettes for drive-time listening, featuring a Reader's Digest-style potpourri

Smart Idea:
The "pits" is what exhausted parents call that last hour before dinner with tired, hungry, fussy kids. If you're not fixing the meal, scoop up the kids for a thirty-minute walk around the block, or clean out a closet or a toy box, or otherwise occupy everybody until the meal is ready.

of five-minute discussions on topics of interest to every dad (published by Family University).

• *40 Ways to Teach Your Child Values.* A practical handbook of ideas for communicating forty important skills, attitudes, and values to children, from toddlers to teens.

• *Famous Fathers.* A two-hour series of four videos featuring fathering stories, comments, and insights from celebrity fathers Stan Smith, Rosey Grier, Bill Gaither, Josh McDowell, Kenneth Cooper, and Noel Paul Stookey.

Other sources of excellent fathering resources are Focus on the Family (8665 Explorer Dr., Colorado Springs, CO 80920, phone 917/531-3400) and the National Center for Fathering (10200 W. 75th, Ste. 267, Shawnee Mission, KS 66204, phone 913/384-4661).

For those who want to build a small fathering library of your own, I suggest the following books and tapes:

• *The Seven Habits of Highly Successful Fathers*, Ken Canfield

• *Missing from Action: Vanishing Manhood in America*, Weldon Hardenbrook

• *Raising Self-Reliant Children in a Self-Indulgent World*, H. Stephen Glenn and Jane Nelson

• *The On My Own Handbook*, Bob Biehl

• *Tender Warrior: God's Intention for a Man*, Stu Weber

• *Fathers and Sons: The Wound, the Bond, and the Healing*, Gordon Dalby

• *Finding Our Fathers: How a Man's Life Is Shaped by His Relationship with His Father*, Sam Osherson

Worthy additions to this list appear regularly. You are invited to write to Family University for additional recommendations.

8

Habit Four: Communicating Life Skills and Principles

The Tire

In a Dads University course, I often ask men to form groups of three or four to introduce themselves to each other—but in this way: Each man is to assume the character of his own father, and introduce his son—that is, himself. (Phil, role-playing his father, says, "I'd like to introduce you to my son, Phil . . .")

The introductions are always animated and broken by laughter one minute, tears the next. Within the first few sentences, most men stop talking *as* their dads and revert to talking *about* their dads—in particular, the skills, lessons, and insights their dads taught them.

A man gets a special sparkle in his eye and pride in his voice when he says, "My dad taught me that—." I overheard my own sons say it recently to some neighborhood friends as they sawed wood and pounded nails on the patio, building something at the workbenches I made for them last Christmas.

As the project progressed, one of the playmates asked my boys more than once, "Hey, how'd you learn how to do that?"

"My dad taught me."

It felt good hearing that. I want to be my boys' primary instructor. I want to keep a clear channel of communication so they'll always know they can ask Dad, and that I'll give every answer my best shot— even if I have to respond, "I don't know, but I'll help you find out."

The fourth key habit of smart dads is that of giving your children a working understanding of the life skills and principles they will need to function successfully as adults.

In our wheel paradigm, this is the tire. Tires come in a great variety of styles and constructions, each suited to handle different weather and road conditions. We select tires with an eye to the roads we travel, the weather and driving conditions we anticipate. The ideal tire is strong and fairly adaptable to most road surfaces.

Five Key Habits of Smart Dads
FATHERING PARADIGM

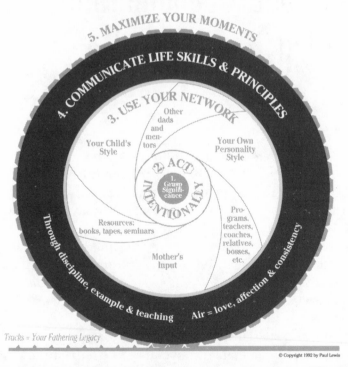

Start with a broad-based approach to communicating life skills and principles to your children. You see the world in which they live, the dilemmas they will face. Your assignment is to shape in your child the necessary character and commitments to safely maneuver through whatever challenges you can anticipate for them.

Today's rate of technological and cultural change is dizzying. But then, most generations feel that life moves faster for them than it did for their forbears. I ran across a small fathering book entitled *Dad, Whose Boy Is Yours?* The preface began, "The speed of modern living is terrific. Never before have there been so many demands upon each ten minutes of a man's time." I checked the copyright page and saw the date—1936.

The sense that modern life is rushing by isn't new, but the rate of change has seemed to accelerate, even by objective standards. One of my fathering concerns is to assess what skills my kids will need when, in a few years, they are on their own in an even more hyper world. How can I prepare them to live maturely in the very different world that ours will be twenty years from now?

The answer is to focus on principles and fundamentals. I must teach them a process for aiming at good answers, rather than giving them answers myself. I must teach them to assimilate timeless principles that ought to govern all decisions, regardless of cultural changes—truth, fairness, love, integrity, loyalty. I must teach them to accept responsibility for their own lives, to practice self-control, to express their feelings without hurting others in the process, to respond to others' needs.

I must help them recognize that, in their power of choice, they control much of their own destiny. I must introduce them to God, who holds their destiny in his hand, teaching them to love and obey him. (Later I will explain the connection I see between my relationship with God and how I relate to my children as a father.)

Teach Them How to Think

Ask questions.

Teaching your child *how* to think and reason is infinitely better than teaching them *what* to think.

Asking questions is the chief way of teaching children how to think. Say you are teaching your son to wait his turn in line. One Saturday morning at the playground you notice him cut in front of other kids. You could say, "Hey, I told you to wait your turn." Or you could ask him, "What have I taught you about taking turns when using the slide?" The question

Smart Idea:
Kidnap your child for lunch this week. Find out the exact time school breaks for lunch, notify the school office, and show up outside the classroom door. A nearby fast-food restaurant will do the trick. When it's your *wife* you kidnap for lunch, take her to a restaurant at the mall.

requires him to find his own answer—based on your instruction—and apply it. Your next question might be about how he should correct his behavior or repair the feelings of others.

It can be a bit trickier with older children, especially when moral issues are involved, but the approach is the same—*what* questions rather than *why* questions yield far better results in terms of shaping character and sponsoring maturity:

- "What is wrong with driving home from a party after you have taken a drink?"
- "What consequence did we agree you would experience?"
- "What are you risking when you choose to cheat on a test?" (or "to lie to me" or "to be sexually active")
- "What will it take to reestablish trust between us?"

Let them choose between good options.

Hone decision-making skills in younger children by giving them options. Once your daughter can talk, ask her, "Do you want to wear your blue dress or your green one?" "Do you want to have an egg or pancakes?" When she grows older and contemplates a poor choice, you can set firm limitations, yet at the same time offer options.

Your teenage girl wants to date too soon, for instance. You can set firm limits with "No, you can't date until you're sixteen." But don't stop there—give her some options: "You can have a boy you want to know better visit with our family at home or go out to dinner with us." This way she can practice making appropriate decisions, though within your limits.

It is essential that rules of behavior in your family are clear and clearly communicated. It's even better when a fair and clear penalty for breaking the rule is attached to each. If established up front, before the infraction occurs, you have the luxury of responding in sympathy with your child in terms of the discipline to be dished out, rather than being in the position of playing judge and jury, making up the penalty on the spot. Post the basic rules you agree on in a conspicuous spot.

Some examples of what family rules might be:

- **Courtesies—if you open it, close it. If you turn it on, turn it off. If you break it, repair it. If you can't repair it, report it. If you use it, don't abuse it. If you make a mess, clean it up. If you move it, put it back.**
- **Personal stuff is private. Get permission first.**

- Homework and chores precede TV and video games.
- Truth rules—we never lie to each other.
- If you won't be home on time, call.
- If your plans change midstream, report them first.
- Family plans and commitments come first.

If you and your spouse don't agree on a particular rule, work out a compromise. A lack of clarity here sends very confusing messages to your children.

Let them tell you why.

Once you establish rules and principles that guide your family, ask questions to help your child think through the reasoning behind your rules. When a child protests "Why can't I?" to a limiting rule you lay down, you can ask, "You tell me: Why can't you do that? Why is this important?" Thinking about reasons behind rules does not spawn little rebels, but cultivates healthy, active consciences.

Help them find their own answers.

Don't give your children all the answers. Help them instead to learn the process for finding answers. My daughter Shelley often asks me to spell a word for her. If I'm busy, I'm tempted to simply spell the word for her. But I do better when I say, "Try it yourself, Shelley, while I listen." Eight times out of ten times she spells it right, and trying it builds her confidence.

If a child has a school project due, go to the library and show her how to find the information she needs. Lead her in trying various paths to follow in obtaining her research . . . in projecting what will likely result from each of the routes she proposes. Suggest whom she could ask for help when she exhausts her own ideas. This kind of teaching does more good than merely giving answers to a child's questions.

In short, ask questions whenever your child—

- **Needs to stop and think about his behavior.**
- **Needs reminding about a rule being broken.**

Smart Idea:

Spring these riddles on your kids:

- What is everybody in the world doing at the same time? (Growing older)
- What is the center of gravity? (The letter V)
- What word is always pronounced wrong? (Wrong)
- What can go up the chimney down, but can't go down the chimney up? (An umbrella)

- Needs to think about the rights or feelings of others.
- Needs encouragement to make the right moral choice.

How you ask questions is important, too:

- Lower your voice and avoid sarcasm.
- Ask only one question at a time.
- Use questions to keep your emotions under control.
- Repeat your question if your child is avoiding the right answer.
- Use questions instead of statements to remind the child of what he already has been taught. ("What have I told you about waiting in line?")

The Importance of How You Communicate

Strong families communicate with each other clearly and regularly. Communication is a set of skills you can develop. You're certainly at an advantage if you came from a family that communicated well; but even if communication was poor in your home, you can learn what makes for successful communication and practice these skills as you interact with your children.

Communicate with a spirit of love.

The tire represents the important life skills and principles your child needs to acquire. Just as the best tire in the world won't take you far if it's flat, so you must inflate the life skills and principles you communicate with the air of your love, affection, and consistency—the fatherly combination that allows this tire to roll. If you try to communicate even the right things, but without a spirit of love, your attempt will be futile.

This point is made eloquently in the New Testament by the Apostle Paul:

> If I speak in the tongues of men and of angels, but have not love, I am only a resounding gong or a clanging cymbal. If I have the gift of prophecy and can fathom all mysteries and all knowledge, and if I have a faith that can move mountains, but have not love, I am nothing. If I give all I possess to the poor and surrender my body to the flames, but have not love, I gain nothing. (1 Cor. 13:1-3)

It's difficult for some men to actively love their children because love, they believe wrongly, is a feeling (although it is true that when you love your children, you will likely generate loving feelings). Love is a verb, not a noun. Love is action. Love is choosing to do whatever is necessary for the well-being of your children. As you love your children, they will become receptive to whatever you communicate to them—including life skills and principles. Yet the most correct instruction in the world won't make much difference in your children if at the same time you do not demonstrate your active love for them.

Demonstrate your love by telling your children how much you love them, listening intently when they talk, showing physical affection (hugs, kisses, wrestling, an arm around the shoulder, a pat on the head), spending time with them, paying attention to them, speaking to them respectfully, and faithfully caring for their needs.

Communicating with a spirit of love means that you—

• **Talk directly to one another.** If you have something to say to your wife or daughter, go to her directly instead of talking about her to other members of the family. Don't rely on them overhearing a comment made about them to provoke them to respond. Couriers of your message will only distort it—plus you'll probably hurt the feelings of the person talked about, or you'll betray a confidence.

• **Don't rely on rumors.** Go to the source. Make sure that what you heard *about* someone is in truth what was actually said or done.

• **Listen very carefully.** Listening deeply shows respect for your children and earns their respect. When a child tries to talk to you, exercise enough patience to let him say what he's trying to say rather than finishing the sentence for him. Take time to listen. Give the child feedback to make sure you understand her—then make sure she knows that you did actually hear her.

• **Keep your conflicts out in the open.** Strong families have fights and get mad at each other, but they keep their conflicts out in the open. They honestly discuss differences and aren't passive-aggressive in punishing each other (like giving someone the silent treatment).

• **Work toward resolution.** Remain committed to talking through a disputed issue until a solution is reached that is best for everybody.

Build communication bridges by blessing your child.

If you want to get across to your children the life skills and principles you have to communicate, actively and regularly bless your child. Authors Gary Smalley

Smart Idea:

A person's last thoughts of the day remain in the subconscious all night. It's a good reason, as you say goodnight to your child, to praise her for a character strength you admire or an act or word of hers that made you proud of her.

125

and John Trent offer this excellent formula for conveying a strong sense of your blessing:

• **Meaningful touch.** Make a habit of touching your child in positive ways. A hug, kiss, or a pat on the back makes your words real to them. Children need lots of meaningful touch; research shows that it actually causes positive physiological changes when you touch your child with affection.

• **Spoken words.** Say what you mean. Say what you feel toward your child. Spoken words, words of instruction, praise, affirmation, are all powerful ways to convey love.

Solomon, acknowledged in the ancient world as enormously wise, wrote that "death and life are in the power of the tongue" (Prov. 18:21). Accordingly, when you say, "Jason, the way you stood up for your sister today makes me proud. That took real courage," you affirm not only the act, but also the value of the child. What commonly keeps fathers from verbally blessing their children are workaholism, withdrawal, simple procrastination, or the fact that they were never blessed verbally by their own father.

• **Express the high value you place on your child.** Tell your child often how much you value him or her. Comment on specific character traits and physical attributes that you admire and appreciate. Let your son know that you like the way he dressed and groomed himself. Express your appreciation for the way your daughter comes home every day and does her homework without being told to do so.

• **Picture a special future.** Envision the best happening in your child's life and express that vision ("Boy, with a pitching arm like that you could be in the major leagues").

• **Be actively committed to helping your child succeed.** When you communicate important life skills, take steps to equip the child to experience success with the skill you are teaching. When you teach your young son how to groom himself properly, for instance, it's not enough to tell him to take a shower and wash his hair if he has never been *taught* to shower and shampoo on his own. So teach him how— and remember that teaching includes helping him overcome any fear he has of the water or of getting shampoo in his eyes, it includes using nonirritating shampoo to *guarantee* his eyes won't burn, giving him the brushes to do his own hair, and so on.[1]

Let your children learn from your experience.

Your children learn how life works when you share your life with them. So let your kids learn from both your successes and your failures. Give them a taste of the struggles you face outside your home. Men tend not to talk about their problems and insecurities with their families, perhaps because we fear we will appear weak or because we want to shelter our family from worry. But when your children see that you're not perfect, then they can more easily share *their* problems and insecurities.

So model not only your virtues, but model also your frankness about your faults. Kids don't expect perfection in you, but they will profit from your doing your best to live true to your own values. Teach them the importance of honesty by acting honestly. Teach them the importance of wearing seat belts by buckling up. Live the values you want your child to learn.

"He was my teacher," Kevin Costner said of his father, "and he taught me about loyalty and friendship and doing your best. . . . Truth and those things are never far out of style."[2]

Demonstrate the skills you want to teach them.

Before expecting your child to do something properly, you must instruct him adequately and thoroughly. You cannot simply assign a young child a new chore, expect it to be completed, and then—when the child inevitably fails at it—deflate her with "If I want something done right around here, I have to do it myself."

Overcome your impatience by working in pairs at a skill. It promotes cooperation, respect, mutual support, and makes large jobs easier. When the pair is a parent and child, furthermore, you have a natural reason to be together and talk—plus your quality-control may be less threatening.

Another way to demonstrate skills you want your child to learn is to take him with you to your workplace and show him what you do there. Not too many generations ago, children saw the work their fathers did; many, in fact, learned trades at the hands of their fathers.

These days, though "work" steals fathers from their children, few children have a clue about what their fathers do at work all day. Yet on occasion—and depending on the ages of your children and the nature of your work—you can take your child to work or on a business trip. (One dad I know takes each child along with him every year on a business

Smart Idea:

As you're tucking your child into bed, get crazy. "Hey, let's camp out in the living room tonight!" Grab two sleeping bags and a flashlight. Make shadow animals on the ceiling, talk about your day, and plan a real campout together in the near future.

trip.) If your children are self-disciplined enough and your work is conducive to having them present, these are excellent times to spend with your child, to communicate how important the child is to you, and to help her understand your job and the realities you contend with.

These reminders have helped me when I plan a business trip with my children:

- **Spell out the ground rules.**
- **If she will miss school, arrange for her to bring homework along to fill up the time when you are busy.**
- **Plan time to visit a historical site or take in a fun activity unique to your destination.**

Release children progressively throughout life.

Practice equipping and releasing your child. From childhood onward, give them freedom and confidence in their own abilities.

It's like teaching him to ride a bicycle. First he graduates from the tricycle. Then he learns to maneuver a two-wheeler with training wheels. When you see he's got the idea, you take off the training wheels—but you still don't just let him go. You hold on, running alongside; as long as he stays up, you keep your hands off the bike (but never far from it). When he wobbles, you catch him. You keep encouraging, coaching, and letting go until he can keep his balance indefinitely and no longer needs you running alongside. What you've done is give him freedom and confidence in his own ability.

Letting go is a process that you need to practice from day one with your children. If they are taught to accept responsibility for their own lives, then step by step we end up with grown children who can cope with life successfully when they leave our care. If we still have to remind our children to do their homework, pick up their clothes, and be home on time well past the age when they should be responsible for these tasks on their own, they will not be prepared to deal successfully with life on their own, when we're not around.

It is during the early years of childhood that these skills are most effectively taught, with only touch-up and fine-tuning during junior high and high school. If you can do this, your children will learn how to monitor themselves and make good choices in most circumstances. A child that comes of age functionally unable to care for himself, on the other hand, will not thank you for your concern and care over the years, but will likely resent you—even blame you when he is unprepared to bear the sudden pressures of responsible adulthood.

Let young children learn from experience.

We need to reverse parents' tendency to overprotect young children and underprotect their teens. Your young children are probably already fairly well protected. Within the controlled, safe environment of your home and under your watchful eye, you can afford to allow your youngsters to feel the relatively minor consequences of their disobedience or poor choices. They can afford to skin their knees a few times or get physically rebuffed if they get aggressive with another child. Your child learns how the world really works by experiencing consequences of his behavior. She gains a rock-solid understanding of what it means to reap what she sows.

Protecting young children from the consequences of their actions fosters unrealistic expectations. They tend to enter the outside world thinking that they can do whatever they want, and expect someone to step in and protect them from the consequences. The evidence is all around us that that is exactly how too many teenagers were raised: widespread experimentation with dangerous drugs, dangerous driving habits, recreational sex—a general avoidance of responsibility for their actions. It is during your child's preadolescent and adolescent season that you must be *more* vigilant in monitoring behaviors with life-threatening consequences.

Monitor teenage children with vigilance.

Teenagers believe they are immortal. They know all the facts about AIDS, drinking and driving, and drug addiction—and assume that bad things happen only to others, never to them. So it is up to you to protect your teenager from whatever behaviors that have perilous, lifelong consequences. Emerging adults gain courage to act responsibly from the strength of the father-child connection—more, in fact, than from the mother-child connection. During this phase parents need to be especially vigilant.

Discipline.

Effective discipline is another powerful way fathers instill in their children the life skills and principles that lead to success. Discipline teaches your children the reali-

> **Smart Thought:**
> Hugs are therapeutic. Would your family become better at expressing love if each member made a point of hugging the others at least once a day? And don't let a week go by without a "family hug."

ties of life's proper boundaries and the self-control to live happily within them.

You've watched it happen often. Young children throw a temper tantrum when told they can't have the cookie or toy. They may lash out at you physically or verbally. An appropriate spanking or canceling a cherished privilege for "acting that way" is an entirely suitable response, as long as you also explain what kinds of negotiations with you are acceptable alternatives.

Children who learn how to control their temper and mouths early in their lives will be way ahead when they become adolescents—and so will you. You'll have teenagers whose first reaction to being denied a request isn't to sneak around you or storm out of the house or abuse you verbally, but to respectfully negotiate with you for the freedoms they want.

Yet each of your children is different, and each responds differently to different kinds of discipline. So study your children for what kind of discipline each child responds to most. One child toes the line if he so much as notices your eyebrow go up at the mere suspicion of a stretched household rule. His sister, on the other hand, may need extended "time outs" to think about her misbehavior. Keep each child's unique nature in mind as you try to achieve balance and fairness in establishing consequences for wrong behavior. Tailor the punishment to the temperament of your child.

As often as possible, set up disciplinary measures (or consequences) in advance of infractions. This helps your children to envision the impact of a bad choice and to take ownership of the outcome. If children can predict the disciplinary measures, then choose their behavior accordingly, you've given them a skill that will navigate them around all manner of bad consequences throughout life. If you bail them out too often, you diminish what they need to learn from the experience.

Here are some discipline guidelines:

- **Adapt your discipline to what works with each child.**
- **Set clear standards for appropriate and inappropriate behavior.**
- **Make sure each child understands your standards.**
- **Decide the penalty for violating a particular behavior before that behavior occurs.**
- **Make sure the penalties are consistently enforced from infraction to infraction and from child to child.**

- As much as possible, allow the penalty to be associated with the natural consequences of poor choices.

Teaching children to get along with others.

In families children learn foundational skills for getting along with others. Plan ways to make the most of the quarrels that inevitably occur. Help your children come up with successful ways to work together, solve their problems, work through differing opinions, and settle disputes. Children need to learn how to negotiate a positive solution—and they gain that skill as you require them to experiment and practice working out the differences between them.

For example, the next time your two children (who are developmentally able to carry out this assignment) are caught quarreling, try this: Send each to a different corner of the room, but sitting so that they face each other. Tell them they must remain there until each is ready to make peace with the other. The resulting negotiations usually quickly lead to peace again. In the process, you have helped your children learn to resolve conflicts through cooperation.

Conduct family councils often, for they lead to fair solutions for problems between members and encourage family participation in rule making and problem solving. Draw up a list of family-council procedures that all agree to. Your list may look like this:

- Anyone can tell parents how he or she feels, and ask for a meeting.
- At the meeting, everyone can say what he or she thinks about a situation.
- Instead of fixing blame, the council must try to understand why there's a problem.
- The council will try to create a solution that's fair to all.

Role playing is another tool for sharpening confrontation and problem-solving skills. It's a creative communication tool that promotes listening, empathy, and new patterns for managing conflict.

Here's how to do it: Describe an actual problem among some members of your family. Recreate the incident, though with switched characters—that is, with various members of your family putting themselves in another person's position. Replay

Smart Idea:
Shake up your mealtime routine by staging an old-fashioned progressive dinner—all at your house. Appetizer in a bedroom, vegetable or salad in the family room, main course in another bedroom, and dessert in the garage or basement.

the situation, experimenting with alternate responses and reactions. Then, over a bowl of popcorn, talk about how each of you felt in the various roles and what was learned from the experience that could help solve the problem.

Role play is also an excellent way to let your children rehearse good decisions (about issues they'll face in the near future) and the words that explain or defend those decisions. At many points, for instance, your child will encounter tough, persistent, negative peer pressure. So role-play situations in which peers try to get your son to do something he shouldn't do. Rehearsing can be good preparation; he can try on comfortable ways to say no without looking foolish. It could spell the difference between being lured into dangerous behavior and having the self-confidence to resist.

Keeping communication lines open.

It's far easier to keep communication lines open than to repair them once they're broken.

I used to do something I called "Monday Night Interviews" with my kids. Every Monday evening after dinner, I spent twenty minutes with cassette recorder in hand, asking each child questions about what happened during the weekend, during that day at school, and what each child expects to do the rest of the week. Any question was fair game; I tended to focus on their friends, pets, hobbies, and achievements.

Or turn the tables and let your children interview *you*. Or play a light-hearted game of "Truth or Dare," in which each takes turns asking questions that must be answered truthfully. The person who is asked the question can then choose to answer or do something silly that the questioner dares them to do.

Another simple communication builder: Give each child the chance to stay up with you an extra thirty or sixty minutes once a week. Younger children especially relish the chance to stay up past their normal bedtime. Spend the time lying on your backs, talking about the family, the kind of day the child has had, or planning a future adventure. The lost sleep is insignificant compared to the relationship you're strengthening.

Before they leave home.

I aim to communicate the life skills and principles I want each child to know by their junior year in high school. This way I have their senior year to watch how well they've got a grip on these skills and make necessary corrections. Setting this deadline forces me to decide specifically what I want to communicate, what skills I want them to be proficient at, what values and attitudes I want to see ingrained in their character. Let these ideas get you started:

Skills

- Handling finances responsibly
- Balancing a checkbook
- Decision making
- How to make, keep, and treat friends
- Coping with guilt
- Accepting criticism and correction
- Dealing with death
- Personal grooming and cleanliness
- Home management skills
- Spiritual life habits and disciplines

Attitudes

- A can-do spirit
- Kicking the blues
- Turning negatives into positives
- Looking on the bright side
- A sense of humor
- Persevering and acting with diligence
- Appreciation of simplicity
- Counting their blessings
- Self-respect
- Servanthood

Values

- Honesty
- Personal integrity
- Taming TV
- Family traditions
- Respect for others' privacy
- Appropriate modesty
- The value of hard work
- Appreciation for the arts
- A love of learning
- Courage

Smart Idea:
"I thought of you when I saw this!" are magic words when scrawled on a note and taped to something—flower, picture, magazine clipping, travel brochure, candy—that you leave out for your child or wife to discover.

When your quarterly father review and evaluation rolls around, use some of your time to chart where each child is in his or her progress toward learning the life skills and principles you want them to learn.

Imagine a scale from one (poor) to ten (excellent) next to each of the above skills, attitudes, and values; now mentally rate their competency. Keep your expectations reasonable, considering the age and development of each child. Then let this evaluation you've compiled guide you into the next quarter as you decide where in particular to help and encourage them.

Celebrate Rites of Passage

Many cultures celebrate rites of passage—positive steps toward adulthood that are celebrated and recognized by society to help children make the transition from childhood to adulthood. In Jewish culture it is the bar (or bat) mitzvah, in which the community comes together to celebrate a young person becoming responsible before God for his or her own life.

In modern American culture, however, rites of passage are virtually nonexistent. Yet just because you raise your children in a culture that doesn't celebrate rites of passage doesn't mean that you can't at least create some markers for your children.

A wise father thinks through important milestones in life, helping his children chart and celebrate their progress. When *you* treat such milestones importantly, your children will similarly attach value to their progress.

The onset of puberty is a key marker in your child's development. I celebrate this rite of passage on each child's thirteenth birthday. I start by writing a letter, acknowledging her uniqueness—what I respect and honor about her life. I affirm him in as many specific ways as I can. In the letter I recognize and honor personal strengths. Writing this letter is a way to express my appreciation of her, to describe him in writing, to recognize his idiosyncrasies I want to applaud.

Over dinner at a special restaurant (of her choice), I read the letter to her. I listen to whatever reponse she has to the letter. We discuss the transition to becoming a young

Smart Idea: These days it's hard to keep extended families in touch. Create an address list of relatives and initiate a round-robin letter. Mail your short family update and a couple of photos to the next address, along with instructions for them to do the same for the next family, and so forth.

woman and the new responsibilities she will soon assume. I recognize that he will want more freedoms, which I tell him I will gladly give— but in exchange for the greater responsibilities that go with them.

I acknowledge her passage into the zone of premarital sexual control. Controlling one's sexuality is a mark of maturity and of one's sense of well-being. I admit to her that many are sexually irresponsible, but I stress the benefits of self-control, of waiting for sex within marriage. I help her see the beauty of genuine sexuality in contrast to the devalued sexual mores in our culture. I express clearly my expectations as her dad.

This may sound heavy, but it's really a festive time of looking both backward and forward. We celebrate the other few rites of passage that are significant in our culture—getting a driver's license, getting their first job, using the family car, graduation, and so on. These are prime moments to talk about increasing responsibility and to reinforce new life skills and principles needed to successfully make the transition.

Have in Mind a Clear Picture of Success

The very helpful book *Raising Self-Reliant Kids in a Self-Indulgent World* lists seven foundational capabilities of successful young people—skills and perceptions found in children who have the ability to consistently make mature choices. According to authors H. Stephen Glenn and Jane Nelson, successful kids will have—

- **The perception that they are significant.**
- **The perception that they are capable.**
- **The perception that they have potent control over their environment.**
- **The skill of understanding themselves.**
- **The skill of understanding others.**
- **The skill to flex and adapt.**
- **The skill to make effective judgments.**

Regularly picture in your mind your child's success and his next stages of development, and then make the most of each opportunity to help your child grow—every day, every week.

A final note about communicating life skills and principles to your children: It is never too late for a father to start doing what is right. Communicating life skills and principles is no exception. Only recognize that it gets proportionately more difficult the later in your child's life you start. So take action today to make the most of the time and opportunity you now have.

9

Habit Five: Maximizing Your Moments

The Tread

I always kissed my father goodnight and we always enjoyed a certain warmth, but we never talked seriously. We were from two different planets. He died in 1964 at age 55 when I was fourteen years old. I felt then, as I do now: that he had labored tirelessly to "get ahead" at the price of never having been able to stop and try to know what it or we were all about. His was a selfless labor for kids he barely had time to know.[1]

—JOE RUSSO,
PARTICIPANT AT MULTICULTURAL MEN'S STUDIES SEMINAR

I don't want my children to write about me like this.

In our fathering paradigm the tread on the tire represents maximizing your moments with your children. Each of those nubs, bumps, and contours represent an incident, a conversation, a Saturday morning at the baseball field or on the lake, an errand a few blocks away, a vacation, angry or loving words of discipline or correction—any of a million possibilities, but each one a moment of relationship and interchange between your child and you.

Five Key Habits of Smart Dads
FATHERING PARADIGM

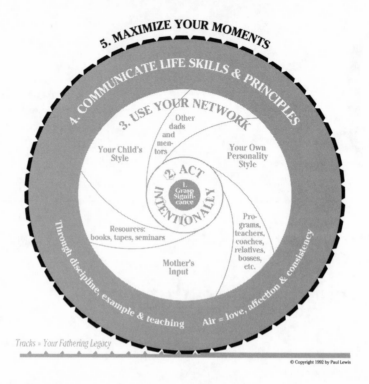

5. MAXIMIZE YOUR MOMENTS

4. COMMUNICATE LIFE SKILLS & PRINCIPLES

3. USE YOUR NETWORK

Other dads and mentors

Your Child's Style

Your Own Personality Style

2. ACT INTENTIONALLY

1. Grasp Significance

Programs, teachers, coaches, relatives, bosses, etc.

Resources: books, tapes, seminars

Mother's Input

Through discipline, example & teaching

Air = love, affection & consistency

Tracks = Your Fathering Legacy

© Copyright 1992 by Paul Lewis

Added together these moments form a noticeable, unique pattern. As a tire's tread leaves an imprint, the time you spend with your children shapes the imprint of your life on theirs. Moments grand and small, magical and mundane—these are the stuff of which memories are made.

How and where you spend your discretionary moments tells the tale. You can use your moments to know your children, to express your love for them, to teach and guide them, to let them know you—or you can invest your moments in other responsibilities, as Joe Russo's father apparently did.

Give your children time to know you. Take lots of pictures and videos, take time to write notes and letters, make audio recordings of your thoughts or of reading stories to your children. Compile a scrapbook of clippings you find that reflect ideas and values that drive your life. Create lots of physical evidence of you, for someday it will be treasured by your children and grandchildren—just as you treasure anything you may have of your grandparents.

Two summers ago Leslie and I celebrated our twenty-fifth anniversary with a visit to Great Britain—and took along my father and mother to celebrate their *fiftieth*. I especially looked forward to spending a day or two in Breckon County, in the south of Wales, from which my great-great-great-grandfather emigrated to the United States.

We called some relatives to learn what we could about my Welsh ancestor before we left on the trip. A cousin of my grandfather finally sent us details about our family tree, including the fact that in 1857 John Lewis—my great-great-great-grandfather—had married Ann Vaughn in Crickhowell, Wales.

Finally locating Crickhowell on a map, we set aside a day to drive there.

We spent a night at a bed-and-breakfast farmhouse in the village of Cum Dee, a short walk from the ruins of a Norman castle that had been partially restored by a Vaughn family. The relatives of Ann Vaughn, we wondered? In explaining our genealogical quest to our Cum Dee host the next morning, we learned that he and the head librarian in Breckon—the county seat fourteen miles away—were good friends.

With this referral we were ushered into the Breckon library, where a clerk set to work. The search eventually took us to the county records office looking for a public record of the marriage of John Lewis and Ann Vaughn. Two hours later on a call to the recorder in a nearby town, the voice on the other end of the line said, "Here it is." The other clerk had in hand a copy of John and Ann's marriage certificate, which named a farm not two miles from the bed and breakfast at which we had stayed.

A couple hours later my father and I pushed open a gate at the end of a narrow country lane and walked toward a weathered, grey stone farm house. The occupants were obviously sheepherders—in the middle of lambing season, at that, for ewes and new offspring were everywhere.

We knocked on the white picket gate, and out of the house came a small man in tattered clothing, though bright, clear eyes set in a sun-weathered face. Dad unfolded the paper on which was outlined John Lewis's branch of our family tree, and handed it to the shepherd with an explanation of who we were and what we wanted. The little man studied it for a minute;

Smart Idea:
Young children can create wonderful stories. Take dictation from your child, then read the story back to him. Keep his stories in a special notebook; they make great reading years later, too.

then, exhorting us not to leave yet, he turned and walked back into the house.

When he returned a few moments later, he held an aged family Bible—six inches thick with deeply embossed covers and brass latches on the side. He opened it to the middle, and there on the family record pages, laid out line by line, was the Lewis family tree.

This sheep farmer turned out to be a distant relative of ours with a keen interest in genealogy. He led us into his small kitchen to show us a keepsake—a tall, plain grandfather clock ticking away up against the wall. This, he explained, was the wedding present John Lewis gave Ann Vaughn. (We got it all on video.)

It was difficult to believe that I was standing in the kitchen of my great-great-great-grandfather, running my hand along the wood-work of a clock he had undoubtedly wound hundreds of times. How I wanted to talk with John Lewis for just a day or two—the John Lewis who loved and married a woman named Ann, who began a family before bringing them all to America.

As it is, apart from a handful of details, John Lewis is only a name to me. The rest I must guess at. What I wouldn't give for a recording of his voice and laughter, a journal of his thoughts, even a clear photo. I wondered about the relatives whose names were list-ed in the sheep farmer's Bible—much like a man's own children and grandchildren will wonder about a father who does not give enough of his time to his children so that he is known deeply by them.

Children Spell Love T-I-M-E

Your time is the currency your children will value most. Gifts of your presence mean more than any presents you may give. Child-ren understand that time is valuable; so when we have inadequate time for our children, they eventually interpret this to mean that we don't value them.

Smart Idea:

Ask you wife to list five things she wants done around the house during the next month—then surprise her by getting all five done.

Quality Time, or Quantity of Time?

How much time does a good father spend with his child? That's a hard ques-tion to answer; most fathers I talk to say they don't feel they have enough time with their children. Only you can gauge the substance of the minutes and hours you invest in your fathering legacy.

Without a doubt, however, any relationship requires time to grow and blossom. It is not enough to say your *life* is committed to your children if you have not committed substantial *time* to be with them. While you can usually add more quality to the time you spend with your children, the quality will always be in direct proportion to the quantity of time.

Time with your kids—and lots of it—is important because teachable moments almost always crop up at odd and unpredictable times. The more you are with your child, then, the greater the odds you'll be there when a teachable moment arrives.

Several years ago when my now-married daughter was in junior high, I listed the family vacation experiences I wanted to share with her before she left for college and wouldn't be home during the summers. I was stunned when I realized I was already two summers short to complete my list.

That got my attention. Although you and I get eighteen or so years with our kids, those years do not stretch on endlessly. I have only a window of time with each child. I began to deliberately look for and guard the times, large and small, I could spend with her.

No Quality
without Emotional Energy

There is scant quality in the time you spend with your children if you drag in the door most evenings, emotionally drained. It's a start at better fathering to get home at a respectable hour. But if the anxieties of your job follow you in the door, the quality of your time with your family plummets. A father must manage his emotional reserves just as he does his time reserves. His family deserves and needs more than emotional leftovers.

It doesn't get easier, either. Older children and teenagers are experts at sensing just how interested you are in what they're telling you when you interact with them. If you're emotionally wrung out, you cannot give and take in your family relationships the way your family needs you to relate. Learn to ration your emotional energy for home as you probably learned to do for work, so that you are prepared to be emotionally present with your wife and children.

Plan to Play

Play is a prime moment maximizer—not to mention a great stress reducer. Playing with your children reduces fathering guilt, helps you relax, restores your emotional energy—and makes your kids very happy.

If by *play* we mean any kind of pleasant interaction, think for a moment what it accomplishes with your child.

Play enhances self-esteem.

Play says, "I like you! You're important to me. You're fun!" Watch the eyes of your ten-year-old brighten when you say, "Hey Buddy—let's go play!" or watch your preschooler's sad expression when you brush off her request "Daddy, will you play with me?"

Play with me or trade me!

Used with permission of Hoest and *Ladies Home Journal*

Play builds bridges.

Whether it involves a sport, dolls, a hobby, or just unhurried, unguarded conversation, play builds bridges of mutual interest and experiences that last a lifetime. Aren't many of your fondest memories the spontaneous times of wrestling with your dad on the floor or just acting silly?

Play builds respect.

When you don't play with your kids, it's harder for them to obey you. Both discipline and intimate talk flow more naturally after playing together, because your child senses your loving heart in your play.

So give priority to playing with your kids. Start with ten minutes of tag before dinner, a bedtime chat over a bowl of popcorn, a joke at breakfast, a game of Chutes and Ladders or Candyland with your preschooler. Even cleaning the attic or washing the car make great play if you simply remain a kid at heart yourself.

Maximize Your Time with Kids

Besides play, here are some other ways to maximize the moments you have with your children.

Choose the right place.

Become aware of the settings in which your child seems to be most open to you.

In one father's master bedroom were two blue chairs, set facing each other. When a time came to talk deliberately to one of his children, he pulled his son or daughter into the bedroom and into those blue chairs. So many good conversations happened there, he began to notice that when one of the kids wanted to talk with him about something important to them, they'd ask, "Dad, can we go talk in the blue chairs?" To the children, the blue chairs were a safe place to communicate.

A mother of a couple teenagers noticed that they talked to her more openly when just the two of them, mother and child, were in the car. She didn't understand what the car had to do with it, but she made good use of the phenomenon anyway. Whenever her daughter or son seemed distant, she contrived a reason to drive them somewhere. And more often than not, once in the car they opened up and talked.

When my now-married daughter was a teenager, we lived in a mountain community an hour out of San Diego. We had horses, too, during that time, and plodding along dirt roads on horseback became an easy setting for conversations. In fact, my most significant conversations with her about sex were during those horseback rides.

Keep your antenna out for a place or setting in which your kids tend to open up—and then, whenever you sense your child wants or needs to talk, deliberately settle into those chairs or take a drive or saddle up.

Choose the right time.

Similarly, watch for those times when your child opens up to you. Some kids

Smart Idea:

Help shape your older child's growing independence by presenting on each birthday a roster of new privileges and responsibilities. Talk over last year's list and celebrate the areas of significant growth.

share more easily at bedtime, when they have quieted down after a busy day. Others are most receptive as soon as you get home, or on Saturday mornings. Notice the time of day interchange seems to flow easiest with your child—and do your best to be there then.

Be prepared to use stray moments.

You can do a lot of fathering during random moments here and there—ten minutes waiting for your wife to finish dressing . . . three minutes of commercials between TV action . . . ten minutes until the game or news comes on. A smart dad harnesses such moments.

Or try the "One-Minute Memo," a note of praise or love on a colored three-by-five card you keep handy for such impromptu - occasions. If you're stumped about what to write, start with these ideas:

• **Praise**—Write three sentences praising one of her qualities.

• **Specific thank-yous**—"Thank you, Casey, for helping me carry in the groceries without being asked. I really appreciate your help!"

• **Inspiration**—Write a favorite poem, a verse of Scripture, or a brief anecdote that reminded you of your child.

• **Catch-up note**—"I've been thinking of you a lot today, Jon. We haven't had much time together recently. How about going out for ice cream this weekend?"

• **Check up**—List jobs you want the child to do, with instructions to check them off when a task is completed and return the list to you—for a surprise reward.

My point is this: You *do* have time with your child, even if it is very little time. Make the most of what time you have with your children.

Maximize Your Moments *Away* from Your Children

Post-It notes.

Keep a pad of them in your desk or in your planner book exclusively for your children. When you think of things to tell them during your day, write them down in short notes: "You looked nice in your green sweater today". . . "Thanks for washing the car". . . "Let's go shopping for new tennis shoes tonight." Before you leave the house for work the next morning, leave these notes where your child will find them—the kitchen counter or their bathroom mirror, for example.

Don't leave unsaid those expressions of love you think of when you are away from them. Write 'em down and let your kids know that you think about them during your day.

When you're away from your toddlers overnight.

Before you leave, photocopy the pages of a couple short story-books. Take the copies with you. At bedtime call home and read the story over the phone while the child follows along in the book. The phone call may cost you more than the photocopies, but the investment pays big dividends in proving to your children that even when you are away from them, you reach out to them with love.

Smart dads who will be away for several nights may find it easier to record several bedtime stories on a cassette tape; Mom can play back your reading of a story at just the right moment with the book propped up in the child's lap. You can even use a whistle or finger snap to indicate when to turn the page.

And there's always the mail.

Before you leave, address and stamp several envelopes and a few postcards and tuck them into your briefcase. This makes it easy to dash off a quick note or enclose a cartoon or news clipping or anything else you noticed that reminded you of your child. Slip in a match book or other memento; if you brought a camera along, use a one-hour photo lab so you can enclose some snapshots of what you have been doing, seeing, or maybe the people with whom you're involved.

Checklist for traveling dads.

• Take a copy of your kid's schedule (including the phone number where she will spend the night on a sleepover, etc.).

• Take postcards, envelopes, stamps—whatever will help you write home frequently. Kids love mail—or a telegram if time is short (or if you'd beat a letter home).

• Leave behind a hidden surprise (pack of gum, a dollar for some ice cream, a brainteaser, etc.) that you can reveal when you're on the phone with your child.

• Plan a special moment to share together when you return home.

Smart Idea:
There's probably a magazine devoted specifically to your child's hobby or interest. Check the library for such lists of periodicals. Then give your child a personal subscription to the most suitable one—and read the issues together.

• Once in a while, surprise everyone by returning early. Get home the day before you said you would or six hours early. Scoop everyone up for an impromptu walk in the park or pizza dinner.

Essentials for long-distance dads.

No one denies how difficult it is to maintain a relationship with your children when you do not live with them—but it can be done. From the experience of fathers and the advice of professionals come several helpful reminders:

• Strive for consistency. Regular, small moments express love far better than infrequent "Disneyland" extravaganzas.

• Make and sustain contact with your child's school teachers. Knowing how they're doing in school will help you better support and encourage them. Direct contact with the school will also reveal any discipline problems and help you learn about academic achievements. This will keep father-son or father-daughter long-distance interactions far more enjoyable and insightful.

• Similarly, an occasional telephone call to their sports coaches and music instructors will display your appreciation for their love and attention to your child.

• Keep your children in touch with relatives and friends on your side of the family as much as possible.

• Guard against letting those hours you used to spend with your children each week become absorbed by other activities. Noting your children's special days or events on a calendar will help you keep in touch. Ask their school and PTA to put you on the parent's mailing list.

• Keep a camera handy and regularly enclose snapshots of yourself at home or at work.

Smart Idea:
Once a week have everyone scour your house for loose change—pockets, dresser tops, couches, car seats (no piggy banks, though). Put the coins in a jar. Once the total reaches fifteen or twenty dollars, vote on an activity for the "Loose Change Party"— miniature golf, buying a new board game or read-aloud book, etc.

Maximize Your Moments of Weakness

Even when you are at your fathering worst, you can enhance your relationship with your child. Your child must know your failures as well as your strengths. It is through your weaknesses that your kids will understand guilt, forgiveness, and rebounding from falling away—however slight or serious your fall was. To let a child see you walk through the consequences of a sorry choice is more powerful than pretending you don't falter morally. Your child needs to observe you facing problems of your own making with courage.

For your kids will need your forgiveness, too. They will seek your forgiveness more readily if they have seen you seek forgiveness for your failings. It is simply not true that if fathers reveal personal weaknesses, their children will lose respect for them. To the contrary: When you are man enough to admit you are wrong, own your mistake, and make the turnaround—then you will garner your children's deep respect.

Maximize the Big Moments in Your Child's Life

We've talked a lot so far about being a presence in your children's day-to-day routine—playtimes, mealtimes, bedtimes. Yet your absence is extra-obvious if you miss the big events—the birthdays, recitals, performances, the big game. Granted, more character is shaped, more life skills are communicated during the seemingly insignificant events in life. Yet children interpret your participation in their big moments as a measure of your love.

How do you know what a "big" moment is for your child? Just look at it from their perspective. How do *they* view the event?

Birthdays may be the most significant celebrations of a child. So invest generous amounts of time—and of yourself—in making special birthday memories. Make it *the* event that tells your child that you're glad beyond words that she is alive.

Plan "Trophy Moments"

These are times of celebrating your child's achievements—and each achievement gives you another chance to heighten his sense of competency. Teetering around the block for the first time on a two-wheeler (training wheels removed), scoring an A on an English test, earning a Boy Scout merit badge, graduation of any sort—these are trophy moments.

Take plenty of snapshots at trophy moments, and keep them in a special photo album—maybe label it "Sharon's Achievements." As she grows up, she can recall the evidence that she is capable and can accomplish the things she sets out to do. This photographic record makes a rare and precious gift for her when she leaves home.

Create your own big moments to reward your kids. I've taken each of my kids to Washington, D.C., with me. We spend two or three or four days together, studying the history of our country. During these trips I have shared my own values more deeply with them and given them my perspective of all we see.

But your big moments don't have to be extravagant—just special for both you and your children.

Maximize the Moments of Crisis

A crisis is opportunity as well as danger. I hope your secretary or receptionist knows that you *always* want a call from your children put through immediately. Do your kids have an extra quarter in a pocket or shoe with your work phone number taped on it? Or do they know your calling-card number? If there's going to be a crisis, be there. Whoever is with your child during a crisis will strongly influence the direction your child's life takes.

Take Time to Beat the Competition

Face it—most of us are competitive. The rap is well-deserved and, probably, one you are proud of. So at least harness it to work on behalf of your kids. A world full of diverse forces are competing hard against you for your kids' minds and hearts. Some of these forces are obvious; they pack a gun or a baseball bat or a pill or a six-pack. But usually the battle isn't nearly as clear as this. And you can't win it by default, either. By maximizing your moments—that is, by spending time with your children—you can monitor the media and peers that compete for your kids' attention. Such forces never let up—and you shouldn't, either.

10

Nicks, Scrapes, and Gouges
Taking Your Habits on the Road

The frenzy had begun just before Wayne arrived home from a three-day business trip. Casper the hamster had somehow escaped from his cage; the kids guessed he was hiding under the couch. The couch was too heavy for Mom to lift, so it had to wait until Dad came home. Wayne had scarcely removed his coat before he got the whole story. So he stepped to the couch and raised one end so his daughter could look for Casper.

There he was, all right. But he darted out of his hiding place and skittered across the living room floor.

No one had noticed Samson trot into the room, attracted by all the commotion. When the black Labrador saw the scurrying hamster, he saw the chance of his canine lifetime. He lunged at Casper and, with a snap of his jaws, killed the poor rodent on the spot.

Horrified, the kids screamed and cried. Wayne yelled at Samson, who was oblivious to everything but his carnivorous instincts and the thrill of fresh blood. In short, the lab dismembered Casper in front of everyone. It took a long while to calm the kids, clean up the mess, and restore a degree of order to the household.

After he comforted his kids, Wayne called a family meeting. The agenda: to determine what had happened and to ensure it wouldn't happen again. Being the latecomer onto the scene, he released a downpour of paternal questioning: "Okay, who left the hamster cage door open? Who played with him last? Who didn't close the back door that the dog came through?"

The kids had some questions of their own: "Why didn't Casper come to me? Why did Samson eat Casper? Why aren't you spanking Samson?" The upshot was, everyone gradually owned up to their responsibilities when the now-docile Samson, sitting off to the side, started gagging. He vomited up the hamster right there at their feet.

There are some moments for which no fathering model can prepare us. There is no textbook way to handle spontaneous domestic traumas, such as Wayne's fiasco with Casper and Samson. Real-life fathering can be messy. Don't think for a minute that the five key habits of smart dads will make your fathering experience neat and tidy. What it will do, though, is assist you to your destination: a mutually satisfying relationship with your kids and, eventually, a positive imprint on their lives.

I don't hang around auto tire stores any more than the next guy. But the other day I took my youngest son with me to have a set of tires mounted on my car. In the waiting area I leafed through a couple brochures and was surprised again by the diversity of rims and tread designs available. Kevin and I ran our fingers along the groove patterns in the rubber. We felt the smooth, shiny contours at the chrome rim display. And Kevin did his usual twenty-questions drill on me: "What's this? What's it for? Why . . . ?"

The tires and rims were showroom fresh compared to the used wheels being worked on in the service bays twenty feet away. Wheels—rims as well as tires—take a pounding from speed bumps and curbs, roads under construction, potholes, the constant stress of starts and stops, intersection drainage dips. Through rainstorms and winter slush, emergency stops and hard cornering, we depend on those lug nuts, rims, tires, and tread to do the job and keep us safe.

After only a few thousand miles, wheels start losing their sheen. But they acquire a different kind of beauty—the look of a well-used tool. Nicked, gouged, and tarnished here and there from the use, but still rock solid.

I see fathering like that. When the five fathering habits are in place, working properly, you can handle whatever family conditions life presents, though you'll inevitably pick up nicks, scrapes, and gouges.

Smart Idea:
Once in a while surprise your family by coming home a day early from a trip. Or cancel a whole day of work (or even just a morning) to be with them. If your wife works, coordinate schedules so that everyone can be together.

Maybe you like what you've read so far about what it takes to be a smart dad. I'll assume that you're sold on the habits. But liking what you see and getting these habits established in yourself are two different things. Let's look at what it will take to get them functioning productively in you.

Balance Those Wheels!

After a tire is mounted and before it's put back on your car, it's usually balanced so that it spins smoothly and doesn't vibrate at high speeds causing excessive stress and wear. Balancing your fathering, accordingly, means examining the strength and balance of the elements in your fathering network to be sure things are in sync.

Try this self-test to check your fathering balance:

Network area	*Current level of strength*
	Poor Excellent
1. I understand the strengths and weaknesses of my fathering personality.	1 2 3 4 5 6 7 8 9 10
2. I have good coping strategies in place to compensate for my natural weaknesses.	1 2 3 4 5 6 7 8 9 10
3. I have a clear understanding of my child's personality strengths and weaknesses and how they tend to play against my own.	1 2 3 4 5 6 7 8 9 10
4. I regularly discuss my child's progress with his mom and value her insight into both the child and my fathering practices.	1 2 3 4 5 6 7 8 9 10
5. I have at least two good friends I talk candidly with at least once a month.	1 2 3 4 5 6 7 8 9 10
6. I have made meaningful contact within the last two months with adults who relate regularly to my child (teachers, coaches, bosses, neighbors, scout leaders, etc.)	1 2 3 4 5 6 7 8 9 10
7. I have read a book, listened to a tape, or attended a seminar about fathering in the past twelve months.	1 2 3 4 5 6 7 8 9 10

Alignment

Unaligned front wheels cause stress, excessive wear, and instability to the entire steering system. Likewise, you need to align fathering with your other roles—husband, employee or owner, son of elderly parents, weekend tennis player, bass fishing enthusiast, soccer coach—that you fulfill in your family, company, and community. Keeping these various responsibilities and pressure points in alignment is what challenges and frustrates most fathers.

You will succeed as a dad only if you take the time to carefully consider how much time, energy, and money you are willing to commit to each of these roles in your life.

You may be like me. Every time I sit down and review where I am in my fathering growth and practices, I uncover more adjustments—more alignments—that I need to make. And I've learned that I can either practice good maintenance and do the alignment *right then*, or I can put it off and try not to think about what I know without a doubt—that someday it will take a lot more time and expense to get the alignment put back where it should have been all along.

Say you realize that things aren't clicking like they should between you and your child. You're not getting the attention and response you expect when you advise or instruct her. Your instincts (or a discussion with her mother) tell you what the underlying problem is: Your schedule over the past couple months hasn't left you with much time with her. Communication levels are consequently down. All the child has been hearing from you are commands and demands. So it's no wonder that her responsiveness toward you in general has shriveled.

What your fathering needs right then is realignment with your other roles. You probably need to spend more time with your child. So being the wise father that you are, you make the tough decision to cut back on the extra hours you are putting in at the office or on a community service project or on the golf course or whatever.

I know what I'm talking about. Three times in the past week I was annoyed with responses I've gotten from one or the other of my sons when I asked them to follow through on a chore. My knee-jerk reaction was "What's wrong with this kid?" A calmer look at their resistance to my fathering revealed that, for the past four months, I've devoted a *lot* of extra time to writing this book. Special times with the boys have been too scarce. Their lackluster response to my commands turned out to be no mystery at all. So now I'm making the adjustments to bring my fathering back into alignment.

Realignment is managing critical and competing responsibilities. That's probably why it's difficult. For instance, you see your overtime hours on the job as discretionary—not a part of your job description. So you figure after all these extra hours at the office for months on end, it's your kids' turn to get some extra attention from you.

Yet just because you adjusted your fathering priority doesn't mean your boss has to agree with you. He may or may not perceive your overtime and extra efforts as discretionary. Your most recent raise, in fact, may have been awarded you with the unspoken expectation of more sixty- and seventy-hour weeks.

Realignment of fathering and career will take some tactful discussion in a situation like this. You may or may not want to explain that you are changing how you work in order to accommodate your new fathering focus. I'd suggest being forthright; you never know the positive effect it may have.

A friend who worked for a savings and loan was assigned a loan analysis by his boss at about four in the afternoon, with the request to have it ready for a board meeting the next morning. Normally he would have stayed late and completed the work. But he had been working hard during the past month to bring his fathering priorities into better alignment. And working that evening conflicted with his son's soccer game, which he had promised to attend.

So my friend swallowed hard and explained it all to his boss: Normally he'd be happy to stay late, but this particular evening he had made a promise to his son that he didn't want to break.

The boss was accommodating—but the real reaction came the next day. The boss told my friend that seeing him make fathering a priority had made him think hard about the way work had become too important in his own life. So, he said, he was instituting a policy that no one stayed beyond six, except for Thursdays. And he was having the building's security system adjusted accordingly, so that if you left after six the alarms would create all kinds of havoc.

You'll always be realigning, because the patterns and habits of our lives always take time, energy, and money. When you adjust or change a habit in one dimension, something will have to give somewhere else.

Good Tire Maintenance

Because your four tires each wear a little differently, you rotate them regularly to get the most wear from them. In the same way, as you cycle through different

Smart Idea:
Ask another dad to tell you the fathering mistakes he wants to avoid and the fathering examples he hopes to emulate.

seasons of life—new fatherhood, career change, your kids' adolescence, a new marriage—fathering will be at the front of your attention sometimes, and be on the back burner at others.

Once you establish the five key habits of a smart dad, practicing them will become much easier. What you do out of habit isn't difficult. Good fathering habits will keep you moving and in control even during those seasons when your attention is required elsewhere.

No Modifications Necessary

I've met fathers who, from what I've observed of their behavior, think of fathering as a competitive sport. They want to be the biggest and the best. So they adopt an attitude akin to putting slicks on a race car. Looks hot, but the down side of this modification is that fathering is not a drag race. Slicks just don't do well in a race of endurance. Whatever habits we acquire should keep working powerfully for a lifetime. So here's my advice:

• **Don't pretend to be more or better than you are as a man or a father.** If you fool everyone else, at least your children will know the truth—and of all people, they're the ones who need to see a transparent, frank father.

• **Don't compete with other fathers.** Nothing spoils a healthy relationship with your network faster. Keep other fathers as your allies, not as contestants.

• **Presenting yourself as a larger-than-life dad wears down you and those around you.** Do you do things more in the interest of your fathering reputation than in the best interest of your children? A friend of mine—father of four and the associate pastor of a church—asks himself that question often. Some in his congregation expect him to be an exemplary father—and he knows how easily he can oblige them, at least in appearances. He says he used to worry more that he *looked* like a good dad than actually *being* a good dad.

It's Never Too Soon to Start Good Fathering Habits

Women get a head start in parenting. The changes in their bodies demand that they start adapting to the baby months before it arrives. Dads, on the other hand, experience no biological changes that demand we start adjusting to the responsibility. It takes a conscious effort for us to prepare for the expectations and requirements of fatherhood.

It's never too early to start the thought patterns and habits that make you a smart dad. In fact, here are some ideas for bonding with your unborn child (if you have the opportunity):

• **Write a letter to your unborn child.** Express the joy and anticipation you feel as a parent. Write of your desire to parent the baby. Verbalize the desires that have led you and your wife to want to have a child. Put into words your hope for the kind of person you trust the child will become.

Then put the letter in a safe deposit box to be opened on the child's twelfth birthday. Your long-term goal is to build your child's sense of self-worth with the assurance that his or her arrival was a welcomed event.

• **Sing and talk to your unborn child.** Unborn babies hear sounds and respond to them. Let that little one get to know the sound of your voice before it sees your face.

• **Feel your baby move.** Take time to lay your hands on your wife's abdomen and wait until your little one makes a move.

• **Accompany your wife on her prenatal visits.** Watching an ultrasound image or listening to the heartbeat of your unborn child heightens the reality of that growing life.

Once your baby is born, take an active role in child-rearing. The new version of Dr. Benjamin Spock's *Baby and Child Care* offers this advice: "The father—any father—should be sharing with the mother the day-to-day care of their child from birth onward. . . . This is the natural way for the father to start the relationship, just as it is for the mother."[1]

Your decision to participate in your child's early development will pay rich dividends. Research regularly shows that when a child's father involves himself early in child rearing, children tend to have higher IQs, perform better in school, and even have a better sense of humor than children whose fathers do not give themselves and their children this advantage.[2]

Specifically, you can bond with your newborn in ways like this:

• **Let the baby learn your comforting techniques.** Snuggle your baby's head up under your chin, then talk and sing to it

Smart Idea:
If you're unsure of the answers to these and similar questions, go ahead and ask your child.
• What most embarrasses your child?
• Who (outside your home) most influences him or her?
• What is your child's biggest fear?
• What is your child's most prized possession?
If you need to get the conversation going, first tell them what embarrasses, influences, and frightens you.

in low masculine tones. Your infant will learn to be comforted by your style just as he or she responds to Mom's touch.

• **Read some child-development literature—or at least some articles in baby magazines.** (Baby mags and mailers will flood your home when infant-product companies learn you've just had a baby.) Become familiar with your baby's coming developmental signs. (In fact, try beating Mom at noticing a new stage in the baby.)

• **Take your shirt off when you hold the baby.** Skin is your newborn's primary sensory channel. Feeling the warmth of your chest, just as when Mom nurses the child, greatly enhances the bonding and the ability to feel comforted by you.

Two Ways to Get New Habits Rolling

Focus on improvement rather than perfection.

Consider each of the five habits as a continuum, as a range. Pinpoint as closely as you can where you currently are in practicing the five key habits of smart dads—then aim for measurable improvement, not perfection. If you aim too high too soon, you will probably procrastinate rather than attempt progress.

List your ideas for putting each of these five key habits into action.

Nothing disciplines one's thinking like the point of a pencil. Written commitments afford you the valuable opportunity of confronting yourself later in your own handwriting about what you did or did not do.

Smart Idea: Reduce petty arguments and sibling rivalry with a "Child of the Week" strategy. The privileged child gets to choose the prime seat in the car, operate the garage door opener, push the shopping cart, and spend Saturday afternoon alone with dad and his favorite game or activity.

You may want to start like this: Divide a sheet of paper into three columns. In the left column list the five key habits. In the center write your expressed goal regarding that habit. In the right column list specific steps you will take to reach that goal. (See page 158 for an example.)

The goals and action steps, of course, will shift in tone and focus the older your child becomes. Brainstorm for action steps with a friend or your wife, listing as many specific steps as you can. Then be very selective, however, and try only a few changes at one time. Biting off more than you can chew only sets you up for failure. It is not how many changes you institute that matters, but the number of habits you develop that become a part of your everyday routine. Start small and exceed your expectations. Regularly building on your last accomplishments as a dad can take you, over the course of a lifetime, to fathering heights you didn't imagine were possible.

This will take you less than a minute, so do it now, before you turn the page or lay this book down: Consider your fathering goals and options. Choose one, simple, workable action step—one that you have listed above, or another than comes to mind. Now get up and do it, right now, before the idea becomes cold.

FIVE KEY HABITS OF SMART DADS

Key Habit	Goal	Action Steps
1. Grasp my significance	Create in my children the positive memory of my being there for them as they grow up.	Remind myself three times today that just being there for my kids and being affectionate makes a world of difference.
2. Act intentionally	Revise my schedule to accommodate new fathering focus and goals.	Set aside two hours, sometime in the next week, to plan how I will apply what I have learned in this book.
3. Use my network	Build primary and secondary fathering networks.	Discuss these five key habits with my wife and ask her to evaluate my strengths and weaknesses. Then find two other fathers with whom I can meet regularly as a support group.
4. Communicate life skills and principles	Have my children know what skills and principles they each are working on, and be proud of their individual achievements.	List the things I want to teach my kids before they leave home. Find and use three teachable moments in the life of each child this week.
5. Maximize my moments	Learn to consistently harness small moments of time in fathering.	Add one item to my daily routine with each child. Play with my kids fifteen minutes each day.

NICKS, SCRAPES, AND GOUGES

Key Habit	Goal	Action Steps
1. Grasp my significance		
2. Act intentionally		
3. Use my network		
4. Communicate life skills and principles		
5. Maximize my moments		

11

Burnin' Rubber

The Tire Track: Your Fathering Legacy

I got hit in a fender bender last Saturday. No one was hurt, but the other car creased my rear quarter panel behind the wheel well. The driver, who had turned out of a shopping-center driveway onto the road without noticing me, was embarrassed and frustrated at having caused her first accident. Skid marks five or six feet long, made by my tires when I was hit, attested to the force she bumped me with.

The skid of an accident or of a panic stop, the cautious progress of a four-wheel drive through mud, raising dust as you bump along on a dirt road—in the right circumstances, tires leave a clear signature. In the same way, your fathering legacy is the record of those moments and experiences you share with your child. An imprint.

I'm famous in my house for recognizing what good fathering means to my kids, framing a plan, putting it in writing—and then gliding along on the strength of my good intentions. Meanwhile, a dangerous gap grows between my great plan and my actual performance. In fathering, as in most aspects of life, it's performance that counts, not wonderful intentions. Tire tracks aren't left behind where the tire never rolled.

It's one thing to admire a showroom tire, glistening black, hard edges on all the tread, mounted on the latest style rim. It's another

Five Key Habits of Smart Dads
FATHERING PARADIGM

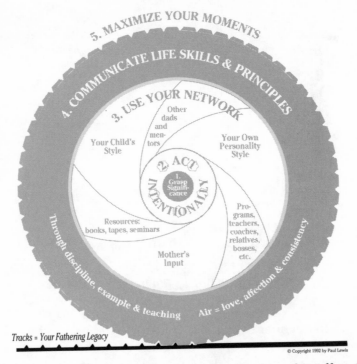

5. MAXIMIZE YOUR MOMENTS

4. COMMUNICATE LIFE SKILLS & PRINCIPLES

3. USE YOUR NETWORK

Other dads and mentors

Your Child's Style

Your Own Personality Style

2. ACT INTENTIONALLY

1. Grasp Significance

Pro-grams, teachers, coaches, relatives, bosses, etc.

Resources: books, tapes, seminars

Mother's Input

Through discipline, example & teaching

Air = love, affection & consistency

Tracks = Your Fathering Legacy

© Copyright 1992 by Paul Lewis

thing, though, to put that tire on a pickup and send it off to thirty or forty thousand miles of daily wear and tear. Then you find out how good it is. Fathering habits, too, look nice when you showcase them. But they'll work for you only if you put them on, use them every day on life's road, keep them in good repair and road-ready month after month, year after year.

Preventive Fathering

Often it's just forgetting commonsense prevention that gets dads into fathering trouble. If you don't practice preventive fathering, you'll end up playing catch-up or trying to compensate for an outright mistake you made earlier.

"It's a whole lot cheaper to prevent disease than it is to treat them," says Dr. Kenneth Cooper, who popularized aerobic exercise. "It's a whole lot cheaper to prevent family problems than it is to heal them. Whether it's drug addiction, alcohol, obesity, heart disease—we as parents should be keenly concerned in the potential of preventive medicine for our families."

Likewise, preventive fathering can protect you from problems that damage father-child relationships.

You've seen the scenario—a scrubbed, cheerful, clean-cut mechanic (or plumber, contractor, etc.) in a pressed uniform hands a customer the bill. "That will be $49.95 for the check-up," he says politely. The appreciative customer drives off, thoroughly satisfied. Cut to a greasy mechanic—filthy jumpsuit, matted hair, a day or two of stubble on his face—who, with a smirk, hands a cowering customer the oily bill. The customer's face registers shock, and you know why. Cut to Mr. Clean again, who warns us that "in maintaining your car, you have a choice: you can pay *me* now . . . or you can pay *him* later."

You can invest in your children up front—it's fairly manageable to attend to each of their stages as they come along—or you can neglect your relationship with your kids when they're young and later pay far more than you can afford.

Preventive fathering means monitoring these habits:

Check the pressure level in your various roles monthly.

You can't avoid pressures in this life—but is your life overinflated? Avoid a blowout—release some of your commitments, even if you have to drop *good* things. Overcommitment, contends Focus on the Family founder James Dobson, is the single most damaging habit of families today. Police yourself so you don't overload your life with too many commitments and activities.

Drive at moderate speeds, observing legal limits.

Safer, more satisfying fathering comes easier as you move slowly. Don't hurry your children to grow up too soon. Let each grow at his or her appropriate pace. Don't rush yourself, either. Take time to develop the skills, knowledge, and habits that allow you to father your children well.

Mistakes happen when we hurry. Discern and accept the natural limitations on you and on each of your children, and you can relax and enjoy the ride *during* their childhood.

Smart Tip:
These rules can lead to fair solutions in resolving problems between family members:
1. Anyone can call a family-council meeting.
2. Everyone is free to say what he or she thinks about a situation.
3. Blaming is not allowed in determining why a problem exists.
4. The solution must be fair to all.

Avoid driving over potholes, obstacles, curbs, or edges of pavement.

Awareness in fathering is like good defensive driving: You anticipate obstacles before they hit you.

Are you now anticipating the issues your child will face in his next stage of life? What type of questions will she begin asking? Are you prepared? Do you have a clue how you will answer her? What will he need most from you? Do you know any of the early warning signs for errant behavior (like substance abuse or depression)? Are you an alert father?

Notice obstacles up ahead, and you will be in the envious position to deal with them before they hit you.

Avoid spinning your wheels.

That is, don't make a lot of promises to your wife and kids that you don't back up with action. Big plans and no delivery is just like burning rubber: You generate a lot of fury and noise, but it doesn't get you anywhere.

Don't spout off about what you plan to do. It doesn't matter if it's swearing off alcohol, a Disneyland vacation, or threats of dire punishment to an erring child. If you have no sure plan of making good your promise or threat, keep quiet. Steady, measured, intentional actions, without fanfare, are usually the better course.

"If you see any damage to a tire," reads the brochure of a tire manufacturer, "replace it with a spare and see a tire-care professional at once."[1]

Few families escape without some kind of serious damage to relationships—medical emergencies, clinical depression, emotional difficulties, addiction, abuse of whatever kind, victimization within the family or from outside.

When it feels like a blowout, don't ignore it and barrel ahead. Pull over and get competent professional help.

Prepare for All Driving Conditions

Be prepared to make necessary adjustments for various driving conditions:

Off-road driving

There will be times in your life when you take an unexpected turn with a child and realize you've turned off the road altogether.

You thought your map had everything marked, but you can't find where you are now. You're off-roading as a father.

I think of the U.S. Army general who testified before the Senate Armed Services Committee, offering his recommendation against allowing homosexuals to serve in the military. The night before, this dad's adult son called him to tell him he was gay.

That was an off-road moment for the father. He had probably never prepared himself for such a situation. Yet the next day before the Senate committee, he responded with love and respect for his son while remaining true to his convictions.

I started some of my own off-roading the day I found proof that my oldest son was smoking marijuana. I never believed I would have to deal with this; the fathering maps I had studied (and taught) didn't chart that territory. I had mistakenly thought that fathers who made good choices were guaranteed sons who did, too.

We were living in a small mountain community—oaks, pines, meadow ponds, country roads—an ideal environment in which to raise children, I thought.

Yet from day one, Jon had been a risk taker. He climbed pine trees higher than you would imagine a six- or eight-year-old could climb. He loved the adventure, the risk of it.

Jon was bright—really—but by junior high, a learning disability diagnosed in third grade was taking a toll. Although he could ace a verbal test, he had great difficulty encoding what he knew in written form—the common measure of classroom progress. His coping mechanisms were no longer handling the volume of written work required.

Few of Jon's friends in this small community shared the values of our family. Combine Jon's love of experimenting, his learning difficulty, the trauma of even a *smooth* adolescence—and you've got the perfect recipe for a problem. Jon succumbed, and it took us a while to figure it all out.

I relied heavily during those two years on my fathering network. I got a lot of good counsel from other fathers who had already navigated this territory. (More about Jon's story in chapter twelve.)

Even if a father does *everything* right (and I didn't), there is no guarantee that

Smart Idea:
Strengthen family ties on birthdays and anniversaries by playing "Family Trivia." Stump the kids with questions like these:
- In what year were we married?
- How old is grandpa?
- Name your great-grandparents.
- Who is your oldest cousin?

all his children will turn out just as he thinks they should be. Such a guarantee is a fantasy that will lull you into a state of denial. You simply cannot control every factor that comes along to challenge your fathering. Reality, on the other hand, teaches me that, while there are no guarantees, I can tilt the odds in my favor by living out these five fathering habits.

Driving when drowsy—nodding off or not paying attention

There's a lot of semiconscious fathering going on, despite the fact that it's a dangerous way to live with a family. If you're not paying attention or are simply too tired (in any sense of the word) to father well, pull over, and get some rest—before you run off the road.

Avoiding road hazards

When I was growing up in Dayton, Ohio, I remember city street crews waging their annual battle against the potholes created by the winter freezing and thawing. A family friend was among the first buyers of a VW beetle, and we'd joke about him getting lost in a pothole.

There are serious road hazards out there. For some fathers, it's emotional (or worse) abuse of wives and children, or workaholism. For your children, it's gang involvement, recreational drug use, alcohol abuse, promiscuous sex, AIDS, abortion, molestation.

Blessed are the children with alert fathers who help them steer clear of hazards that can maim the body and the spirit.

When road signs point in the wrong direction

Road Runner, you remember, would flip the road sign so that Wile E. Coyote, mistakenly following the arrow, careened off the cliff.

Among modern road signs that misdirect our kids:

• **Evolution.** When we tell children that life began as blind chance, that their significance lies in being simply the latest play in a huge survival-of-the-fittest game, we shouldn't be surprised when they abuse each other or join racist groups that vaunt their own superiority. If evolution is your philosophical core, there is little reason for shaping a sense of positive worth and self-esteem, or for valuing the person next to you. We must teach children that each of them are special because they have been created by God and endowed with a unique purpose for their lives.

From this premise—the purposeful creation of all life by God—springs all other values that make life sacred.

• **Safe sex.** We put kids at great risk by teaching them that condoms eliminate the risk of AIDS and of sexually transmitted diseases. Condoms fail at an astounding rate. If, as a hundred passengers prepared to board a plane in Los Angeles for Chicago, the attendant announced that about eighty-three would make it safely and the rest would die, how many passengers would go aboard?

Only abstinence is absolutely safe. The safe-sex sell is a tragic hoax. For a score of other reasons besides catching a deadly disease, what loving father wouldn't strongly warn his children that choosing to be sexually active before marriage is a monstrous risk?

Modern society has flipped lots more warning signs, so that now our children are told that whatever is legal is moral, that pornography is a harmless adult pleasure, that gender roles are interchangeable. Your job as a dad is to hear where society wants to escort your children, clearly interpret it, and carefully and tactfully lead children to see through the illogical, fuzzy thinking.

Fathering Myths and Mistakes

I've been a father now for a quarter century. More important, I've listened to the perspective of thousands of fathers. From their combined experience, I have identified several myths and mistakes that are poised to defeat us. When repeated consistently—or even when left unexamined—these four myths and four mistakes can run you off the fathering road.

Myth 1: Big Moments Count Most

When I feel like I'm behind in my relationship with my children, I tend to look for some grand moment I can create to catch up, to fix the problem—to at least absolve my sense of guilt about not being there enough. It's the whole evening we'll spend together (later in the week), the big Saturday outing (in two weeks), the extravagant vacation together that will make a lifetime memory (next summer)—anything to make up for the time I'm not investing in the relationship right now.

Smart Tip:
Manage TV viewing time. Balance it with reading, chores, music practice, homework, whatever. Track a child's TV time with a jar of marbles on top of the tube: A marble is deposited in the jar for each half hour of reading, chores, etc. A glance at the jar lets people know how much TV watching the child has earned.

Big moments are important, but not as much as you think. It's fantasy to believe that they count most in shaping a relationship with kids. The truth is that lots of small moments count for more. Children's values, memories, and habits are shaped one moment and one day at a time. When a question is on your son's mind, he'll ask it—then. They're around twelve before they can put an emotional need on hold for a few days until you are around to respond to it. Small children can't wait for even a day. They need you when they need you. To wait for tomorrow night is an eternity to them.

If we're not around to answer their life questions, others will be. That's reality.

Myth 2: Strong Fathers Stand Alone

American lore says that a real man always knows what to do in every situation. He handles crises without consulting anyone or anything. Dads like to pack this myth home—so we work in isolation, seldom asking each other about what makes for strong fathering and healthy marriages.

We take the one shot we get at raising each of our kids—a high-wire act without a net of other strong fathers and mentors who can coach us. For whatever reasons, we honor independence, not interdependence.

The truth is, every man needs connections to others. A network of healthy relationships enriches his ability to father. I am a better father because of the hours I've spent across a table with other dads (a point I made in chapter seven about using your network).

Myth 3: Pain Is Pointless

Love for our children makes it almost understandable to want to shield them from every pain. Yet in so doing, we also shield them from powerful lessons learned only through making their own mistakes and slugging it out through consequent difficulties. Saturated in our culture with the message that sacrifice and suffering are needless, we are not encouraged to lower the shield. Yet if we believe that pain is pointless, we lose a great source of wisdom. Mistakes are powerful tutors.

Every family and individual will experience pain, in some form or another—physical, emotional, mental. Pain is regularly the natural consequence of a poor choice or mistake. And, of course, some pain just happens.

If we respond positively to suffering, it has a beautiful and refining effect on our character. While never engineering a trauma for his child, a wise father nevertheless knows that his child's suffering is a painful, valuable opportunity to learn life skills and values. So with a careful eye to what is enough and what is too much, he usually allows the logical and natural consequences of his child's mistakes to fall on him or her.

The child who learns that lemonade can be made from life's lemons—that there is a point to life's pains—has a huge advantage over individuals who seek to avoid every difficulty.

Myth 4: Great Fathering Is Just Around the Corner

This myth seduces young fathers in particular, although at careless moments I still give in to it.

Here's how it often works. We deliberately choose imbalance ("just for a while") to make the career move, win the promotion, close the big deal, get the new business up and running. Time with our children? Well, you'll get right on it—as soon as you finish this *really* important project.

The truth is that as soon as you get around this corner, you're probably looking at another corner, no less critical to get around than the last one.

Today's economic climate makes things less certain than ever. Companies downsize, folding two or three jobs into yours—and twenty people lined up for your job are perfectly willing to put in the overtime if you aren't. If you hustle less in order to be available to your children, somebody else will win the contract or close the deal.

Life is compromise—and there will be seasons of compromising fathering time. But at least you can keep your thinking clear and recognize the downside of any decisions to temporarily postpone time with your kids.

If we're lucky, we get about twenty years of fathering a child. Just one shot. I've talked to too many fathers who regret moments they wish they could have shared with their children. Your kids are two years old just once. They're five, then nine, then fourteen just once. Questions burn in their heads, begging for answers—at just this moment, just that day. Only once do they hit their first home run, turn sixteen, or endure their first romantic breakup. A wise father learns to value each

Smart Idea:
Ask "seesaw" questions at dinner tonight:
• Did you feel today more like a heart or a brain? A washer or dryer? A steak or a hamburger?
• Do you think our family is more like a factory or a farm? A TV or a newspaper? The city or the country?
• Why?

day as if it was the only one he will have with his children. He avoids pretending that he'll have more time later, when he'll be freed up to be a great dad. He values most the moments he has now with his kids.

When I ask older dads what their greatest regret is—and I ask this often—I've never heard, "I regret I didn't pursue my career more intensely." But lots of men say, in one way or another, "I regret that I didn't take more time for my kids when they were young and available to me and craved the interaction. What I traded for those moments wasn't worth it."

Four Common Fathering Mistakes

Mistake 1: Demanding Common Ground on Your Turf

Don't push your children into activities that are more *your* interest than your child's. We all know the caricature of the dad who lives out his athletic fantasies in his child. None of us wants that.

Yet kids so love their dads' involvement and approval that they will push themselves to excel at what they guess (usually accurately) will earn them Dad's admiration—even if it's not what they genuinely enjoy or want to do.

That's as unhealthy as the overtly pushy father. Instead, look at your children's abilities and interests, then find some authentically common ground—an interest, a pastime, a recreation that both father and child sincerely enjoy. Athletics may not be the best common turf. Maybe it will be piano or photography or electronics or modeling or collecting. It may be something you find boring; for when there seem to be no areas of overlapping interest, a dad needs to be sufficiently wise to choose the child's turf over his own.

Since he was two, my youngest son's passion has been mechanical things—in particular, cranes, earth movers, even the fork lifts at the wholesale building-supply warehouse we shop in. So I made Kevin the perfect invitation: to come with me to the Caterpillar dealership's used-equipment lot. Acres of earth-moving equipment, waiting to be mauled and scrambled on by a young boy enthralled with machinery.

Sure, the equipment interested me—for a few minutes. Hydraulic fluid and grease aren't my idea of a great Saturday morning. But Kevin's delight poking around those machines with me tells me we're on common ground—which is where an effective father needs to spend some time.

Mistake 2: Expecting Adult Behavior and Reasoning Too Early

A dad usually expects more mature behavior than his kids are able to deliver. So he gets all exasperated about something they should have done and didn't, or at least didn't do to his expectations. *They* knew exactly what he wanted done, and yet they didn't do it. So he raises his voice and launches into an adult's classic string of interrogatives: "How many times have I told you . . . ?" "How come you never . . . ?" "Why can't you ever . . . ?" "Why don't you act your age?" and "Surely you realize . . ."

These are nothing less than put-downs, and they seldom spur children toward mature behavior. The most they usually accomplish—besides making us feel better about getting it off our chest—is to make our child feel as capable as a whipped puppy.

The problem is usually mine, not my child's. When I tell my daughter, "Your room is a disaster—clean it this afternoon," I set up Shelley for failure. Unless she and I have established beyond doubt what constitutes a clean room, her idea of a clean room and my idea of a clean room can be far apart. So she produces an award-winning clean room, by her definition. Then I show up to inspect, only to end up yelling, "Shelley, get in here! I thought I told you to clean up your room!"

That's when I let emotion overwhelm logic. That's when I belittle my child.

All I needed to do to avoid the misunderstanding was to clarify my expectations up front. When I first assigned the clean-up task, I should have asked Shelley to stand with me in the doorway of her room for a moment and describe the way the room will look when clean. I should have let her talk me through the job as she sees it. If she missed something, I could have simply asked, "And what about those clothes hanging out of the drawer—is the room 'clean' if they're still there?"

Questions like these clarify a task for your child and help her succeed in living up to your expectations.

Once you have taught her how to perform the task, it is fair to expect her to do it as you have taught her. If she doesn't, you have a legitimate gripe. Then you

Smart Idea:

When you know you'll arrive home after your child's bedtime, ask her to jot on a Post-It any questions, requests, or comments for you—and stick it on the bathroom mirror. And if you leave in the morning before they awake, leave your response on their mirror.

calmly ask her what standards she agreed to, and ask her to finish the job.

Mistake 3: A Short Fuse and Explosive Anger

When I talk shop with experienced dads, I ask them what they are least proud of in their fathering. By far, the most common answers are uncontrolled anger and a quick temper. "I can have a very short fuse," they'll say, "and I'm not proud of it." Repeated outbursts of anger usually reflect an internal problem—his own impatience or suppressed rage. Though he blows up at his child, the child was hardly the fundamental cause of his anger.

Adult anger is seldom a productive emotion in the presence of children. Uncontrolled anger at a child tears at her respect for her father and erects instant barriers against him. You don't go out of your way to confide in a person who has vented his anger on you a number of times already.

If you have a short fuse, get help—and start with your spouse. Some couples have a subtle signal they use to help him keep a lid on his anger. Some agree that, when she senses him losing control, she will get his attention by slamming a door somewhere in the house, or by humming "Dixie"—*anything* that can remind you that you're skating on thin ice.

A couple years in Vietnam left a dad I know with a hair-trigger temper. He feared what damage his tirades might do to his relationships with his three daughters. So after discussing what their dad was grappling with, they made a pact together: Whenever he blew his stack, they would simply grab his hand and, without saying anything, hang on. It was amazing, he told me, how over a few months that one simple act helped calm him.

Whatever approach you adopt, include with it the healthy habit of asking for forgiveness. No matter how justified your anger toward your child may be, logic won't dispel her *feeling* of rejection. Contrary to instinct, a father never stands so tall in his child's eyes as when he admits he's blown it and seeks forgiveness.

Keep short accounts with your family. Don't let years of angry outbursts build walls between you and your children.

Mistake 4: Failure to Choose Your Battles Wisely

If you fight over every little thing with your child, you will eventually lose him. Choose your battles wisely, for it's the important battles you want to win.

Too many dads I talk with are unhappy with the tension between them and their son or daughter—and the cause is merely style. A distinct style (you may call it a horrible style, a decadent style, a silly style) is a normal part of growing children's efforts to express their unique identities. Her current tastes in clothes, music, hair, and room decor may offend you; but these external issues are far less important in the long run than character and integrity. An absence of either can damage your child.

Regardless of how you cringe at being known as the father of a child who dresses or wears her hair as she does, it's better to swallow your pride and save your energy for battles about issues that matter—integrity, loyalty, honesty, keeping your word, choice of friends, education, unsafe or immoral sexual behavior, using drugs, and so forth. Your goal is not compliant, but committed behavior—actions that flow out of the child's personal convictions. You'll gain a lot more of your child's respect when you defend unflinchingly only those things that truly matter.

You don't know what lies ahead on your fathering road. Yet if you instill critical life skills and principles in an atmosphere of love, affection, and consistency through many thousands of encounters and investments of time in the relationship, you will leave behind a clear and strong fathering legacy. The imprint of your life will be clear; your grip into the next generation will be strong and positive. Listen to your network; let them support and encourage you never to give up, especially when the road is rough and your confidence plummets. Every father has those moments. Talk about the journey with others on the fathering road. Lots of fathers have been down the stretch of road you face next.

With the five key habits of smart dads well in place, you are on your way to arriving at your fathering destination safe and secure. But before we part company, there is one other issue I must discuss with you. Your views on this subject affect not only your approach to each of the five fathering habits, but also the level of ultimate success you will experience as a dad. At issue is your foundational view of life and your spiritual moorings.

For me it has been a very personal encounter with God—the heavenly Father—that has enormously impacted in a positive way the quality of my work in each of the five habits. I believe that wise choices in the area of this "supra-factor" produce outstanding results and are key in energizing all the rest.

Let's take a look at how it works . . .

Smart Idea:
Discern where it is that you and your wife or children most easily talk—your bed, their bed, the couch, the car, the back yard, wherever—and return to that setting often.

12

Authentic Father Power
Tapping the Supra-factor

Whew! It was 1:30 A.M., and we were relieved to see our daughter Shona walk in the door. But the tremble in her voice signaled trouble. She had been on a date with her boyfriend—traveling some fifty miles away to San Diego. No call had come to tell us they were going to be late.

More was fueling our anxiety than the lateness of the hour. Shona and Mike had been dating several months. Shona loved Mike's sense of humor, and he was good looking and popular at school. But to us, his troubled background left much to be desired, and it was hard to tell whether he had left all of that as completely as he had assured Shona he had. Even though Mike treated her like a queen, we still weren't thrilled that Shona seemed blind to the dangers we saw in the relationship. I had tried in several conversations to press our views, but to no avail. Although I could lay down the law, I couldn't change Shona's heart about this guy.

Over some hot chocolate the story of the evening tumbled out. It had been a fun date—until the highway patrol pulled them over on their way home. The officer told them cordially that they were driving too slow. As a matter of routine he ran a check on Mike's license number.

When the office returned to the car, his demeanor had changed radically. "Move away from him," he instructed Shona. Then he turned to Mike. "Place your hands on the dashboard," he said. "Do you have any dangerous weapons in your possession?"

He was acting on an outstanding warrant for Mike's arrest, and Shona was pretty sure it wasn't just an unresolved traffic citation. She watched her boyfriend handcuffed and taken into custody on the spot.

The officer asked her if she could get herself home. "Yes," she replied. Shaken to the core, she drove the last twenty-five miles home on an unfamiliar winding mountain road.

Tears were streaming down her face by the time she finished her story. Amid hugs and reassurances, we acknowledged the reality of the situation. Shona had thought that Mike was a neat guy who loved her and had put his past behind him. But our perception as two caring parents that this boyfriend wasn't a good choice had proved to be correct.

Perception vs. Reality

In fathering, just as in every area of life, our perceptions daily dictate what we do and how we respond to each moment and situation. I hear a child's scream from the backyard. My *perception* of its tone and intensity cues me about whether to smile at the good time the kids are having or to run to see who's hurt. When my daughter Shelley says, "You're wrong, Dad," it's my perception of her attitude that either makes me proud of the young woman she is becoming, or makes me worry about a sullen attitude.

Your perceptions about fathering are acted out daily in the judgment calls you make. Can you afford to work late tonight and miss dinner with your family? This one time won't hurt, you figure. It will allow you to give the whole weekend to the kids.

That's a judgment call based on your perception of realities at your house. Fathers make hundreds of these decisions every month, and each one is based on fundamental perceptions about life and how it works.

Your Worldview and Fathering

The collection of ideas, axioms, principles, and beliefs that daily guide your thoughts, decisions, and actions is your worldview. It is how you believe life works. You use this frame of reference to make choices. Even without conscious evaluation, every choice flows from an operating premise you believe will work out best.

Your worldview is also the supra-factor that shapes and impacts your fathering—that overarching element that transcends all other components of your fathering. Your worldview, your belief system affects the quality of your fathering. It's like buttoning a shirt. If you get the top button right, the rest fall in line. If you button that top button in the wrong hole, however, the shirt will be out of alignment.

All this to say that you want your fundamental beliefs, your worldview, your supra-factor, to be as firmly rooted in truth and reality as possible.

I think it is only fair—even important—that I reveal to you my belief system. It seems to me to be the most realistic explanation of the world I experience as a man and father. This worldview honors my role as a father, promotes respect for my wife and children, and guides my understanding of how to act in their best interests. It provides the motivation and power to do what is right when I frankly don't want to do the right thing.

I found this worldview, which in my perspective is firmly rooted in truth and reality, in the Bible. This book explains the selfishness I work so hard to root out of my children, my selfcenteredness that tears at my marriage and fathering. The Bible also explains how to escape from such vices.

I've looked at the historical facts surrounding the birth, life, death, and resurrection of Jesus Christ long and hard. I have carefully weighed the evidence, for I have no intention of being duped or fooled about this. In the process I've been forced to the conclusion that it would require greater faith to disbelieve the Bible than to accept it. The case is simply that strong to me. My decision is to accept it and to encourage my children to do the same.

Your belief system, like mine, colors how you approach each of the five key habits of a smart dad. Let me explain.

The Five Key Habits' Supra-Factor

Among the several definitions of *father* is "Father God"—in my understanding, the true and living God described in the

Smart Idea:
Play "Hug Tag" with your children and the neighborhood kids. Follow regular tag rules, except that players are safe only when they are hugging another player. Then play it again, this time requiring that huggers must be in a *threesome* to be safe; and so on. It's magic!

Old and New Testaments of the Bible, the one who created us, our wives, our children, and who alone is capable of giving family and fatherhood complete and deeply fulfilling meaning. I have found that God is the source of authentic father power.

In fact, God is the ultimate father—his love for his children is unsurpassed, he opens his arms to wayward children who come home, he disciplines his children for their own good.

A little abstract, you say. Agreed—which is why God sent his son, Jesus, into humanity. "Anyone who has seen me has seen the Father," Jesus told his followers (John 14:9), driving the point home even plainer with this declaration: "I and the Father are one" (John 10:30).

Based on a *Psychology Today* survey a few years ago, the magazine's readers named Jesus Christ as the "New Ideal Man."[1] Whatever *Psychology Today's* reasons for elevating Jesus to that modern pedestal—and despite the fact he had no biological children himself—I find Jesus a perfect role model of the ideal father.

A Christian worldview puts its own spin on how a father understands and practices each of the five habits.

Grasping Your Significance

If you are a follower of Jesus Christ, you recognize the truth that no person is a biological accident, regardless of the circumstances of his or her conception. Each child's unique features, gifts, and personality bear the imprint of a personal and creative God. That new life, the Bible says, is created in the image of God—which includes a *yearning* for God. The Psalmist reminds me that I was known by God even in my mother's womb and that nothing about me is by chance (Psalm 139:13–16).

Therefore both I and my children are significant—and no person or circumstance can take that away.

Neither is any child (including adult children) fatherless or without a fathering model, even if his or her biological father is gone. This is evidence of God's sensitivity to the fact that life isn't perfect; yet he will be there for a child when an earthly father is not.

By divine design you are and always will be significant to your children, whether you are actively present in their lives or not. This explains the fathering power you innately possess. You can use it positively or negatively, but you cannot turn it off.

The Impact of Your Father

No matter what kind of dad you had, your worldview will deeply color the place he holds in your thinking. If you didn't know the man, even that absence made an imprint just as if he had been there during your developing years. If your father's relationship with you (or lack of one) was disappointing or even painful, you have recourse in God, your heavenly Father, to acquire a perfect substitute and a healthy fathering model.

There is also God's spiritual power to heal and put behind you the dull ache or vivid anguish you still may feel because of your father. In God your Father is the hope that you can yet understand and forgive your dad. Whatever his failings or sins against you, he was overwhelmed by the same human condition you and I face in ourselves each day—selfishness and self-centered thinking.

A word about sin: In biblical terms sin is not a laundry list of unapproved behaviors—a cosmic Dirty Dozen or Negative Nine— but an attitude of ignoring God, either passively or actively. I have observed in each of my children an instinct to sin from the earliest days of their lives, in spite of Leslie's and my enormous efforts to make our home a positive and wholesome place to grow. This bent to ignore God is darkly instinctive within each person.

If your belief system does not account for the negative, troubling, unfair, and dark aspects of life, sooner or later you will be visited by confusion and emptiness when your worldview cannot explain or help you face a devastating life situation—a violent act against you or a loved one, a death in the family, a crippling or terminal disease, an unfair or humiliating defeat. What will you do then? What will you say to your children to prepare them for such eventualities? They need to hear it from you.

The biblical worldview squarely addresses the evil that even well-intended people do to one another—including my shortcomings as a dad—and offers a realistic, personal healing.

Acting Intentionally

"It's not hard to make decisions when you know what your values are," asserted Roy Disney (yes, Walt's brother).[2] The trouble is that we are fathering in a culture plagued with fuzzy thinking about bedrock values—especially the question of just how responsible individuals are for their choices and actions. We are all too ready to excuse personal responsibility or else find a scapegoat for it.

Smart Idea:
Discipline yourself to write to your out-of-the-nest children every week. It may be only a cartoon clipping, a two-sentence greeting, or a "What's up with you?" question—but the frequency will keep your relationship growing.

In the car the other day, I caught a news clip on the radio. The city had apparently announced a get-tough approach to its graffiti problems. In the sound bite, a city official explained that they would begin charging parents of "taggers" for the costs of repairing their kids' damage. "It will no longer be acceptable for a parent to argue, 'I just can't control my child,'" the official said.

When did it become tolerable for a father to default on his civic responsibilities to his children—not to mention his emotional and spiritual responsibilities? Where is his intentional action toward the training of his children?

The worldview called Christianity encompasses intentional action somewhat ambiguously. On one hand, Jesus requires a father (as he requires all people) to follow him—to act intentionally "toward" him, so to speak. Yet he makes it equally clear that Christianity is *not* subscribing to a code of conduct, not even a biblical code. This is because to genuinely, consistently follow most codes is beyond any human. The Ten Commandments, Christ's Sermon on the Mount—the worldview advocated by God in such edicts is accurate but unattainable.

Hope lies in one of the meanings of *Christian*—"Christ in one." That is, only by Christ living in me am I able to acquire the spiritual dynamic to father my children as Jesus Christ fathers me. Jesus Christ lives spiritually in me, changing my desires to ones more compatible with effective fathering, empowering me to make tough fathering choices. Faith applied like this, within a Christian worldview, becomes a supra-factor to positive and practical fathering.

Using Your Network

Although I value and celebrate the talents and personality that God gave me, I still don't possess what I need to get through life. I love the clear, haunting tones of a well-played French horn, but that sound does not thrill me like a full brass ensemble. It is realistic, not pessimistic, to admit that I don't have all the answers and gifts and talents that my children need. A Christian worldview assures me of this reality, as well as of the absolute need of the support and balance I receive from others. Worldviews that place me at the center of the universe instead of in the center of friends—that is, dependent—do not easily sustain realistic fathering.

"Be kind and compassionate to one another, forgiving each other, just as in Christ God forgave you," wrote the apostle Paul (Eph. 4:32) in an ancient endorsement of modern networking. When I am as dependent on others as they are on me, I can let my hair down. I don't have to always be right. I can admit that, as a mature and reasonably savvy dad, I still don't know what to do in a given situation. I can admit to other dads my failures and struggles without losing face. And in return I can receive their genuine support and encouragement.

That is networking.

A biblical worldview also helps me select and support other adults who help my child grow up—teachers, neighbors, coaches, bosses. A biblical worldview deepens my appreciation for them and gives me objective criteria for reviewing and evaluating their input.

Communicating Life Skills and Principles

A biblical worldview, of course, offers the wisdom of the Bible as a prime sourcebook for living—a proven, full, and integrated set of life principles, with hundreds of stories that illustrate and exemplify those skills and principles for myself and for my children.

Take the Old Testament book of Daniel, for instance. After a three-month siege late in the seventh century B.C., Jerusalem surrendered to Nebuchadnezzar, who marched many Jewish captives off to Babylon—including a young aristocrat named Daniel. The dilemmas of this nobleman and his companions in the king's court are timeless stories of peer pressure, resisting temptation, and salvation from whatever lions happen to be stalking you at the moment.

Some of God's clearest instruction about what principles a father should teach his children are in Deuteronomy.

> These commandments that I give you today are to be upon your hearts. Impress them on your children. Talk about them when you sit at home and when you walk along the road, when you lie down and when you get up. Tie them as symbols on your hands and bind them on your foreheads. Write them on the doorframes of your houses and on your gates. (Deut. 6:6-9)

Tell your children about how life works. Our society is drifting into destructive ways of interacting because too many fathers are either silent or telling their children the wrong message.

In the previous chapter I told you about the discovery that, despite all my supposedly good parenting, my son Jon became involved with marijuana and substance

Smart Idea:
Encourage a habit of critical thinking and activism in your kids by keeping postcards or stationery and a supply of stamps by your TV. When a program, newscast segment, or political report pleases or annoys you, express your sentiments in writing.

abuse. There are no ironclad guarantees in fathering, I found out. It was the low point so far in my experience as a dad. What had become of all those values, skills, and principles I tried to instill in Jon?

Once the abuse was discovered and we confronted Jon, it took a couple years before we felt somewhat certain that the battle with substance abuse was a winnable war. Prayer to a personal and powerful God was a mainstay during this time. Ultimately, it was our capacity for deeply loving Jon (when his actions were so terribly offensive and unlovable) and God's gentle pursuit of his heart through a variety of circumstances that turned things around.

Once the immediate crisis passed, there began the long process of restoration in the relationship . . . of desiring to see Jon experience real freedom from this season of his youth . . . of desiring to see the life values we thought we had taught all those years be expressed in his daily choices and personal confidence.

I had to bite my tongue sometimes so I wouldn't say what would probably distance us again. At other times, I found myself scrambling for something wise to say as I confronted Jon with my expectations and disappointment about what he was doing.

The phone rang one day, and Leslie recognized the voice as one of Jon's friends who had encouraged his drug abuse. We had prayed that God would either help or remove this friend from Jon's life. In a brief conversation with Leslie, the boy mentioned that *he* was praying about something. Through the influence of a girl he was dating, he had apparently experienced a very real personal encounter with Jesus Christ himself. It had changed his life, and now he was calling Jon out of concern for his old buddy.

In a month of Sundays I wouldn't have guessed that God would choose to work through this friend to tug Jon back to faith. But that's what happened. Jon spent the next weekend with this friend and his girlfriend—attending church with them, learning about the reality of spiritual faith in their lives. It was an important marker in Jon's return to wholeness.

Today Jon is the delight of my heart. He has just about completed his three-year certification as a locksmith and has returned to school to finish college. He's living on his own; we usually meet on Wednesday mornings before work for breakfast. Jon and I both look forward to those times of conversation—sometimes lighthearted, sometimes very serious—but always engaging. I see in his life and conversation, his spiritual interests, the way he treats his girlfriend, and in his desire to help people all the major values Leslie and I had tried to teach and model over the years.

I still believe there are no guarantees. Yet the probability of a happy ending, should you find yourself off-roading as a dad, is vastly improved if the supra-factor or spiritual faith is guiding both your choice of life skills and principles and your ability to live them in front of your kids.

Maximizing Your Moments

You may have heard about the father's trip to the supermarket with his four-year-old son. They found themselves waiting in line at the register, packed into the narrow checkout aisle immediately behind a man who was plainly obese. The youngster took one look at the girth looming over him and said, too loudly, "Hey, Dad, that man is really fat!"

Thoroughly embarrassed but recognizing a teachable moment when it was thrust upon him, the father bent over and told the boy, in one of those intense parental whispers, "We don't talk about people that way! He may be large, but we must be kind in how we talk about him."

The boy missed the point completely. "But, Dad, he really *is* fat!"

The corpulent customer, annoyed now, attempted to turn around in the narrow aisle and see who was raising such a racket. In the process he bumped against the youngster. At the same moment his pager started beeping.

"Look out, Dad!" the kid shouted. "He's backing up!"

Teachable moments, it seems, arrive when you least want them, they're too public for your comfort, and they lack all appearance of Christian charity.

A biblical worldview urges fathers to detect teachable moments wherever and whenever. Without in any way diminishing the freedom of personal choice, a Christian worldview contends that God knows and cares about every detail of every life. God numbers the hairs on my head, Jesus taught, and a sparrow cannot fall to the ground without his knowing. That kind of all-knowing and caring God can coach a father to maximize his moments and number his days with his children.

Your High-Stakes Choice

That is my worldview—ordered by God, personified in Jesus, revealed in the Bible. Whether or not you agree with my belief system, of how I perceive that life works,

Smart Thought:
A famous man is one whose children love him. (French proverb)

you sense the priority and importance I attach to choosing carefully one's personal belief system.

One cannot afford to be wrong on this point. You cannot evaluate this question casually, put it off too long, or leave it to chance. The stakes are just too high, for it concerns heaven and the afterlife.

Jesus was not vague or uncertain about heaven. He came to earth from there, he said. We are to pray to our Father who is listening from heaven. Reliable witnesses—some 500 at one time—saw Jesus ascend into heaven following his resurrection. Far from wishful thinking, heaven is a real place for which there is highly defensible evidence.

I would lay odds on heaven if only for this reason: *If* there is a heaven, I don't want my children to miss it. Like any father, I love my children deeply and want for them the best of everything, including the afterlife. I've never forgotten what a friend remarked to me some years ago. "You realize don't you," he said, "that your children are the only earthly possessions you can take to heaven with you?"

Jesus clearly taught that when he left this earth he was returning to God the Father in heaven, where he would prepare a place for every one who believes in him. And if my children whom I love so much are going to be in heaven for all eternity, I want to be there with them, too. Compared to this, I don't care about my questions and doubts about other Christian teachings. I just wouldn't want to miss an eternity with my kids—and I don't think they want to miss it with me.

Wherever you are or whatever your circumstance at this moment, God wants you and your family to spend eternity with him in heaven; the box office to heaven is always open and your ticket has already been purchased for you by Jesus Christ. All that remains is for you to decide you want to go there and to step up in a simple prayer of gratitude and receive from Jesus Christ his forgiveness for your sins and your paid admission to heaven.

God listens and responds to the prayers of his children, the Bible teaches. Prayer is a secret weapon for a father, a powerful tool for protecting them fully and providing what they need most.

The Power of Praying for Your Children

Look at what a father's prayers accomplish:

• **Prayer keeps me dependent upon God.** Fatherhood can be baffling. Was I too strict or too easy? Were my words loving enough? Will they forgive me for my temper? Will I someday regret how much time I now give to my job?

Prayer guarantees that I am seeing my fathering role for what it really is—a spiritual calling—and confirms that I'm seeking God's power and the wisdom in the Scriptures to overcome my weaknesses.

• **Prayer sets the stage for successful living.** In instructing followers of Christ to "pray continually" (1 Thess. 5:17), the apostle Paul was saying that prayer ought to create a backdrop for everyday living. Whether it is a misunderstanding with my wife or children or a simmering dispute with a colleague at the office, prayer changes a fractured relationship into a spiritual project.

• **Prayer protects my children.** I'm not in my daughter's classroom to counter a false value served up by a favorite teacher. I can't be there on the playground to contradict a painful, excruciatingly timed remark directed to my child. I can't monitor the billboards, magazines, or commercials that tug at my son's sexual desires.

I really have no option but to ask God to guard my children's minds and emotions from being captured by the evil forces in the world. I must pray, as Paul did for his followers (whom he cared for, he wrote, as a father cares for his children), that they "may be able to discern what is best and may be pure and blameless until the day of Christ" (Phil. 1:10). This is a battle I cannot afford to lose by default.

• **Prayer provides for my children.** At the top of my list of things I want provided for my children, way ahead of the others, is the gift of a spouse they will live happily with for a lifetime. Beside finding their own personal faith in Jesus Christ, I can't think of a more important gift in this lifetime. Ironically, it's a choice I will watch them make when they are probably young and inexperienced.

Yet miracles of a sort can even happen here. Sam was a teenager in southern Oregon when someone presented the story of Jesus Christ to him, and he made a personal spiritual commitment. His spiritual growth took off with a bang and stayed strong. Someone got him his own Bible (with *Sam* stamped on the front cover), which he read voraciously, underlining portions that connected with him, writing notes in the margins.

So it was a particularly dismal day when he lost his Bible somewhere along a

Smart Idea:
Challenge your family to take a vacation from complaining. Dare them to go twenty-four hours without a complaint. It's not as easy as it sounds; you'll all discover how easily complaining becomes a habit.

trail during a summer backpacking trip. When he got home, he bought another Bible and forgot about the loss.

Four years later Sam was attending college in Southern California and seriously dating the daughter of a Christian family. The weekend her family moved to a new house across town, Sam helped. He was carrying an overfilled book box out the door to the trailer when a book tumbled out of the box onto the sidewalk. Sam set the box down and reached for the book—and in disbelief recognized it as his long-lost Bible.

"Where did you get this Bible?" he asked the family. During a family vacation to southern Oregon a few years earlier, they found it on the trail during a hike. The girl's parents searched for an address so they could mail the Bible to its owner, but all the I.D. they found on it was the imprinted *Sam* on the cover. The more they flipped through it, though, and read through the handwritten notes in the margins, the more they were impressed with the spiritual insight of this "Sam." If only a man with this kind of spiritual heart would marry their daughter, they thought. So they had begun praying, "Please send a man, God, to marry our daughter—a man who loves you as much as 'Sam.'"

In one way or another, your prayers will provide what your children need.

Let's Stay in Touch

The five habits of smart dads aren't clever. Yet I have found in the courses I teach at Dads University—and through conversations with many, many fathers—that this model helps fathers understand their role and stay on track as they leave a positive imprint on their children, a legacy of fatherly love.

My hope is that you will adopt the five key habits of smart dads for yourself. I hope that your fathering is satisfying for both you and your children.

If these five key habits of smart dads help get your fathering on the right road, please write and tell me:

Paul Lewis
Family University
P.O. Box 500050
San Diego, CA 92150-0050.

Notes

Chapter 1

1. Ellen Goodman, "Life without Father: Lost and Found," *The Boston Globe*, April 10, 1992.

2. Henry Biller and Dennis Meredith, *Father Power* (Garden City, New York: Anchor Press/Doubleday, 1975).

3. *The Role of Fathers in America: Attitudes and Behavior*, a Gallup national random sample conducted for the National Center for Fathering, April 14–17, 1992.

4. Nancy R. Gibbs, "Bringing Up Father," *Time* (June 28, 1993), 55.

5. Nina J. Easton, "Life without Father," *Los Angeles Times Magazine* (June 14, 1992), 15.

6. Gibbs, "Bringing Up Father," 55.

7. Alvin Toffler, *The Third Wave* (New York: William Morrow & Co., 1980), 139.

8. Gibbs, "Bringing Up Father," 54.

9. Easton, "Life without Father," 16.

10. Myron Magnet, "The American Family, 1992," *Fortune* (August 10, 1992), 45.

11. Magnet, "The American Family, 1992," 42–47.

12. Easton, "Life without Father," 18.

13. Gibbs, "Bringing Up Father," 54.

14. Magnet, "The American Family, 1992," 46.

15. Ibid.

16. This collection of statistics is found in Barbara Dafoe Whitehead, "Dan Quayle Was Right" (*Atlantic Monthly*, April 1993); Magnet, "The American Family, 1992"; and Gibbs, "Bringing Up Father."

17. Gibbs, "Bringing Up Father," 58.

18. Asa Baber, "The Decade of the Dad," *Playboy* (January 1990), 33.

Chapter 4

1. *The Role of Fathers in America: Attitudes and Behavior,* a Gallup national random sample conducted for the National Center for Fathering, April 14–17, 1992.

2. Dotson Rader, "'I Want to Be like My Dad'" (interview with Kevin Costner), *Parade Magazine* (January 20, 1991), 5.

3. *The Role of Fathers in America: Attitudes and Behavior.*

4. Sam Osherson, *Finding Our Fathers* (New York: Macmillan, 1986).

5. Easton, "Life without Father," 19. The parenting program is conducted by New York's nonprofit Manpower Demonstration Research Corporation.

Chapter 5

1. Everett Kline, on growing up. Kline's essay is part of *Men's Stories, Men's Lives,* a collection of reminiscences gathered from the National SEED (Seeking Educational Equity and Diversity) Project's first Multicultural Men's Studies Seminar, October 30, 1991.

2. From a 1990 National Center for Fathering news release.

3. Easton, "Life without Father," 16.

4. Shasta L. Mead and George A. Rekers, "Role of the Father in Normal Psychosexual Development," *Psychological Reports,* 45 (1979), 923–24.

5. Mead and Rekers, "Role of the Father," 924, 926.

6. Mead and Rekers, "Role of the Father," 923, 927.

7. Alston & Nanette, 1982; Bach, 1946; Biller, 1976; Biller & Baum, 1971; Carlsmith, 1964; Covell & Turnbull, 1982; Daum & Bieliauskas, 1983; Drake & Mc Dugall, 1977; Fry, 1983; Gershansky, et. al., 1980; Goldstein, 1982, 1983; Hetherington & Deur, 1971; Lynn, 1974, 1976; Matther, 1976; McCord, McCord & Thurber, 1962; Mead & Rekers, 1979; Nask, 1965; Micoli, 1985; Parish & Taylor, 1979; Reis & Gold, 1977; Rekers, 1981, 1986; Shill, 1981; Stoklosa, 1981; Stolz, 1954. All appeared as cites in testimony given on June 12, 1986, Capitol Hill hearing on "The National Family Strengths Project." Testimony given by George A. Reekers, Ph.D., and available from U.S. House of Representatives, Rayburn Office Building Room 2325, Washington, D.C.

8. Whitehead, "Dan Quayle Was Right," 47.

9. Alston & Nannette, 1982; Covell & Turnbull, 1982; Gispert, et al., 1984; Lancaster & Richmond, 1983; Parish & Nunn, 1983; Pomano & Micanti, 1983; Lewis, Newson & Newson, 1982; Hoffman, 1981; Park, 1981; Russell, 1983. See note seven, above.

10. Easton, "Life without Father," 16.

11. Gibbs, "Bringing Up Father," 61.

12. Ibid.

13. Ibid.

14. Ibid.

15. Magnet, "The American Family, 1992," 43.

16. Whitehead, "Dan Quayle Was Right," 47.

17. Qualitative research from a stratified study of 2,066 religious fathers surveyed between October 1988 and February 1990. Comments were compiled from a random sampling of that group.

18. Stephen Covey, *The Seven Habits of Highly Effective People* (New York: Simon and Schuster, 1989), 42–43.

19. Qualitative research of 2,066 religious fathers.

20. Sam Keen and Ofer Zur, "A *Psychology Today* Survey Report: Who Is the New Ideal Man?" *Psychology Today* (November 1989), 54.

21. Rader, "'I Want to Be like My Dad,'" 4.

22. Paul Lewis, *Famous Fathers* (Elgin, Ill.: David C. Cook, 1984), 112.

Chapter 6

1. Qualitative research of 2,066 religious fathers.

2. Ibid.

3. *The Role of Fathers in America: Attitudes and Behavior.*

NOTES

4. Barna Research Group, commissioned by Josh McDowell Ministry in preparation for the Why Wait? Campaign. The study regarded the sexual attitudes and behavior, personal interests and lifestyle, relationship with parents, spiritual beliefs, and demographic traits of 1,483 youths, ages twelve to seventeen.

Chapter 7

1. Covey, *Seven Habits*, 50.
2. Qualitative research of 2,066 religious fathers.
3. Covey, *Seven Habits*, 49.
4. Tom Black, my associate at Family University, is a specialist at helping parents understand motivational patterns and the personal style of their children. His recently published book *Born to Fly!* (Grand Rapids: Zondervan, 1994) is an excellent guide to discerning the strengths, drives, and patterns in yourself as well as in your children.

Chapter 8

1. Gary Smalley and John Trent, *The Blessing* (Nashville: Nelson, 1986).
2. Rader, "'I Want to Be like My Dad,'" 7.

Chapter 9

1. Joe Russo. This writing is part of *Men's Stories, Men's Lives*, a collection of reminiscences gathered from the National SEED (Seeking Educational Equity and Diversity) Project's first Multicultural Men's Studies Seminar, October 1991–May 1992.

Chapter 10

1. Cited in Gibbs, "Bringing Up Father," 58.
2. Gibbs, "Bringing Up Father," 61.

Chapter 11

1. From a brochure from Grand Auto Supply & Tire Service, SKU #890243, November 1991.

Chapter 12

1. Keen and Zur, "The New Ideal Man," 57.
2. Roy Disney is cited by H. Jackson Brown, Jr., in *A Father's Book of Wisdom* (Nashville: Rutledge Hill Press, 1990), 131.